WHO

BY

FIRE

WHO
BY
FIRE

A Novel

DIANA
SPECHLER

HARPER ● PERENNIAL

NEW YORK ● LONDON ● TORONTO ● SYDNEY ● NEW DELHI ● AUCKLAND

HARPER ● PERENNIAL

P.S.™ is a trademark of HarperCollins Publishers.

WHO BY FIRE. Copyright © 2008 by Diana Spechler. All rights reserved. Printed in the United States of America. No part of this book may be used or reproduced in any manner whatsoever without written permission except in the case of brief quotations embodied in critical articles and reviews. For information address HarperCollins Publishers, 10 East 53rd Street, New York, NY 10022.

HarperCollins books may be purchased for educational, business, or sales promotional use. For information please write: Special Markets Department, HarperCollins Publishers, 10 East 53rd Street, New York, NY 10022.

FIRST EDITION

Designed by Jan Pisciotta

Library of Congress Cataloging-in-Publication Data is available upon request.

ISBN 978-0-06-157293-7

08 09 10 11 12   OV/RRD   10 9 8 7 6 5 4 3 2 1

*This book is for my mom and dad
and for my sister and brother.*

April 24, 2002

AT THE BACK of the plane, twelve men bow and mumble and sway, masked by thick beards and crowned by black hats. They wear angelic white shawls over demon-black suits. Their eyes are shut. They hold their prayer books closed, using their thumbs as bookmarks. I face the front of the plane again, and return to the article my mother e-mailed me: "How to Cope When Your Loved One Joins a Cult." For peace of mind, I'm supposed to get a support group, to eat whole wheat bread and peas, to breathe deeply and remind myself that I'm not to blame. I inhale sharply through my nose. The air smells stagnant—transatlantic airplane air. I try to exhale some blame.

After Alena disappeared, my mother was brimming with blame. She blamed the state police for not making enough effort. She blamed other families for not understanding. If my father sat down to watch TV, she would say, "You think your daughter has the luxury of watching television?" She started grinding her teeth so hard, she had to wear a mouth guard. For a year, she dragged Ash and me all over New Jersey, making us tape flyers to telephone poles, as if we had lost her favorite cat. She never directly blamed us, her two remaining children, but she often began a thought with, "If it had been you, instead of Alena . . ." Of course, she always followed that up with "Don't give me that look. I never said I *wished* it had been you. God forbid. What do you take me for?" But we have always understood: Alena was the baby. Alena was the favorite. Six-year-old Alena, with the paint brush–black hair and the chin dimple and the jeans rolled halfway up her calves, Alena imitating our eighty-four-year-old neighbor's smoker voice, Alena whizzing through the kitchen on roller skates with pink wheels—Alena was the irreplaceable one.

After losing its baby, its best member, especially if a family can't properly mourn, it begins to decay like a corpse. At ten years old, I didn't know yet that my father would leave us, that my mother would grow old while she was still young, or that Ash would swing from obsession to obsession like a child crossing the monkey bars. All I knew for sure was this: we had lost everything we had been.

Ash might remember it differently. Perhaps he remembers the voice of God saying, *No one will ever forgive you.*

I wait a while before unbuckling my seat belt and making my way to the bathroom at the back of the plane. The praying men have dispersed, but as I walk down the aisle, I can pick them out. I can see their hats towering over the seat backs. I can see their plain wives, their squirmy broods of children. I want to tell them that they are no match for me, that for ten days now they have been no match for me, ever since I heard the news that I know will get Ash to come home.

I plan to catch Ash off guard, to show up at his yeshiva, to tell everyone there that he used to eat baseball stadium hotdogs that couldn't possibly have been kosher; that he fidgeted restlessly during *Schindler's List*; that at Yom Kippur services, he used to fart on purpose during the silent meditation. I will tell them, *This is my brother you've taken! And now I'm taking him back.*

Go as a voluntary exile to a place of Torah. . . . Do not rely upon your own understanding.

—from *Ethics of the Fathers*

On Rosh Hashanah it is inscribed, and on Yom Kippur it is sealed: How many shall pass on, and how many shall be born. Who shall live, and who shall die; who in his time, and who before his time. Who by water, and who by fire; who by sword, and who by beast; who by hunger, and who by thirst; who by earthquake, and who by plague. Who shall rest, and who shall wander. . . . Who shall fall, and who shall rise. . . .

—from the Rosh Hashanah prayers

PART I

April 12, 2002

I'M SITTING IN Friday evening rush-hour traffic, staring out the window at the Charles River, and listening to the news. A bomb detonated in Jerusalem. A man speaks in panicked Hebrew. Another man talks over him in English: "How are we supposed to live like this?" they say in overlapping languages.

It's been eleven months since Ash clapped a yarmulke on his head, dropped out of college, went missing, and then one week later turned out not to be missing. Where he turned out to be was Israel, at a yeshiva, ready to spend the rest of his life studying Judaism. (Judaism! In Israel! A real pioneer, my brother.)

I call Ash from my cell phone and get his voice mail. Ash's voice mail annoys me. It's in Hebrew, for one thing, which is absurd considering he almost didn't get to have a bar mitzvah because he wouldn't learn his Torah portion. I don't know Hebrew, but I can tell by the way he speaks it that it's not right. It sounds distinctly American. In his message, he calls himself Asher. That's what he goes by now.

Maybe he's traveling. His last letter said something about traveling during Passover vacation. Is it still Passover vacation? I'm trying to remember that letter, but I can only remember the package that he sent with it: dried prunes, dried apricots, bright orange sticks of dried papaya.

On his voice mail, I say, "Isn't this getting a little ridiculous?

Isn't it about time to come home?" I don't hang up right away. I listen to the silence in the phone, half-expecting an answer and hating the feeling. You can waste your whole life half-expecting the impossible.

The phone is ringing when I get to my apartment, and I know it's Ash. I can feel him sometimes.

But it's not Ash. It's my mother, calling from New Jersey because she just heard the news.

"I can't reach him," I tell her. "But I'm trying. Don't worry."

"Bits," she says, "don't do this. Don't do this to me."

"I'm sure he's fine," I say. "Don't cry."

"You're sure? Here I'm about to have an attack, and you're sure! Call his yeshiva," she says.

I sit on the kitchen floor and lean back against the stove, propping the soles of my feet on the refrigerator door that I've never decorated. My apartment, in general, is kind of austere. I've just never known whose pictures to display, what sort of artwork I love enough to live with. Looking out my window at Allston, at the CITGO sign flashing and the traffic I'm not sitting in and the umbrellas in a million different colors on rainy days . . . it's enough for me. How much can a person ask from a place? "I'm not calling his yeshiva, Mom." I tell her that we should keep the lines free, in case Ash calls us. You can still convince my mother that she needs to do things like keep the lines free. "Good Shabbos," I say, even though that's not the kind of thing I say.

My mother says, "What's so good about it?"

Once I hang up, the gnawing feeling hits, like I've forgotten to do something or I'm supposed to be somewhere. It's the feeling I used to get as a child, when my mother would stand at the kitchen sink, her back to me, screaming at the window, "Where is she? Where the hell is she? Just tell me that!" It's an anxiety that my mother still ignites in me, although it's not about Alena anymore; these days, it's about Ash.

A familiar urge starts poking at me like a finger. *Don't call Wade,* I tell myself. *Don't start cruising through chat rooms. Chat rooms are for weirdos. People with hobbies. Child pornographers. Do something else. Anything else.* I drag the vacuum cleaner into my bedroom and turn it on, but I'm afraid I won't hear the phone ring, so I turn it off. I should exercise. Exercise is supposed to be calming. But I'm not much of an exerciser. After ten push-ups, I can't go on. I lie on my stomach, listening to my heart beat through the carpet. I get up and pick up the phone.

Oh, fuck it. I'm entitled. Just this once won't kill me. I dial Wade. "Come over," I say. Wade and I work together at the Auburn School. As my mother would say, he's no rocket scientist. But he serves a purpose.

"What's wrong?" he asks.

I press the phone harder to my ear, feeling my skull throb against the receiver. I squeeze my eyes shut and see explosions of color. "Just come," I say. "Hurry."

When I hang up, I go through the junk drawer in the kitchen until I find Ash's letter. It's dated by the Jewish calendar: 16 Nisan 5762.

Bits, I went to Rosh Hanikra. The waves blow against the grottoes at night. It's so beautiful. I was really close to Lebanon. You could look through a fence at it, but you couldn't cross over. Back to Jerusalem tomorrow. I just learned this: When we die, G-d will ask, why didn't you taste all My fruits?

He won't spell out "God" anymore. In my head, I start composing a letter to him. I'll sign it, *Love, B-ts.*

The intercom buzzes. Maybe Wade is one of God's fruits. So I will taste him. Whatever.

Wade hasn't changed from work. He's still dressed up like a

gym teacher: a Red Sox sweatshirt, warmup pants with a stripe down the side, a whistle around his neck. He smells faintly of perspiration. I reach up and put my fingers in his short brown hair. He asks again what's wrong. "You sounded—"

"Nothing's wrong," I say. "It was a trick. I just wanted to get you here quickly." I grab a fistful of his sweatshirt and pull him toward me. We sink to the hardwood floor in the entryway. I straddle him.

He whispers in my ear that I'm a weird girl. A weird, weird girl. Wade's vocabulary isn't very big. He uses the word "weird" a lot. He says it with a Boston accent. He also knows the words "hot," "cool," "totally," and a few others.

I close my eyes, but I feel like a barbell, lying like this on top of Wade. I try to make my mind blank, cold and numb as a snowball. But it's not easy; I'm listening for the phone. When I open my eyes, I see sweat on Wade's upper lip, a string of little jewels. His eyes go out of focus. His chin twitches. His face turns red. When he finishes, I feel like I should offer him Gatorade.

For some reason, I think of a birthday party I once attended at a Japanese restaurant. Sushi, arranged in little wooden boats, circled the bar on a conveyor belt. Everyone frantically grabbed the passing sushi so it wouldn't get away, but within ten minutes, the food that had just looked so appetizing was turning our stomachs.

I don't want to look at Wade. I resist getting up to open the front door. I resist screaming "Bye!"

Wade is grinning. "Why do I feel used?" he asks. "Why do you always make me feel used?" He holds my face with one hand, thumb hooked in front of my ear, fingertips pushed into my hair. He kisses me. "You're a weird girl," he says, and I remind myself not to feel bad. I remind myself that although Wade means nothing to me, I might mean even less to Wade. It's just sex. Normal people have sex all the time.

2 Iyar 5762
(April 14, 2002)

W E'RE ALL STANDING together in the *beit midrash*, the main room in the yeshiva that we use for study and prayer. Our evening prayers complete, we hold our prayer books closed at our sides or pressed to our chests. Rabbi Berkstein is reciting the blessing for counting the Omer. *Today is eighteen days, which is two weeks and four days of the Omer.* Out the window, the sun has gone down. The sky is sapphire blue, like the footrest of God's holy throne. Where else in this world could I ever want to be?

Before 70 C.E., the year the Second Temple was destroyed in Jerusalem, every year on the second day of the Passover festival, the priests offered God an omer of barley. Once the offering was made, all of Israel would begin counting the forty-nine days until the next holiday, Shavuot. Today, even though the temple is gone, we still count. Those forty-nine days are called the Omer.

After Rabbi Berkstein finishes the blessing and the counting, we repeat him. We thank God for allowing us to count the Omer. And then we count. I can feel the words, the numbers, filling my chest, vibrating on my tongue. We count loudly; we want God to hear us. I'm probably the loudest of anyone. Rabbi Berkstein smiles at me. He is smiling at Asher. (I chose that name from Torah—Jacob's eighth son.) No one here knows much about Ash, the son of a man who's not even worthy of mention. It might sound like I'm hiding things, but it's not that. I just see no reason to dwell on the past.

Since Yeshiva Hillel caters to North Americans, a lot of the guys here grew up on the East Coast as I did, but mostly in Jewish sections of New York, and they all went to Jewish day schools, then yeshiva high schools. Well, not me. I started learning at age nineteen. Of course, as a child, I went to Hebrew school and became a bar mitzvah, but that doesn't count; it wasn't kosher. Our synagogue was Reform. Membership was expensive. Men and women prayed together, and for an hour a week at the most. There was even a female rabbi, which I now know is an oxymoron. Like jumbo shrimp: contradictory and *treyf.*

So these are the things I keep to myself: that I joined a fraternity my first year of college, that Bits's childhood nickname was Whore of Babylon, and that my mother draws connections between yeshiva life and Jonestown. ("I should sit on my hands and say nothing?" she says. "I should wait until my son drinks poison Kool-Aid?") I don't talk much about how I became religious either or about the hippie Jews I used to learn with in Boulder, Colorado. People are much more straitlaced here. More committed. Stronger. Which is what I wanted, of course, and why I came, and why I've been here nearly a year and have no plans to leave.

Lastly, I don't talk about my little sister Alena, who's been missing since 1989. I am a Ba'al Tshuva, which means I'm returning to God, so I'm in a constant state of repentance. I am always returning, always repenting, but it's a private thing, repentance; no one but God needs to know what I did.

I AM IN A stranger's living room. The stranger has cats. Cat hair and a line of dust on each slat of the blinds, and not enough light. The group moderator has a doughnut crumb in his beard. He is patting a crying woman's shoulder. The woman's daughter is a Jehovah's Witness. "It's not safe for a pretty nineteen-year-old girl," the woman is saying. "A pretty girl knocking on strangers' doors at all hours? Something is going to happen." The woman shifts in her folding chair and blows her nose. I stare into her eyes, searching for myself. She has mascara on her face. Am I like her?

Maybe. We've both let our children escape us. I let Alena become a statistic, and I can't let the same thing happen to Ash. I know, I know: Ash is already a statistic, one more eighteen-to-twenty-four-year-old who fell prey to a cult on his college campus. But with my son, I can still strive for a happy ending.

I should have known better than to let Ash go off to Colorado, where there was no one to take care of him. Bits can barely take care of herself, and their piece-of-shit father . . . well. God help us all. Their piece-of-shit father.

The man beside me checks his watch and sighs. He runs a hand over his bald head. His eyes are murky with impatience. He is handsome. He has a Jewish face, a strong, sharp nose, intelligent eyes. A Jewish Mr. Clean in a necktie.

It was my sister, Viv, who talked me into joining a support group. She's always trying to get me to join things. She still thinks I might meet a man. Me. At my age. I can tell you how much I need a man. But I took her suggestion and found a support group for families of cult members. "Ellie!" she said when I told her. "Ash isn't in a cult!"

Is that a fact? Please. Can't we call a spade a spade? I am the mother of a cult member. And I want to know how other parents cope.

Now I'm finding out. With tears. With doughnuts. With affirmations from strangers. The crying woman blows her nose. Mr. Clean cracks his knuckles. I wonder which cult has split his life open.

Most Jews are like Viv: They find Orthodox Judaism more acceptable than Scientology, than the Moonies, than the Manson Family. Why? Because at least it's Judaism. That's what my friends from the JCC and the synagogue say. But Orthodox Judaism meets all the cult criteria: For one thing, it's apocalyptic. For another thing, Orthodox rabbis tell people like Ash that rational thoughts are bad, and crazy thoughts are good. (Okay, maybe they don't use those words, but their message is clear: Moses was wonderful! So what if he talked to bushes? Eve used to be not a fetus but a rib! God is good and kind and fair, even though the world is a crisis zone!) I can just imagine what those rabbis must have told Ash to lure him in: that Torah would solve all his problems, that if he followed it to the letter, his guilt would go up in a puff of smoke.

Only a cult would promise such claptrap. Who *doesn't* have guilt? Who doesn't want an instruction manual for life? I could certainly use one. But you don't see me sitting here pretending to have one.

Look, I'm as Jewish as the next person, the daughter of a Holocaust survivor. I'm very active in the synagogue. And I *know* how important Israel is. I know the Jews need a place. But does my *son* need a homeland so far from home? Has *he* been persecuted? Does he need to set up camp halfway across the world to wait for the Messiah, like a child waiting for the Tooth Fairy? What have I done to deserve this, I'd like to know? One child kidnapped, another *meshugena*, and Bits.

A black cat jumps onto Mr. Clean's lap. He doesn't move, doesn't touch it. He and the cat stare at each other until the cat bristles and leaps to the floor. It disappears into the kitchen.

Most people at this meeting seem to agree on one thing: if your child joins a cult, it doesn't mean you were a bad parent. I know I haven't done everything right (I let Alena out of my sight long enough to lose her), but I've been a wonderful mother to Bits and Ash. I went back to work after Ben left us. I made sure my kids got their educations. I fed them and clothed them. They have a lot to be thankful for. And how did they thank me? They left me. You'd think that kids who lost a sister and a father would want to stick with their mother. But the second she had the chance, Bits moved to Colorado. As soon as Ash finished high school, he did the same. And now! Ash isn't the only guilty party. Who knows what Bits has been doing since she moved to Boston? I'm certain she has secrets. I hear them in her silences. Mothers know these things. We just know.

At the end of the meeting, I don't want to talk to anyone. What would I say to these schmaltzy people?

Everyone is standing up, smoothing wrinkled skirts, hugging one another, accepting coffee refills. I hurry outside to my car and extract my keys from the black hole of my purse. I'll clean my purse out one of these days; I'll become the kind of woman who has a clean purse, an organized date book, fresh lipstick; a woman who joins groups that are interesting and fulfilling. But for now, all I know is that support groups aren't for me. I plan to tell Viv that coming to a stranger's house for a big group cry is nothing but a headache. I don't need it. Ash will come around. He's just going through a phase. Life will continue. Not that I have a say in whether or not life continues.

Someone is behind me, breathing close.

"Ellie, right?"

I turn. It's Mr. Clean.

"You're running out of here like someone's chasing you." His speech is quick and clipped, like he's both trying to sell me something and trying to escape me.

I clear my throat. "And you are?"

"Listen," he says, glancing over his shoulder. The sleeves of his suit jacket are too short. He stands before me like an overgrown child. "I know about the Orthodox Jews." He scratches his shiny scalp—a fast, jerky, ape-like movement. "A cult hiding behind the shield of religion. They invite you to a Shabbat dinner, right? What could be more innocent? 'Come to my house for Shabbos. Stay the night. Come to shul in the morning. Here. Eat this. Drink this. Play with my children. We're *family*.'" He squares his shoulders, his jaw set, his teeth clenched.

"Well, I've never had that ha—"

"And they reel you in just like that," Mr. Clean interrupts.

Who is he to interrupt me?! As if I'm not even here! As if we're not having a conversation!

"Do you have a child who—"

"I specialize in the Orthodox Jews, Ellie. Okay? I have connections. Have you heard of Ted Patrick, Ellie?"

I don't know why he has to keep repeating my name. It makes me feel like I owe him something. And what does he mean, "specialize"? What is he, a doctor? I fish through my purse for my sunglasses. There's a cough drop wrapper stuck to one lens. It flutters to the ground at our feet.

"Have you?" Mr. Clean asks.

"Ted Patrick?" I inch toward my car and lean against it. I put on my sunglasses.

"Black Lightning? The anti-cultist movement? Deprogramming?"

"Deprogramming?"

Mr. Clean laughs in a way that makes me think he hasn't laughed in years. No smile. No inflection. It raises goose bumps on my arm. "Ellie, are you willing to do anything to rescue your son?"

"I don't know if—"

"Has he stopped calling you yet? Does he preach to you?"

I don't say anything. I don't know what to say. I should ask him about his own son or daughter, ask him what he's doing here, but I hesitate. I have the strange sensation that I am standing on a precipice, that I can either step back and keep my balance, or take Mr. Clean's giant hand and step off into nothingness. Why do I feel myself reaching for him?

"Ever seen an athlete break a bone?" Mr. Clean asks.

"No, and I don't plan to," I say, hugging my purse to my body.

"What do they do on the playing field?" he asks. "Athlete breaks a bone, coach snaps it back into place." He demonstrates by putting his hands over his nose, as if he's readjusting the bones of it. I see that he's not wearing a wedding ring. "Snap!" he says.

I shiver.

"Listen," he says. "The mind works that way, too. Brainwash is like a bone snapped out of place. All we have to do . . . are you listening to me?" He glances over his shoulder again.

I lean toward him. I can't help it. He smells like a clean cologne, a nice, neat ocean wave.

"All we have to do," he says, "is make the brain snap back." He snaps his fingers. "Snap," he says.

I touch my thumb to the tip of my middle finger. The ground gives way beneath my shoes.

Mr. Clean takes hold of my arm. "I'm talking about reversing brainwash. Are you listening to me, Ellie? We can do this. You and I. You just have to want to."

April 13–14, 2002

M Y FRIEND MAGGIE, who teaches fifth grade at the Auburn School, is having a party. I'm standing out on her balcony, trying to get drunk, talking with a guy named Tony whose hair is blond and silky. I notice without much interest that he's missing a thumb. There's just a stump, smooth and round. He catches me looking at his hand and does the trick my uncle used to do: tucking each thumb inside a fist, then pretending one thumb separates at the knuckle. But Tony doesn't have to tuck.

I look away, out over Boston Harbor. The water glitters under the city lights. What if Ash's thumb is lying in a pile of rubble on a cobblestone street, the rest of his hand several yards away?

Okay, I know it's not. I know Ash is probably just ignoring us. It wouldn't be the first time. The first time was eleven months ago when he disappeared from Boulder. That time, I took it all in: the wide-open door of his dorm room, the stripped bed, his confused roommate, my mother screaming at anyone who would listen, *My children keep disappearing!* That time, I was worried. This time, I'm skeptical. I'm not like my mother, who always thinks at least one of us is dead. If she calls me and I don't call her back within three hours, she calls me again. And again. Every half hour until I pick up.

"What," says Tony, "never seen a guy without a thumb?"

"I'm not thinking about your thumb," I say.

Tony slides closer to me. "You're hot," he says. "Such curly brown hair. Big brown eyes. That smooth olive complexion. You remind me of my relatives from Sicily."

I smile and say nothing. I think of my mother saying, *Always smile. You never know when you'll meet your husband.*

"But you're not fat like my relatives."

"Thanks," I say.

"You're thin. You have perfect . . ." Tony cups his hands in front of his own chest, as if he's pressing two invisible balloons to his nipples. "You afraid of heights?" he whispers.

"Afraid?" I shrug.

"We're twenty-two floors up."

"Are you going to push me?"

"Are you going to jump?"

I imagine my body falling through the night sky, growing tiny as an action figure.

"You seem sad," Tony says.

"Nope."

"Distracted?"

"From what?"

Tony is quiet for a minute. Finally, he says, "You know, it wouldn't take as long as you'd think. To fall. It's a long way down, of course, but weighted objects fall fast."

Weighted objects. I think of Ash wearing his first yarmulke, something that looked more like a beret. Then wearing the black velvet yarmulke. Then dropping out of college. Then running away to Israel. All in six months. A slippery slope. Ash fell fast. I squeeze my eyes shut. Why am I doing my mother's worrying? Let Ash disappear into the desert. What is it to me?

I open my eyes and look at Tony. His Adam's apple is striking. It moves up and down. I want to rub it like a worry stone, to press my lips against it.

Later, on his mattress with no sheets, I see the moon through the window, silver and cheap like a nickel. Tony climbs on top of me, his gold cross swinging on its chain, knocking on my forehead. I watch with interest the way his face clenches, the way creases form between his eyebrows, the way his lips cinch up into a tight drawstring. He's older than I am. Forty? Forty-five? He has crow's feet, blond beard stubble laced with gray. He collapses on me. I can hardly breathe. I feel the cross between us, boring into my sternum. I wrap my arms around him and squeeze. *Don't think about Ash,* I tell myself, as the image I invented, the thumb in the street, begins seeping, full color, into the dark. I run my fingernails up the pebbles of Tony's spine.

Seconds later, he's snoring. I see a birdcage hanging directly above our heads. It's draped with a ratty beach towel. It could fall. My heart races at the thought of climbing out from under it. I push Tony carefully aside, quietly untangle clothes from afghan, locate socks, and run.

The next afternoon, I keep glancing at my phone. I know my mother's going to call. She'll want to know if I've talked to Ash. She'll cry when I tell her I haven't. It's been like this for two years. As soon as Ash moved to Boulder, she started saying things to me like, "Well, he's your responsibility now. That's what you both wanted, isn't it?" and "You two obviously don't need me, so you'd better look after each other." She tried to sound indifferent—so convincing! an arresting actress, my mother!—but whenever she called me at school, her first question was "When was the last time you saw Ash?" When Ash disappeared the first time, it was my fault. I'm sure it's my fault this time, too. My fault that two of my mother's children are missing. My fault that she's stuck with just me.

I log on to the Internet and search the headlines for at least the fifth time. The bomb detonated in an outdoor market, someplace where Ash probably bargains for dried papaya in his dumb broken Hebrew. I can practically hear the glass shattering. I can see raspberries, kiwis, pomegranates exploding, splattering on stone like jelly. Six people are dead. Two of the six are Chinese men. That leaves four dead people and sixty wounded people who could be Ash. Some of the wounded are critically wounded.

I read about the siege at the Church of the Nativity. Palestinian gunmen. Catholic hostages. Israeli tanks rolling through Bethlehem. Inside the church, an Armenian monk has been shot. The wound didn't kill him. But he's still a hostage, so he can't call his family to tell them he's alive.

I read about something that happened hours before the bomb: a shooting on the Gaza Strip. Palestinians died. Israelis died. The article says nothing about Americans.

I go into a chat room called AddictionNet. "What's everyone addicted to?" I write.

Someone writes, "Klonopin."

Someone writes, "Ovaltine."

Someone writes, "And you?"

"My brother's the one who's addicted to stuff," I write. "God, for instance."

A guy I know from a chat room called Boston Night Forum sends me an instant message. His name is Fin. We've been chatting for weeks. He's a medical student. He's very philosophical. We talk about everything without talking about it. "Busy?" he asks.

I want him here right this second, lying on top of me, filling me in, smelling of latex gloves and sterile instruments. "Are you dangerous?" I ask him. I know that he isn't. I feel it intuitively that he would never hurt me.

"I'm a medical student," he writes. "How many dangerous medical students do you know?"

I'm clawing at my legs, my ears are ringing, my throat is dry. *What if he's not a medical student? Or what if he's a medical student who's also a sociopath?* My heart thuds in my chest. I attempt a deep breath and fail. Maybe I'm having a heart attack, in which case, a medical student would be the perfect guest. "Come over," I write. I give him my address.

Within the hour, Fin's buzzing in from downstairs.

He has a goatee and two hoop earrings. He's wearing a white T-shirt with the sleeves torn off. In the living room, we watch a movie about a mobster, who takes a bullet for a woman and dies.

"My father left my mother," I tell Fin, who looks nothing like any medical student I've ever seen.

"Today?"

"No. I was eleven." I think about that early morning, when Ash and I watched from the top of the stairs. Our father didn't know we were watching. We didn't call out to him. Ash reached a hand out. I pulled it back and put it in his lap.

"You're interesting," Fin says, stroking his little goatee. In the dark, the television reflects on his shaved head. Shaved or bald? I can't tell.

"Interesting is dull," I say.

"No," he says, "it's the opposite." He closes the gap between us on the couch, peels off his shirt, climbs on top of me. He is unzipping my jeans. Now his hands are in my hair. He's winding my hair around his finger, tighter and tighter.

"What are you doing?" I ask, but he doesn't answer. He just tugs harder at my hair and keeps winding. I push at his pierced nipples with my fists. "Seriously," I say. "Stop." He continues to ignore me. How different this is from my first time. Ten years old. A boy with shiny red hair. His body weight replaced the invisible weight that had been bearing down on me all summer, had been crushing me since Alena disappeared. It wasn't real sex—back then, I guess we weren't capable of real sex—but it was some simulation of what we understood sex to be. It was euphoric, enlightening, sweet relief. This is the opposite. Fin is the reason people warn against sex with strangers. Tears are blurring my vision. My scalp feels like it's separating from my skull. "You're not a medical student," I say. It comes out like an accusation, even though I'm the one who has made a horrible mistake; Fin is just the person he's probably been for many years: a guy most women would never let into their homes.

On the carpet below us are the construction-paper clocks I've been making—on Tuesday, I'm going to teach my first graders to tell time. The clocks don't have numbers yet. They're just blank circles, faces that haven't chosen expressions. And next to all that construction paper are my scissors. The sharp ones with the blue handles. I reach to the carpet, stretch my fingers toward them. The handles are in my fist. The pain is sickening, but I stop resisting Fin. His hipbones mash into mine. With one quick motion, I lift the scissors and stab him, hard, in the upper arm.

"Fuck!" He smacks my ear so hard, it rings. He rolls off me to the floor. "Fuck!" he screams again, cradling his arm.

My heart is chopping in my chest, but I feel a little thrill. I've never stabbed anyone before. I am in awe of myself. It's like I'm starring in a movie about a very brave girl. I rub the sore spot on my head. I notice a small drop of blood on the carpet. I stretch my leg out to touch it with my toe.

Fin starts dressing. He is smiling, just his mouth, not his eyes. He bends down abruptly to push his nose up to mine. "Memorize my face," he hisses.

It's ugly. He has razor-burned cheeks. Chapped lips. None of the smooth softness of that redhead I once knew. I miss the softness of childhood, the comfort of inexperience. What do I want with razor burn and nipple rings and a grown man who pulls hair? "Get out," I say. I stand and walk around him to the front door, hold it open with one arm.

He doesn't argue, but he takes his time dressing. And he steps on my toes on his way out.

The movie is still going. There is gunfire, then the phone rings. At first, I think it's a phone in the movie, so it rings three times before I stumble into the kitchen and grab the cordless. *Ash, if this is you, I'm going to kill you. . .*

It's my mother.

"I'm still trying him," I tell her. "I'm sure he'll call back soon."

"No," she says, and her voice is small. "Bits. Listen."

I sink into a chair. I'm shaking. My teeth are chattering. Did I lock the front door?

"Bits."

"What?"

"Honey . . . it's not good."

Is she talking about Ash? He's dead. How could he be dead? No. My mother always just *thinks* we're dead. Shouldn't that keep us from dying?

"She's . . ." my mother says, and I understand then that she's not talking about Ash. Could she possibly be talking about Alena?

"They found her body," she says, and her voice is strange. "It's over," she says again and again. "It's over. It's over. It's over."

SUNDAY NIGHT I wind up at a bar in Migrash Harusim (the Russian Compound, in English) only because my roommate Todd's band, Arbahim, is playing. Since everyone at Yeshiva Hillel is *shomar n'gia*, meaning we don't touch girls, we're all trying to keep our distance from this cluster of girls up front near the stage, which isn't really a stage, since it's level with the floor. The girls, probably study-abroad kids, probably Jewish, but definitely secular—not to mention drunk—are dressed in a way that reminds me of frat parties, all skimpy and sparkly. They're dangerously close to Todd and the other guys, and I guess they're not observing the Omer period since they're dancing with their arms up over their heads, hips twitching, wrists circling in the air. The Omer period is a time of partial mourning. We're mourning the deaths of Rebbe Akiba's 24,000 students, who were struck by a plague 1,850 years ago. The plague was a punishment because they were jealous of one another, but we have to mourn them anyway. That means, among other things, no dancing.

I notice one girl dancing alone, about six feet away from the rest of the girls. She's dressed like they are and looks as though she could be one of them, but something about the way she dances is different, slightly off, as if she's never danced before, as if she's trying to mirror the other dancers. I watch her pile her long yellow hair on top of her head with her hand, then let it fall. Todd looks uncomfortable. He sings with his eyes closed, but he keeps open-ing one of them and peering down at the girls. In between songs, he presses nervously on his hearing aid, the way he does when we're learning a really difficult tractate of Talmud. I can't say I feel sorry for him. We're in a bar! With music. What does he expect people to do, have a minyan? I've tried to explain to him, "Todd, bars are for secular people. We shouldn't be hanging out in bars." But he says, "I just want to play my music, Asher."

That's Todd for you. He's also one of the only guys in the ye-shiva who won't go by his Hebrew name, or at least by a more Jew-ish name. He says he's already got a name. But it's not Todd who's rationalized playing music during the Omer period. It's David, the drummer. David's practically a professional at finding loopholes. He says that playing music isn't festive, as long as no one's dancing, and that, in fact, Arbahim's songs are mournful.

I shove my hands into my pockets and survey the room. I'd never tell Bits this, but whenever I'm in public, I find myself glanc-ing around for suspicious people. Bits is always looking for con-firmation that Israel is dangerous. She's in love with the American media. A few weeks ago, when I called her after the first of the Passover suicide bombings, I tried, after assuring her I was alive, to get off the subject of terrorist attacks and talk about meaning-ful things. Like the Omer. She said, "How you can sit around counting goddamn *barley* while there are *bombs* exploding out-side your window is beyond me." She loves to say "goddamn" and "Jesus Christ" to me as much as possible.

Anyway, tonight, I don't see anyone suspicious. There's an Is-raeli couple sitting at a table in the back, smoking nargileh. There's the bartender, a bald guy who looks bored. He's examining his fingernails. Now David is in the middle of one of his many gratu-itous drum solos. The rest of the band watches him and fidgets.

Truthfully, I'm not nervous most of the time. I guess that's partly because I understand the Arab-Israeli conflict: It's not just a land dispute like most people think. It didn't start in 1948 when World War II ended and the UN sanctioned the creation of a Jewish state. It started in Biblical times, when Jacob and Esau became enemies over the issue of their father's birthright. The Jews are Jacob's descendants. The Arabs are Esau's. And Jacob's people are the ones with the birthright. It's in the Torah. How much more evidence do people need? It wasn't the UN that first promised Israel to the Jews. It was God, thousands of years before, when He told our forefather Abraham, "I will give this land to your family forever." (He also said, "I will curse anyone who curses you," and that obviously includes anyone who participates in or supports the suicide bombings.) We can't deny what's written.

The risk of living in Jerusalem is nothing compared to God's will. That's partly why I'm not in Colorado anymore, where I did less than a year of college before realizing that college was pointless. How could I focus on serving God if I was an American college student?

Bits can think what she likes. I don't call her anymore. Some people might judge me for that, but look: something just happened to me, something awful, at the end of my Passover vacation. Well, it didn't happen to *me* exactly, but I was there. . . . I do my best not to think about it, there's no sense in thinking about it, but when you have a terrible experience, you figure out your priorities. So here's what I figured out: I'm through with my past. That includes my mother and Bits.

One of the dancing girls bumps into me. I turn and walk out of the bar. I want to get back to the yeshiva.

IN ASH'S MIND, "secular" (his word) means weak. By which logic, I'm weak. But since our father could win a medal for outstanding acts of weakness, it surprises me that Ash can throw the word around so casually. And he does! Take the last time I talked to him, for example, right after a suicide bombing. I told him what I thought about his living in Israel when there are bombs blowing up every five seconds, and he said, "Bits, what do you want me to do? Not believe in what I believe in?" He said, "Only weak people believe in nothing, Bits."

You want weak? Okay. How's this? My father almost let Ash and me drown. It was late August 1990, a little over a year after Alena disappeared, on what turned out to be our last-ever attempt at a family vacation. We had driven from New Jersey to Boston, and stayed a few miles from Cambridge in a synagogue, right in the sanctuary, our sleeping bags rolled out on the wine-colored carpet; we slept on top of them because of the heat. We slept in the synagogue because of my father, who never willingly set foot in a synagogue with religious intentions but would have slept in a sewer before paying for a hotel room. "We're Jewish," he always said. "That ought to count for something."

When we woke up in that synagogue, my parents fought. I can't remember the particulars, only that, after Alena disappeared, they always fought. My mother decided to go shopping in

Harvard Square, and my father took Ash and me canoeing on the Charles. We didn't have life vests, even though my father couldn't swim. Ash and I were eight and eleven and couldn't swim either. About twenty minutes into the whole affair, my father dropped his sunglasses into the water, then impulsively lurched after them, tipping the boat almost forty-five degrees and letting in a cold surge of water. He reeled back, and the canoe promptly flipped. We all splashed into the water, clinging to the overturned canoe, not an easy task for little kids with little arms. I arranged Ash in front of me, draped his arms over the hump of the canoe, and squashed in behind him, wedging my arms around his, pinning his hands down with my own.

My father's lips went white around the edges. Ash and I screamed and screamed, each waving an arm over our heads, but our father just clung to the canoe, pressing his cheek to it, his eyes squeezed shut, whimpering, "There are so many things I haven't done yet."

Eventually, we were rescued. One of those eight-man crew boats, filled with Harvard students, rowed right up to us. The coxswain yelled, "Weigh 'nuff!" and then, "Set the boat!" and one by one, someone from the boat jumped into the polluted water and helped one of us in. First my father (who had shouted that he needed to be saved first so he could help his children), then Ash, then me.

The rest of that day, my father looked dazed. My mother about killed him when she heard what had happened: "We go on a family vacation to get a break from the hell we live in. And what do you do? Almost take my other two children from me!" We drove home to New Jersey in silence. Ash and I held hands in the backseat, staring out opposite windows.

It was one week later, on a Sunday morning, when my parents had their final fight. My mother was making pancakes. My father was telling her it was time to give up on Alena. My mother threw a spatula at him. Batter splattered on his plaid shirt. He looked down at his shirt, then back up at my mother. He said, "Life is too short. It's time to move on."

My mother said, "She's our daughter, Ben! How can you move on when nothing's definite yet? What's wrong with you?"

Ash and I sat at the kitchen table, our heads rotating from parent to parent. Our father said, "I can't take this." He said, "Kids, your mother and I don't love each other anymore." In my memory, he's cheerful when he says it, as if he's telling us to get packed for Disneyland. He was gone a day later. He stopped helping my mother search for Alena. He stopped contacting us, with the exceptions of a birthday or holiday every few years. He moved to Colorado, met a divorced woman who had three daughters, and raised them as if three of someone else's kids could make up for the one he was missing.

He popped up again during my last year of high school, offering me his address so I could get in-state tuition at the University of Colorado. "Get out of New Jersey," he said. "Have some new experiences. There's nothing like the mountain air."

I was happy, of course. Who wouldn't want to leave New Jersey? But I knew it wasn't an act of goodwill on my father's part. It was a gesture not unlike staying in synagogues instead of paying for hotel rooms, not unlike stealing Life Savers from the 7-Eleven, which I saw him do sometimes when I was a kid, not unlike cheating on taxes, which, according to my mother, he also did. My father doesn't suffer from garden-variety cheapness; rather, it's his belief—it's always been his belief, as far back as I can remember—that the world owes him something. Which means he owes nothing to anyone.

So don't tell *me* about weak.

4 Iyar 5762
(April 16, 2002)

IT'S TUESDAY AFTERNOON seder, the second time in the day that Todd and I learn together in the *beit midrash*. The *beit midrash* is the biggest room in the yeshiva, the walls lined with thousands of Jewish books. Half of the room is filled with tables for studying; the other half, where we stand to pray, is empty except for the holy ark. Todd and I are sitting at one of the tables, talking about Moses' older sister, Miriam, who committed *lashon hara*, or evil speech, during the Exodus by wondering aloud why Moses wasn't sleeping with his wife. When she learned that God had told Moses to remain celibate for spiritual reasons, Miriam committed more *lashon hara* by pointing out that everyone else was sleeping with their husbands and wives, so what made Moses so special?

It sounds like something Bits would do. Wouldn't Bits love the opportunity to insist that I'm no purer than she is, or to accuse me of being selfish rather than pious? Wouldn't Bits love to get involved in my personal business, to make herself look like a hero, a one-woman sexual revolution?

To punish Miriam, God gave her *tzaraat*, a skin disease that some scholars think might have been leprosy, and banished her to confinement. According to one source, Moses defended Miriam by drawing a circle around himself and telling God that he wouldn't leave the circle until Miriam was healed.

If you ask me, Moses wasn't defending Miriam for her sake (he obviously knew she was wrong); he was defending her to show God how humble he was, how righteous, how forgiving. He wanted to ingratiate himself. But Todd doesn't see what I see.

"Moses confined himself in a little circle to show God how impractical confinement is," he says.

Todd's one of those redheads who has more freckles than normal skin. He has to slather SPF 50 sunscreen all over his face whenever he goes outside, but it doesn't seem to help. He leans toward me now, over the polished wooden tabletop, and I can see where his nose is peeling, right across the bridge.

"Moses was saying to God, 'Look, I'll stay stuck in this circle until You release my sister. And if I'm stuck, I can't keep leading Your people toward the Promised Land.'"

I snort. "You think Moses was trying to teach God a lesson? Are you crazy?"

"Not a lesson." Todd bites his lip and shakes his head. "That's not what I mean. He just wanted to *remind* God that confinement is impractical."

"It's not always impractical," I say. "Confining ourselves from the secular world, for example. That's practical. Then we don't have to worry about people offering us ham sandwiches or calling us on Saturday mornings or acting like it's cool to be atheist. . . . I hate when people act like it's cool to be atheist!"

"Well . . . what if the secular world is your family?" Todd's fidgeting with a pencil, twirling it around his knuckles. I see where this is going. Todd's infatuated with his family. He calls them every day. They're always saying stuff to him like, "We support you, Todd!" It's like *Leave It to Beaver*. Todd thinks everyone's family is like his, so ever since I made the mistake of telling him that I'd stopped calling my mother and Bits, that I wanted nothing more to do with them, he's been letting me know what he thinks of my decision.

Todd and I became both roommates and learning partners, or *chavrusas*, almost as soon as we met. I couldn't see a good reason not to. We were already so lucky: Most yeshiva boys in Jerusalem have all kinds of housing problems—apartments all the way across town, eight guys to one room, expensive housing—but Yeshiva Hillel's dorms are right inside the yeshiva. It seemed so convenient, living in my yeshiva with my *chavrusa*. So when everyone said, "You'll see too much of each other—it's not healthy," we didn't listen. But lately, I'm starting to see their point. Something has changed between Todd and me.

I don't get Todd's obsession with loyalty. It's naïve, if you ask me. Who, besides God, deserves my loyalty? My father, the opposite of Moses, who shed his family like a scratchy sweater, who, the morning he decided to leave us, the morning my mother threw a spatula at him, turned to Bits and me and said, "Kids, I don't love you anymore"? (Bits always tells me I'm wrong; she swears he said that *he and our mother* didn't love each other anymore, but I don't know . . . I remember what I remember.) Does my fraternity brother Chris Rue, who came on to Vanessa Barletta, my last girlfriend from the secular world, deserve my loyalty? (I was right there! I was the one who had brought Vanessa to that party. I watched Chris back her into a wall, their noses barely an inch apart.) Does Vanessa, who said to me the next night, "Ash, this isn't working out anymore," and left me sitting on my bed in my dorm room staring at my roommate's Magic Johnson poster on the closed door, listening to Ben Harper—I don't even like Ben Harper; I'm pretty sure he's a Christian—thinking that, at least, *at least,* she'd come back for her Ben Harper CD? Does *she* deserve my loyalty?

"There is no loyalty in this world," I say. "We can only pledge loyalty to God, because people can't be trusted."

Todd laughs. "Asher! These people—Miriam, Moses—they were just human. Miriam only did what she did because she was jealous. Haven't you ever been jealous of your sister?"

"No! My sister—" I almost said, *My sister's a slut!* I bite my lip.

"Okay. Well, I used to be really jealous of my brother. I was always good at music, but he was better at sports. My friends and I would sit around and make fun of jocks. You know, how people do. And we'd say bad things about my brother. My own brother! I kind of hated him," Todd says. "I told myself I was better than him, wasn't as shallow or something. But really, I was jealous. . . . Anyway, it was my sophomore year of high school when suddenly . . . I lost my hearing."

I never asked Todd about his hearing aid. I've been wondering about it since I met him, and now suddenly he's talking about it like it's no big deal. I'm not sure how to act. Should I say, "It's okay to have a hearing aid"? Should I pretend I never even noticed he had one? I look down at the soft green carpet, at the worn toe of my black shoe.

"That was my *tzaraat*," Todd says.

I look up. He's tapping his hearing aid.

"Especially back then. No one really cares if you wear glasses, for example, but for some reason, when you're fifteen, a hearing aid's almost as bad as a wheelchair. Everyone started treating me like a leper. And it came on out of nowhere, Asher. The deafness. I mean, it wasn't medical." He taps at his hearing aid a couple more times. "If God punished Miriam for being disloyal to Moses, then maybe He was punishing me for being disloyal to my brother."

I wind one of my *payos*, or earlocks, around my finger. I'm one of the only Yeshiva Hillel guys with *payos*. I've been growing them for months. It's usually Hasids who grow their *payos*. Hasids are different from the kind of Jews you find at a place like Yeshiva Hillel, but God commands Jewish men not to mar the corners of their faces, so I don't trim my *payos*. End of story. I take a deep breath and decide to be honest. How else will Todd learn? I tell him what I've been suspecting since I met him: "God took your hearing," I say. "He took it so you would become religious. He took your hearing so you would stop hearing the noise of the secular world and hear Him instead."

"Well, I don't know—"

"He gave Miriam *tzaraat* so she would fear Him," I continue. "And look what happened to you and to Miriam. You both came to fear God. Right? But whatever. We're getting off track. We were talking about Moses' strength, Moses' loyalty to God. That's what we should focus on."

"You think my family's in trouble," Todd says after a minute, "because they're not religious."

In fact, I'm not thinking about Todd's family. Todd's the only one who's thinking about his family every second of the day. What I'm thinking is that God knows what I did to Alena, and I'm sure He's waiting for me to slip up again. I'm thinking that anyone who turns his back on God should prepare himself for the worst.

"I just can't quite buy that," Todd's saying. "I mean, they're my family! We're supposed to honor—"

"Our parents? Yes. Honor thy mother and thy father. Unless they ask you to violate Torah. You only have to honor them if they honor God."

"I don't know, Asher."

"Listen," I say. "This is our family." Todd won't meet my eyes. I open my arms. "These people. Torah is thicker than blood."

April 16–17, 2002

I DIDN'T THINK I would grieve. I guess I believed all the people, all those years, who said, "If they find evidence that Alena is dead, it will be a relief. You'll finally get some rest." People who knew nothing about loss gave my family unsolicited sermons on "closure," on the bright prospect of one day being able to move on. Now my sadness has caught me by surprise. I can't believe I digested those people's stupid opinions. Of course they were wrong! "Dead" is so much more final than "missing."

We think we know who took Alena. We've suspected since early 1991. That year, a man who had been convicted of armed robbery in New Jersey was released from prison on parole, on the condition that he not cross the state line. He broke his parole and hid at his uncle's place in Connecticut until someone tipped the police off. From inside the house, the man saw two cops walking up the front steps and promptly shot himself in the mouth. Right in his uncle's kitchen.

The man's name was Buckley Quinn, a name that to me, still now, sounds oddly innocuous. Buckley Quinn is a Pilgrim name. The name of a well-heeled boy with a Nantucket summer home. Not the name of a child-killer. Turned out, since his release from prison, he had buried the bodies of two little girls in his back-yard. In a town eleven miles away from ours. When my mother heard about Buckley Quinn, even after hearing that the two little girls unearthed from his backyard weren't Alena, she said that she was sure: Buckley Quinn had taken Alena. Mothers know these things, she said.

And then, the kicker: There were two hairs on the floor of Buckley Quinn's brown Cadillac that matched the hairs my mother had submitted to the police from Alena's pillow and hairbrush.

At that point, we had to accept that Alena was probably dead. The searching became less intense. My mother stopped making regular calls to the state crime bureau, to the governor, to the FBI. She stopped spouting alternately depressing and hopeful bits of missing-child trivia: *Forty percent of all children abducted by strangers are killed. . . . Only ten percent of missing children aren't found within the first year.* She stopped constructing press kits to send to news stations. She started referring to Alena in the past tense. Then she talked about Alena less and less, as if rather than having been suddenly abducted, she was gradually fading away.

So we've known for years, but thinking you know and knowing for sure are two very different things. Confirmation is more painful than suspicion. Alena's death never felt real before, at least in part because when she was alive, she seemed like the most alive person in the world, or at least in our family. She used to gather us all into the living room after dinner, sometimes even passing out construction-paper flyers beforehand, and perform for us, plays and musicals, using my father's neckties, Ash's hockey jerseys, whatever she could find, for props and costumes. The story lines never made sense, and she made all the songs up as she went along. She would freeze with her arms spread out at the end of each scene, as if a heavy velvet curtain might drop down in front of her. Our parents and Ash and I, squeezed together on the couch, cheered for her as if she were Elvis, and I still remember how that felt, my parents on either side of me, holding hands in my lap, their wedding bands shining. Later, we were never that close.

My mother wants to have a funeral. The prospect, to me, is repugnant.

"Do we have to invite Dad?" I ask.

"Invite?! What, I should send invitations?"

The evasiveness of her answer makes me wonder if she already called him. I hate the thought of my mother and father in the same room, of my mother oozing anger, even after all these years, because my father left her, left us, and she never moved on. My father will act indifferent toward her, not because he'll be playing it cool but because he honestly feels indifferent.

A funeral seems gratuitous anyway. There's hardly anything to bury, just small bones and black hair, which a dog dug up in a park half a mile from the house I grew up in, the house my mother still lives in. The house we all lived in for all those years, wondering where on earth Alena was.

"You do realize Ash needs to know," my mother says. She's given up her Ash-is-dead campaign, now that she has something bigger to focus on. She's accepted that he's healthy and safe and snubbing her in her time of need. "He doesn't call his mother."

"He's not calling his sister either."

My mother sighs. "He needs to be at the funeral. Bits, do you understand me? It's up to you to get him there. I don't mean to put pressure on you, but . . ."

"Right. Uh-huh."

"We all need to be there."

All. It's the saddest word in the world, once it no longer includes everyone it used to include. I remember Alena's last birthday party, a magician in a black cape with red lining who made things disappear. I squeeze my eyes shut and press the phone hard to my forehead. I try to draw a breath.

"Promise me you'll get him home for the funeral," my mother is saying. "We'll have it here. At Beth Shalom."

I open my eyes, return the phone to my ear. "I'll tell him," I say.

"Promise me."

"Okay," I say. "I promise."

At night, I call Ash for what must be the eight thousandth time. I've memorized his outgoing message, and I start to recite it along with his voice: "Shalom," I say, collapsing onto my living room couch, but then I realize that I'm listening to something I've never heard before. In English, Ash's voice says, "You've reached Asher. Please leave a message. Todd, if this is you, wait for me. I might be late."

I hang up and sit up straight. I set the phone in my lap. For some reason, I think of fourteen-year-old Ash in his Save the Whales cap. Ash's great love hasn't always been God. For a while, it was whales. Then animals in general (Militant Vegan Ash). Then his fraternity (Awkward Frat Boy Ash).

I sit on my hands because I'm afraid I'll call Wade. I eye the phone warily. Then I think I should try to relax. "Relax," I instruct myself aloud. So weird how people say that: *Just relax.* Then they say, *Just breathe.* Right. No problem. I try to be happy that Ash is alive and well enough to change his outgoing message. I even stretch my mouth into a wide smile. "What a relief!" I say the way someone might say it on a detergent commercial, upon seeing the red wine stain disappear. But my voice is shaking. Relaxation eludes me. Of course, I know now that Ash survived the bomb in the outdoor market. He survived the shooting on the Gaza Strip. He did not die inside the Church of the Nativity among the Palestinian gunmen and Catholic hostages. I do not have two dead siblings. But now my suspicions have been confirmed: he's ignoring us on purpose.

⌒∽⌒

I wait up until two in the morning, even though I have to work tomorrow, just so I can call Yeshiva Aleph (I found the number on the yeshiva's Web site) at nine a.m. Israel time.

A man answers in a different language, ostensibly Hebrew, and I ask him to please speak English. When he does, he has my mother's Brooklyn accent. "How can I help you?"

"I'm looking for one of your students," I say. "Ash Kellerman. Well, he goes by Asher now. But that's not his real name. But maybe you think it is."

"We don't have an Asher Kellerman."

I cross the room to my bed and lie down. I examine the spider-web crack in the ceiling. Has it grown? It looks bigger than usual. I wonder if one day the ceiling will split apart and fall on my head. I wonder if Ash will think, *Oh well, it's God's will.*

"You don't understand," I say, and my voice breaks. "I have to tell him something important."

"That may be so, but I don't know who this person is."

"Can't you check?"

"This yeshiva is very small," says the man. "I know all of our students."

"That's not possible!" I spring out of bed and go to the kitchen. I take Ash's last letter out of the junk drawer and check the return address, and that's when I remember: He uses a P.O. box. "Please," I hear myself say.

The man starts to get annoyed. "There's no one here by that name," he says. "All right? Good-bye."

When he hangs up on me, I think I should call my mother, to tell her that Ash is hiding from us, that Yeshiva Aleph is not his yeshiva. But I won't call my mother because there are things I could have done, things I didn't do, to change the course of our family's history: I could have tried harder to make Ash stay in college. I could have begged my father not to leave us. Minutes before

Alena was kidnapped, when she and Ash asked me to play goalie in the driveway, I could have said, "Sure," instead of, "Get out of my room."

I won't call my mother because this could be my final chance to do something for my family. I can't remember the last time I did anything for anyone, unless I count giving people orgasms. Once, back in Boulder, when Ash was accusing me of being a bad Jew (those were the kinds of conversations we were having before he left), he said to me, "God gave us six hundred thirteen command-ments. Do you fulfill even one of them?"

Getting my brother to come home for our sister's funeral must somehow fulfill *at least* one. So I'll be the one to tell Ash that the uncertainty we've lived with for thirteen years, the blanket of gray that has covered his life, that drove him to the black-and-white world of religion, no longer exists. We have answers now.

I go to my computer and start searching for yeshivas in Israel. I will find Ash. I will find him and bring him home and we will laugh about this one day, about the time he moved to Israel to be an Orthodox Jew.

M Y KIDS THINK I've never had an exciting moment in my life. They think I've always been the grieving mother, the abandoned wife. But, of course, they didn't know me in my prime. My life, my marriage to Ben, once held the promise of backpacks and foreign transportation systems and sunrises in deserts halfway around the world. I'm not saying that those are realistic things to expect from a life. I'm just saying that I was a kid when I met Ben, and yes, our marriage vows warned me of the bad times ("for worse," "for poorer," "in sickness"), but I must have thought it would be cute to have problems, the way it is in romantic comedies—an opportunity to cry and eat chocolate chip ice cream in bed and have a best friend, as fun and fat as a beach ball, pick me up and dust me off.

Does Ash remember that his parents met in Israel? Back when I was a college student, I received a scholarship for children of Holocaust survivors to study at Hebrew University for a summer. That same summer, Ben was traveling through Eastern Europe with a friend. They wound up in Jerusalem. And then there we all were, taking those all-day intensive Hebrew language classes. I would stare at Ben in his cutoff jeans and leather jewelry, loving the way his mustache moved when he tried to sound out the Hebrew words for the plastic fruits and vegetables the teacher brought to class. He had thick hair to his shoulders because it was the early seventies. (I used to wear my hair long, too, parted down the middle. I hated it because it was so frizzy, but now, of course, I know it was beautiful.)

One day after class, Ben invited me home for lunch, and I went with him and his friend to the house they were staying in (some hippie friends of friends of friends). As we were approaching the house, an Arab man in a white kaftan appeared out of nowhere, yanked every pair of jeans off the clothesline in the front yard, and ran. (Back then, in Israel, jeans were expensive.)

Without a moment's hesitation, Ben and his friend sprinted after the man, tackled him, and wrestled the jeans away from him. I stood in the middle of the street, watching, my heart pounding in my chest. When the man in the kaftan ran off, his empty hands in the air as if the two hippie American guys might be carrying guns, Ben and his friend headed back to me, arms full of blue jeans, goofy grins on their faces because they had just out-machoed the thief. I looked at Ben and thought, *This man will take care of me. This man will protect me. My life will be fulfilling—exciting and safe all at once.* I knew right then and there, on a residential street in Jerusalem in 1971, that I would marry Benjamin Kellerman.

Like I said, I was a kid. I ignored the fact that Ben wasn't on speaking terms with his parents (he had borrowed so much money from them without paying them back, they had cut him off, and then he wrote them off and never—still to this day, as far as I know—forgave them). I ignored the way his eyes would dart around the room when I talked. I ignored it when he met my mother and chewed her ear off for forty-five minutes about transcendental meditation, not noticing that she was yawning. ("What is he, a professor?" my mother asked me, jerking a thumb at Ben.) I even ignored it eight years later when I was six months' pregnant with Bits, and he took off traveling again with the same friend, this time to South America. I ignored and ignored and ignored, and look what wound up happening: I realized too late that I had married the wrong man. Bits and Ash don't even know how wrong. I've spared them a number of details. He is their father, after all.

But, more important, I am their mother. So with Mr. Clean's help, I'm doing something about Ash. Maybe I'm overstepping my boundaries, maybe I'm supposed to let my kids make their own mistakes—that's what the self-proclaimed experts say—but I know about mistakes, about how indelible they can be.

O N T H E N O. 6 bus (that's something my mother and sister don't know: I do take buses), an Israeli girl sits down beside me. She's talking with the girl across the aisle from her. They are laughing loudly, practically screaming. The one next to me is wearing pants so tight, I can't imagine how she got them on, not that I want to imagine that. The one across the aisle has her bra straps showing; they're pink and lacy. I inch away, still unaccustomed (I pray I'll always be unaccustomed) to the way Israelis treat personal space.

We pass the police headquarters, then Ammunition Hill, the Six-Day War memorial. We pass an Arab neighborhood where a barefoot man is carrying a basket on his head, then the outskirts of Mea Shaarim, one of the most religious neighborhoods in the world, where tzitzit, the fringe religious men wear under their clothes, swing from the clotheslines.

The girl beside me shrieks with laughter and leans back against my shoulder. Her coarse hair brushes the side of my neck. I cringe and inch closer to my window. *"Slicha,"* I mumble, even though I'm not the one who should be excusing myself. The sight of her naked back, that space in between the hem of her shirt and the waist of her jeans, makes me queasy.

The bus climbs a hill, and I lean my forehead against the window. We pass the Museum on the Seam, where I've never been—

who has time for museums?—then another Arab neighborhood where men stand selling sesame bread and ice cream, children's clothing and spices. We turn right on Haneviim Street.

When I get off the bus in Migrash Harusim, I can still feel where the girl leaned against my arm, as if she left wet paint there. The world outside yeshiva feels like that now—wet paint, messy and unwelcome. Sometimes the smell of it, of *treyf* food, of strong cologne, literally makes me feel sick. As I walk toward the bar where Todd's band is playing tonight, I see the secular world all around me: on fluorescent flyers taped to the walls of buildings, in the litter on the streets and in the sewers, but I can almost ignore it. All year, I've been building an invisible filter around my body, I don't want ungodly things touching me.

When I pass the alley, just inches from the door of the bar, someone says, "Hey."

A blond girl is leaning against the brick wall. She looks familiar. I stop walking and squint at her. It's the girl who was here Sunday night, dancing by herself.

"You speak English or Hebrew?" she asks.

I clear my throat. "Both," I say, which isn't quite true. I can talk about *arvads* and red heifers with the best of them, but my conversational Hebrew is pretty limited.

"I grew up bilingual," she says. "We spoke Hebrew at home, but when I hear it now, I pretend I don't understand." She flips her hand back and forth as if she's waving away cigarette smoke.

"Why?" I ask. I step into the alley, into the shadows.

Her eyes widen, as if in surprise. "You really couldn't pay me to speak to you in Hebrew," she says.

"Fine," I say. "Whatever. I don't have any money anyway."

She introduces herself as Monica and holds out her hand to shake.

"I'm Asher," I say. I look at her hand, which is pale and thin with brown freckles, then at her face, which is the same, and shake my head. "Sorry. I only shake hands with my mother and sister."

"How formal. Do they shake hands with each other, too?"

Monica laughs, and when she does, she looks strangely familiar to me.

"Well, you know what I mean. I, um, hug them." I cross my arms around my chest. I would go inside right now, just walk out of the alley and into the bar, I really would, but back at the yeshiva, we just counted twenty days, which is two weeks and six days of the Omer. Each day of the Omer, except the forty-ninth, represents one path to learning Torah. The twentieth day is the day to practice the art of conversation, so it would be irreverent to walk away. "You know what I mean," I say again.

She takes a swig of her drink. Something in a clear glass. I wonder if she's allowed to have her drink outside the bar, if she hid it as she slipped outside, or if she's just not the type to worry about getting caught. "I was testing you, to see. I thought I could trick you," she says, "like in Simon Says, when you get so used to doing what you're told, you wind up forgetting to wait for 'Simon says.'" She tips her head back and shakes ice into her mouth. I can't tell if she's insulting me. She crunches ice and I shiver. "Want some ice?" she asks, holding her glass out.

I put my hands up like a shield. "No."

She shrugs. "I'm not trying to poison you." She tips the rest of the ice into her mouth.

I stuff my hands into my pockets and take a small step back from her, remembering the serpent in the Garden of Eden, who weakened Adam and Eve: *Go ahead,* said the serpent, *eat from this tree. You certainly will not die.*

"Where are you from?" Monica asks.

"South Jersey."

"I'm from California. Bay Area."

The Bay Area. Like Chris Rue, my fraternity brother who stole Vanessa from me. He was from San Francisco. He wore a baseball cap backward with sunglasses resting on the rim, the picture of cool. He rode his bike everywhere without holding the handlebars. He said "hella" instead of "very." He held Vanessa's hip with one hand and pressed his other hand against the wall beside her face, his arm outstretched.

"I've been studying at Hebrew University all year," Monica says. "I probably won't go home. I'll probably make aliyah, join the army." She makes a gun with her hands and pretends to shoot it at the opposite wall. Then she drops her skinny arms to her sides and looks at me, slowly moving her eyes from my head down to my shoes and back up again. Her lips are pursed and pushed to one side. "I trust you," she says. "You have a look I trust. It's your coloring, maybe. You're dark. I don't trust people who are too fair."

"You're fair," I say, and then I feel my neck get hot. I don't want her to think I'm checking her out.

"It's also that you're not too big. You're not, like, one of those muscle guys."

I stand up straighter before I can tell myself not to.

"I mean, not that you're scrawny. You're just regular. A regular guy with brown hair and brown eyes. I like that."

"Okay," I say. "I mean, I never asked you."

"Do you trust me?"

"Why would I—"

"Are you some kind of yeshiva boy or something?"

I nod. She has glitter on her chest. I glance at the ground. It's dirtier in the alley than it is out on the sidewalk. We're standing in candy wrappers and cigarette butts.

"The kind who just decided to be a yeshiva boy, or the kind whose parents make him go to yeshiva when he finishes high school?"

I don't answer.

"You know it's Yom Hazikaron today?" she asks.

"Sure," I say.

"In case you didn't know, that's the Day of the Fallen Soldier."

"Yeah," I say. "I know." But I'm not sure if I knew that. What do I need with secular holidays? They shouldn't even be called holidays. What's holy about them?

"You yeshiva boys. You all think you can just study and pray, study and pray."

Monica's holding an imaginary prayer book, bowing up and down over it.

"You hate the Israeli government for being secular. You resent having to fight in the army, but who do you think is protecting you?" She puts one fist on her hip.

"Hashem protects us."

She nods, inspecting me like I'm something under a microscope. "So you think without the IDF, you'd be safe? God would keep the Arabs off you?"

I open my mouth to respond, then close it. I can think of a thousand things to say, but I don't know where to begin. It's not that I've never heard this rhetoric; it's just that I'm not used to having to defend myself to someone who's not related to me. "We did fight," I finally say, "back in '48. Plenty of religious men fought."

She snorts. "How old are you?"

"Twenty. Why?"

"I thought maybe you were seventy. Seventy-five. You said 'we' like you were there."

"Look. Religious men join the army. The government doesn't give out enough exemptions for every religious Israeli. Besides"— I back away a couple steps—"now Israel doesn't need us as much. There's no shortage of soldiers. The physical danger Israel's in is nothing compared to the spiritual danger."

"Spiritual danger!"

"Look at all these secular people," I say, throwing my arms out as though we're surrounded by irreverent Jews brandishing pitchforks. In fact, we're surrounded by nothing out of the ordinary—wall and alleyway, colorless Jerusalem stone, a starry sky. "Breaking Shabbat," I say, "breaking kashrut . . . the list goes on and on. Religious Jews keep the Torah safe."

"You know," she says, "I resent the term 'secular.' You religious people call everyone who doesn't wear a black hat or shave her head 'secular.' Why are we secular? Maybe we feel religious inside."

"That's not enough."

"Who are you to say?"

Would Bits ever claim to feel religious inside? It sounds like something she might say if she were drunk. ("Inside, I feel so religious!") Of course, she wouldn't remember saying it. The thought makes my jaw clench. I remember an older guy in high school who once said to me, *I'll bet your sister has crabs.* I remember the parties Bits used to drag me to in Boulder, where she would let guys in concert T-shirts get her drunk. I remember how those guys looked at her, like criminals looking at a bank before they rob it.

"You have to express your spirituality outwardly," I say. "You have to follow the laws of Judaism. Stick with your community."

"A lot of your people see prostitutes," Monica says. "What's religious about that?"

"That's not true."

"Oh," she says, laughing. She covers her mouth. "You're so naïve!" She pulls her ankle up to her opposite knee and bends to inspect something on the bottom of her shoe. I can see her cleavage. It's the sort of cleavage skinny girls have, more rib cage than breasts. She should be wearing a sweater, something to cover up. I look away.

"If it's true," I say, "they're an exception to the rule. We don't condone prostitution. Obviously."

"Oh no, of course you don't. Because you have so much respect for women."

"We do," I say. "We have all the respect in the world."

She narrows her eyes at me again. "So much respect that you make them cover every inch of their bodies so you don't get a hard-on."

I force a laugh. "No one's *making* anyone do anything. They cover because they're modest. Because they're God-fearing! They cover because th—" I stop myself. Why am I fighting with this girl? She's spouting every cliché in the book. She doesn't understand a thing.

"You want to be a rabbi or something?"

"No," I say. "I don't think I do. It's more like Torah Lishmo. You know, learning for the sake of learning."

"I saw that suicide bombing last Friday," she says abruptly. "The one at the outdoor market? At Mahane Yehuda? I was there. I almost tripped over a head. I'm not kidding. I was walking to that bus stop when it happened. The bomber was a girl," she says. "Did you know that? A *girl.*" The way she says it gives me the creeps; her face is expressionless. She sounds like she's reading from a script.

Through the wall, I can hear Todd singing a song he wrote. He was composing it for days in our room, sitting on the edge of his bed, hunched over his guitar, the side of his head with the good ear tipped down toward his lap. The lyrics, in Hebrew, are "I love you, I love you, don't you know I love you?" Musically, Arbahim sounds sort of like a Hebrew-speaking version of the Grateful Dead, but lyrically, I guess they're more like Whitney Houston, not that I would share that analysis with Todd.

"Do you like trying to prove me wrong?" Monica asks.

"What?"

"Does it make you feel powerful to be more religious than I am?"

Looking at Monica, I realize all at once what's familiar about her. Her eyes. They remind me of Vanessa Barletta. Monica's eyes are very blue, and Vanessa's were sort of green, but still. Something's similar. Maybe it's the way she's looking at me, the same way Vanessa used to, as if she's trying to peek past my eyes into my brain.

"I don't feel powerful," I say. "I'm not judging you."

"Right."

"I don't know you," I say, and suddenly I'm seized by the fear of being caught out here, talking with a strange, sparkly girl in an alley.

Monica's smiling and rubbing an ice cube along her bottom lip. "Hey," she says. "Would Hashem protect you if I screamed 'rape'?"

My heart lunges in my chest. "I'm going home," I say quickly.

"You just got here."

"I shouldn't have come." I glance over my shoulder. My teeth are chattering. This isn't right. I feel self-conscious, instead of proud, of the *payos* that curl around my ears; of the tzitzit, or fringe, that hang past my belt in honor of God's six hundred thirteen commandments.

Monica presses her glass of ice to her cheek, to her neck, the other arm draped over the top of her head. "Are you happy, Asher?" she asks.

"Happy?"

"Happy."

"Now?"

"In general."

"Yes," I say. "Of course." I clear my throat. *"Baruch hashem,"* I say. *Praise God.* I back away, my hands in my pockets.

"You should call me."

"Uh . . . maybe I'll see you."

"You'll be out tomorrow night," Monica calls, "won't you, for Yom Hatzma'ut? It's going to be a major party. You can't miss it."

Rabbi Berkstein already told us what happens on Yom Hatzma'ut, Israel's Independence Day. How the streets are so crowded, you can't move, how people spray one another with silly string and get drunk, right in the middle of the Omer period. Secular people say that Yom Hatzma'ut is the day Ben-Gurion declared Israel's independence in 1948. But what's so great about anti-religious Zionists spitting on the Omer period, in favor of sacrilegious celebration? Secular Zionists are an insult to us, to the real Jews who serve God the way He's meant to be served.

"I'll be studying tomorrow night," I say.

"Well, that's a shame, Asher," Monica says, but she's smiling a little. She walks right past me, veers left, and holds her arms out to her sides for a security guard. Her shirt is backless, except for one tiny pink strap that makes a cross with her spine. She disappears into the bar, flicking her blond hair over her glittering shoulder.

April 18, 2002

I DRIVE TO WADE'S apartment after work like someone in a dream—the kind of dream where you have decided to do something stupid and nothing can stop you. I am fueled by these facts: I am in debt. My credit cards are nearly maxed out. I had to borrow money from my mother last month to pay my rent. I need to buy a plane ticket to Israel. Wade has a trust fund.

Once, at a party, I overheard him say, "My buddy borrowed it out of my trust fund . . . but it's all good; he paid me back."

Who *says* things like that? Most people do not.

I never thought before about how tiny Wade's apartment is. It's like an elevator. No privacy. No room to be sneaky. If I had a trust fund, I would live in a castle. But Wade has different financial priorities: on his dresser, he keeps a coffee tin full of cash, sort of like the piggy bank I had when I was little—that plastic pink thing I hammered open the day I got it because I was dying to see its insides—except Wade's coffee tin holds hundreds of dollars. I'm not kidding: He uses the money for things like ordering pizzas.

I follow Wade into his bedroom.

Wade's bedroom is like a little boy's: trophies everywhere, clogging the bookshelves, lining the windowsill. He flops belly-down on his bed, on sheets printed with primary-colored football players, and shoots the TV with the remote control. He pats the space beside him. "Want to watch with me?" he asks.

"I can think of nothing I'd rather do," I say.

"Are you being sarcastic?"

"No."

"I can't ever tell with you," Wade says.

"I resent that. I can be very serious."

"Do you like hockey or not?"

I shrug. "My brother used to play in our driveway."

Wade laughs. He shakes his head at me. "You're weird," he says.

I leave my backpack strategically beside the dresser. Then I sit next to Wade on the edge of the bed. On the TV, the camera zeroes in on a little girl whose face is painted maroon. Over the face paint, she has a beard of crumbs. She waves a maroon flag.

Wade buries his face in his hands and shakes his head. "They're playing like shit," he says, his voice muffled.

This is what I call bad street smarts: closing your eyes when someone's in your apartment among all of your possessions. How does Wade know I won't steal his credit cards? Read his journal? Thump him over the head with one of his big gold trophies? I could get up right now and take his coffee tin. Can't he sense that?

The ends of his hair are wet, freshly showered. When he turns his head and looks up at me, I lean down and kiss him lightly on the lips. I trace a line with my thumb down his arm, then around the waist of his pants. He puts a hand on my thigh. I take a deep breath and say, "Wade."

"Yeah?" He smiles his wholesome, all-American, popular-guy-from-high-school smile: well-cared-for white teeth, symmetrical dimples, sparkling brown eyes.

"Wade," I say again in my most confident, clear-headed, authoritative voice. I tell him, "I'm going to blindfold you."

His eyes get a little wider. "Yeah? Okay." He sits up and peels off his shirt, as if that's the natural next step. Wade loves himself naked. He frequently takes his clothes off, unsolicited. He's always the guy at parties who has his shirt unbuttoned after a few drinks. The first time he ever kissed me, he undid his belt buckle. "Go ahead," he says, squeezing his eyes shut. He smiles bravely. "Blindfold me."

Beside the dresser that holds the coffee tin sits a dark green laundry basket, full of clean laundry. I extract a long white athletic sock that looks like a sweater for a tree trunk, return to the bed, and tie the sock around Wade's head, double-knotting it in the back. Then I move away and look at him, and even though he had no intention of eliciting such a feeling in me, I pity him. I can't help it. He looks so vulnerable, naked from the waist up—I know he took off his own shirt, but still—blindfolded by a sock. And those perfect flat abs with those tiny folds of skin over them . . . I don't know . . . there's a tinge of violence to the whole scene that makes me think of Alena. An abrupt surge of nausea forces me to grab the corner of the bed.

Quickly, I steer my attention to the coffee tin. The edges of bills stick up from the mouth of it. My vision clears. The nausea passes.

"So," Wade says.

"So."

"Do I look like a pirate?"

"No," I say. "Do you *feel* like a pirate?"

We both start giggling, nervous giggling, he because he thinks this is some kind of sex game, I because I'm terrified—this is my debut as a thief, after all.

Keeping my eyes on Wade, I move toward the dresser.

"If anything," I say, "you look like you're about to go in front of the firing squad."

"If anyone's going in front of the firing squad tonight," Wade says, "it's you." He wiggles his eyebrows above the sock.

"This sounds like bad porno."

"Bits Kellerman," Wade says. "What do *you* know about porno?"

Can he see me? Whenever I've been blindfolded, mostly years ago at birthday parties during Pin the Tail on the Donkey, or when Ash and I would play Marco Polo in our cousins' swimming pool, I always found a way to peek—either over the top of the blindfold or underneath it, or else the blindfold was sheer enough to see through. My blindfolds were always as ineffectual as diary locks.

"Don't cheat," I say. "Can you see?"

Wade pats his eyes through the sock. "No."

I take a step closer to the dresser. Wade stands up. He's grinning. My backpack is at my feet. "Stay where you are," I say, trying to keep my voice from shaking. I stick my trembling hand inside the coffee tin. No. Bad idea. I remove my hand and grab the whole tin. Some change inside clanks together. Shit. I clutch the tin to my chest and suck in my breath.

Wade steps closer to me.

"Hey," I say, backing toward the wall, "go sit down."

He ignores me. Still grinning, he starts turning in slow circles, groping the air in front of him like a mime. His wallet has imprinted a faded white rectangle into the back pocket of his jeans. I catch a glimpse of it each time he turns. The glimpses make me sad. Wade moves closer to me, still turning. He's so close, he could fall on me. All I have to do is squat down and dump the contents of the coffee tin into my backpack. But I lose my nerve. Slowly, quietly, I return the tin to the top of the dresser. Then I step around Wade and go back to the bed.

"Forget it," I say as I sit. "Just take the thing off."

Wade stops turning. He frowns and pulls the sock down from his eyes so it hangs around his neck. "What's the matter with *you*?"

"We were playing a game," I say. "It was my game. You ruined it." I sound like one of my first-graders.

"Don't get all pissed," Wade says.

The crowd from the television erupts into cheers. Wade goes to stand in front of the television, his hands on his hips, his fly open. *Of course* his fly is open.

"Fuck, fuck, fuck," Wade says. He pulls the sock over his head and unties it. "Fuck!" He whips the sock against the side of the television, then slides a hand over his hair, shaking his head.

"Want to go to sleep?" I ask abruptly, affecting a great yawn.

Wade doesn't turn from the television. "What is it, like seven or something?"

I take off my black boots and leave them on the floor by the bed. I slip in between the football player–printed sheets. I do another big yawn. Wade is shaking his head at the TV. He chucks the sock at the laundry basket.

"Good night," I call.

Wade turns around to look at me. He looks very confused. "What the hell was that all about?" he asks.

"What? I'm just so tired."

Wade looks down at his open fly. "The whole blindfolding thing . . . that's over?"

"For now," I say, turning onto my side and closing my eyes.

I hear him come toward the bed and sit behind me. "Why do you want to sleep here?" he asks. "You never sleep here."

"Maybe just a little nap."

"You can sleep over," Wade says. "I mean, I'd like you to."

"Good idea. I'll sleep now, then get up early and drive home before work. . . . Climb in," I say, scooting toward the edge of the bed to make room for him.

"Well, I'm not really tired," he says, but I feel him lie down and get under the covers. He snuggles in behind me, his face pressed to my back. I hear him fumble around for the remote control. Then the TV goes silent. "Too depressing to watch," he says. "Maybe I *should* go to sleep. Maybe while I'm sleeping, good things will happen." He plays with a piece of my hair. "Remember when you were little on Christmas Eve how you'd go to sleep and then in the morning, it was like everything had changed overnight? Everything had gotten so *good* overnight?"

"No," I say.

"Oh yeah, you're Jewish."

"Right. No Christmas memories. . . . But . . . Purim was fun," I say brightly. "We sent packages to the poor. I guess that's not as fun as Christmas. But it's important to give to those less fortunate than you." I glance toward the coffee tin. "I mean, if you can spare it. Right?"

It occurs to me that we're in the Purim season. Did it pass without me? It used to be one of the fun holidays. Ash, Alena, and I would dress up in costumes for the Purim carnival at Temple Beth Shalom, bake hamantaschen with our mother, and shake noisemakers at the mention of Haman, the evil Jew-hater. My mom and I made the packages up every year, hamantaschen and marzipan, and little kosher chocolates wrapped in foil, and sent them anonymously to Jewish charities. I feel a pang of jealousy that Ash won't ever miss Purim again, that he gets Purim and I don't, and that Wade has Christmas memories and will celebrate Christmas for the rest of his life.

To my surprise, Wade starts to snore. I wait a few minutes before untangling my limbs from his and slipping out of bed.

The year the Ethiopian Jews were airlifted into Israel, my mom and I sent Purim packages to the children. "We're welcoming them home," my mother said, tears standing in her eyes. She would never do that now—refer to Israel as home. She wouldn't want to give Ash the satisfaction. Does Ash consider Israel home?

Is he comfortable there? It's hard to picture my awkward brother comfortable, shuffling around the yeshiva in his disgusting brown slippers, the ones with the holes in both toes. If Israel isn't his home, then what is? Not Colorado. Not New Jersey. Really, he and I don't have a home. The thought makes me feel very sorry for us. Maybe Ash is better off in Israel, living in the homeland, cut off from the world, believing that Alena might be alive.

No. That would mean that ignorance is bliss, or that Orthodox Judaism is the recipe for happiness. I remember now: Ash needs my help. If I don't accept my obligation to help him—and I realize, of course, that he's not asking for help, but his not asking seems characteristic of people in need, like all those people who got our Purim packages, who had never asked us for a single thing—there will be very little left of my family. I don't care that Ash hasn't invited me. I don't need an invitation; Israel is my land too! Wasn't it also promised to me? First by God, and then later by the UN?

When I reach the dresser, I look back at Wade. He's snoring and still, visions of sugar plums dancing in his head. What does he need with so much cash? Pizza? I'm the one who just found out that her only sister is dead. I'm the one whose only brother is living in a war zone. If the situation were reversed, I'd give up a couple months of pizza to let Wade go to Israel. I peer into the coffee tin. The city lights out the window cut through the darkness. I can make out twenty-dollar bills, fifty-dollar bills. I grab everything except the singles. Wade groans and rolls over.

I freeze, my heart pounding in my throat, but he doesn't make another sound. His snoring has stopped. Is he awake, watching me? Should I say something nonsensical and then pee in the laundry basket to make him think that I'm sleepwalking? I stay still as the seconds tick by and gather into minutes. Finally, I peer into the coffee tin again. It looks depleted. I slowly unzip my backpack and retrieve my wallet, pull a few singles out of it, and stuff them into the coffee tin, fluffing them a little to create the illusion of fullness. I put the bigger bills in my wallet, and shove my wallet into my backpack, zipping the backpack closed and leaving it on the floor in the doorway. Wade stirs in bed. Then he sits up. My stomach seizes.

"Bits?"

"Yeah," I say. "Um, I changed my mind. I can't sleep. I need to go home." My voice is shaking.

"What are you doing over there?"

"Looking for something," I say. "In my backpack." I act like I'm looking for something in my backpack. "Found it," I say lamely.

I go back to the bed, sit on the edge of it, and stuff my foot into my black boot. I zip it up the side. I can feel Wade's eyes on my back.

"Why do you always do this?"

"Do what?" I ask, pulling the other boot on. My mouth is dry.

"You're so . . . *shady*. What do you want from me?" Wade asks. But he doesn't seem to expect an answer. He lies back down and pulls the top sheet and comforter over his head.

I cross the room again and stand in the doorway for a second, watching the lump of him under the covers. I force out a laugh. "Why do you assume that I want things from you?" Then I sling my backpack over one shoulder, slip out the door, and pull it closed.

I'LL TELL YOU when things got good for me: the day I met Yosi, the first Orthodox rabbi who ever talked to me. It was early Kislev 5761—or late fall 2000 on other people's calendars—four weeks after Vanessa broke up with me. I was walking through what everyone in Boulder called the UMC, the University Memorial Center (memorializing what, I couldn't tell you), between the rows of club-recruitment booths. I'd been consumed all morning by the feeling that every person I saw was unreachable, as though I were walking through an aquarium, past glass barriers and tight-knit schools of fish. In my old life, I usually felt like that.

At all the tables, students clustered in twos and threes, wearing matching T-shirts, whispering with each other until some tentative freshman approached, then smiling in an obligatory way and handing over a clipboard. They all looked the same to me, a blur of sameness, until a guy in a dark suit and hat sitting behind a folding table squinted at me and said, "Hey. You Jewish?"

I stopped walking. There was something magical about him, the magnification of his green eyes, perhaps, behind his thick glasses, or the unruliness of his beard. He looked like what I'd always thought God looked like, only younger. "Yes," I said, mainly because I was afraid to ignore him.

"I'm Yosi," he said, pumping my hand. "You look lost."

"Me?"

Gripping my hand more tightly for leverage, Yosi leaned toward me and lowered his voice. "You're looking into your past, instead of looking ahead. That's not healthy for the soul, you know. The Holy One wants you to grow, not to grieve for things that can't be changed."

I looked down at the scuffed brown floor, at the aisle formed by two neat rows of booths like the parted Red Sea, and totally forgot where it was I'd been headed. To this day, I can't remember.

Prior to meeting Yosi, I didn't even really know what Orthodox Judaism was, besides something my mother rolled her eyes about. If you asked her, Orthodox Jews were fanatics, who walked to shul on Saturdays, who wouldn't eat in Chinese restaurants. From Yosi I learned that Orthodox Judaism was a real lifestyle, for real people. Yosi told me all about the Zeff House, where he had been praying every day for seven years. Internationally, the Zeff Movement is a niche for artistic hippie Jews. A musician/rabbi, Yudel Zeff, started it up back in the sixties. He died in 1994.

At the Zeff House in Boulder, I couldn't follow the service that first Shabbat evening. I just flipped helplessly through my prayer book, watching everyone else—long-haired men in brightly colored prayer shawls and *kipas*, short-haired men in black hats and suits—sway and mutter incomprehensibly. They broke into sporadic song and dance, grabbing one another's hands, throwing their heads back, moving in circles, and I just watched, amazed. On the other side of a Japanese scrim, I could hear the women singing and dancing too. I could see their shoes, their ankles, the hems of their skirts. Everyone seemed so happy, overjoyed to be serving God. Finally, someone began chanting something familiar, the Sh'ma, the essence of Judaism—Hear O Israel, the Lord our God, the Lord is one—and the sound of it made my head pulse, like something was pushing against the walls of my scalp from inside; the voices joined and rose until the floor vibrated beneath us. That's how it was at the Zeff House: the singing felt like electricity.

I swear I lifted out of my body, trembled like God had sent an earthquake, and I couldn't stop trembling, couldn't stop hearing those voices in my head for weeks afterward. I can still hear them if I try.

I can explain what I felt that night only by comparing the experience to a far lesser one: Once, a few years ago, Bits and I started talking about old TV shows, and she asked, "What was the name of Alice's boyfriend in *The Brady Bunch*?" Neither of us could remember. We must have racked our brains for an entire day, until suddenly the answer hit me like a bus: I shouted, "Sam the butcher!" and then we both sighed in great relief. Magnify that relief a thousandfold. I felt it that night at the Zeff House, but it was Alena who had been haunting me, for years rather than hours, and it was the singing of the Sh'ma that lifted her from my thoughts, that provided relief I had never thought possible. In fact, I hadn't even known the extent to which Alena had been haunting me, hadn't known she'd been resting under my skin like a hard-to-reach itch, until I saw what my heart felt like when I could finally fill it with something new.

"I *want* this," I told Yosi later, over roast chicken and potatoes that I was too worked up to eat. He nodded, pleased. I wanted to grab his wrist, to point to my eyes, to make him see in them what I was feeling. I wanted to scream, "This is urgent!" I was afraid that if I waited, if I resumed my old life for even a second, then whatever it was I was grasping at would disappear like smoke.

"Eat," he said. "Enjoy. Then we'll talk."

"I'm not hungry."

"Ah," he said, chuckling. "The spirit of Shabbat sustains you. What is food compared to Torah?"

I nodded, pressing my shaking hands to the white paper table-cloth. "I need a fresh start," I said hoarsely. "I can do this. I know I can."

Yosi shrugged. "It's not so complicated. All you need to do is start learning."

After I met Yosi, I lost interest in my secular studies. How could I not have? It was my freshman year; I was taking Intro to everything, skimming every surface, when all I wanted to do was dive. I lost interest in my friends, too, but no one had exactly been banging down my door in the first place, not even my fraternity brothers, with whom I'd endured "hell week" the previous semester, when we'd all had to wear purple and yellow sweatsuits and Burger King crowns and throw up on each other.

I had found my real interest. I had found God. I had found God's Torah.

Yosi and his community satisfied me for a while, but something was never quite right about it. Take, for example, the time Bits showed up at the Zeff House during the Shabbat evening service. She came in through the men's entrance, instead of the women's, and stood in the doorway behind the holy ark, trying to get my attention. Everyone always tells Bits and me that we look alike, so here I was, trying to pray, standing across from a girl version of me who saw no problem being in shul in a skin-tight sweater. I was so humiliated. All I could do was bury my nose in my prayer book and pray harder. She was trying to rescue me, she told me later, trying to get me to lay down my prayer shawl and go to happy hour with her for two-dollar margaritas. Happy hour! So I was ignoring her, of course. But then I glanced up and noticed Yosi.

He had quit praying, mid-prayer, and was staring at Bits. This was a married man. A religious man. But he was staring at her, smiling faintly, his eyes behind his glasses out of focus. I fixed my eyes on my prayer book and continued to pray. I prayed as hard as I could. And when I looked up again, Bits was gone. Yosi had resumed his prayers. I wondered if perhaps I'd imagined it all.

But I began to grow restless. It was as if I'd been starving before I met Yosi, and then I'd begun eating, only to have my food whisked away before I was full. I was grateful that I had found Judaism, of course; it was just that I knew, somehow, that something was still missing.

One spring afternoon, Yosi and I were learning together in the *beit midrash* of the Zeff House, sitting on beanbag chairs, talking about a passage in Exodus that begins, "And Yitro, the Priest of Midyan, heard all that God had done for Moses and Israel." After that line, Yitro goes into the wilderness to join the wandering Israelites.

"What did Yitro hear?" I asked. "What did he hear that made him want to drop his comfortable life and wander into the wilderness?"

Yosi pulled off his glasses by the stem. "Tell me, Ash," he said, leaning close to me. "What do *you* think he heard?"

I looked down at the page again. "It would take news of a great miracle to make a prince run to the desert and join a bunch of homeless people," I said. "I think he must have heard that God split the sea."

Yosi's jaw dropped.

"What?" I said.

"How . . . how do you do that?" he asked.

"Do what?"

Yosi pressed his fingertips to his scalp, like he was trying to keep his brain from falling out. "You ask Rashi's questions," he said in a hushed voice.

"What do you mean?"

Rashi, a biblical commentator in the Middle Ages, was the greatest Jewish scholar of all time. People don't just offhandedly compare each other to Rashi.

"I mean, every question you ask is one of Rashi's questions. And you answer the questions with Rashi's answers."

"I just ask the obvious questions," I said, inching away slightly.

"No." Yosi shook his head firmly. "No, Ash. These questions you ask are not obvious."

Something really shifted then. Was I learning from an inferior? Yosi began to repulse me.

The next Shabbat, for a change of pace, I attended a shul in Denver. I had spoken to the rabbi the day before, and he had set me up with a family so I would have a place to stay. The father of the family, Avram, met me at the shul and walked me back to his house. As we walked, we talked about the week's Torah portion, and I liked Avram right away, trusted him because of the way he paused before he said anything, proving that he was really thinking. Later, over dinner, when I told Avram and his wife about the Zeff guys I was learning with, Avram said, "Zeff? There's a Zeff shul in Boulder?" He and his wife exchanged quick glances.

"Sort of," I told him. "It's more like a house."

"Listen," he said, wiping his mouth with his napkin, "maybe this is none of my business, but I can see that you're smart, and dedicated, so I feel I should tell you this. That movement is *treyf*, okay?"

"What do you mean?" I asked. But even as I asked the question, I knew, without knowing why, that Avram was right. There was something *treyf* in the air at the Zeff House. I just hadn't been able to put my finger on it. "I mean, how so?" I asked.

Avram and his wife looked at each other again. His wife pushed her plate away.

"I don't want to speak *lashon hara* about the dead," said Avram. "Look. Zeff is better than nothing, of course, but there's a whole world out there of proper learning for you to do. Zeff is a catch-all for people who would otherwise leave Orthodox Judaism altogether. Don't settle. You're young. Go to Israel."

His words hit me as powerfully as if he'd shoved me up against a wall. I looked around Avram's quiet Shabbat table, at his wife in her neat wig, her eyes cast down toward the table; at his six children, well scrubbed and well behaved. Here, there was none of the raucous singing and dancing and bright colors of the Zeff House. These were pious people. Of course Zeff was *treyf*. How could I not have seen it before?

Back in Boulder, I did some of my own research about the Zeff Movement, and what I learned made me sick. Back in the 1960s and 1970s, Rabbi Yudel Zeff had sexually assaulted young Jewish women and molested Jewish girls. He never even got in trouble for it. *This* was the man Yosi was so starry eyed about?

I kept showing up at the Zeff House for a while, but my feelings had changed and I couldn't foresee them changing back. Every time I looked at the photograph of Rabbi Zeff on the wall, I felt like punching through the glass. He was no different from the guy who had taken Alena.

Yosi acted worried about me. "What's wrong?" he kept asking. "You were ascending rapidly! What's happened to you?"

"You're the ones who have something wrong," I finally told him. "This isn't Judaism. You make a joke out of Judaism, with your music and your hippie stories. And the way you idolize that"—I gestured toward Rabbi Zeff's picture —"that *pig!*"

Yosi's smile faded from his lips. "You've been listening to rumors," he said. "Don't believe everything you hear."

"I want the real thing," I said. "I want real Judaism."

"Ash," Yosi said. "We're not trying to keep you here. We welcome you, of course. We love you, but if this feels wrong for you, then by all means—"

"You're phonies. Hashem is ashamed of you!" I said. Anger rose inside me like a tide. "And stop talking about love all the time. You cheapen it. You cheapen one of Hashem's greatest gifts!"

Yosi took a step back from me. And it was that step back, and the look in his eyes—fear—that made up my mind once and for all: I needed redemption, forgiveness, guidance, and I wasn't going to get it at the Zeff House. Not from Yosi. Not from singing and dancing around and practically worshipping a sex offender. I remembered what Vanessa had said to me, *This isn't working out anymore,* and how those words had cut into my heart like razor wire. "This isn't working out anymore," I told Yosi; then I turned on my heel, the thrill of power making me heady, and walked out of the Zeff House forever.

That was the last time I spoke to any of them, until I got a letter from Mendy, one of Yosi's friends, back in August. But that's a whole other story, a disquieting one, not a pleasant thing to think about. I know I will have to think about it again one day. Maybe next August, I'll light a *yartzheit* candle. But until then, I would rather think of the beautiful parts of life. Israel. Torah. Yeshiva Hillel.

After I walked out of the Zeff House, I started calling yeshivas in Israel right away. The only yeshivas that wanted me were the ones geared toward Ba'alei Tshuva, new Orthodox Jews. I didn't want to go to a yeshiva for amateurs. Yeshiva Hillel is one of the more liberal yeshivas, in that it's geared toward life-long Orthodox Jews, but not so adamantly opposed to Ba'alei Tshuva as long as they're fast, dedicated learners.

Over the phone, Rabbi Berkstein told me, "We are very serious here at Yeshiva Hillel. Many of our students have been learning their whole lives. You will have a lot of catching up to do."

"I don't want casual Judaism," I promised.

"No," he said, "it's not meaningful, is it."

I pictured Rabbi Berkstein as Avram. I wanted him to understand that I was like him, that I'd be everything he'd ever wanted in a student, that I knew how precious and pure Judaism was, and that I wanted to help protect it, to build a fence around the Torah. I wanted him to know that he could trust me not to ruin things, and that he'd never find a reason to write me off. "I promise I'll be just as pious as anyone there," I said. "I won't pollute your yeshiva with pieces of my old life. I don't even *like* my past. Or my present. Please believe me. I'm ready for change."

I haven't made anyone sorry yet.

I'LL TELL YOU when things got bad for me: just over a year ago, during the spring semester of my senior year of college. I lived with four girls then, one of whom was my best friend, Kyra, who was engaged to a guy named Ross. Really. Engaged. In college. In my circle, that was unheard of. But Kyra had been born for marriage. For example, she liked to walk around furniture stores and fantasize about buying an expensive couch. I was going to be the maid of honor in her wedding that summer. Until I did something not so honorable, which consisted of having relations with her fiancé.

My housemates and I were having this wild Saint Patrick's Day party, complete with green jungle juice, and I was coming out of the upstairs bathroom and Ross was standing in front of me. I don't know if he'd been waiting for me or what, but there he was—Hawaiian shirt, green lei, bloodshot eyes, his hair a mess, like he'd been in a wind storm, and the air around him reeking of liquor. He was swaying like a blow-up doll in the breeze, clutching the banister for support.

"Did you know that Saint Patrick was born in Scotland?" he asked me.

"No."

"He was a *slave*," he said, emphasizing the word "slave" by poking my shoulder with his index finger. I stumbled backward. "His captors brought him to Ireland from Scotland. Then he escaped," he said, which sounded like "skate" because he was slurring. "Escaped to Britain, then went back to Ireland and converted everyone to ca-hallsm."

"To what?"

"Ca. Tha. La. Siz. Umm." Ross burped. "March seventeenth is the anniversary of his death." He stumbled a little, and looked like he was about to fall over the banister.

"Really," I said.

Ross burped again. I giggled. Then I worried that he might throw up on me. "It's fucked *up*," he said. "We're celebrating his death! A slave's death!"

"It's kind of cool," I said. "I mean, it's impressive for a slave to become famous."

"People are so fucked," Ross said. He raised his red plastic cup in an imaginary toast. "Three cheers for the dead slave!" Green jungle juice sloshed over onto his fingers. He slurped it off and I saw a red stamp on the back of his hand. "It's like celebrating a wedding. You know? Like, congratulations! You're a slave!"

And then I understood. "You won't be a slave," I said.

"I already am one." Ross clapped a hand on my shoulder. He left it there too long. And even though I didn't want to, I knew at that second that I was going to sleep with him. And guess whose fault that was. Ash's.

Okay, not really. I know. But I needed something that night, something to take my mind off my brother, who was becoming a weirdo, who had begun wearing peasant shirts and a kind of yarmulke that looked like a fez. When he'd first gotten to Boulder, I'd been able to get him to come to parties with me. But that had changed. He wasn't a partying sort of guy anymore. At first, he'd made up excuses. Then he just started saying no flat-out. "Why do you always have to go out and get drunk?" he would say. "There are other things, you know. Other ways to have fun." He talked like a youth-group leader. It made me cringe. Save the whales, okay. Veganism, okay. But Orthodox Judaism? I couldn't believe what I was seeing. He had developed a constant expression of anxiety in his eyes, like he was running to catch a speeding train. I didn't trust these hippie Jews any more than I trusted the homeless kids on University Hill who begged for money to get their dogs vaccinated.

Earlier that day, I had invited Ash to our Saint Patrick's Day party.

"Bits, I can't go to a Saint Patrick's Day party. How can you throw a Saint Patrick's Day party? What, are you Catholic now?"

"Oh, lighten *up*," I'd said, even though he had a point. Who was Saint Patrick anyway? Was he really someone to celebrate? Now, coincidentally, I had just found out. Saint Patrick was a dead slave.

"I'll tell you something else about Saint Patrick's Day," Ross said. "You know how the Catholic Church has a conspiracy?"

"No."

"Well, they do. Like, they try to get people's money. And they try to make people believe in Jesus. I know these things. Do you know how Catholic my parents are?"

"No."

"Catholic. Very Catholic."

"Do you have, like, nine brothers and sisters?"

"Seven."

"Oh. Wow."

"Guess what the shamrock is," Ross said.

"I don't know. The shamrock? It's like the leprechaun. It's a symbol. It's green and festive."

"It's the trinity. The father, the son . . ." Ross started crossing himself, but his finger got stuck in his lei. "Fuck it," he said, hiccupping. "I'm not having any sons any time soon. . . . Religion is the backbone of evil, you know."

I thought about that: how my brother could chase after religion like a butterfly hunter, and how Ross could run from it, spit on it, hate it with all his strength. I wondered if either of them would ever be satisfied.

"The candy cane, too," Ross was saying. "Another conspiracy. What letter does the candy cane make?"

"'J'?"

"'J' for Jesus. With his blood striped all around it."

"That's not true. That's gross."

"It *is* true," Ross said. He downed the rest of his jungle juice. "I'm too young to get married," he said.

I agreed with him but didn't say so. Ross was one of the least mature people I knew. I heard Kyra's laugh from downstairs. I heard her screech, "That is hilarious!" I saw Ross wince at the sound of her voice.

"I love her," Ross said, "kind of. But I love lots of people."

"Maybe you can be a swinger couple," I said. What a horrible thing to say to your best friend's fiancé.

"I love you, for example," Ross said. He punched my arm too hard. "I mean, we're buddies, right?"

"Um . . ."

"Let's go somewhere," he said.

He took my wrist and pulled me. Okay, he didn't drag me kicking and screaming. All I'm trying to say is that I didn't instigate it. Didn't even want it. Just went with him because I wasn't thinking about how disgusting he was. I wasn't thinking about Kyra. I wasn't *thinking*. I didn't want to think anymore. I was sick of thinking and worrying. Anyway, we wound up in my room, with the door closed, in my bed. Ross's lei made crinkling diaper sounds between our bare chests. We were stupid, of course, because Kyra walked right in a few minutes later. (Of course she did. You don't have to knock on your best friend's door.)

The whole scene was like something from a movie, the way she was laughing when she opened the door at something someone else had said, the way her eyes adjusted to the semi-dark until she saw us—her fiancé and her best friend—naked in bed, the way her hand flew to her mouth, the way Ross said, "Kyra, wait," and the way she ran from the room and down the stairs and screamed for our other roommate, Pearl. It was a violently bad cliché. And even though I was drunk, I knew immediately that I'd lost my best friend, and I felt that loss like an amputation.

She approached me the next morning, as I vacuumed cigarette butts from the living room carpet. "Don't you think about anyone but yourself?" she shrieked at me. "Don't you have any empathy?" She was working for a crisis-intervention hotline at the time, so terms like "empathy," "active listening," and "cognitive dissonance" were part of her daily vocabulary. "Can't you ever put yourself in someone else's shoes for two seconds?"

I wasn't sure what to say because I had an answer to her question, but it would have sounded like an excuse: At one time, I had given a lot of thought to what life would be like in someone else's shoes. And then I had stopped. Because if you put yourself in someone else's shoes too much, especially in the shoes of someone you love, especially if you don't know where that person is, but you suspect that the person has been raped, tortured, and killed, you will come apart at the seams.

"No," I said to Kyra, switching off the vacuum cleaner. "I have no empathy. I'm really fucked up."

"You're the worst kind of fucked up," Kyra said, and she sounded sad when she said it, but she never spoke to me again.

That spring was a season of loss. In addition to losing Kyra, I lost my home. No one explicitly kicked me out, but no one would talk to me either. Only my friend Maggie stood by me. She wasn't one of my roommates. She was closer with a different crowd and didn't care about Kyra. When I showed up on her doorstep, home-less and distraught, she said, "Bits, you followed your heart. Were you supposed to ignore your feelings forever?" Then she folded me up in a big hug.

I didn't tell her that my heart had had nothing to do with it, that I had never even *remotely* loved Ross. Maggie bought me a T-shirt that said VIXEN on the front. She made me burn sage to rid myself of the negative energy that bad friendships can leave on the soul. I crashed on her couch until graduation, grateful for the burden-free friendship of a person who didn't understand me at all.

As for my other friends, I ran into them a few times, at bars or on campus, and I watched the cluster of them, saw what we had always looked like from the outside, and understood things about them as if I were still on the inside, but it was like looking through one-way glass. They simply stopped seeing me.

Maggie had just accepted a job at a new private elementary school in Boston. "They're still doing a lot of hiring," she said. "Forget grad school for a while. Come with me." I was supposed to stay in Boulder to get a master's degree in U.S. history, and even though the program was competitive and I was flattered to have been accepted, I hadn't been completely sold on the idea of going straight to grad school, and now especially, I had to get out of Colorado; most of my former friends were planning to stick around. So I eagerly accepted Maggie's advice, called the Auburn School, and requested first grade. The grade Alena was about to enter when she disappeared. I don't know why I thought that was a good idea.

The other thing I lost was, of course, my brother. Without warning, he packed up everything in his dorm room and shipped off to Israel. For a week, until he finally called home, we thought he was missing. I guess I don't know whose fault that whole episode was. My mother secretly blamed herself, at least in part. I could tell, even though she kept calling me and screaming, "What do you *mean* he hasn't called you? How could you have let him disappear?" Once we found out where Ash was, she called me at all hours of the day and night to ask me more questions she wouldn't let me answer. "Is he crazy?" she would scream. "Has he totally lost his mind?"

She asked me, "What about sex? Doesn't he like having normal, healthy sex? A nineteen-year-old boy!"

She said, "Football games are on Saturdays. He'll miss football games for the rest of his life?"

"When has he ever gone to a football game, Mom?"

"I begged him, Bits. I told him, 'I'll never ask anything of you again. Just don't do this! Don't stay in Israel! Don't be an Orthodox Jew!' One small favor I ask of him, and what does he do? He stays anyway! In a war zone he lives. He lives among the crazies. It's a phase," she decided, "isn't it, Bits?"

I didn't know. I had my own questions. Would Ash have gone to Israel if he didn't blame himself for Alena's disappearance, if our father had never left us, if our mother had handled things differently? It's so hard to pinpoint the sources of things. And what about me? Could I have prevented Ash's transformation if I'd provided more for him in Boulder? Couldn't I have tried to accommodate his needs, instead of just inviting him to parties all the time? I had known he wouldn't be comfortable at parties. Couldn't I have been less selfish, less judgmental, more invested in my brother's happiness? But you can make yourself crazy, you know, with questions. Everyone's a little to blame for everything.

I'LL TELL YOU how odd things have gotten for me: I am utterly consumed by a man. Me! With the cellulite on the hips and the osteoarthritis I got for my fiftieth birthday. Mr. Clean's name is Jonathan. I'm trying not to mention that to Viv. Or to mention that, within two hours, Jonathan managed to convince me to give him $5,000 of the money that Ash was supposed to use for college. Not that Jonathan will profit. The $5,000 barely covers the expenses for the rescue mission. That's what he's calling this: "the rescue mission."

Viv and I are in the cologne department at Macy's, shopping for a birthday present for her husband, my brother-in-law, who I have suspected for some time now is missing a pulse, who spends his Sundays attending boat shows, whatever those are, God help us.

Everything reminds me of Jonathan.

Viv hands me a white strip of cardboard. I close my eyes and inhale, and there he is, the lines around his mouth, the sharp jut of his nose, his voice forceful in my memory: *Don't ask too many questions.* I know enough to say nothing to Viv. Then, of course, I can't literally say *nothing,* so I talk around him. Mentioning him without mentioning him.

"Have you ever heard of Black Lightning?" I ask, opening my eyes.

"The one by Armani?"

I hand the strip back to Viv, and she holds it under her nose. "I'm not talking about cologne," I say.

"Let's try the men's clothing section." Viv crumples the strip in her hand. "Everything's starting to smell the same."

In fact, nothing smells the same. Nothing looks the same or feels the same or is the same since I met Jonathan. It's been so long since I've felt anything like this, so long since I've met anyone so intense, intense the way men were when we were young—practically shooting sparks from their ears—in the years before life intervened and threw buckets of dirty water at them.

"What's wrong with you, El?" Viv takes my elbow and guides me past the glass fragrance counters. "You're acting . . . strange."

"I don't feel strange."

"You're definitely strange today."

"Why? Because I want to talk about something of substance?" I lift a perfectly folded V-neck sweater from a stack. It is cashmere and soft and lovely in my hands. I resist pressing my cheek to the cashmere, resist closing my eyes to pretend that I'm burying my face in Jonathan's chest. I return the sweater to the pile and glance at Viv. "I'm talking about cults," I say, fingering the alligator decal on the sweater's front.

"Give the kid a break, Ellie, would you? He's not in a cult."

I ignore that. "Don't you remember that black man back in the seventies who snatched kids from cults and deprogrammed them?"

Viv squints like she's trying to remember. "No."

"You really don't?" In fact, I hadn't remembered him either, but Jonathan brought me home with him, showed me pictures and newspaper clippings from the shoebox in his basement, and now I feel as though I do remember. "Ted Patrick. They called him Black Lightning."

"And?"

"And nothing, Viv. I just think it's interesting. Can't I have an interest?"

"Do you like this color?" Viv holds a sweater up to her chest, stretching one sleeve out like she's dancing with it. "It looks like Phil, doesn't it? He can always return it. Use the gift receipt. He's impossible. Let's go. I've got a hundred things to do."

I follow her to the cash register. "But how many of those things do you think are really important?"

Viv stops and turns to me. "What's with you? I'm not kidding."

Behind us, heavily made-up women stand in a row, smiling like robots and shooting clouds of perfume at strangers' wrists. The music coming through the speakers is a Muzak version of a Big Bopper song.

"Don't you think we waste our time worrying about silly things?" I ask. I want my sister to understand me, but I also feel superior with the knowledge that she won't, that she is married to the man who goes to boat shows, and I have just met Jonathan.

"You sound . . ."

"What?"

Viv adjusts her purse on her shoulder. "Brainwashed," she says. "You sound brainwashed."

I OPEN THE DOOR of Yeshiva Hillel and step outside. The grounds are green and manicured, hugged by a wrought-iron gate. Some of the work-study kids do the landscaping. I'm here on work-study, too, but I work in the kitchen, where I've learned a lot about kosher laws. For example, I've learned that many over-the-counter medications are *treyf* because they're made from pig. I've learned that in certain situations, the only way to make a *treyf* kitchen utensil kosher again is to use a blowtorch. I've learned that an egg shell is porous, so it doesn't protect an egg from *treyf* influences. That means, even if it's in its shell, you can't boil an egg in a nonkosher pot, unless you want a *treyf* egg. So many Jews don't know these things. So many Jews are eating *treyf*.

When my eyes adjust to the bright sunshine, I see that blond girl I met outside the bar Tuesday night. Monica. I blink hard because at first I think she's an illusion, one of those weird negatives you see behind your eyelids on sunny days. But it is Monica, her skinny legs below the hemline of her shorts like two lengths of rope, knotted in the middle. She's on the other side of the gate, holding a bar in each fist.

"Hi," she says, wedging a flip-flop between two bars. "You looked like someone from a commercial for dryer sheets." She imitates me by closing her eyes, holding her arms out wide, and inhaling deeply. Then she opens her eyes. "*Good* day, *Sun*shine," she sings. She giggles and wraps her fists around the bars again, then rests her face between her fists.

I hurry toward her, my heart flapping in my chest like a terrified bird. *Go,* I have to tell her. *Get out of here. Right now.* Don't I? I know what Rabbi Berkstein would probably do: explain to her, nicely, why it's inappropriate for her to come here wearing shorts, what the yeshiva means to its students, those sorts of things.

"Can I come in?" she asks.

I make a visor for my eyes with one hand. "What are you doing?"

"I figured I'd find you here."

"But what are you *doing* here?"

"Yeshiva Hillel. I know who Hillel is. The rabbi who said, 'If I am not for myself, who will be for me?' Pretty selfish, if you want my opinion. He's all, 'Well, if *I* don't take the last cookie, who'll give it to me?'"

"He wasn't selfish. He was a great—"

"He also said, 'If not now, when?' Right?"

I cross my arms over my chest and look away from her.

"I know more than you think," she says. "I even know that you guys might change the name of the yeshiva, because you don't want anyone to confuse you with the real Hillel organization."

"What's the 'real Hillel'?"

"You know . . . the organization that helps Hasidic runaways assimilate into Israeli society? Anyway. Sometimes people assume I'm ditzy because I'm blond. Also because I'm friendly and cute. But then they talk with me for a minute and they're always like, 'Wow.' You know? They're like, 'She's *smart*.' . . . Hey! Come on, Asher." She kicks a bar. "Open up."

I glance behind me again, then go to her. "It's— No. I can't."

"Then you come out. I want us to do something together."

"What is it?"

She bats her eyes at me. "If I told you, that would ruin all the fun," she says, pulling her face out from between the bars. We look at each other for a long moment, then I look away and shove my hands into my pockets. "I win the staring contest," she says. "Know why? Because you don't have as much self-confidence as I do. That's how you win," she says. "By believing in yourself."

"Shh!" I put a finger to my lips. "People are studying."

"What are you, a librarian?" she says, but she lowers her voice slightly. "I can make eye contact forever," she says. "It's crazy. I'm like a frog."

"How so?"

"Frogs don't blink. And neither do fish. And that's what everyone calls me back home: Fish."

I pull my shirt away from my body and fan my skin with it.

"My aunt's boyfriend, Jon—that's who I live with back home because my parents are dead. . . . Actually, he's not my aunt's boyfriend anymore." She blows her bangs back dramatically, as if she's being forced to explain something I'll never understand. "It started out I was living with my aunt and Jon, but then she bailed on us, so now I just live with him. Well, I lived with him until I came out here, I mean. But the point is, Jon has always called me Fish."

"Because you don't blink?"

"You wouldn't find a soul in my hometown who'd go along with calling me Monica. They'd be all, 'Hello?'" She reaches between the bars to knock on my forehead. I recoil slightly. "'Her name's *Fish*.' My hometown's kind of like a big family—"

"San Francisco?"

"—and I'm like everyone's favorite cousin." She twists her long hair around two fingers and holds it to the back of her head. She

has a thin white neck, like a swan. She frowns. "Not San Francisco, for your information. I'm from a smaller town. In the South
Bay. You're a detective, huh?"

"I just know when people are lying."

"Oh," Monica laughs. "Well, that's ironic."

"What's that supposed to mean?"

"Anyway. Jon thinks I'm nuts. He's all, 'Leave it to you, Monica, to move to Israel now.' He's all, 'There's a *travel advisory.*'" She
laughs and rolls her eyes.

I don't ask her why Jon called her Monica instead of Fish. "I
have to go. . . ." I gesture vaguely past her head. For some reason,
I'm embarrassed to tell her I was leaving to buy socks.

"Come on, Asher. Come out and play." She lets her hair fall. It
forms a cape around her shoulders, makes her face look smaller.
"Have you ever lit an ant on fire?"

"No," I say. "Why would I—"

"I really want us to do this thing together. Please? Please,
please, please?"

"Light an *ant* on fire?"

"No. It's better than that. I was just trying to get a feel for you,
for your tolerance. Look. I know you want out of here. I mean,
who *doesn't* want to have a little fun? . . . You're an open book,
Asher, you know that?" In her eyes, I see Vanessa again. It makes
my breath catch in my chest. "So come with me. You don't know
how many people would pay to have this opportunity. You have no
clue. . . . You're staring at me," she says.

"You're talking."

"You're hypnotized."

"You just . . ." I unhook my eyes from hers, embarrassed. "You
look so much like someone . . . I mean, you do and you don't."

"Who?"

"You won't know her."

"Tell me her name anyway. I like to know as many things as possible."

I look over my shoulder. The building stares back blankly. I face Monica again. "Vanessa," I say.

"Ex-girlfriend?"

I scratch at an invisible stain on my cuff.

"Bet anything it's your ex-girlfriend. People are always telling me I look like some ex of theirs. It's because of how feminine I am. I have this feminine part of me, you know, like a real girly part, that loves to go shopping and wear red nail polish. I don't mean for it to come out all the time, but it does. I, like, personify femininity. Honestly, I'm embarrassed by it, because I'm so strong . . . stronger than you, I bet. How much can you bench press?"

"I don't bench press."

"Well, I used to try to be a tomboy, but I wasn't any good at it. I'm too naturally feminine. Anyhow, the girly thing makes me stick in men's minds. They think I'm just like their ex-girlfriends, but all it really is, is they miss having a feminine presence in their lives. And then along comes little old me." She sighs.

I smell cigarette smoke. A streak of panic runs through me. There's only one smoker in the whole yeshiva: David, the drummer in Todd's band. I know he's behind me, standing on the front steps, watching us, smirking. Everyone's a little afraid of David. He's a giant, huge with dark curly hair all over his body, unevolved-looking, like Esau. He's got that loud, back-slappy way about him, where the friendlier he is to you, the more uncomfortable you feel. You always walk away from a conversation with him playing and replaying it in your mind, kicking yourself for acting like a tongue-tied idiot.

I look down at my feet and, to my horror, see that Monica's hands are between the bars and she's gotten hold of my tzitzit. She's braiding them! I yank them away from her.

She laughs. "Excuse *me!*" she says.

"Don't touch," I say, and I hear the way my voice trembles.

"Don't push me away," Monica hisses.

I back away. I hear David's shoes on the concrete, drawing closer. He's right behind me. My stomach turns to quicksand. His shadow covers me like a shroud. Monica notices him too. Her expression goes blank.

"Asher, my boy," David says.

I turn to him, try to affect pleasant surprise. "Oh, hi, David." I cross my arms around my chest, then change my mind and put my hands on my hips, then finally jam them into my pockets.

"What's this, a *shidduch?*"

I glance at Monica. Does she understand him? A *shidduch* is a set-up, a date arranged by a matchmaker or a mutual acquaintance. Who in their right mind would arrange a date for Monica and me? What could we possibly have in common? "I think she's here for you," I say. I laugh too hard and it rings in my ears like a wrong note.

"I'm *not* here for him," Monica says.

David looks at her, smirking condescendingly, and flicks his cigarette butt between the bars of the gate.

"She was asking about your band," I tell David.

"I was not!"

"Groupie," I say, forcing another laugh. "You have a stalker on your hands."

David turns his smirk to me. "No need to be rude, Asher."

I keep laughing, showing Monica that David and I are actually in on the same joke.

David ignores me and looks at Monica again, looks her up and down in a way Rabbi Berkstein would disapprove of. "What are you doing here, Monica?" He strokes his beard.

I look back and forth between them, confused. "You know each other?"

"'Course he knows me," Monica says. She turns to David. "I was just telling Asher that men can't forget me. It's like, what *always* happens. It's embarrassing, when people are like, 'Hey, Monica,' and I'm all, 'Uhhh . . . ?' It's probably kind of how movie stars feel."

David snorts. "You visiting Asher?"

I laugh. "No! She's—"

"I was in the neighborhood," she says. "Last time I saw Asher, he was like, 'Next time you're in the neighborhood, stop by.'" She reaches through the bars and yanks one of my *payos*.

My vision goes momentarily fuzzy. I feel like I might pass out. David looks at me, his thick eyebrows raised. They are caterpillar eyebrows. I want my mouth to form the words "She's kidding." I want to laugh again, laugh and laugh, until David laughs, too, until our laughter forms a protective layer around us, a cocoon where women aren't welcome.

I want to tell David that she's lying, that she showed up out of nowhere, that I never invited her or encouraged her or wanted her, that I don't even *know* her. But I can't say anything. Mixed with my embarrassment is the feeling I had when I first met Vanessa, when she absentmindedly lifted up her T-shirt to scratch her belly; the feeling I had when I was twelve and one of my classmates brought a *Playboy* to school. It is a feeling typical of men who are not properly immersed in Torah, who aren't focused and holy. A feeling that doesn't belong in Jerusalem.

I turn my back on Monica.

"I thought you said you'd come with me!" Monica calls.

No! I want to scream. *I will never go with you!* But I say nothing. I just hurry up the steps and go inside.

I LIE TO MY mother. I tell her I finally spoke with Ash. I tell her he's fine. I tell her, "If you can wait a couple weeks for the funeral, he can be there." I'm cradling the phone between my ear and shoulder and lining up Wade's bills like Monopoly money on my desk: first the twenties, then the tens, then the fives.

My mother says, "Two weeks?! Jewish law says she should be buried right away." She sniffles, collects herself.

I can't tell her that I'm going to Israel to find Ash because I don't want to have to explain to her that he needs to be found. But I'm going in a week. Ash will be at Alena's funeral.

"All right, we'll wait if we must," my mother says. "Do you *swear* he'll come?"

"He's coming."

She sighs. "I won't be able to bear it if he's not there."

"Is Dad coming?"

"Will you stop asking me that?"

"I need to mentally prepare myself," I say.

"Oh, cut the theatrics, would you? I'll give him the date. If he wants to be there, he'll come."

"Fabulous. Will he bring his wife?"

"I don't need this, Bits. Don't start with me."

I'm tempted to tell her about my plan, but I know what she

would say: *A week! You can't plan a trip to Israel in a week!* And I would say, *Why not?* And she would say, *Why not?! Because it's crazy! That's why not!*

And she would be right. It's crazy to plan any trip a week in advance, let alone to a place where the buses explode, where the pizzerias go up in flames during the lunch rush. However, there are far crazier things than taking a trip to Israel during the Intifada. For example, Wade has been keeping more than five hundred sixty dollars in a coffee tin on his dresser.

I stack the piles together and stuff them into a deposit envelope.

"What does Ash want with such a life?" my mother asks. "Life isn't complicated enough as it is? He needs to live in Israel and add bombs to the picture? He should make his life more simple," she says, "not more complicated. Look at me. Your Aunt Viv and I go to yoga together twice a week. Is yoga beneath him?"

"I think yoga might be against his religious beliefs," I say.

"His religious beliefs! What's sacrilegious about peace of mind?"

"Mom," I say, "what's Ash's yeshiva called?"

"His *farshtunkeneh* yeshiva," she grumbles. "Don't get me started. The Sexist Pig Society of Jerusalem."

"I'm serious."

"I raised him with good values. He grew up around women. A number of women love him. What's with this life of his that only accounts for men? . . . It's Yeshiva Aleph," she says.

"That's what I thought."

Even though I'm exhausted, even though I have been worthless at work since the first time I stayed up until two a.m. this week, I do it again, waiting for nine a.m. Israel time. While I wait, I search the Internet for yeshivas in Jerusalem, eliminating the ones whose Web sites are in Hebrew (I can't read them and I know Ash wouldn't go to a Hebrew-speaking yeshiva anyway), eliminating the ones that don't look terribly religious, and eliminating the ones whose students are girls. I write down the names and phone numbers of ten yeshivas, then start making calls. I figure after calling the first ten, I'll write down ten more, and so on.

But on my sixth try, when I ask for Asher Kellerman, the man who answers the phone, instead of saying, "*Who* do you need?" says, "I'll take a message and have him call you."

"That's okay," I say. "Never mind."

I hang up and write down the address. Yeshiva Hillel. Ash's yeshiva is Yeshiva Hillel. I go online and reserve the $600 plane ticket I found. Airfare to Israel is at an all-time low. No one in his right mind wants to be anywhere near the Middle East.

7 Iyar 5762
(April 19, 2002)

DISTRACTION IS A dangerous thing. You should have seen me in class this morning, staring out the window at the wind shaking the trees, the leaves beckoning like fingers. I don't know how many times Rabbi Berkstein called my name, but when I finally heard him and jerked my chin off my fist, he was waving both arms above his head like he was stranded on a desert island and I was a helicopter. "Asher," he sang. "Earth to Asher."

Believe me: I don't want to be thinking of Monica. I would do anything to clear her from my thoughts. But she is a virus, spreading through me, mutating, staking her claim in my bloodstream.

One thing I've learned is that Jews are destined to be guilty. After all, we committed the ultimate crime. I'm talking about the golden calf. I'm talking about the Israelites, right on the verge of receiving the commandments, spitting in God's face, pulling off their gold earrings, their bangle bracelets, and spilling them like sand into Aaron's open palms, so he could build them an idol. I'm talking about *my own ancestors*. And I am ashamed. We should all be ashamed!

But for me, guilt is not just about the golden calf. For me, there is also Alena. Everyone always talks about Alena's "disappearance," because people don't like to say "kidnapped." They don't like to say, "Her brother watched someone kidnap her." But that doesn't mean no one's thinking it. It happened right outside our house. It was a sunny day. Alena and I were playing hockey in the driveway when a brown car pulled up. I thought it was Mrs. Palmer from down the street. It looked like her car. I could have sworn. We loved Mrs. Palmer because she always baked something called tuxedo brownies—white and dark chocolate—and invited all the neighborhood kids inside to eat them while they were still hot. Alena must have thought it was Mrs. Palmer, too, because she ran up the driveway to the car. I ignored Alena and kept hitting the puck against the garage door. Then I heard a car door slam. I still didn't look up. I heard the car drive away. I ignored that too. Next time I looked up, the car was gone. Alena was gone. The street was empty.

A little over a year ago, I asked Yosi about guilt. We were sitting on those stupid beanbag chairs in the Zeff House. In Israel and in New York, the Zeff Movement is thriving, but the Zeff House in Boulder is small and obscure; I never would have known about it if God hadn't brought me to Yosi.

I do still believe that God brought me to Yosi, even though I wish now that I'd never met him. Yosi, like most of the Zeff guys in Boulder, was a late-thirties/early-forties ex–Dead Head, who had exchanged LSD for Kabbalah, Jerry Garcia for God, whose eyes betrayed all the drugs he'd done in the past, as if the strings that kept most people's eyeballs tight in the sockets had been loosened like shoelaces. God guided me to Yosi like a foot to the first rung of a ladder. And then I'm sure He expected me to keep climbing.

"Ash, guilt is just your *nefesh habehamit*, you know," Yosi said. "Your animal soul, tricking you. Stop feeling guilty. Hashem doesn't want you to feel guilty." He wound part of his straggly beard around one finger.

"I'm not talking about me," I said. "I wasn't there."

"Where?"

"At Mount Sinai."

Yosi clucked his tongue. "Of course you were. Your soul was there."

"Well, right, but . . ."

"Ash, do you know what complete repentance is? Complete repentance is when you atone for a sin, and then when you're presented with the opportunity to commit that sin again, you refuse. We reject idolatry. Every day. So we've come a long way from the golden calf." Yosi leaned toward me. "The Rambam states it clearly. There are two steps to Tshuva. Isn't that encouraging?" He held up two fingers. "Just two steps to return to God!"

Now, just over a year later, I know that Tshuva is not nearly as easy as Yosi led me to believe, that it's a life-long process, a constant effort, that all your life you're returning every single second, but you will never have completely returned.

Yosi said, "One, you regret your misdeed. Two, you vow to never commit that misdeed again." He wiggled his two fingers in the air.

I looked up at the framed picture on the wall of Rabbi Zeff and Yosi. Rabbi Zeff had a bushy gray beard. The top of his head was bald and covered with liver spots. He wore a black vest over a white button-down shirt. His eyes were closed. He was holding Yosi's head to his cheek. In the picture, Yosi's eyes were closed too. I looked at Yosi across from me. He was wearing a vest like the one Rabbi Zeff was wearing in the picture.

"What if you committed your first really bad sin when you were a child, and you haven't exactly had an *opportunity* to commit it again?" I asked.

"Ash." Yosi had taken off his glasses and was rubbing his eyes.

"I mean, were the little kids at Mount Sinai less guilty than their parents?"

"We have no proof that the children even participated in the sin of the calf."

"But they might have," I said. (I still believe that they did, that the children, drawn to its shininess, its sturdiness, must have swarmed it.)

"Children aren't as accountable as adults."

"Children know certain things."

"Ash, what are we talking about?" Yosi asked. He chuckled gently. "I think you're having a private conversation with yourself. I think maybe I'm being excluded."

"I just want to know what God does with people's guilt. That's all. When does He accept remorse?"

"The Holy One forgives," Yosi said. "After the golden calf, He still gave us the Torah. And He still let us into the Promised Land."

"But then He let us get exiled later," I said. "So we obviously weren't completely forgiven. Plus, He constantly reminds us that we sinned."

Yosi nodded. "Every punishment that befalls the Jews," he agreed, "has some of the sin of the calf mixed in."

"So what are we supposed to do with our guilt?" I asked. "Bury it, even though God has only sort of forgiven us?"

"Not bury it, Ash. No."

"Beat our own chests with it? Atone once a year and let the guilt slowly creep back over the next twelve months?"

Yosi held up one finger, signaling me to wait. "Before I became Ba'al Tshuva," he said, "before I found the Zeff shul in Jerusalem, before I met Reb Yudel—may his name be bound up in the world to come—I followed the Grateful Dead on their concert tours." (Most of Yosi's stories began that way.) "Now I see clearly that I was lost, groping, but at the time . . ." He opened his palms, as if checking for rain.

"So we went to a concert in Kansas," he said, "a whole busload of my friends. Between sets, we were walking around. Wandering, you might say. And a boy . . . a child, really, couldn't have been more than fifteen, bumped into me with his shoulder. I looked at him. He opened his fist." Yosi demonstrated. "And he showed me a sheet of LSD wrapped in tinfoil." Yosi closed his fist and rested it on his knee, then kept his eyes trained on his lap. "So one of the girls—her name was Janie—said, 'One second, Rob'—at the time, I was still called Rob—she said, 'One second, Rob. Don't buy that. I have a bad feeling about it.' But we'd been looking for LSD all day, and now? Here it was." He trailed off for a second. He seemed to be looking at something in the distance. "So I ignored her." He looked up at me again. "We all took LSD—"

"Janie, too?"

"Janie, too. I convinced her she'd be okay. In fact, if I remember correctly, what I said was, 'I'll make sure everything's okay.' No person has the power to promise that, Ash. You know that, don't you? I wish I had known that then. You are so lucky. Nineteen and already finding the truth." He smiled at me, and adjusted the black *kipa* that was slipping from the bald spot on the back of his head. "But anyway, we all started coming on and suddenly the crowd was too much for me. That's what people say when they take psychedelics: This is too much, that is too much, and so on. People were twirling all over the place, and the air smelled like whiskey and it was full of colors. . . . I can't really explain this."

I looked out the window. Some kids below were playing Frisbee on the grass. They kept turning to look at three girls who were sitting nearby, watching. All three girls had dark ponytails. I wondered if one was Vanessa. I turned back to Yosi. "So what happened?" I asked.

"Well, we were standing by a chain-link fence. I remember this because I had to climb over it a minute later to get to the Red Cross station. I was saying, 'This is way too heavy,' I was telling this to someone, and suddenly, beside me, Janie collapsed to the ground. She was standing next to me one second, and the next second she was gone. We all looked down and she was lying there with her eyes wide open."

"She died?"

Yosi rubbed his forehead with the inside of his wrist. "At first, I thought she'd been shot. What else would have knocked her to the ground?" He opened his arm out toward the floor, as if she were sprawled at our feet in the Zett House. "But it wasn't anything violent," he said. "The drugs had just reacted badly with her body."

"Like . . . an overdose?"

Yosi nodded. "She had taken other drugs. Things got mixed up inside her. . . . She was a beautiful girl, Ash. Lost, of course, like we all were, but beautiful. She had bright red hair, like King David. It's been said that King David had bright red hair. Anyway." He tried to smile.

"Were you . . . like, dating her?" I asked.

Yosi said nothing. I wasn't sure if he'd heard me. Then he waved away something invisible with one hand. *"Zichrona livracha,"* he said. *May her name be blessed.*

You know about guilt, I thought. The realization made me strangely uncomfortable, like meeting someone who has your same name. My eyes moved to that window again. Now one of the guys was spraying the girls with a fluorescent green water gun. The girls were huddled together, covering their heads with their arms. I could hear their muffled shrieks. Was that Vanessa? The one in the gray T-shirt. . . . Was it? Had God planted her there to tempt me, the way He planted the Tree of Knowledge in the Garden of Eden?

I looked back at Yosi and told him nothing. I didn't tell him that he and I had something in common. Even back then, before I really knew better, I must have known, at least unconsciously, that I didn't want to be the same as Yosi.

"I've written her father since," Yosi went on. "Janie's father. When I became religious . . . it wasn't long after that, in fact . . . I wrote to her father three times. Apologized. Asked his forgiveness."

"Did he write you back?"

Yosi shook his head sadly. "But what do we do with this guilt? Guilt isn't something to carry around." He grinned. "Guilt is for Jewish mothers, no?" He winked.

Oh? Was that what my mother was feeling all those years? Guilt? Was that why she dragged me all over town, tacking flyers to telephone poles, harassing people in town hall, acting as if I were responsible for finding Alena? That's funny. I had assumed it was blame.

"If you wrong someone, Ash, you must apologize three times. Then, there's no more for you to do."

"Kind of selfish, isn't it?" I didn't mean to say that, didn't want to get into it with Yosi. But I was suddenly throbbing with rage. "We apologize three times and if we haven't been forgiven, we have permission to *feel* forgiven? What if what we did was really bad? Three apologies can't always be enough. A million apologies might not be enough for some transgressions. Now that you've apologized three times to Janie's father, do you honestly believe that you're absolved? Honestly?"

Yosi's eyes dimmed for a second, as if a cloud had passed through them.

"Plus," I said, "you can't apologize to Janie, and she's the one who really deserves an apology."

I thought I'd crossed a line then. I immediately regretted it.

But the cloud disappeared from Yosi's eyes and he smiled. "Let's go back to the golden calf," he said. "Think about it. How many times do you think the Jewish people have repented for the golden calf? We remember it every day, yes?"

I stood and glanced out the window. It wasn't Vanessa. I could see that now. No, it wasn't her at all. I let out a shaky breath and reminded myself that I was lucky to have lost Vanessa, that God had seen me clinging to her and lifted my eyes to Him. I smiled. "Of course," I said with a newfound calm. "We always remember the golden calf."

"But we don't kill ourselves over it," Yosi said.

"What?" I didn't turn from the window.

"We don't kill ourselves over our mistakes."

"No," I said.

I heard Yosi stand. He came up behind me and clapped me on the shoulder. "No," he repeated firmly. "This we must not do."

April 19, 2002

WHEN I SEE Wade leaning against the plastic cubbies outside my classroom early Friday morning, his muscular arms knotted across the front of his AUBURN SCHOOL ATHLETICS T-shirt, I feel an overpowering impulse to pull him into my classroom, push him inside the coat closet, and sink to the floor with him, to climb on top of him and pull his mesh shorts down to his striped tube socks and do it just like that in the dusty dark beside the white cardboard lost-and-found box, the naked wire hangers rattling together above our heads like wind chimes. It's an impulse born of anxiety, of course, because his lips are pressed tight together in two pale, thin lines and his eyes are hard and cold. It's not a pretty picture: angry Wade. Wade doesn't usually get angry with real people, only with professional athletes on television, who fumble or foul or go out of bounds when they should know better.

I say hi like it's normal that he's waiting for me outside my classroom, like I didn't tie a sock around his head last night and make him go to sleep at seven p.m. so I could steal his money and sneak out of his apartment. How does he already know he's missing money? Did he order a pizza for breakfast?

He follows me into the classroom. "I'll have you know," he says, "that I'm not an idiot." His words sound rehearsed, like he was practicing a speech in the car on his way to work as he inched through traffic.

I set my backpack on the floor beneath my desk and start pulling the orange plastic chairs off the kids' desks. "Of course you're not an idiot," I say unconvincingly.

Wade follows me. "You're not a good thief or a good liar," he says. "For your information, lots of people think you're crazy. Crazy like with a mental illness. And I agree. I always thought the sex thing was weird. But this is even weirder."

I cringe at those words: "the sex thing." I don't want to hear what he thinks "the sex thing" is. I'm reminded of junior high, when I pretended to think it was funny when girls made fun of other girls for being sluts. I'm reminded of my freshman year of high school, when some of the senior guys started a rumor that I'd had three abortions. People are always so quick to judge. I don't want to hear it from Wade.

"You keep your eyes closed while you fuck," Wade says. "You don't even look like you're enjoying it."

I pause, one cold metal chair leg in my fist, and look directly at him. "So if I don't enjoy sex with you, I must be mentally ill?" I lift the chair from the desk and set it on the floor.

"You fuck like it's medicine," Wade says.

"Medicine for mental illness?" I go to the whiteboard and begin erasing things that aren't even there.

"You can't make this go away," he says.

I stop erasing. Go to the windows and push them open. I stick my head in the crack for a second and suck in fresh air. The crows call to me like an omen. "Make what go away?"

"You're not fooling anyone, Bits. The money was there before you came over and gone when you left. Did you really think I wouldn't notice hundreds of dollars missing from my own bedroom?"

I'm addressing myself to the window, scratching at an invisible mark on the glass. I laugh. "I have no idea what you're talking about."

"You stole money out of my coffee tin! Five, six hundred dollars."

"Wade, you're kidding," I say, turning around to face him. "Right?"

Wade's eyes change, like a lightbulb that can't decide whether or not to burn out. Then he heaves a big sigh. "Look," he says. His voice sounds tired. He puts his hands up in front of him like I might shoot him. "Just pay me back, okay, and we'll—"

"Wade?" I smile at him. "You're joking, right?"

He frowns and drops his arms to his sides. "No!"

"You're . . . really?" I try to look very puzzled. I stare deeply into his eyes. "You think I *stole* from you?" I shake my head. "Are you mad at me for leaving your apartment last night? Is that what this is about?"

"Stop it." Wade curls his hands into fists and presses the fists to his temples. "Don't even— I'm not falling for this."

I walk to my desk at the back of the room. I wish I weren't wearing high heels. They aren't obscenely high or anything, just two inches or so, but when you're self-consciously aware of someone watching you walk, and you're wearing two-inch heels, you wobble like a drunk. The heels threaten to pitch you forward onto the cold floor, threaten to land you on all fours like someone begging.

When I finally reach my chair, I sit without looking at Wade and begin arranging papers, paper clips, the colored pencils blooming from the little glass jar.

"You'll get fired," Wade says, approaching my desk.

"You should know that doesn't scare me."

"You think you don't care about this job. But you'd care if you were unemployed."

I smile mildly, like this is all a big joke, like he's a big excited dog jumping around me while I'm trying to read the mail. Is this how I would be acting if I were innocent? I can't decide. I'm not quite sure what that would be like.

"I'll call the cops."

"Call 'em," I say flippantly, but my heart starts racing. Is he serious?

"I know you just took time off to go overseas."

I swallow and say nothing. I don't change the expression on my face.

"You're broke," Wade says. "You always say so. So how did you—"

"Frequent flier miles."

"You're not a frequent flier."

"How do *you* know?" I say. Then I wonder if I should just tell him. Maybe it would inspire some sympathy: *My sister is dead. I need to get to my brother.* No, that would be disloyal, exploitative. I don't want to exploit my family.

Wade places both hands on the surface of the desk and leans down to push his face up to mine. He smells like aftershave, the nice kind, not too strong, which complicates things. "I have a lawyer," he says. "A good one."

I laugh like I still think he's kidding, but really I feel sick. People with trust funds can *get* lawyers to fight for five hundred sixty dollars. People with trust funds can do anything. They're like superheroes.

"This isn't about money," says Wade. "It's about principles. I'll sue you on principle. I'll sue you for everything you're worth."

"That should be lucrative," I say.

"You'll be out on the streets, though." His voice rises and trembles. "You won't even have rent money!"

A threat. Wade is threatening me. Like Fin did last weekend: *Memorize my face.*

I've memorized it. I can see it in front of me, in the texture of my wooden desk, clear as a photograph. My life is full of messes. I'm more sure than ever: I need to get to Israel, to set at least one thing right. Wade stomps across the room and pauses at the threshold. "I hope you had a good reason," he says. "I hope at least in your mind, you can *act* like you had a good reason for stealing from someone who's supposed to be your friend." He stomps out. The door slams so hard, the windows rattle.

I had a very good reason, I want to tell him. *I'm going to salvage my family.*

I AM BORDERING ON crisis. I should know the first thing about a romantic dinner for two? Me? Please. I'll tell you what I know: how to cook for a family of three or four or five. Lasagnas and casseroles and Crock-Pot stews that turn into the next day's leftovers. There is nothing romantic about shepherd's pie, nothing seductive about my ex–mother-in-law's noodle kugel recipe. And mood! This is something I'm supposed to "create," according to the *Romance After 50 Handbook* I found in the dollar bin at Target. How do you create mood in a house filled with more than two decades of clutter? What kind of mood can I set in a dining room with peeling wallpaper, in a house that still holds a wicker chest of Bits's decapitated Barbie dolls, including the naked Roller Skating Barbie that Ash drew nipples on? What kind of mood can I set when I don't know the first thing about selecting a bottle of wine, when the only candles I have in the house are the kind that fit in a menorah?

The pasta is boiling. The doorbell is ringing.

Jonathan is not holding flowers in a paper cone. He is not holding a bottle of champagne. These are things the *Romance After 50 Handbook* prepared me to expect. *Mishugas*, if you ask me. What do those authors know from anything? Jonathan isn't like most men. He can't be categorized or filed away. He is not typical or predictable.

When I open the door, he is typing something into his cell phone. Watching his fingers, the furrow in his forehead, and the tiny dots of sweat on his upper lip makes me shiver because Jonathan and I are lovers. I've been rolling that word over and over in my head like taffy. We have been lovers since the day we met, the day he told me he could help me, then took me back to his house, literally lifted me into his arms and carried me into his bedroom.

"There are things we can accomplish together," he told me, as he worked a shoe off my foot, unzipped the back of my skirt, released the clip from my hair. And I let him do all of those things as if I were in a trance, as if all my life I had been moving toward that moment, and it had finally arrived. I'm losing it. I know. But it felt like arriving.

Is this out of character for me? You bet. The last man I slept with was my husband, well over a decade ago. Bits and Ash think I made no effort to move on after their father left, but I dated a few men. I tried. I went through the motions: dinner at depressing restaurants, evenings of fighting off sleep while listening to the Philadelphia Pops or to long, boring stories about other people's divorces. After a while, you start to see it: everyone is the same.

Except Jonathan.

"Ellie," he says, slipping his cell phone into his pocket. He takes my face in both hands and looks at me hard with those brightly lit eyes—a crowd of candles at a vigil. "We have so much to talk about," he says.

And suddenly, there is no mess in my house, there is no pasta on the stove, there is nothing, nothing, nothing but Jonathan's face and the smell of his neck. I breathe him in. "I'm stressed," I hear myself say. "I wanted to make you a nice dinner." Of course, he and I both know I'm not just talking about dinner. I hold his arm so I don't unravel.

"Ellie," he says. "You're doing the right thing. *We're* doing the right thing."

I lead him to the kitchen, turn off the burners. He comes up behind me and puts his hands on my hips and I almost melt all over the linoleum. Steam from the pasta rises into my face. I close my eyes.

"Why are you doing this?" I ask. I'm surprised to hear how breathy my voice is. It sounds . . . sexual. What I'm asking is, why is he helping me, why is he invested in me, but he thinks I'm asking why he's touching me.

"Because you want me to," he says matter-of-factly, and, of course, that answers all of my questions.

I know that Jonathan has a past. Not that anyone doesn't at my age. But something catastrophic must have happened to him. The day I met him, I felt it in his house, in the way parts of it felt cluttered (dishes in the sink, piles of papers on every imaginable surface), and other parts felt uncomfortably bare (mantels empty of pictures, whole rooms without furniture).

Jonathan's arms slip around my waist. Not that my waist is small enough for anything to slip around it, but that's how Jonathan makes me feel: small, protected.

"Let me set your mind at ease," he says, resting his chin on my shoulder. "I've learned a few things." He is unbuttoning the front of my dress. "One," he says. "Your son's yeshiva is not Yeshiva Aleph."

"What?!" I say, but I react with emotion only because I know I should be shocked and outraged, that I should care more about where my son is than about how Jonathan's fingers feel on my skin.

"He's lying to you, Ellie. They're making him lie to you." He runs a finger over the front hook on my bra. "Two. Your daughter is on her way to Israel."

I spin around in his arms. "You're crazy. There's no way. Bits doesn't even have enough money to buy socks. Last time she was here, I had to take her sock shopping. She had holes in her socks. You could see her toenails."

"Speaking of money," Jonathan says. He closes his eyes and sighs, opens his eyes and runs a hand over his hair. He steps back from me. "Look. You know I hate asking."

I take his arm, pull him toward me again.

"This is more expensive than I had anticipated," Jonathan says. "Look. I'm a simple man. You know that. This is a labor of love."

Love. He said *love.*

"If you need the money," I say, "there's nothing I wouldn't do to accomplish our goal, but . . ."

Jonathan leans into me. "Shh," he says. "Relax. It's working." He kisses my forehead and smiles widely, his teeth big and white and straight like piano keys. I hear music. "Don't you see that?" he says. "It's working. Now you just have to let it work."

MY CELL PHONE'S ringing because I forgot to turn it off before sundown. It's probably Bits, calling to deliver her weekly lecture on how America is the only safe country in the world. What does she know about safety? What does she know about Israel? The American media would never let on that there are happy Israelis, or that children in Israel actually play and run around like American children, or that life in Israel isn't just a string of bombings, that things are usually, for the most part, normal.

Ordinarily, the thought of having to call Bits back would weigh on my shoulders until I did it. But ever since a couple of weeks ago when I decided to stop calling her, to stop calling my mother, to stop calling anyone who resents my Torah-centered life, I feel liberated. I don't have to answer my sister's phone calls. I don't have to answer to anyone but God.

The ringing stops, then starts again. I sit up in bed. Everyone else is having Shabbat dinner downstairs, but I was feeling restless and couldn't concentrate on any of the conversations going on around me, so I slipped out early and came up to my room, even though I should have known better: throughout the Omer period, we've been reading a chapter of *Pirkei Avot, The Ethics of the Fathers* every Shabbat, and one piece of advice I've learned well is "Don't separate yourself from the community." But tonight, I separated, and now I'm alone and it's stuffy in here. Dark, too, because not only did I forget to turn off my phone, I also forgot to turn on my lamp. To properly observe the Sabbath, once the sun goes down on Friday, you can't use electricity again until sundown on Saturday. So I'm stuck in the dark with a ringing phone and Todd's not even around because he's visiting family friends in Haifa for the weekend, and I can't help remembering my life in Boulder, when aside from learning with Yosi at the Zeff House, I spent most of my time in my room.

The phone keeps ringing and I feel like throwing it out my window—a message to everyone in the world who isn't observing the Sabbath, who thinks Friday night is an appropriate time for phone calls. I stand and adjust my *kipa* on my head. This isn't Boulder. This is my new life, my real life, and there are sixty people downstairs who would be happy to share the Shabbat meal with me.

I open the door and almost walk straight into Monica, who is standing at my threshold, holding a cell phone to her ear. She's wearing a short gold dress. She looks like a Jetson. The hallway is dark except for a few candles perched on wooden ledges, painting ungainly shadows of me, of Monica, on the walls. For a second, I think my eyes are playing tricks on me. There's no way Monica could have gotten past the gate, let alone through the door and upstairs to the dorms.

The voices from the dining hall are louder from out here. Everyone's singing, banging on the tables—but not the way it was at the Zeff House; this is singing that's *truly* directed to God, singing with no ego, not singing just for the sake of singing, which is basically idol worship.

Monica pulls the phone away from her ear, then presses a button and drops it into this big canvas bag she's got strapped across her shoulder. She puts her hands on her hips. Her elbows strain against her white skin. "Finally!" she says, throwing her hands up. "Don't you answer your phone?"

Downstairs, the singing ends, and I hear plates and forks clinking.

"I've been calling you! I've called you like five hundred thousand times."

"How'd you get my number?" I whisper. "What are you doing here?"

She smiles mildly.

"It's Shabbat!" I sputter.

"Well, Shabbat Shalom," says Monica, pinching the gold skirt of her dress on both sides and spreading it out. She curtsies. "Let me in, okay? Everyone's eating dinner, right? Hey. Know what? You'll probably think I'm lying, but cross my heart and hope to die?" She actually stands there and draws an invisible cross over her chest. Crosses herself! Inside Yeshiva Hillel! "This is my first time inside a yeshiva."

"You would have no reason to ever be inside a yeshiva," I say. "This isn't a joke, you know. It's not a stop on your sightseeing tour."

Monica takes the canvas bag from her shoulder and sets it on the hallway floor between us. Then she takes a few steps back, stretches her arms up, rests her palms against the opposite wall, bends over backward, and starts walking her hands down the wall, folding herself into a backbend. Her hair hangs; the tips of it almost brush the floor. The hem of her dress rides up her thighs.

"What are you *doing*?"

"I'm stretching," she says. "I stretch three to four times a day. . . . Please, please, please let me in?" She walks her hands back up the wall until she's resumed a normal standing position. Her eyes twinkle in the candlelight.

Vanessa's eyes used to twinkle, too, like brand-new silver. The first night Vanessa and I spent alone in her dorm room, listening to Ben Harper and drinking root beer, I couldn't stop watching her eyes. Vanessa always drank root beer. She stored cans of it in her mini fridge and, during the day, kept a water bottle full of it clipped to her backpack with a carabiner. She was six feet tall and addicted to root beer. So when we met, in the very beginning of the fall semester, I thought she was a misfit like I was. I thought I was the only person who could see her strange beauty, who could love her huge feet and her hairy arms. As it turned out, Vanessa's quirkiness was the kind that drew people to her. She was one of those people whom other people imitated, whereas I . . . well, I'm just not.

Alena probably wouldn't have reached six feet, but otherwise, I think she would have grown up to be a Vanessa type: quirky, free-spirited, beautiful.

Monica steps closer to me and I stretch my arms out to the sides, blocking my doorway.

"Let me into your room or I'll scream," Monica says matter-of-factly. She yawns, picks up her bag, and slings it over her shoulder.

Suddenly, I understand what it means to watch yourself from outside your body. "Are you spying on me or something?" I hear myself ask.

"Oh, get over yourself, Asher," Monica says. Her bottom lip is chapped. She licks it. "This isn't a secret club. Anyone can find out anything they want about your stupid yeshiva." Her hair is staticky at the top, raised, as if she's picking up signals no one else can hear.

I open my mouth to speak, then close it. I slip into my room and quickly close the door, closing myself inside, shutting Monica out. I lean against the door, catching my breath, press my fists into my eyes, and whisper, "Please, God . . . please renew my strength. Dear God, I so badly want to serve You." I open my eyes and look around the room, from Todd's bed to the window behind the desk, to my bed, to my closet door. I listen to the faint sounds of singing from downstairs. "Send me a sign," I whisper. "Send me a sign so I know that You're with me."

I hold my breath.

Monica starts knocking on my door, louder, louder. "Let me *in!*" I feel the vibration of the knocking in my spine. If the singing stops, someone will hear her. Exhaling, I turn around and fling the door open. Monica pauses, mid-knock, on the threshold. With her free hand, she is playing with her hair.

"Better let me in," she says, "unless you want me to go downstairs and tell everyone you already did."

My sweaty palm slips from the doorknob. Monica smiles brightly and pushes past me into the room.

"How did you get through the gate?" I ask.

Monica pulls the canvas bag off her shoulder and sets it on the desk chair. "It wasn't hard," she says. "Someone left the side gate open. I've never seen that happen around here before. But that's all it takes: one slipup and your whole security system's breached."

I hold my head in my hands, watching her shake out her hair and tuck it behind her ears, smooth the front of her dress down with her hand, stretch her arms over her head, and yawn like she's ready for a good night's sleep. I'm squeezing my head so tightly, I'm afraid my fingers might push straight through my scalp. I say another quick prayer: *God, give me strength to resist this.*

Minutes later, Monica has settled beside me on the edge of my bed, leaving about an inch between us, and I can't bring myself to get up, to make the awkward switch to Todd's bed. I can feel the heat off her skin, the way it comes off grass in the summer. She's still making a big show of stretching, her legs stuck straight out in front of her, her upper body curved over, her hands around her ankles. There's a moon out the window, glaring as a search-light. Monica's gold dress shimmers in the white glow. She sits up straight. "I wa—"

"Shh!" I hiss. "You have to whisper."

"I want to see the rest of the yeshiva," she whispers. "I want the full tour. I can borrow your clothes as a disguise. I'll be like Barbra Streisand in *Yentl*." She interlaces her fingers and stretches her arms over her head, starts rolling her head in a slow circle. I see the blond stubble in her armpit and quickly look away.

I get up to open the window, but it's stuck. I push and pry a little, but the necessary effort feels like too much work for Shabbat, so I slip my hands into my pockets and watch the wisp of my reflection on the glass. I hear Monica stand, feel her behind me. "I don't get this," she whispers. "Is it like boarding school or something? You'd get in trouble? Like suspended?"

"Expelled."

"That's so . . . oppressive."

"I'm not oppressed. What, you think someone's *making* me live this life? I choose to be here."

"It's like how my aunt used to be to me. *You can't do this, you can't do that,* and I was all, *Then get out of my face.* Eventually, she did, and me and Jon are glad." I feel her step closer to me. I walk around her, back to the bed, and sit. She starts rummaging through her canvas bag. "I brought you something," she says. She pulls out a stack of magazines.

I look away. "You think I have time to read *magazines*? Why would you bring me—"

She drops them on my lap. I hear chairs scrape linoleum downstairs. Dinner is over. Now everyone will scatter, some to Rabbi Berkstein's house—he has an open-door policy on Shabbat—and some back to their own rooms or to each other's. The stack sits on my legs like a cinder block. The magazine on top has a naked woman on the cover. She has huge nipples. I set the magazines on the floor. Sweat slides down my back. After Shabbat, I will go to the *mikveh*, the ritual bath. I will sit in rainwater and be purified.

Monica sits beside me and I smell her coconut shampoo. I'm having one of those daydreams I used to have in school, when I would zone out and imagine myself doing the most inappropriate thing possible—standing up and dropping my pants or charging the teacher, throwing her over my shoulder, and running from the room. I would always have to grab my desk or pinch my leg to assure myself that I was still sitting in my chair. Now I'm envisioning taking Monica's hair in my cupped hands, bringing it to my lips, sliding it like cool silk through my fingers. I slip my hands under my legs, pinning my fingers down.

"Let me guess about you," Monica says, crossing one leg over the other, letting her sandal drop to the floor. "I have a very good sense about people. I bet I can see right through you." She cocks her head and squints like a fortune-teller. "You went to college." She leans back on her elbows.

"Yeah? So?"

"Couldn't fit in, right? You were too smart for everyone. Felt like you had to bite your tongue all the time so you wouldn't use big vocabulary words. You were like"—this she says in a British accent—"'Guys, I've been cogitating, and I've concluded that we must implement some reforms in the dormitory.'"

I hear David's laugh, loud and hearty, above the general din downstairs. If David found Monica in my room, he would probably act infuriatingly unsurprised, like it had always just been a matter of time before my commitment to God wore off. David's so conceited about having been religious since birth, thinks anyone who's Ba'al Tshuva is beneath him. (Rabbi Berkstein says different. He says we're elevated, because we chose. All David did was emerge from the womb of a religious woman.)

"Maybe you had your heart broken," Monica says. "Or maybe you're one of those guilty types. Guilt can get very heavy, right? It's practically the heaviest thing in the world. Maybe you have, like, a shady past. You used to rob banks or kill people."

"Right. You figured me out. I'm a killer."

"Then you met someone. Probably a rabbi. You think you found him. But really, he found you. He preyed on you because you looked like a lost soul. You found"—she makes quotation marks with her fingers in the air—"a *community*. And a light bulb popped on in your head. You should be religious! Your family never understood you anyway. You could have a *new* family! Pretty soon, you learned how to act like them, the religious guys, and you felt all cool for being part of something so righteous. You'd always known you were righteous anyway, and now it was, like, confirmed."

I hear shoes pounding in the stairwell, voices, laughter.

"But you know what, Asher? You're a poseur."

The sweat is at my temples now, too, and above my lip. I taste it as it drips into my mouth. The pounding shoes grow louder. All they'd have to do is turn left at the top of the stairs, take three or four steps, and they'd be at my threshold.

"You'll never be like these guys," Monica says, nodding toward my door.

I hear David singing an Arbahim song. He's got an excellent voice, but he shouldn't be singing an unholy song on Shabbat. His voice grows louder as he gets closer to my room.

"Know what studies show? You can only change your personality point nine percent. That's it! That's, like, hardly anything!"

"I've always been this way," I whisper, staring at the door. "Always. Deep down. Now I'm finally the real me."

"You're the *new* you. Not the real you. You're like the 'after' part of a before-and-after picture. You know, those fat ladies who get all skinny?" Monica's face is turned toward the ceiling now, eyes closed, like she's sunbathing. "Know what happens to them?" She yawns, sits up, then slides to the dusty wooden floor, sits at my feet. "They gain the weight back." She stretches her legs out in front of her and folds her body in half. "My hamstrings are so cramped," she says into her knees.

"Plenty of people get religious at nineteen, twenty, and stay that way forever," I say. "You don't even have your facts straight."

"How long after you broke up with that girl . . . Vanessa? The one I remind you of. How long after that did you convert?"

"I didn't convert."

"You know what I mean." She sits up straight, and then, I swear, she opens her legs into a wide straddle and leans over her left leg, her right arm arced over her body. "Convert, sign up, whatever you did."

I stand quickly and go to my closet for a towel. "I returned," I say. "I didn't convert. I've always been a Jew. It's just that my parents didn't raise me properly. But I was born Jewish, so now I've returned to Hashem."

Monica stares at me and says nothing.

"Look," I say. "I don't know. I don't know which came first."

"She's a shiksa, isn't she."

I hear footsteps again, louder, closer. I wipe my temples, the back of my neck, my mouth, then press the towel to my forehead and close my eyes.

"That girl, Vanessa. She's not Jewish, right? *Vanessa?*"

Vanessa. I can see her in the dark behind my eyelids. Can hear the crunch of her hairbrush running through her wet, tangled hair. I can see her on that first night we spent together, the way the backs of our hands touched, the electricity between our skin. Vanessa lying beside me, our heads dangling over the edge of the bed, her hair pooling like ink on the floor, blood rushing into our faces; I remember how she looked upside down, no more than an inch between our noses, how she said, *Now I know what you would look like if you were pink.* She pressed a thumb to my face and said, *I just left my mark on you.*

Monica says, "Answer me, Asher. Is she Jewish or not?"

I'm starting to feel dizzy from the heat; there's a sandstorm in my head. I lean my palm against the hard, cool wall, remembering one morning in Boulder several months after Vanessa and I had broken up. My roommate was in class, and I was alone in my dorm room, wrapping tefillin around my arm—I had just learned to lay tefillin—saying my morning prayers, my prayer shawl draped over my shoulders. I had my door cracked, and I was hoping—this is pathetic, I know, but it's true—hoping Vanessa would walk by, would peek in, would see me praying, would see me caring about something that wasn't her. Caring about something so much bigger than her. I thought the sight of that—of me!—might melt her. I was such an idiot.

Monica starts plucking imaginary petals from an imaginary flower. "She's Jewish, she's Jewish not. She's— No, wait. She's Jewish, she believes that Jesus Christ is her personal savior. She's Jewish, she recognizes organized religion as a xenophobic institution designed to perpetuate segregation. She's Jewish, she's . . ."

I hear David right outside my door. He's not singing anymore. He's talking with Reuven, who lives across the hall. Aside from the advantage Reuven has from having been born to Orthodox parents, he's also a genius, a luminary, or as everyone in the yeshiva says, a *gadol.* Supposedly, Reuven knows twenty of the sixty-three volumes of Talmud by memory, commentary included. But you'd never know that he's a genius because he's so shy and modest, the type who's more likely to laugh at everyone's jokes than to contribute his own thoughts to a conversation. The rabbis adore him. Really, everyone does, except for David, who seems to want him dead.

David's words are indistinct at first, but then his voice starts to rise. He's arguing with Reuven. "*Rashi* admitted he didn't know things. So who are you? Moshe Rabeinu?"

"I just think there's more to it," Reuven says, and he sounds weary, defeated, unconvinced that he should even bother trying to explain himself. "I mean, I think there are exceptions."

"And whatever *you* think must be true, right? Your thoughts are so precious. You have superhuman intelligence."

"I'm allowed to speculate, David, aren't I? I think some distractions are okay. That's all I'm saying."

I know what they're talking about: the third chapter from *Ethics of the Fathers*, the part that says that if a man stops learning Torah to comment on how nice a tree is or how well plowed a field is, he is sinning and deserves to die.

Of course, these days, when Jews talk about people deserving to die, we don't mean it. Ever since the Holy Temple was destroyed a couple thousand years ago, we haven't had a court, so we don't sit around sentencing one another to death (although, if we did, I'll bet the secular Jews of the world would think twice about desecrating Torah).

"*You'd* like to think there are exceptions," David says. "I know what goes on in your head, Reuven. You act all high and mighty, but I see you around. I see the way you look at girls. If you had the opportunity—not that any girl would give you the opportunity—you'd take it. In a heartbeat you'd take it. You're no better than anyone."

David is wrong! Reuven is the most focused person I know, and the least pompous. But I wonder if he's really addressing Reuven, or if he's addressing me. He knows I'm within earshot. David's and Reuven's voices are so close, it sounds like their mouths are pressed to my door. I fold the towel into quarters, my hands trembling. I set it on the foot of the bed. Monica has apparently finished stretching. She is sitting on her knees on the floor. I sit on the bed at a safe distance.

"They know you're in here," I whisper, more to myself than to her.

"You're paranoid," Monica whispers back. "You're being like a schizophrenic, like my aunt. She's schizo." She cranks a finger in front of her ear. "She always thinks everyone wants to poison her. This one time, Jon made her a pot of soup, and she wa—"

"We'll get caught."

"We won't get caught. But if we do, you'll have bragging rights. Do you honestly think there's a single guy in your yeshiva who wouldn't want me in his room?"

"No one wants you! Please!" I say. "Just be quiet."

Now David is shouting, "I had no idea you were so important."

"I never said I was important. Just listen. Sometimes, some distractions can be—"

"You're a genius," David slurs. He sounds drunk. "So let's go tell everyone. Get some wine. *L'chaim!* It's Reuven! The resident genius."

Monica reaches up for my face and I jerk my head away. "Shh," she says. I suck in my breath. She pinches one of my *payos* at the root, her fingertips barely grazing my scalp, then slides her thumb and index finger, slowly, down to the end of it. In the dark, her touch feels like a million little bugs hatching all over my face. I gulp involuntarily. It sounds impossibly loud. She lets go, watches the hair fall back against my jawline, then lifts it again and starts over.

"This could ruin my life," I say, but my words sound far away, out of my reach, like things that used to belong to me. "If we're caught," I say, "my life will be over." I see the shadows of shoes in the dim strip of candlelight beneath the door. I shudder.

"Don't confuse your yeshiva with your life," Monica says. "They're two different things."

"You don't understand," I say.

"I understand perfectly. Look. Don't you think it's strange that you have to worry so much about being seen with me? You're a grown man, aren't you? Legal voting age. Old enough to be a soldier. Can't you make your own decisions? Don't you think there's something wrong with being afraid of people who are supposed to be your friends? Your 'community'?"

"What are you doing?"

"I'm getting you to think. It's uncomfortable, isn't it? Thinking in ways that aren't in line with what you've been taught here?"

"I think perfectly well on my own, thank you. I do more thinking here than I've ever done. Yeshiva life is incredibly intellectually stimulating."

Monica considers that, then seems to dismiss it. "I'm going to straighten this curl," she whispers, her face now so close to mine, I can see flecks of light in each of her irises. She reaches around me and takes hold of the other earlock, too, as if she's holding the reins of a horse.

"Maybe it doesn't want to be straightened," I say.

"Uh-huh," Monica says. "Whatever you say, Asher."

Outside the door, Reuven says, "We have an obligation to try to understand."

"But then there's you," says David, "the scholar. You don't have to try to do anything. You're just naturally omniscient."

"All I ever do, David, is try to understand. I'm not omniscient. No man is omniscient. Why are you saying these things?"

Monica's pale eyebrows are wrinkled together, her blue eyes focused. "They're almost straight now," she whispers. "Because you're so sweaty. It's the sweat that's doing it."

David's voice grows louder. "Let's ask Todd," he says. "He'll agree with me."

It takes me a second to grasp the meaning of his words. Then every muscle in my body clenches like I'm having a seizure.

I grab Monica's wrists. A long silence stretches as I watch the shadows in the threshold light. The shadows shift and the floor creaks. What is David *doing*? He doesn't even study. I've seen him at night. He doesn't. So I know practically for a fact that he wouldn't bother asking Todd a question about *Ethics of the Fathers*. He doesn't ask questions *period*, come to think of it. He's above questions.

"Hey, Todd!" David yells, and then the pounding comes, loud and insistent against my door, which I realize all at once I forgot to lock—I'm not in the habit of locking it. I squeeze Monica's wrists harder. They are thin wrists. Girls' wrists are thin. Fragile like crepe paper. I'd forgotten that.

Monica whispers, "I can hide under the bed. Why don't you—"

I let go of a wrist and clap a hand to her mouth. "Stop it," I whisper. "This isn't a game. I don't want you to hide. I don't want you to move. Just stay still and be quiet."

"Todd! Open up! We need a third opinion."

"I don't think he's around," Reuven says. "Isn't he in Haifa?"

David knocks again anyway. "So where's Asher, then? Hey! Asher!" I can't see David, of course, but I can picture him there, just as clearly as if the door has dropped away to reveal him, powerful in a rectangle of candlelight, wind blowing his hair back, maybe some smoke swirling around him. The brass doorknob twists back and forth. He's messing with me. He knows the door isn't locked. He knows he could walk right in. I feel a pulse between my palm and Monica's wrist. I can't tell whose it is.

"Probably asleep or something," Reuven says. "Let him rest. Come on." The doorknob goes still. "I'm going to bed." I hear Reuven's door across the hall open and close.

After a minute, I remove my hot palm from Monica's mouth. I release her other wrist and exhale shakily. "You have to go," I whisper. "I have to get you out of here."

"Asher?" David yells. Monica and I both turn our heads to the door. The doorknob starts twisting back and forth again. "Asher. Hey. I just heard you. What are you, talking to yourself?"

I close my eyes and begin to pray. The Sh'ma. I am mouthing the words, sweating like someone lost in the desert. Like Yosi in the sweat lodge in Arizona. That's where he found God, he always said, in a sweat lodge, as he muttered the Sh'ma into a clump of sweet grass for no apparent reason. But that's the kind of story all those Zeff guys tell—romantic hippie stories that link their flower-child days to their faith without acknowledging the obvious fact that they're still hippies. Hippies dressed up as Jews.

I finish the Sh'ma and begin it again. *Hear O Israel, the Lord our God, the Lord is One.* If the whole nation of Israel—not just religious Jews, but all Jews—*could* hear me, and if they believed me that God is One, then Moshiach, our Messiah, would come. Then I wouldn't be in this ridiculous situation right now. I wouldn't be forced away from my studies by a distraction I never invited. Everything would be perfect.

It's strange how you can sense light better when your eyes are closed. Or at least, you're most conscious of light that intrudes on your darkness. A blindfold falls away. I open my eyes. The door is cracked. There's a shaft of muted gold candlelight and David is standing in it.

"What are you guys doing?" he asks.

I am clutching my bedsheet with both hands, digging my fingertips into my palms. "Studying," I say. I don't know why I say it, where it comes from, only that David quite possibly thinks Monica is Todd. The way the darkness is falling, he might not be able to make out details, to wonder why Todd is wearing a shiny gold dress. I pray he's as drunk as I think he is. "Good night," I blurt.

David doesn't move. His expression is hauntingly blank, his dark eyes dull, his thick caterpillar eyebrows and beard as fixed as a disguise. The quiet freezes like it does in the movies right before an execution, when there are soft, insistent drums, a man with a pillowcase over his head, heartbeats like a hailstorm. Three people breathe out of sync with each other.

Finally David says, "Study hard." Is there a smirk in his voice? He stands there for one moment more before pulling the door closed.

After a few long seconds, I hear his shoes clop down the hallway. He starts singing the Arbahim song again, as if the events that took place since he left off occurred on some other plane, or in some other universe, and don't matter at all.

After a minute, Monica asks, "So did you piss your pants or what?" She laughs.

"Keep your voice down," I say, getting up to lock the door, then returning to the bed, several inches away from her.

"Are you *afraid* of David or something?"

"How do you know him anyway?" I ask.

She flicks her blond hair over her bare shoulder, ignoring my question. "He's so annoying. He's always showing up, you know? Whenever we're hanging out."

"We don't hang out," I say. "Monica. You need to go."

"If you were smart, you'd wait until everyone was asleep." She moves closer to me and reaches for my *payos* again.

I push her arms away. "I don't touch," I say weakly.

"You're not touching. I'm touching. And I'm not even really. It's just your hair. I think your hair and your fingernails shouldn't count because they're just, like, dead cells." She folds her hands in her golden lap and sits back on her heels. Then she stands and goes to my desk, picks up the framed picture there, one of Bits and Alena from so many years ago. They're both in sweaters and turtlenecks and long skirts. It's the only picture I have of my sisters that makes them look Orthodox. No one has to know it was taken on Thanksgiving, right before a huge *treyf* dinner, or that they were dressed that way only because it was freezing out. "You have little sisters?"

"One. Well, I did. My other sister's older. That picture's from a long time ago."

"What happened to the little one?"

"She's . . . missing."

"Missing?"

"Yeah, well, she was kidnapped. But they never found the guy who took her."

"How do you know it was a guy?"

"Oh, come on," I say. "I think it's safe to assume."

I don't want to tell her about Buckley Quinn. I don't want to tell her about the hairs from Buckley Quinn's car. That kind of evidence is inconclusive anyway. It's just hair. It's not enough. I don't want to tell Monica anything.

Monica blows dust from the frame, then replaces it on the desk. "You always sound like you're hiding things," she says.

"I'm not."

"You probably are. Not that I care. I'll find out anything I want to know." She comes back toward the bed and stands over me, lays her hands on top of my head like she's blessing me. I feel her trace my *kipa* with her finger. "Shh," she says, even though I haven't spoken. "I'm not touching you. I'm touching your *kipa*."

"Monica—"

"I'm surprised you have a sister," Monica says. "Do you like her?"

"Like her?"

"Love her?"

"Of course."

"Strange then, that you hate women," she says.

"I don't hate women."

"You do. You're like, a total pig."

"I am not."

"Huge pig. State fair winner–sized pig. You subscribe to an extreme form of a patriarchal religion. Even your God's a man."

"He isn't a person."

"But He's a 'He.' You're angry with the opposite sex. You all are."

"You're stereotyping," I tell her. "I mean, your criticisms aren't even original. I'm not angry with anyone. Is it so hard for you to believe that some people are just happy?"

"Shh," she says again. "Let's just lie down," and she crawls around me toward the wall, peels back the green army blanket and the top sheet, and climbs in. She lies on her back and yawns, covers pulled up to her chin, her hair a yellow scribble on the pillow. She closes her eyes. "Climb in," she murmurs. "I won't touch you. I promise."

I push my shoes off, but I don't lie down. I watch her for a long time, as her breathing evens out and her chapped lips part slightly. She eventually rolls over to face the wall, her back to me. I cross the room to Todd's bed, lie on top of the covers, and smell him on the pillowcase, overwhelmingly male: SPF 50 sunscreen and the kosher shampoo everyone at Yeshiva Hillel uses. David's still walking around out in the hall. I can tell it's him because of how loud the floorboards creak, as if they're about to split under his weight and drop him into the *beit midrash*, like if they were any weaker, even just a fraction weaker, they wouldn't withstand such pressure.

WITHIN MINUTES, WADE has launched his smear campaign. As I walk my students to the library for reading time, and then later to art class, I half expect to see my face printed on people's T-shirts, slashed with a big red X. It's obvious that everyone is talking about me. Even while I teach, I can practically feel the whispers coming through the walls like pollen, invisible things floating through the spring air, making it difficult to breathe.

Being the subject of gossip is nothing new for me. There was the time I slept with Kyra's fiancé. There was high school, when everyone was deeply interested in my sex life. There was junior high, when everyone was deeply interested in my sex life. There was okay—fifth grade, right after Alena disappeared, when I started fooling around with a seventh-grader named Teddy—the sweet boy with the red hair—lying naked with him behind the big maroon curtain on the auditorium stage. That was way before sex-ed classes, way before puberty, even before armpit hair. So kids talked. But at age ten, what could I do? Explain to my fellow fifth-graders what it felt like to lose a sister, and to have parents who, instead of trying to sew the hole up, ripped it open wider every day? Tell them about the rush of white noise in my head, the throbbing in my chest; the way sex, or whatever it was Teddy and I were doing, felt like the only way to dull the edges of things? So I said nothing. I let them talk.

But still, you never get used to being treated like a leper. Plus, I keep thinking about what Wade said: *I hope at least in your mind, you can act like you had a good reason for stealing from someone who's supposed to be your friend.*

It's been a while since someone called me a friend.

There's Maggie, of course, good old Maggie, who is kind enough to slip a note under my classroom door telling me to meet her at Dora's Bar later for a drink. But I think Maggie's sort of bipolar or something. Which shouldn't matter. Doesn't matter. I'm scared of Wade, the angry trust-fund baby, and I need all the friends I can get.

"Holy fuckoly, Bits," Maggie says, the second I walk into the bar. "Why didn't you *tell* me?"

She's drinking a draught beer. I order a bourbon and water. I know I'm going to hate it, but it seems like a drink I would order if I were sophisticated, if I were a person with money and a well-organized closet.

"Who drinks bourbon and water? What are you, an old man? And who sleeps with Wade Gordon and doesn't tell their best friend? He's hot, Bits."

"He is?" I stare at Maggie, who spends a lot of her time constructing theories about men—how they think, what they like, what they need. The way she talks, you get the impression she's never really met a man. She talks about them like they're fragile toys. Or toddlers. I can't tell if she's bored or horny or insane. Whatever she is, I think she would pretty much hemorrhage if she knew the details of my sex life. I would never tell her. I never even told Kyra. Never told anyone.

Maggie sips her beer and examines me. "Listen," she says. "I think Wade made up this story because—"

"What story?"

"That you stole his money and all that. He made it up because he's in love with you and he can't have you."

"He did?" It's not a bad theory, really. Why wouldn't Wade be a liar? Why is Wade's dishonesty any less plausible than mine?

I glance at an old guy in a mesh baseball cap who's standing by the pool table. His pants are falling down. He's conducting an invisible orchestra.

"Go to him," Maggie says, and for a second I'm confused about whom she means. She takes both of my hands in hers. "Do you love Wade?" she asks, with no trace of irony.

"No."

"Stop lying to yourself."

"Okay." I order two shots of tequila in quick succession and pour them down my throat.

"Go to him," Maggie says. "Let him see that you love him, and he'll melt in your arms."

Right. Where did Maggie *come* from? How does she convince herself on a daily basis that although men don't want to date *her*, per se, they are, as a species, lovesick? In Maggie's orbit, men keep diaries. They stuff love letters into old beer bottles and cast them out to sea. They spray women's perfume on their pillows to combat loneliness.

"Don't be afraid," Maggie says.

Ridiculous. But maybe she has a point. If Wade sees me, if I'm right in front of him in his apartment where we have so many memories together—well, a few memories anyway; sex memories mostly—why wouldn't he melt? Why wouldn't he admit that he's overreacting, that nothing I do could really be all that bad? Can't I make him forgive and forget? "Okay," I say, taking a deep breath. "Okay, Maggie, I'm going."

8 Iyar 5762
(April 20, 2002)

WAKE UP! WAKE up to do the work of the Creator! It's Shabbat. *Boker tov!*"

My eyes snap open and everything feels backward. Upside down. It takes me a second to realize that's because I'm sleeping in—on—Todd's bed, and because a few feet away from me, Monica is sleeping in mine. She's snoring obscenely. The voice of the *rosh yeshiva*, Yeshiva Hillel's dean, fades out down the hall: "Wake up! Wake up!"

I sit up straight. "Monica!" I hiss. I stand on stiff, exhausted legs, feeling around my head for my *kipa* and adjusting the bobby pins. I squat beside my bed. "Monica!"

She rolls over onto her back and groans. Her eyes stay closed. Her hair is in her face. Her mouth drops open and the snoring resumes. I reach instinctively to shake her, but my fingertips hesitate just above her shoulder. Now I remember touching her last night—my fingers encircling her wrists like cuffs, my palm against her hot mouth, her hands in my hair.

"Monica!"

She snores once more, emphatically, and opens her eyes halfway.

"Don't say a word," I hiss. "Just listen."

"I have to pee."

"Shh!"

She groans again and rolls over to address herself to the wall.

"I'm going downstairs, to pray," I say to her hair. "Monica. Listen to me. When I think it's a good time, I'll come back up and get you out of here." I wait for her to respond, and when she doesn't, I stand, smooth my wrinkled clothes down with trembling hands. "You shouldn't still be here," I mutter. "What are you still *doing* here anyway?"

"What the hell was I supposed to do? You fell asleep too. God!"

"Shh!" I rub at my eyes with the heels of my hands. "Just . . . *shh!*" I slip quickly out the door, locking it behind me.

In the *beit midrash*, I stand in the back and go through the motions, turn pages and move my lips, but every little thing distracts me: the volumes of commentary on the giant bookshelf beside me, the dust on their spines, the backs of everyone's heads, black *kipas* on short haircuts like a sea of dilated pupils. I'm guessing the sizes of windows, silently evaluating the way sounds echo in each stairwell. And then I hear something snap loudly, and a splintering sound like wood cracking.

A few people glance up, just barely, then go back to praying. Amazing how distractions roll right off of them. They used to roll off me, too, back in the Zeff House *beit midrash*, where I would spend hours firing question after question at Yosi about God, about Torah, mostly about halacha, Jewish law. Back then, I could hardly wait for him to finish an answer, I had so many more questions bubbling inside me. Outside, the sun could have fallen out of the sky and I wouldn't have noticed. I retained everything too.

"Why is this so easy for me?" I asked him once.

"Because you've known it all before," he said. "Right before you were born, an angel pressed a finger here," he pointed to the groove above my upper lip, "and took all your knowledge. For the past eighteen years, instead of working toward relearning the information you really need, you've been learning a lot of useless, secular information that has kept you from opening your heart to the Holy One. Of course, that's not your fault. You were a child. But understand that you once knew everything," he said. "You once knew all the right things." He leaned toward me. "We all want to return to that. The time before we were born. When we hadn't made mistakes yet."

David is standing with his prayer book closed, smacking it into his open palm. He's looking around at everyone, a smirk on his face. I wish he'd pray for once in his life. I can't slip out of the *beit midrash* while he's just standing there like a security guard. Another snapping sound. This one seems to come from above. Then quiet. I look up at the ceiling. The sound comes again: *snap, snap, snap,* louder and louder, and suddenly, there is a shadow closing over me, something hitting my left shoulder—

"Watch out!" someone screams, but the voice is muffled and drawn out, like a record at slow speed, and wood-hard objects are bouncing off my head like rocks and the next thing I know, I'm on the floor, my cheek against the green carpet, and there's a small house or something sitting on my shoulder blades.

I hear counting: *"Echad . . . sh'dayim . . . shalosh."* The weight is lifted, the light comes in, and I am lying in an ocean of books, staring at a circle of shiny black shoes. I blink hard and look up through the dust in my eyes.

"Are you okay?" Reuven asks. He reaches his hand down to me.

I take it and let him pull me to my feet. Rabbi Berkstein wraps an arm around me. "Are you hurt?"

"I don't think so," I say slowly. My shoulders ache, my head aches, my left heel feels like it's been hit with a hammer. I look behind me. The bookcase, mostly empty now, is propped up against the wall. I flex my hand, make a fist, open it. I wiggle my fingers.

Reuven goes to the bookcase and touches it. "It's so strange," he says. "The bookcase just . . . fell on you."

I try to smile. "That's called being in the wrong place at the wrong time." I brush dust from my sleeve.

Everyone laughs, relief laughter, and I glance around to see who else got hit. But everyone's eyes are on me.

"So the Holy One has sent Asher a wake-up call." Rabbi Berkstein squeezes me. "Tell us what he's waking you from."

Everyone laughs again.

Rabbi Berkstein chuckles and releases his grip on me. "Maybe Asher has some secrets," he says.

David snorts.

I bend down to retrieve my prayer book from the floor, brush my hand over the cover, and kiss it quickly.

"It was screwed to the wall," Reuven says. He's running a knuckle down the line on the wall where the bookcase was. "Screwed to the wall! It doesn't make any sense." But, of course, it makes perfect sense. Of course God would hurl a shelf of holy books at me while I am fake-praying and Monica is waiting upstairs in my bed like a concubine.

For the first time in months, an old feeling takes hold of me like a straitjacket, and I remember with glaring clarity how I felt before I met Yosi, before I moved to Israel: the deadening gauze over everything, the shackle of guilt. If I drift away from Judaism, I'll be right back where I used to be.

"I have to lie down for a few minutes," I tell Rabbi Berkstein. "My head hurts." I'm thinking about what Monica said: that people can't change, that even if someone does change, he always changes back. That can't be true. It can't be. There's no reason I can't be high on Torah for the rest of my life. Torah doesn't wear off; it doesn't get boring like an overplayed song; I still have so much of it to explore.

"Reuven, go with him," Rabbi Berkstein says.

"No!" I hold a hand up in front of me and start backing away toward the door. "No. I'm fine." I press two fingers to my temple. I'm remembering the way I felt at that first Zeff Shabbat, the way my veins pulsed with energy. Why does that feel like another lifetime? It wasn't that long ago. That was me. That *is* me.

David is watching me, looking suspicious.

"*B'seder,*" says Rabbi Berkstein, shrugging grandly. "He gets flattened by a bookcase and he wants his privacy." He dismisses me by waving both hands. "So give him his privacy." From behind me, he grips my arms affectionately and gives me a little shake. "*Maichoyil el choyil,*" he says. *Go from strength to strength.*

I run. Down the hall, up the stairs, and into my room, where I find Monica lying on my bed with her knees bent and her legs open. She's reading one of the magazines from her stack. There's a pistol on the cover. I catch a glimpse of Monica's turquoise underwear before I close the door and lean against it. I feel heat creep up my neck, up my cheeks. "I've got to get you out of here now."

"What was that crash?" she asks, turning a page. I can't see her face. "I thought it was a bomb." She yawns. "I thought you were dead."

"I never wanted you here," I say.

"Who are you trying to convince? Yourself?"

"You have to go. Monica. Listen. The work I'm doing here . . . I mean, what I'm doing here, I can't let anything . . . anyone . . . get in the way of it. My life depends on this. Do you understand?"

"It would have been really ironic if that was a bomb, and if you died, because remember how I told you I wanted us to do something together? The other day?" She turns another page. "What I was going to ask is if you wanted to build a bomb with me. It's easy. Tells how in this magazine. Bombs aren't usually anything fancy. Just nails and some explosive stuff." She drops the open magazine facedown onto her chest and looks at me. "You know, I have fifty-six magazine subscriptions. That's a lot, huh? I found a way to get them for free. I can show you how if you're interested. I get them shipped overseas from the States. Couple from Britain."

"Go," I say. "I need you gone."

Monica raises her eyebrows. "Who taught you to talk to a lady like that?" She sits up, legs crossed in front of her, and smooths her staticky hair. "I just think it would be really fun. We could blow up something small at first, you know? Like a trash can. And then . . ." She waves her hand in the air in a vague way. "Well, we'll see."

"You're sick," I say. "Talking about bombs. In Jerusalem. In a yeshiva."

She laughs.

I touch the back of my head, feeling for a bump. "Who do you think you are?"

"I know who *I* am."

I cross the room to the desk, rest my hands on the chair back, and look out the window at the courtyard.

"You know, the suicide bombers have wires coming down both arms," she says, "out of their sleeves, and they just press the wires together, just these straggly red wires, and *boom*."

I wince. A word from the Intro to Psych class I took in college pops into my head: "sociopath." I swallow hard, my throat as dry as rope.

"Remember that old TV show?" Monica says. "About the girl with the alien father who she talked to through a cube? She'd touch the tips of her index fingers together and time would freeze? Dumbest show in the world, but anyway, suicide bombings are kind of like that. Just one quick touch. One quick moment and the world explodes."

"That's just fabulous," I say. I mean to sound sarcastic, but instead I sound scared.

"Not all bombs are the wire kind. Others go in a backpack, and the bomber just has to move his neck in a certain way to pull the cord. There are all different kinds."

My knuckles on the chair back are white. "They're cowards!" I say. "Suicide bombers are cowards. What's wrong with you? You think it's romantic or something to ruin people's lives? Think of the victims' families."

"They're the opposite of cowards." Monica laughs. "They know there's more to life than just staying alive. They have a cause! They're tremendously brave. They don't do it because they hate life. They love life. They don't even consider it suicide. I don't either. I mean, I don't want to commit suicide, Asher. I'm just saying, it's so nice and neat. Just touch your wrists together and—"

"If you go down the back stairs," I interrupt, "I'll be able to watch from here, to make sure you get out. From the time you leave my room, I should be able to count to twenty and then see you in the courtyard. If you go quickly."

I hear her stand. "And then what?"

"And then you go back to Hebrew U," I say, the words pushing out of my lungs like a long-held breath, "and do whatever it is you do there, and stay as far away from me as possible."

"You can't just keep closing the door on the real world," Monica says.

"You're not the real world!"

"You'll throw all your weight against the door, and then one day . . . one day you'll go to open it and no one will be on the other side. Then how will you feel?"

"I mean it," I say. "You need to stay away from me."

"I'm not a violent person," Monica says. "I just like to talk about things. We should talk about things that make us uncomfortable. No subject should be off-limits. The only thing that's dangerous is a closed mind."

"Other things are dangerous Much more dangerous."

"Buddhists meditate on their own deaths. Did you know that? I think that's really cool."

I don't turn around. I'm wondering if she has planted a bomb in the yeshiva, in my room perhaps. "Don't come back," I say. "No more showing up here. Understand? Now hurry," I say, "before everyone comes out of the *beit midrash*. I don't want you offending everyone."

"*Offen*—"

"You look offensive!" I explode, even though today is twenty-three days, which is three weeks and two days of the Omer, the day to focus on having a good heart. My hands curl into fists; my thumbs massage my knuckles. "Go to a club if you want to strut around in a miniskirt. Go to Tel Aviv. I don't care. Just get out!" My shoulders and head still ache. My knees too. All I want to do is crawl into my bed and fall asleep and wake up knowing that last night was a dream, that Monica was never here, that she didn't leave long blond hairs and the scent of coconut on my sheets.

I brace myself for what I know is coming: a barrage of insults, a long-winded story about her Uncle Jon or some guy who's in love with her, a threat of some kind. I wait, listen to her pick up her bag, sling it over her shoulder, and then I hear her footsteps, and then the door opening—all this in the space of five seconds—and she doesn't say a word. The door doesn't even slam. She pulls it shut so softly, I have to strain to hear the click. But I do hear it. I know exactly what it is. I am well acquainted with the sound of someone leaving.

I touch the window and start to count. One . . . two . . . Monica is tiptoeing to the top of the stairwell, resting a skinny freckled hand on the banister. The floorboard on the first step is a real squeaker. *Please take your shoes off,* I beg her silently. The court-yard is perfectly still. Not even a breeze in the trees.

Why am I remembering Vanessa?

I always seem to wind up remembering Vanessa. Such a waste of mental energy, thinking about girls. At least right now. Maybe in a couple of years, I'll want to get married. Someone in the community will find me a girl, a good, religious, modest girl, a girl who wouldn't leave me just because one of my friends hit on her at a frat party (there won't be any frat parties!) or because I tell her the secret that I've never told anyone but Vanessa: that after Alena disappeared in the brown car, I didn't run inside to tell my mother, that it was at least an hour before my mother even asked me where Alena was, that when she did ask, I shrugged and said I had no idea, that it took me a whole week to admit that I'd seen a brown car, that if I'd spoken up earlier, something might have been done. Alena might have come back to us. I was a child, but I knew better. I didn't want to take the blame for letting Alena get into that car. After all, how many times had I heard my mother tell me to keep an eye on my sister? I preferred to lie than to give my parents, the police, and the neighborhood search party the information that might have saved Alena's life.

Vanessa didn't leave me because of Chris Rue. She left me because I told her what I had done to my family. She left me when she found out who I really was.

Twenty-five . . . twenty-six. . .

Monica, where are you? Thirty . . . thirty-one . . . thirty-two . . . It's time for breakfast. I listen to the drone of voices downstairs, but can't make out words, can only follow the path of the noise, moving from the *beit midrash* to the dining hall. I hear glasses and forks clinking. I hear footsteps running up the stairs . . . thirty-seven . . . thirty-eight. . .

A knock on my door. I stop counting. She came back!

But of course she didn't. There she is below me, a tiny dot running across the grass, her yellow hair flying out behind her like a flag. She's holding her sandals in one hand, running in bare feet, and for a second, I forget that I just banished her from my life. I forget about her magazines and her bombs. I have an uncomfortable urge to fling the window open and yell, "Monica!"

Another knock on my door.

I watch Monica for a few more seconds, and then sit in the desk chair, trying to look natural. I know I don't look natural. I get up and lie on my bed. That's not right either. I stand, stare at the door, and finally go to it and pull it open.

It's Reuven. He has his hands in his pockets, his prayer book pinned under one arm. "Just wanted to make sure you're okay," he says. He scrunches his nose to nudge his glasses up the bridge of it. "I don't think you should go to sleep. You might have a concussion. I just wanted to tell you that. Do you feel strange at all? I remember once my brother got a concussion and he kept thinking all day that he'd lost his wallet, even though it was right in front of him."

"Lost . . ." I feel my back pocket instinctively, then lean against the door frame and let out a shaky breath. I start curling one of my *payos* around my finger, undoing the damage. "I haven't lost anything," I say.

PERHAPS I'M SUFFERING from the arrogance that comes with falling in love, the assumption that no one else on earth could possibly understand how I feel when I throw my arms around Jonathan's neck, bury my face in his shoulder, stand on his feet, squeeze him with all my strength, and still can't ever get close enough to him. Do my children know that agonizing ecstasy? Will they ever? I worry about my children—show me a mother who doesn't—about their capacity for love, about the relationships they might have or will have. After all, I'll admit it: they didn't have the best role model. Their father treated me like a discolored mole, something to ignore until it was time to remove it.

My kids don't know all the sordid details of what their father did after Alena disappeared. They know certain things, of course: that he became increasingly remote and unavailable, that he packed up and left us a year later like we were a motel that had turned out to be infested with fleas. But they don't know everything.

This is something Jonathan and I have in common: our spouses traded us up for better offers. I don't know the details of Jonathan's marriage; details don't matter much. Disloyalty is disloyalty. It's always the same story really, that one person falls out of love with the other and finds someone else to love. Bits and Ash think that their father left me, and then took up with a new woman. I'll never tell them the truth, but I've been tempted. I've been *very* tempted.

After Benjamin left me, my sister Viv told me that his actions were typical of parents who lose a child, that she'd read about this, one parent being unable to cope, seeking companionship outside of the marriage. Know what I think of that kind of psychobabble? I'll show you where to shove it. *I* would have liked to have had an affair! *I* would have liked a little excitement in my life, a little distraction. But I had two other children to raise! I was busy raising them. And where was my husband? A year after we lost Alena, he left me for some New-Agey blonde he met at a self-healing workshop. I hadn't even known he was going to things like self-healing workshops. I had never even *heard* of self-healing workshops. What kind of nonsense is that? So he and his new woman self-healed and healed each other and who knows what else, and then picked up and shipped off to Colorado like a couple of teenagers trying to find themselves.

My kids don't need to know that their father, on top of being a deadbeat, cheated on their mother. But he did! I was the jilted wife! So can anyone blame me for staying single after that, for guarding my heart with thick metal bars? What I'm doing now with Jonathan—it's a risk. He is a man, after all, and I know what men are capable of. Anyway, maybe I shouldn't worry so much about my kids. What do I know? It's not like anyone tells me anything. Maybe my kids were born with talent for love. Neither of them got any musical or mathematical talent, and they have to be talented at something (don't they?), so maybe Bits and Ash are love prodigies. Maybe their relationships are deep and fulfilling.

I DRIVE, HALF DRUNK, to Wade's apartment building. I smile at the doorman and follow a tenant into the lobby, take the elevator to Wade's floor, and knock. He opens the door quickly, as if he's expecting someone, then starts to close it as soon as he sees that it's me. I stick my foot in the door. He's wearing a dark blue button-up shirt unbuttoned, a necktie untied, collar turned up. His hair is wet.

"What's the occasion?" I ask, gesturing to his tie.

"Get out of here," he says, waving an arm at me. "It's my dad's birthday. My parents are coming to pick me up soon to go out to dinner."

I push the door open wider with my foot and fold my arms across my chest. "Let me in," I say. Gentle but firm. Like scooping an injured bird from its nest. "We need to talk."

Wade won't look me in the eye. He leans in the doorway. "Go home," he says, "or I'll call the cops. How'd you get up here anyway?" He begins buttoning the front of his shirt, his fingers shaking slightly like he's had too much sugar.

I try to sound sane. "I'd very much like to come into your apartment," I say. "And talk to you." I sound so polite, I almost curtsy.

Wade laughs without smiling, without looking at me. "Oh, yeah, just give me a minute and I'll put everything in my safe. And then maybe . . ."

"That's what I want to talk to you about."

"You have my money?"

"I want to talk to you seriously," I say. "I didn't take your money. Okay? I know I was being evasive this morning, but I guess I didn't really think you were serious. Then you started talking about me to everyone . . ."

"Everyone had already been talking. Everyone's always talking about you. Everyone thinks you're a psychopath, Bits."

"I don't know why you're doing this to me. Are you upset with me about something?" I touch his elbow as he buttons his cuff.

He yanks his arm away and glares at me. "Yeah, I'm upset with you for blindfolding me and stealing hundreds of dollars out of my bedroom."

"I didn't—" I bite my lip quickly. What I almost said was, *I didn't steal it while you were blindfolded.*

Wade's cell phone rings. He pulls it out of his pocket and turns his back on me. "Happy birthday," he says. "Yeah, I'll be ready. No . . . I'll meet you downstairs." He glances over his shoulder at me. "Let me meet you down there, okay?"

I focus on the slope of his shoulder blades inside his shirt. I want to touch him. How cozy it sounds: a dinner with Wade's parents, probably at a nice restaurant, maybe a seafood place on the water. Maybe they'll even drive to the North Shore for lobster. He and his father will probably smoke cigars. His mother's purse will match her dress. They'll ask about Wade's old friends. He'll tell them about them, about their lives at law school, their box seats at Fenway Park. The light from the birthday candles will sparkle in his father's eyes. His eyes will be brown like Wade's, the color of fall leaves. I feel a deep, incomprehensible pang of sadness.

Wade stuffs his phone back into his pocket, then turns around to face me. "Ten minutes," he says. "Okay? You can come in for ten minutes, and then I have to go. Don't try anything."

"What kind of thing would I try?" I push past him into the apartment. Wade closes the door, and I feel suddenly shy, awkward, unsure of myself. I didn't exactly come here with a plan.

As he sits on the edge of his bed, using a shoehorn to put on his shoes, the lamp on the bedside table casts a dim glow on his face, and I realize that this is the first time I've been in his apartment when the TV isn't on. Inexplicably, the silenced, blank screen makes me want to weep. I feel like I've been left out of some decision. It's like watching someone grow up when you wish that person wouldn't.

As Wade slides the shoehorn out of his left shoe; as he looks at it in his hand, turns it over, runs his fingers over the shiny smoothness of it; as he sits there with his shoes untied and his shirt untucked, for a fleeting second, I love him. I love him for stroking that shoehorn like it's the head of a kitten. I love him for *having* a shoehorn, and for putting on a tie to have dinner with his parents. I love him for not wanting his parents to see me. I want to sit on his lap and throw my arms around his neck and tell him things. I take a step backward.

He looks up at me. "Bits," he says. "Listen."

I put my hands over my ears and close my eyes. I want to tell Wade that I'm different now from how I was yesterday. I've changed. Yesterday, he was an object to me. Now, I see him for what he is: He is the son of two parents. He might be someone's brother. He is many people's friend. I want to explain to him that I don't mean to be the way I am, that I'm reckless sometimes, but that I'm going to change. I want to tell him that I'm going to Israel to repair the holes in my family. But I can't tell him any of this because then he would know I stole his money.

After a second, I feel his hands on my wrists. I open my eyes. He's standing in front of me. I let him take my hands away from my ears.

"We have nothing in common," he says.

"Yes, we do," I say. "We work at the Auburn School. Over ninety-nine percent of the world works somewhere else, but you and I . . ."

"You think differently from how I think."

"You don't know how I think."

Wade drops my wrists and sighs. "Are you going to give me my money back?"

"How many times do I have to tell you I—"

He holds up a hand. "You know what? Have it," he says, "if it means you'll leave me alone. I'd pay six hundred dollars to be rid of you."

"This is unfair," I say, and in this moment, I really believe that it is. People deserve second chances. I'm not as horrible as he thinks I am. "You're treating me unfairly," I say loudly.

Wade snorts. "I don't understand what goes on in your head, what your problems are, what happened to fuck you up so bad, but there's something"—he taps his forehead—"there's something seriously wrong with you. I don't *want* your problems. Okay? I'm not interested in trying to figure you out." He finishes closing up the buttons on his shirt. "It's like you think life is a play or something. *The Bits Show.* You love drama. But I've got my own shit. Everyone does. I've had enough," he says. "It bores me."

I reach for his face. He turns his head away. I reach for his belt and try to unbuckle it. He pries my hands off.

"You need to go," he says.

I start to cry. I sink to the floor and put my face in my hands. I hear him sigh above me, but I can't stop crying. I cry and cry. Not the attractive kind of crying. Not the kind of crying people do in movies. No. There is snorting. There is snot. There is moaning and there is wailing. But despite the unbecoming picture I know I have painted, I wait for him to squat down next to me, to touch my cheek, to apologize for being so callous. Part of me is perfectly aware of how I'm going to feel tomorrow, how I'll hate myself for doing this. But I keep crying, like that might make things better instead of worse.

I hear his footsteps, then I hear his front door open. Is he leaving? And then, I feel his arms around me, one around my back, one under my knees, and then I'm being lifted off the floor. Is he going to bring me to his bed? Is he going to lay me on his football-player sheets and dab my eyes with a tissue and whisper, *Why don't you get cleaned up and let my parents buy you dinner?*

I open my eyes, still sniffling. Wade is carrying me through his front door.

"Hey!" I say.

He sets me on the floor in the hallway near the elevator. Then he wipes his hands on the front of his pants like he was handling garbage. He turns around and walks back to his apartment.

"What are you *doing?*" I watch the door close. "Wade!" I sniffle.

That door will open again. It has to. He has to come out here, at least eventually to meet his parents. I'll wait. And when he comes back, I will tell him everything. I will apologize. I will start over. I will tell him that just as soon as I get Ash out of Israel, I will pay him back every penny I stole. He'll understand. He probably would have done what I did yesterday had he been in my position. If he had credit card debt. If he didn't have a trust fund.

I have to pee. All that bourbon and tequila. I hiccup and try to stop crying. Leftover convulsions course through me. I wipe my eyes and lie back on the pajama-striped carpet, staring up at the stucco ceiling. After a few minutes, I hear the elevator ding. I turn my head. The little red arrow is lit. The door opens. Two security guards in uniform step out. One is about my age; the other is much older. Of course Wade would live in an apartment building with security guards.

"Let's go," the young one says to me.

I sit up quickly and inch away from him without standing. I hold one hand out in front of me. "Go away. I'm waiting for my friend."

He beckons to me with one arm. "Come on."

"He let me up," I say, pointing to Wade's closed door. The brass knocker mocks me like a face with its tongue stuck out. "Is that what this is all about? Did he call you to come get me? He's lying. God. He *let me up*. How else would I have gotten up here?"

The younger guard takes my arm, pulls me to my feet. "You gonna make this difficult or you gonna cooperate?" he asks. He escorts me into the elevator, one hand planted firmly on my shoulder.

"You don't understand," I say, as the doors slide closed. My stomach drops as the elevator sinks. "Nobody understands me." I rest my head against the mirrored wall and wonder which of the two security guards I can get to sleep with me.

The older one smiles kindly. He has a perfect half halo of white hair around his otherwise bald head. "Everyone thinks that 'bout themselves," he says, pinching my cheek, "that no one understands 'em. But I'll tell you something I know 'cause I'm old." He cups a hand around his mouth and stage-whispers, "It's hardly ever true."

PART II

16 Iyar 5762
(April 28, 2002)

I AM ON MY way to pray at the Western Wall, the Kotel, a wall from the actual Second Temple that has miraculously remained intact for two thousand years. Jews all over the world face the Kotel during their prayers, so of course, the first time I ever saw it in person, my legs shook so much, I thought I'd fall over. You can't help but shake if you're that close to the Holy of Holies, the holiest place in the temple, because God's presence has never left it.

Unfortunately, the Holy of Holies rests inside a big golden dome now, which the Arabs built to cover a rock. The Muslims think it's the rock Muhammad ascended from, but really it's where Abraham bound his son Isaac as a sacrifice to God, a thing my own father never would have done, not because he thinks I'm so wonderful but because he's weak and squeamish, not to mention a terrible Jew.

My first time at the Kotel, almost a year ago now, I saw a sea of men with their black hats tipped back on their heads so they could press their faces to the stones; I was too shy to get that close. I felt as self-conscious as if I were on a first date, more so because of all the people around, as though they were all going to lift their heads at once and burst into laughter: *Don't you know God is out of your league?*

The most I could do was reach out and brush the Wall quickly with my fingertips, then bring my trembling fingers to my lips.

Today, I go right ahead and lean my arm against the Wall and rest my face on it. I love *mincha*, the afternoon prayer service. I love picturing the doctors at Hadassah Hospital, the shopkeepers in the Jewish Quarter, a man in Mea Sharim fixing a broken sink, all coming to a standstill, putting everything aside, because not one thing in the whole entire world is more important in the afternoon than praying *mincha*. My favorite part is the line in Ashrei (the prayer recited twice in the morning and once at the beginning of *mincha*) that says, "God preserves all who love Him." It means that as long as you're pious, as long as you pray and pray and mean every word, everything will be okay for you. And it also means that if you slip, God won't pretend He hasn't noticed.

Beside me, two soldiers stand praying in their green uniforms. The sight of them makes my shoulders tense. How can they stand there asking God for things, while they defend Israel in the name of secular Zionism? They're not even wearing *kipas*! I close my eyes, slide my palm over the smooth stones, feeling the cracks, and wait. I wait to feel God's presence course through my bloodstream like caffeine. But instead, it's as if I've opened a two-liter bottle of Coke that I didn't know had gone flat: Where is that satisfying fizzing sound?

During the Amida, I bow as deliberately and slowly as I ever have. If you don't bow during the Amida, your spine turns into a serpent. The serpent, like the one in Eden (and like Monica, my personal serpent), tries to use sexual energy to draw you away from God. Above me, a baby pigeon coos from his nest and I think of my baby sister. Today is Alena's nineteenth birthday, and it's also, insignificantly, the eight-day anniversary of Monica running across Yeshiva Hillel's courtyard in a flash of straw-colored hair and gold.

I press the pages of my open prayer book to my eyes. I have to concentrate. I have to concentrate. But when I finish my prayers, I feel as though I haven't prayed, like when you read a paragraph from a book, then realize you have no idea what you read. I walk backward from the Wall—you should never turn your back on it—out of the plaza, up the stone steps, past an old woman in a chair selling red string bracelets, past a man selling charcoal drawings of the Old City, and onto the street. I am wondering: Once your spine becomes a serpent, can it go back to being a spine?

As I walk, I see Monica everywhere: in a purple sundress, sifting through a barrel of dried dates; outside a souvenir shop, handing out flyers, her face hidden by a big floppy hat; in an IDF uniform, an Uzi strapped across her chest; holding a baby on her hip, pointing to the Dome of the Rock. "See?" she asks her baby in Hebrew. "Gold like Mommy's earrings." And here's Monica with a scarf over her head, eyes turned down, modest shoes, long skirt—an Orthodox Jewish Monica. It's not so unreasonable, is it, that Monica could become an Orthodox Jew? If you'd told me two years ago that I was going to live a Torah-centered life, I would have laughed. But people have transformations. Monica might. She could learn about the revelation at Mount Sinai. She could learn modesty. She could keep a nice Jewish home one day.

Not mine, of course. Just someone's.

And here's yet another Monica, wearing an airy white dress. As she walks toward me, a breeze flattens the dress to her left calf and causes it to billow out around her right calf like a sail. The closer she gets, the more clearly I see that she's actually much younger than Monica, probably about twelve or thirteen years old. She walks very slowly, one foot in front of the other in a straight line, and behind her, walking twice as quickly, is a tall, broad-shouldered Hasid, wearing a heavy black winter coat that makes me sweat just looking at it. The cuffs come down all the way over his hands.

Something is wrong. I stop in my tracks beside a shop window, where papier-mâché puppets of a religious family sit around a papier-mâché Shabbat table, and a papier-mâché religious couple is frozen in dance, a papier-mâché handkerchief between them.

The girl in the white dress arranges one foot in front of the other like Miss America. The Hasid is gaining on her. Yes, something is *definitely* wrong. Things are moving in slow motion and the world is on mute and all I can hear is my own pulse.

The man hurries past the girl. But he doesn't step to the side, the way I've seen Rabbi Berkstein do, to avoid brushing up against her. His arm collides with the girl's arm so hard, she stumbles. Of course, Hasids are a little different from the Yeshiva Hillel guys; they're more mystical, less academic, but they are still observant Jews to the greatest extent. A Hasid wouldn't brush up against a girl like that. I turn to watch the Hasid hurry past me, past a postcard rack, past a faded Israeli flag, past a tour group clad in matching blue polo shirts. I see something poking out of his cuff, something the color of blood, and I remember what Monica said about suicide bombers, what she told me just last week about the wires in their sleeves.

"That's red wire," I say.

I don't realize at first that I'm speaking aloud. Why is the Hasid wearing a *shtreimel*, one of those big fur hats men wear on Shabbat or holidays? Today isn't a holiday. No other men are wearing *shtreimels*.

"Red wires are sticking out of his sleeve," I say more loudly.

My arm lifts of its own accord. I'm standing frozen, pointing at the big fur hat as it slithers through the crowd, and every single hair on the back of my neck, every synapse firing through my brain, clearly understands: that man is no Hasid.

I search the crowd for an IDF uniform and run. I can't remember Hebrew. I am shaking a soldier's arm and shouting in my broken high school French. *"L'homme . . . l'homme . . ."* I take a deep breath and try English. "That man," I say, pointing to the black figure moving through the crowd toward the Kotel. "I think that man has a bomb." I point to my wrist. "I saw a red wire coming out of his sleeve!"

The soldier's lips turn pale. He tears off running, and I watch him go, and I am blinded by a memory of a brown car, an empty street, a silence peppered by the echo of a hockey puck hitting a garage door. How could I have been so critical of those soldiers at the Kotel for praying with no *kipas*? Those men defend the land! And what do I do? Do I tackle the man with the bomb? No. I tap a soldier on the shoulder and tell *him* to tackle the man with the bomb.

I should be running after that man. I'm the one who saw him, the one who could identify him most easily. Holding my *kipa* to my head with one hand, I take off running, past the tourists and the tiny preschool boys with *payos*, past the shop windows and the falafel stands, even though I can't see the *shtreimel* anymore, can't even see the soldier anymore, even though I'm not quite sure where I'm going. I run and run, because it's so much better than standing still, because it's what I should have done years ago when Alena got into that brown car. Had I at least run inside to my mother, had someone chased the car down before it left the neighborhood, then maybe the story of the day I let Alena get kidnapped would be a dim memory in the family lore, like the time Bits fell into a sliding glass door and needed stitches in her leg.

I round a corner into an alleyway, and all at once, I am flying through the air. My face is suddenly . . . something. Either hot or cold or wet or burning. A woman is screaming. Surely, something has exploded. This is what it feels like, I guess. Fire so hot, it feels cold. So painful, it feels wet. This is what it feels like to die in the fire of a bomb.

But actually, nothing has exploded. I'm on all fours on the ground and a woman with her hair in a gray knob at the back of her head is screaming at me in Hebrew. She's holding an empty wax-paper cup. Coke, or whatever she was drinking, is dripping from my hair, my eyelashes, the tip of my nose. I'm soaked, but for some reason, she's the one screaming, wagging a finger in my face.

"Slicha," I apologize. But why am I apologizing? Can't she see that I was running with a purpose? *"Slicha!"* I say again, annoyed now, but her yelling only grows louder. Finally, I shout, "I'll buy you a new one!"

"Ach!" she says, throwing up her arms and storming off.

I start running again. Of course, the terrorist must be headed for the Kotel. My knees hurt. My face is sticky. But I run. People who scoff at observant Jews, people like Monica, could see now just by looking at me that religious men are in fact braver than anyone, because we are so confident that God is protecting us.

But then I round another corner and find myself face-to-face with a blockade of soldiers. "You cannot go past," one says, shoo-ing people away.

I stop running, despite all the Jews who are praying *mincha* at the Kotel, oblivious to the danger they're in, despite their families whose lives will be wrecked in the wake of such loss. I lean against a wall to catch my breath. I think of all the other people through-out history who have stopped running at the first little obstacle, who ultimately chose to save themselves instead of saving others. It's a long list of nameless, forgotten people.

I turn and start walking back to the bus stop, wiping Coca-Cola out of my eyelashes and the front of my hair. My back is tense, my shoulders hunched up near my ears. I realize I'm expecting an explosion. I'm always half-expecting an explosion. The horrible experience I had a few weeks ago during Passover break? I heard a suicide bombing. No sound in the world is more horrible, more penetrating; I swear it went straight through my skin, clutched my bones, plunged into my very organs.

I had just returned from traveling up north. I was a couple of miles from Yeshiva Hillel, looking for a place to get something to eat, when I heard what sounded like a sonic boom, followed by high-pitched screams. Panic formed like a bubble in my chest. Then I heard the ambulances. Five different sirens.

By the time I got to the grocery store where a woman had blown herself up, the area was already surrounded by police tape. People stood around weeping, doubled over as if in pain, their arms hugging their own stomachs. One man walked in robotic circles, his eyes wide open. He was holding his ear. Someone covered his shoulders with a trench coat and led him away. This thought came to me then, as bright as a camera flash: *the Arabs could scare us all out of Israel.*

In that moment, I realized I could never leave. Even if everyone else leaves, I'll refuse to go. I'll be the last guy standing, like those environmentalists who tie themselves to old trees. Every Jew should come to Israel! The land would expand to fit us all, and then we'd be stronger, more unified. We'd be a nation again, like we used to be.

I don't care what Monica says; the suicide bombers *are* cowards. If they were strong, they'd stay alive to stake their claim. When you're dead, you don't have to face your problems anymore. So what's so brave about dying? Is a guy who's sick enough to dress up like a Hasid and strap a bomb to his body brave? How can Monica call that brave?

Why am I thinking of Monica?

Tonight I will count the thirty-second day, which is four weeks and four days of the Omer, the day to think about the dynamics of love. If I'm going to love God with all my heart and soul, I have to clear the clutter from my mind, get rid of anything that obstructs my view of Him. All the hippie Zeff stuff—that was an obstruction. And now Monica is an obstruction. I'll go to Migrash Harusim tonight with Todd so that I can confront her. I will tell her again that she needs to stay away from me, that she's crazy, that she can take her magazines and her bombs and leave God's land, if she's so set on desecrating His commandments. Then, with my hands washed of her, I will buckle down and pick up where I left off a couple weeks ago. I will resume my studies, renew my commitment.

I keep walking. I try to stand up a little straighter.

Dear God, please don't let the worst happen: That terrorist might hear the soldier's running footsteps behind him; even if he hasn't made it to the Kotel, he might get nervous and detonate. I envision a sudden orange fire, and I think of the prayer we say on Rosh Hashanah and Yom Kippur: *Who by water, and who by fire; who by sword, and who by beast.* Every year after Alena disappeared, my mother would cry when we got to that part in the service. It's about God's having already decided who will die that year, and how. I remember the way my mother's knuckles would go yellow against her prayer book, and I would look up at her and know what she was thinking.

Last fall, during the holidays, I learned the origin of that prayer: During the eleventh-century Crusades, a great rabbi in Germany, Rabbi Amnon, was reluctant to convert to Christianity, which made the cardinal and the ministers so angry, they amputated all four of his limbs on the eve of Rosh Hashanah. After the amputation, the bloody, dying rabbi asked to be brought to the synagogue. Someone actually carried what was left of him there in a basket. Once he got to the synagogue, he recited that prayer that we now say every year on Rosh Hashanah and Yom Kippur: *Who by water, and who by fire; who by sword, and who by beast. . . .* Then he died.

It's a morbid story, of course, and it's probably no more than a legend, but that's not the point. No one can deny that many Jews have been forced to convert, to suffer at the hands of their captors, to struggle to stay alive just because they were Jews. No one can deny that the Jews, as a people, are strong. We refuse to worship false gods, we choose agony over defeat, we pray with or without our limbs. If we weren't a strong people, we would have vanished centuries ago. As if I needed another reason to thank God for making me a Jew.

April 28, 2002

I'M STANDING OUTSIDE Ash's yeshiva for the second time. Although I flew out of Logan Airport on a Wednesday, by the time I landed at Ben-Gurion Airport, it was already Friday in Israel, meaning that, because of the Sabbath, I wouldn't see Ash until Saturday night at the earliest. At the airport, I climbed into a shared van headed for Jerusalem, and as I listened to two Orthodox men beside me discuss their Shabbat plans, my heart started racing at the thought of all I had to do before my Tuesday flight back to Boston: find Ash, break the news to him, and get him to Alena's funeral, which was eleven days away on the other side of the world.

Why hadn't I considered this time constraint when I was booking my ticket?

Because you're reckless, my mother would say, *that's why. Because you don't think.*

When Shabbat finally ended Saturday evening, I spent three hours outside Yeshiva Hillel, my fists around the wrought-iron bars, staring at the building. No one ever came out. I even tried to climb the gate at one point, but it wasn't that kind of gate.

Today, Sunday, nothing is different. No one is standing on the front lawn. No one is hanging out on the front steps, the way they would be at a normal school on a sunny day. The only difference between the way Yeshiva Hillel looked last night and the way it looks today is that a blond girl wearing binoculars around her neck is crouching behind a tree on the sidewalk. Now she is peering through the binoculars at the building. Now she is lowering the binoculars and shielding her eyes with one hand and staring at me.

"Hi," I say. She keeps staring at me and doesn't respond.

It's fitting, really, that there would be a strange person lurking around Yeshiva Hillel with binoculars. This place is weird, the kind of building where you'd expect to see a KEEP OUT sign with the silhouette of a pit bull. It's so empty and still, so immaculate and fenced-in, I worry I'm going to set off an alarm just by looking at it.

"Um," I say to the girl with the binoculars. "Can you just"—I gesture toward the gate—"go right in?" Of course, I already know the answer to that question. But I feel like I have to say something since she's staring at me. Anyway, maybe she has insider information.

"Right," she snorts. "Just walk right into a men's yeshiva with your arms and legs bare. I'm sure you'll receive the warmest welcome."

I look down at my sundress, then back at the girl's light blue T-shirt and cutoffs. The girl climbs to her feet and brushes off the back of her shorts. She has the kind of eyes that crazy people have: wide and blank. They jiggle back and forth.

"I don't get it," I say. "Why can't you ring the doorbell?"

"That's why there's a gate. They don't *want* you to ring the doorbell." She folds her skinny arms over her chest. I can see through the skin to her green veins. Her limbs are practically translucent. "It's like a jail," she says matter-of-factly.

I look around, surveying the jail's surroundings. One of the strangest things about Ash's yeshiva is that it's just in a plain old neighborhood, not unlike any neighborhood. Not unlike the neighborhood we grew up in. The houses are a little boxier, there are more buses, there's a better view (you can see what I guess is the skyline of Jerusalem, except it's more like a bird's-eye view, a spread of sparkly gold like the inside of a treasure chest), but basically, it's a quiet residential neighborhood. What's so great about it? That's what I'd like to know.

"What if I'm family?" I ask the girl.

Her eyes widen. One hand flies to her mouth. Then she grabs my arms. "Are you Asher's sister?"

I shake out of her grasp. Does Ash know I'm in Jerusalem? Did he pay this girl to stand guard outside the yeshiva, to make sure I couldn't get in? It's a crazy, paranoid thought, but the coincidence just seems too great.

"You are!" the girl says. "I'm psychic! Oh my God. Don't you think I am? People always tell me I'm psychic."

"What makes you think I'm . . . that guy's sister?" I ask her.

"Well. You look exactly alike."

Oh. Right. Of course. I take a deep breath and let it out. This girl is no guard. She's just . . . well, what is she? A friend of Ash's? Is Ash friends with girls? Even before he was an Orthodox Jew, he was never really friends with girls. There was that tall girl from his dorm in Boulder—I think he dated her, I think she had a mustache—the one he used to stare at like an overheated dog. But other than that. . .

"And I'm psychic," the blond girl says. "I just had this *feeling.* You know?"

I shake my head and turn back to the gate. I close a hand around one bar. The grass is mowed to eerie perfection. A long gray tongue of stone steps rolls out from the front door. "Here's the thing," I say. "I'm sort of . . . surprising him." I turn to the girl, who has folded her body in half from the waist. She is holding the binoculars in one hand, reaching for her toes with the fingertips of her other hand. "How do you know him?"

She ignores my question. "Let me guess," she says. "You're here to rescue him." Her blond hair grazes the sidewalk. Her spine sticks out at the base of her neck.

"That's ridiculous," I say.

"I know your type," says the girl.

"My type?"

"I know what you're up to."

"Look," I say, "if you talk to him, you can't tell him I'm here. Can you promise me that? It's very important that you keep your mouth shut."

She snaps up straight and hooks her thumbs into the binocular straps. She's so fidgety. More fidgety than my first-graders. "He's my boyfriend," she says.

"Ash doesn't have a girlfriend!"

"Wanna bet? I sleep in his dorm room! Go look in his desk drawer and you'll see my toothbrush." She steps closer to me, smiles like a knife blade, and lowers her voice to say, "You'll see our box of condoms. They're glow-in-the-dark. They say *Chag sameach.*"

I step back. "What does that mean?"

"*Chag sameach?* Happy holiday."

"Are you for real?"

"Totally."

"Ash is your boyfriend."

"Well . . . don't tell him I told you. It's this big secret; he's all weird about it. . . . Wanna go around back and see into his room? We can't get close, but it's a better angle. I know which room is his. Third floor. Far left."

I have a strange memory then, from a few months after Alena disappeared, when my mother somehow got it in her head that the old loner at the top of our street, Mr. Maloney, was Alena's kidnapper. She was convinced for about a week that he was hiding Alena in his basement. She made me go with her late at night to peer into his house. She made me look through his kitchen window with binoculars. I saw the door of Mr. Maloney's refrigerator close-up. There was a picture of his wife, who had died of some blood disease. There was a YMCA tennis schedule.

"Ash can't have a girlfriend," I tell the blond girl. "Isn't that the whole point of being Orthodox? No touching? No sex? No dating unless you're ready to get married?"

"I don't think it's the *whole* point," she says. "I don't know what the point is."

"But if he's dating someone who's not even Orthodox . . ." I don't finish my sentence: *Then why did he move to Israel and cut off his family and stop eating cheeseburgers?* I don't ask because I don't want answers from this girl.

"Orthodox Judaism is a crock of shit," the girl is saying. The swear sounds strange, calls attention to itself somehow, as if she's never sworn before. "You and I are on the same page," she says.

"You think so?"

"So you want to go spy with me or not?"

"Not," I say, inching away from her again, suddenly deflating from sadness for Mr. Maloney, for my mother, for Alena.

The girl starts rolling her head in a slow circle. "Don't get all sniffy," she says. "We're all spies. Deep down. Think about when you're walking at night and people have their shades up, and you can just look into their houses, see them eating dinner and watching TV—nothing extraordinary—but for some reason, you can't stop looking."

"I don't look," I say, turning away from her to face the yeshiva. I feel unnerved, like I'm talking to my id. I cross my arms over my chest.

"Ha!" she says. "You're skulking around outside your brother's yeshiva, and you're all, 'Me? A spy?'" She chuckles. "Ha!" she says again.

Then the front door of the yeshiva swings open.

At first I think I'm hallucinating—I was beginning to think the door was purely decorative—but behind me, I hear the blond girl swear again, under her breath, and I turn around in time to see her duck behind the tree. When I turn back toward the yeshiva, I see a guy walk out the door onto the front steps.

He's the hairiest person I've ever seen. He has a thick, dark beard, a single eyebrow like a fuzzy caterpillar. He sits on the top step, those white tassel things that Orthodox men wear hanging over the front of his black pants. He bangs a pack of cigarettes against his wrist.

So this is Ash's house of God? A place where people smoke cigarettes and have secret girlfriends who spy on them? A place where you're either locked in or locked out? I wave to the hairy guy. He looks at me with no expression, then peels the cellophane back from his pack of cigarettes. Without taking his eyes off me, he shakes a cigarette out and lights it.

"Is Asher Kellerman here?" I call.

The guy blows a cloud of smoke in my direction. He unbuttons the cuffs of his white button-down shirt and rolls them to just below his elbows, revealing furry arms. He takes his time getting to his feet and strolling to the gate.

"You don't believe in evolution?" I ask him, because I just can't believe that someone who bears such a resemblance to early man could favor the creation story. God fashioning Eve out of Adam's rib is more plausible to him than our gradual descent from hominids?

"Which should I answer first?" the guy asks. "You want to know about Asher, or you want to know about Darwin?"

"You know who Darwin is?"

"Haven't you read *Genesis and the Big Bang*? Evolution doesn't discredit creation."

"Interesting. I'd like to talk about that with you when I have more time," I say, which I hope makes me sound like a cryptic, yet industrious, scholar, rather than like someone who's never read the book he mentioned.

"Asher's not here," the guy says.

His hair would feel coarse against my skin. Scratchy. We would have caveman sex, lots of grunting. But that's really not important right now. What's important is whether or not this guy knows who I am, whether or not Ash warned everyone at his yeshiva that one day, his mother or sister might show up, and that they were not to be allowed inside, no matter what. I wonder if my picture is taped to the wall in the Yeshiva Hillel bathroom, like a "Wanted" flyer in the Wild West.

"When would be a good time to come back?" I ask.

"Dinner's at seven," the guy says, glancing at his watch. His arm hair curls around either side of the watchband. He brings his cigarette to his lips, staring at me, fighting a smirk behind the bush of his beard. He's *smirking* at me. This big, hairy Bible-thumper is *smirking* at *me*.

I'd like to grab hold of that beard and yank on it, so his forehead knocks against the bar of the gate. Instead, I ask calmly, "How will I get in?"

But even as I ask, I'm wondering what I'll do once I'm inside. Will I storm into the dining hall while everyone's eating their kosher dinners? Will I stand on a chair, bang two pots together to get everyone's attention, and scream, *Hand over my brother*?

The hairy guy jerks a thumb over his shoulder. "We leave a door open on that side of the gate from six thirty to seven thirty. All the rabbis are in and out during that part of the evening. Just come around back and ring the bell. Someone will answer."

"Look," I say. I instinctively reach toward him, but he raises his eyebrows in amused alarm and I go back to holding the bars.

"I've been trying to see my—" I cut myself off. "I've been trying to see Ash for days," I say. "I got here on Friday. It's Sunday and I still haven't seen him."

"So you'll see him," the hairy guy says, holding up his hands. "What are you blaming me for? God willing, you'll find him at dinnertime."

"Dinner then," I say. I step back a little, caught off-guard by his casual reference to God. "I'll see him at dinner, God willing."

He gives me a strange look

"Can you promise me?" I ask.

"I make promises only to the Holy One," he says.

"How about a pinky swear?"

He doesn't answer, just locks his eyes to mine and stares until I force a cheerful wave, turn from the yeshiva, and hurry down the sidewalk. On my way, I glance behind the tree. The girl with the binoculars is gone.

DAVID IS STANDING on the front steps, his head tipped back, his lips rounded, blowing smoke rings like tiny nooses. He looks up when he hears me coming and grins, tapping ash from his cigarette. "What'd you see a ghost?" he asks. "What's the matter with you?"

I hesitate, trying to decide how and what to explain. The girl in the white dress? The strange breeze around her? The red wires? "I feel a little sick," I say finally. My hands are trembling. I stuff them into my pockets.

Still grinning, David shoves my shoulder, hard, and I stumble. "Stay away from *me* then. I've got a gig tonight."

"Not contagious," I say. "Just, like, sick to my stomach."

"You got *shil-shul*?"

"What?"

"The runs?" He's looking at me with mock concern.

"Whatever. Like I want to discuss it with you."

"Someone was just here looking for you," he says.

I stiffen. Monica? No. Monica hates me. I sent Monica away. Monica wouldn't come looking for me.

"A girl," David says.

"Must have been a mistake," I say, looking down and kicking my toe into a brick.

"Okay, then. I'll just assume it was a mistake."

"I don't really know any girls out here," I say.

"Fine. Consider it a closed subject."

I try to brush past him to the door. My face is sticky with Coke. I want to wash up before class.

"Hey, Asher." David takes one last drag off his cigarette, then pulls another one from his pack and uses the butt to light it. "You have a minute?"

"Well, we've got class." I look at my watch.

"In ten minutes. Just relax a sec, okay?" He sits on a step and pats the space beside him. I start to lower my body and he ashes on my seat.

I sit on the step below his.

"So how's your *b'sheret* these days?" he asks.

Quite a stretch, of course, to call Monica my soul mate. He's just trying to get me to talk. "I barely know that girl," I say, and then I feel my face get hot, because I just admitted that I knew he meant Monica.

"Look, it's nothing to me," David says, rolling his cigarette between his thumb and index finger. "You want to mess up your life for a girl? *B'seder.*" He holds his cigarette up to look at it. "But we're friends, you and I." He claps me on the back. "So I have to tell you."

"Tell me what?"

He leans back on his elbows and yawns.

"We're going to be late," I say, glancing at my watch again.

David takes a long drag off his cigarette, and I watch the gray smoke escape from his beard. Even his neck is hairy. "Your girl-friend—"

"She's not my girlfriend."

"She's trouble, Asher," David says. "Nothing but *tzoris*. You have to trust me on this. Look. I don't mean to speak badly of her. I wouldn't do that, you know. I'm the kind of person who's protective of people's privacy. I'm not about to tell you every single thing I know about her. I'm a good person."

I don't answer. What am I supposed to do, agree with him that he's wonderful?

"But this is a special case," he says, "because you're my friend." He turns up both his palms like a scale. "On the one hand, I don't want to speak *lashon hara*. On the other hand, I don't want to withhold information from you. If you had information that pertained to me, you'd tell, wouldn't you?" He's affecting a very earnest face, eyes wide, unibrow raised. When I don't answer him, he sighs. "Did you think she was Jewish?" he asks, and he looks at me as though whatever my answer is will be endlessly fascinating. He blows another stream of smoke, just to the right of my face.

She is Jewish, isn't she? Didn't she say so? She was raised bilingual. She wants to join the army. She wants to make aliyah. But with David, the definition of "Jewish" gets a little blurry. Jewish, to David, doesn't just mean you were born to a Jewish mother. Jewish means Orthodox.

"Who cares if she's Jewish?" I say. My voice cracks. "It's not like I'm planning to marry her. Like I said, I barely know the girl." I feel something tighten in my throat.

"Well, if the slutty clothes didn't give it away, she's not a Jew."

"So she's not," I say. "Fine." But it doesn't feel fine. I feel a band tightening around my head.

"Well, I mean, she's a Jew by birth," David concedes. The band loosens. "But she may as well be a shiksa at this point."

"I don't care," I say, climbing to my feet. "She's just some girl. She said she goes to Hebrew U. If she doesn't . . ."

"Hebrew U?" David chuckles. "She doesn't go to Hebrew U. You can take my word for that. Her name's not even Monica, you know," he says. "She started making everyone call her that when she moved to New York. That's how she would introduce herself. But her name's Malkie."

Malkie? Malkie is Rabbi Berkstein's portly wife who bakes parve cheesecakes every week for Shabbat lunch. Monica and Rabbi Berkstein's wife couldn't possibly have the same name.

"New York?" I say. "She's from California. Are we talking about the same person?"

"She used to live in California. But that was a couple years ago. She moved to New York. By me. And then Jerusalem, like everyone else. She was at seminary earlier this year," David says. "Her parents sent her, just like all our parents sent us. Well, maybe not your parents. . . ."

"Monica's parents are dead," I say.

David laughs again. "Dead, huh?" He shakes his head. "They're very much alive. They raised her properly, believe it or not. Anyway, like I said, she went to seminary. Same as all of us. Started last summer. A seminary for troubled girls. But the second she turned eighteen, she ran out the door, started wearing pants and doing who knows what else, and that was that."

"She ran away? From her seminary? Her parents *sent* her to seminary in Jerusalem and she ran away? Why would anyone . . ."

"This is nothing new," David says. "She ran away once before. Last year. When we were seniors in high school."

"She went to your high school?"

"Well, of course not. She went to the girls' school. But her family davens at our shul. I know about her, okay? Look. What I'm trying to tell you is that our senior year of high school, she ran off to live with her aunt's boyfriend. Some weird guy. You can guess what went on there."

I think about that for a minute, and I concede: David must be telling the truth. After all, Monica told me that she used to speak

Hebrew, but she won't anymore; she's hates Orthodox Judaism; and she does talk a lot about her aunt's boyfriend, Jon.

"I mean, like I said, I'm not going to dig up every rumor I've ever heard about the girl," David says. "This I wouldn't do. But she's up to no good. She's a self-hating Jew." He shrugs like he's given up, like Monica's a lost cause and he can't waste his energy constantly worrying about her anymore. "She's against us," David says simply. "She's a Nazi."

I swallow hard. That's what David calls secular Jews: Nazis, Jew-haters, self-hating Jews. My eyes are watering, not for any particular reason. I look away. "What do I care about her?" I say. "She doesn't follow Torah. You either do or you don't, and she doesn't. I don't care what other people do with their lives. If they don't follow Torah—"

"Of course you care," David says. I turn to look at him. He laughs and sits up. "You care a lot. Her lifestyle reflects on you."

"It does not reflect on—"

"People see you hanging around her. They make assumptions. And you do care what they think. If you didn't care, why would you have gotten all religious in the first place?" He turns his head to look at me.

"What does that have to do with—"

"What, you found God on your college campus?" He grinds out his cigarette on the bottom of his shoe. "I mean, it's fine if you did, Asher. You find Him where you find Him. It's none of my business. And it's not your fault you lived *treyf* for nineteen years. But my guess is that you weren't having much success in life before you became *frum*."

"Success . . ."

"Otherwise, why would you have done it?" He doesn't wait for my answer. "I see how it happens. All you Ba'alei Tshuva . . . you're all messed up in the head. Nowhere to turn, so you turn to us. Of course you're searching for acceptance. Of course you care what we think. It's nothing to be ashamed of. Anyway, I'm just looking out for you. The biggest favor you could do yourself is to stay away from Monica. That girl's pathological, okay? A little *meshugena*." He taps his head. "She lies about everything and everyone knows it. Or figures it out. Except you. So I'm telling you. You don't have to thank me."

"How do you . . ."

"She's a freak, Asher. *B'seder?*" He looks furious for a split second, but then he grins at me, making me wonder if I imagined it. "She's not even really blond. She dyes her hair. You see? Self-hating Jew. Look. I'm just trying to help you out. I like to be a good friend. It's just how I am." He hits me hard between the shoulder blades, more like he's trying to stop me from choking than show me affection. "Now, if you'll excuse me," he says, "I've got to get to class." He pushes past me and goes inside.

I HAVE TIME TO kill before dinnertime, before I make my
second trip of the day to Ash's yeshiva, so I decide I should
see things. After all, this is the nation of my grandparents'
dreams, the backdrop of Sunday school stories, the land people
willingly die for. I hail a cab to the Western Wall.

When the driver leaves me at one of the city gates, I take a
detour through the dim stone cave of the Arab market. Young
men push wheelbarrows. One has a dead goat in it. The air smells
of spices. I buy crystalized ginger in a clear plastic bag and eat
it as I walk. The shops are tiny and crammed together, mostly
selling souvenirs—silver replicas of the Western Wall, I LOVE
JERUSALEM T-shirts—and dried fruit out of barrels. I buy a pack
of twenty postcards for my students and tuck them into my purse.
One man follows me a few steps and asks, "You like?" He holds a
silver chain in his open palm. "For you, with special eyes, twenty
shekels." There is a chaos to it all, a swirling of colors, the way the
world looks if you spin around and around as fast as you can until
you fall to the ground. Like we used to do when we were kids on
the Jersey Shore. We used to play this game called Disaster.

Seeing as none of us could swim, I guess the beach was a
strange choice for a vacation spot, but Ash, Alena, and I loved it.
We'd tell our parents, "Give us a disaster," and they'd name one: a
tidal wave, a hurricane, a forest fire inching toward the city limits,

and we would act it out. Every disaster looked about the same: the three of us shrieking and twirling around with our arms open, knocking one another over into the sand. We never entertained the idea of letting firefighters into the game, smoke-jumpers, rescue teams, any figures that might have made our disasters less disastrous. It's not like they were *real* disasters; it's not like they were permanent.

My first impression of the Western Wall is that it's sexist. It's divided so that men can pray on one side and women can pray on the other, but the men's section is about three times the size of the women's. I hang back in the plaza. I know that this is supposed to be a holy site, but I don't feel any holiness. I don't think I've ever felt holiness before, so maybe I wouldn't recognize it, but I'm pretty sure I just feel hot and tired and annoyed.

The Western Wall has the commotion of any tourist trap. Children run in circles, screaming in Hebrew. Tourists wear cameras and canteens around their necks and take pictures of each other pretending to pray. Some people bow up and down, their prayer books pressed to their faces. Others sit in chairs pushed straight up to the wall, their heads in their arms, their arms against the stones. A voice chants through a loudspeaker in a foreign language that couldn't be Hebrew; somehow, it sounds distinctly not-Jewish.

The women are crammed in like people at a concert. At first, I can't even make it to the Wall. I have to wait until someone finishes praying, then squeeze into her spot. Once I'm there, I'm not quite sure what to do. I picture myself crowd-surfing back to the plaza. But I suppose I should pray. Everyone around me is praying.

On the stone to the right of me, a bird has relieved itself. I avert my eyes, press my palm to the smooth, clean stone in front of me, and focus on the notes stuffed into the cracks, the edges of paper trembling in the slight breeze.

Beside me, a woman in a long blue skirt, one of those knit snood things that holds her hair like a sack, and a sweater—a sweater in the desert!—is praying so hard, her face is scrunched up. She seems to be begging: *Please, please, I'll do anything!* She even pounds her fist into her chest a few times.

"Christ," I mutter, then I cover my mouth quickly with my hand. You can't say "Christ" at the Western Wall. I shut my eyes and try to concentrate on what I need, try to focus on a God I've never seen, never heard, never felt. He looks a little bit like Jerry Garcia. "God," I begin silently, but I feel like I'm performing, like I'm practicing a sexy smile in a mirror. It's like the feeling I used to get after Alena disappeared, when I would talk to her in bed at night because someone—a friend of my mom's, I think—had encouraged me to. I would say things like, "Hope you're okay, Alena," and then feel ridiculous because she'd been kidnapped, which was the opposite of okay.

"God," I say, "I would like You to help me find Ash." I pause. "Please," I add.

It seems a fair request, something God can meet me halfway on. After all, I flew all the way out here. For the first time in a year, Ash and I are in the same city. I don't ask God to help me drag Ash out of his yeshiva. I don't want to push it.

Beside me, the praying woman begins to sob loudly. I open my eyes. She's freaking out, shaking with sobs, her fists pressed to her chest. I remember how a year and a half ago, when Ash and I went home to visit our mother over winter break, Ash prayed constantly. He talked about Torah like it was a good book he was reading. He wouldn't go out to lunch with us on Saturday because of the Sabbath. Our mother was irritated: "Must you make such a spectacle of yourself?" she wanted to know.

"Jews don't eat in restaurants on Shabbat," he said.

"The hell we don't," she said.

To hear Ash say those things—Jews do this; Jews don't do that—was a strange echo from the past. Our father used to talk like that, too, to excuse himself from things: *Jews don't wear tuxedos. Jews don't go to Sunday brunch at the Marriott.* If he didn't feel like doing something, he simply wouldn't do it.

I remember the search party the day Alena disappeared, way before Ash told us about the brown car. A whole town of people, a long, unbroken chain, walking slowly, eyes on the ground. My father didn't join the search party. He volunteered himself to stay home and "man the phone." I'm not saying he didn't love Alena. He loved her the best. At night, we used to all take turns reading her bedtime stories, but on my dad's nights, she told *him* stories. I always came into her room to listen, and to watch my father's face. Sometimes Alena made the stories up. Sometimes she just summarized stories from the books the rest of us read to her. And my father was consistently charmed, so charmed, his eyes would get glassy. He would ask her questions to egg her on: *And then what happened? Oh, yeah? So what did you do?* She would sit perched on his lap in the rocking chair, her knees bent so they touched her chin, the shirt of her pajamas pulled over her legs. She would twirl a piece of her long black hair around her finger, and talk, burrowing a hole into our father that would stay hollow for the rest of his life.

But still. *Man the phone?*

I stare at the praying woman, remembering the self-healing workshops my father went to after Alena was kidnapped, and it occurs to me how ineffectual people can be. The praying woman can pray her knit snood thing off, but if she doesn't work for results, nothing in her life will change. Sometimes things are difficult—like keeping a family together after losing a child—but that doesn't make them optional. I want to ask her what it is she's praying for—a husband? a new house?—and

give her some old-fashioned secular advice: *This isn't the way.*
No one's listening to you.

So where does that leave me? What am *I* doing, standing here
talking to a wall? The wall is not going to get Ash out of Israel.
I am. That's why I came to Israel. Not to talk to God but to talk
some sense into my brother.

I turn from the Wall and make my way through the crowd
back to the plaza. I approach the table with the slips of paper and
golf pencils. What's the sense in writing notes to God? I'd rather
write notes to people, who might actually respond. Specifically,
I'd like to write to the rabbis at Ash's yeshiva. My heart pounds.
It's a horrible thing to do. But at least I'm doing something.

To Whom It May Concern,

Asher Kellerman has a girlfriend. I pause, remembering the
Happy Holiday condoms that girl told me about. No way she was
telling the truth. No way. But just in case: *You might consider*
searching his room.

Sincerely,

a concerned party.

I fold the slip of paper in half, shove it into my purse, and head
back up the stairs toward the Jewish Quarter, past an artist selling
charcoal drawings of Jerusalem. At the top of the stairs, a cluster
of IDF soldiers stands, shooing people away. I peek past them and
see more soldiers, standing around a barefoot man in a big fur hat.
Three Orthodox men stand beside him, arguing in Hebrew with
two soldiers, one of whom is holding a pair of shiny black shoes
and looking perplexed. The soldiers glance at one another. They
scratch their foreheads. They stare at the ground. The barefoot
man is wearing one of those red string bracelets Madonna wears.
He's alternately fingering it silently and pointing to it as he yells
at the soldiers. His forehead is pinched beneath a rim of fur. As I
step a little closer, I see that his lips are trembling. His eyes meet

mine. *You heathen,* his eyes seem to say. *Stop looking at me, you detestable woman!*

But I don't stop looking. I stare at him until a soldier ushers me along—*"Yalla! Yalla!"*—and then I stop a few feet away and keep watching. The man reminds me of my father. I'm not sure why. Do they look alike? Or is it his sad, naked white feet, the anger on his face not quite concealing the fear in his eyes? I reach inside my purse to feel for the note. I pinch the crease of it. I wish Ash were here to see what I see: that a black hat—even a fur hat—is not a helmet, that a black suit is not a coat of armor.

I GO TO THE bar early to help Todd set up. He's unusually reticent on the bus, staring out his window, humming a tune I almost recognize, pressing sporadically on his hearing aid. Does he know that Monica was in our room? Did he find one of her hairs? I almost just tell him: *I'm done with her now. I swear!* But it's probably best to say nothing.

Walking from the bus stop to the bar, I recognize the tune he's humming: a song that was in the Top Forty last year when I lived in Boulder, a song that has nothing at all to do with our lives as committed Jews. A goyish song, an immoral song. Panic grips my shoulders, as if I'm holding something fragile that's too heavy for me. I almost blurt out, "You should go to Tsfat." They say the air is sweeter in Tsfat, the mystical city up north in the Galilee. Maybe Todd just needs a vacation.

But before I can open my mouth, Todd turns to me and says, with much more self-assurance than I'm accustomed to from him, the words I immediately realize I've been dreading: "Asher," he says. "I've been wanting to tell you, I'm thinking of moving back home."

I watch our shadows on the sidewalk. Todd's is a little longer than mine. I speed up to walk a step ahead of him. *"Home?"*

"Not *home* home. Probably not even back to Connecticut. But maybe New York or something."

"To go to YU?"

Some guys come to Yeshiva Hillel for a year or two, then go to New York to study at Yeshiva University, but by Todd's silence, I know without him telling me that he's not thinking about YU. Anyway, he's already finished college.

"I mean . . ." I glance at him. "Well, what did you have in mind?"

Todd presses on his hearing aid. "Music school, maybe."

"*Music* school?"

"Yeah, there's Juilliard. And there's the Conservatory in Boston."

"Yeah, but—"

"Nothing's definite yet."

We keep walking without looking at each other. "You'll have to wait a while, won't you?" I ask. "Aren't applications due in January?"

January's a long way off. Todd will have plenty of time to realize he's making a mistake. By January, I could become a better learning partner.

"Well." Todd clears his throat. "I've been accepted to two schools already and—"

"You've already applied?" I scratch at the back of my neck, trying to keep the conversation casual. I can't believe we're even talking about this. Music school is for the goyim!

"I'm sorry I didn't tell you, Asher," Todd says, switching his guitar case to his other hand. "I should have. It was just . . . well, I didn't know how you'd . . ."

"You won't even finish out the semester? I mean, we only have until July."

"Oh, sure," says Todd, a little too quickly. "I didn't mean I'd leave before July."

"What are you going to do?" I ask. "You've barely begun learning."

"Yeah . . ."

"You'll need to find a *chavrusa* group."

"Well," Todd says. "New York's full of them. So's Boston, I'll bet."

"But you'll get sucked in, Todd!" My fingers curl up and my nails dig into my palms. "You'll get sucked in by the secular world! You'll have your beliefs challenged every single day."

"My beliefs . . ." Todd trails off.

We stop outside the bar and turn to face each other. "I think it's a bad idea," I say, even though I know this isn't the way to change a person's mind. I sound like Bits, who screams on my voice mail, "Your life is so stupid!" But what else can I do? This is serious. Todd is turning away from the Holy One. "What about Hashem?" I ask. "Secular music is paganism!"

"Asher." Todd smiles so kindly, I have to look away from him. "What are you going to do? You know we can't stay here forever."

I tighten the bobby pins on my *kipa* and keep my eyes on the ground. Why *can't* this last forever? Yeshiva life is so fulfilling and dynamic. I look forward to us all raising kids in Jerusalem, gathering in the mornings for minyan, learning together on Saturday afternoons. This life I have right now—I'd like to preserve it like the insect collection I had before my vegan years: all those perfect, tiny wings pinned to clean white cork.

"You do know that," Todd's saying. "Don't you?"

I don't answer. Even though we've had our differences lately, Todd is my closest friend, maybe my only real friend. We've been roommates and *chavrusas* for almost a year, so I haven't gotten to know anyone else the way I've gotten to know him. If he could have given me some warning that he was just going to pack up and leave, maybe I would have tried harder to get to know the other guys.

"Asher," Todd tries again. "You and I are different."

Different?! We both wound up here, in Jerusalem, at Yeshiva Hillel. We are just the same: lost once, now seeped in *emet*. Seeped, finally, after all these years, in truth.

"I'm sure you came out here for the right reasons," Todd says. "You came because you wanted to devote your life to God. I'm sure you did. But I don't think I did."

"What do you mean?"

"I think I came here to get away from things. Does that make sense?"

"No." I shake my head vigorously and look past his shoulder. I see Monica. No, that's not Monica.

"Okay, I guess I wasn't trying to get away from *things*. I wanted to get away from myself, get out of my own head. I was driving myself crazy. I still kind of drive myself crazy." Todd chuckles.

"That's not reason enough," I say. "I don't believe you. If you were just trying to get away . . . you could have gone anywhere. New Zealand. Tokyo. Millions of places."

"But I was looking for something meaningful," he says.

"Of course."

"And it turns out this isn't it."

My stomach starts to hurt. "What isn't?"

Todd looks worried. He brushes his red hair away from his forehead.

"What isn't meaningful?" I ask again. I lower my voice. "God?"

"That's not what I mean."

"If God isn't meaningful, nothing is! Who *are* you? I don't know how you can do this after . . ."

"After what?"

I grab my earlobes. "After God took your hearing, Todd! How can you go back to your old ways? What if you go completely deaf?"

"That's not logical." Todd sets his guitar case on the ground. He lays his hands on my shoulders. "Asher," he says. "You're freaking out."

"What if He takes your vision?" I shout, shaking out of his grip. I throw my arms out to the sides. "Your life!"

Todd sighs. "Look."

"I'm serious. I'm worried for you." I can hear the confidence in my voice breaking off like chipped paint. I'm worse than Bits now; I sound like my mother—hysterical, irrational. "I know you think I'm overreacting," I tell Todd, who is nice enough to protest. "But I can't just stand by and—" My words feel like a rock in my throat. I stop talking and swallow. I know that this is pointless.

"I've got to set up," Todd says, glancing at the door. He lifts his guitar case from the ground. "We can talk more about this later, but Asher? Please don't tell anyone. Okay?"

I nod slightly, try to unclench my fists.

"Okay? We'll talk about it." He claps me on the back and smiles. Is his smile condescending? Pitying? Does he really think I'm the one who needs to be pitied? I try to smile back, to let him know we're cool, that I'm nothing like my mother, but my face feels like it's been shot up with Novocain, so I just show my identification to the security guard, then follow Todd inside.

THE HAIRY GUY was right: At six thirty, Yeshiva Hillel's gate is open on the right side of the building. I walk through it and knock on the side door. If people generally leave the yeshiva through the side door, then cut through the courtyard to the road behind the building, that would explain why I never saw anyone leave Saturday night when I stood out front for three hours. I wonder if the blond girl with the binoculars has figured that out.

The boy who answers the door needs a suntan. His face is fragile like baby skin. A pair of glasses sits delicately on his face. He is delicate. I could break him. He would crumble beneath my weight like potato chips. He glances at me, then looks down at his toes.

"Is Ash . . . Asher Kellerman here?" I ask him.

"I don't think so," the boy tells the ground.

"You don't *think* so?"

The boy starts twisting part of his beard around his finger. How strange for someone so young-looking to have a full beard. It makes him seem simultaneously wise and retarded, like those genius children who go to college when they're eight. "I saw him leave with his roommate a while ago," he says.

"Leave for where?"

"I don't know."

"You don't know."

"I didn't ask."

"Are you lying?" I ask him. I take a step toward him like a mobster, like I'm going to cut off each of his toes until he tells me where he's hiding my brother. "Ash told you not to let me in."

"No, he didn't. I don't know who you are."

"Well, I'm not going to tell you who I am," I say. I sound like my students—*I'm not telling. You're not the boss of me*—but I don't want to blow my cover, if I have a cover, and I don't want to admit that who I am is a member of Ash's original family, the one he chose to replace with a bunch of bearded twenty-year-olds.

"Okay." The boy shrugs without looking at me.

I'm beginning to wonder if Plan A—surprise-attacking Ash at his yeshiva—simply isn't going to work, if I'm going to have to resort to Plan B, which entails calling Ash's cell phone. I really don't want to do that. I'm pretty sure that if there's one way to get Ash to avoid me, it's to leave him a voice mail telling him that I'm in Jerusalem, calling from a pay phone across the street from his yeshiva.

I'm not ready to resort to Plan B. "Where's Asher?" I ask, like we haven't already been through this.

"Look," says the boy, "I don't know Asher that well. I—"

"Don't *know* him? You study together every day," I say, as if I've been watching their lives through a window. I take another stab: "You sleep a few doors away from him. You see him more than you see your own family. You're going to stand there and tell me that you don't know Asher Kellerman?"

The boy has been holding the screen door open with his foot. Now he looks back over his shoulder and steps outside. "Are you upset?" he asks quietly. "Is there something we can do for you?"

"*We!* Don't you see what they do to you here? They've swallowed you whole. You've lost your individuality," I say, even though I have no way of knowing whether or not he had any individuality to lose.

The boy frowns. "Would you like a glass of water?" he asks.

"Someone told me to come at dinnertime, that he'd be here."

"I don't know what to tell you. I'm sorry."

I feel like I'm screaming in a sound-proof room. So I fish the note I wrote at the Western Wall from my purse and thrust it at the boy. "Please give this to the rabbi," I say.

"Are you o—"

"I'm *fine*," I say. "I'm perfect. Why even ask? God doesn't care if you're nice to me or not. He'd probably prefer it if you weren't, right?"

The boy nudges his glasses up the bridge of his nose with a knuckle. "Which rabbi?"

"What?"

He waves the note in the air. "Who should I give this to?"

"Who's Ash's rabbi?"

"Asher learns with all of the rabbis, but mostly with Rabbi Berkstein, I think." The boy runs his thumb and forefinger along the fold in the paper, deepening the crease.

I stare at the note, remembering the rabbi Ash used to hang out with in Boulder. Yosi or Yofi or something. Some stoned-looking guy with a beard who used to gaze at me like a pervert at a peep show. I've changed my mind. I don't want to conspire with a rabbi against my own brother. Loyalty grips me like a fist.

I snatch the note from the boy's hand. "Never mind," I say, turning away from him, away from the yeshiva. "Look," I say, my back to him. "I know you're lying, okay? None of you are fooling me. This is my third time here in the last day and a half. I know he's here. I know you're hiding him."

I shove the note back into my purse, half-expecting to feel the boy's hand on my arm, to hear his voice admitting that I'm right, that he is part of a giant conspiracy to keep me away from my brother. But all I hear is the door closing. And then I hear it lock.

To my right, the gray street lies like a flat empty promise. To my left, behind the building, a courtyard sparkles in the sunlight. I turn and walk into the courtyard. I don't want to be on the other side of that gate again.

I feel small among the trees. The bricks on the building leer at me like so many rows of teeth. I count four floors, four windows on each. I remember what the blond girl said, that Ash's room is on the third floor, far left. If that really is his room, his window is open. I walk toward the bricks and feel them. They are rough and hot, nothing like the smooth stones on the Western Wall. I feel the drainpipe, the long, slender, white J of it. It strikes me as old-fashioned, a drainpipe from the past. Like an icebox. An out-house. Aren't drainpipes different now? Better connected to the building? Less flimsy?

I try to measure how many inches span between the drainpipe and the open window. If I can climb the drainpipe to that floor, I'll at least be able to peer in, won't I? And if Ash is in there, if that really is his room, then maybe I'll see him hiding from me. I can just picture the look on his face if I were to knock on his window. It's worth a shot. People climb drainpipes in movies. I shake it once; it feels sturdy enough. I step on the curved tip of it, slowly put all of my weight on it. A wind sweeps through the grass like a warning. I grip the pipe in my hands and start shimmying up, defenseless in a sundress, unsteady in flip-flops. My knees scrape against the brick. But with three or four good pushes upward, I'm level with the first row of windows.

I pause to catch my breath, then push on. One, two, three. I look down. Am I high enough to break my neck if I fall? I hear my mother in my head: *What do you need to do that for? You want a broken neck?*

Broken necks probably aren't as common as she seems to think, but the idea of having one spreads goose bumps over my scalp. I think of Alena. In my mind, I see black hair and white bones, and strength seeps out of me like pus. I hug the drainpipe more tightly, rest my face against it. I look at Ash's open window. It's so far away. The window shade is half-closed—a sleepy eyelid. A picture frame stands on the windowsill. I can see the back of it, the little black velvet leg.

Another breeze comes, sending a round of applause through the trees, and I have a flash of clarity, a moment of blade-sharp focus.

What am I *doing*?

I see myself as someone standing below me might: a girl in a sundress, clinging koala-like to the drainpipe of a men's yeshiva. I slowly loosen one arm and reach for the window. My arm feels like it's about to pop out of its socket, my fingertips barely brush the bricks beside the window, and just like that, my plan fails. The window is simply too far away. It's over. I'll have to slide down like a fireman and go back to my hostel and try to see Ash tomorrow.

No! I'm so sick of failing. I cling more tightly. If I just rest for a minute, I'll think of something.

But what I think of is Alena's funeral. For the first time, I really picture it, the stained-glass windows in the Temple Beth Shalom sanctuary, the slippery, polished pews. And I imagine it without Ash: my mother, my father, and me. The last time I saw my father was when I first got to Boulder nearly five years ago and went to his house for dinner. There were pictures all over the walls of his three stepdaughters playing soccer and posing before homecoming dances. His wife was cold to me. I tried to help her in the kitchen, but she made me feel like a dog, constantly underfoot. My father's stepdaughters, tow-headed high school girls whom I'd never met, stared at me like I was a museum exhibit. My father's relationship with them seemed . . . well . . . healthy. They were dismissive of him in the way teenage girls would be of a father. He had pet names for them. To compensate, I guess, he awkwardly called me Kiddo, and once, Pumpkin, which made me laugh out loud.

I don't think I can handle sitting between him and my mother while a rabbi who probably doesn't even remember Alena recites a Mad Libs–like eulogy, for which he has gathered information from my mother to fill in the blanks: Alena loved squirrels. She used to wake everyone up in the morning by running into our rooms and sitting on our heads. She made puppets out of paper bags. I realize that I don't *just* want Ash to leave the war zone that is Israel, to grow out of his God phase, to be part of the family again; I also don't think I'll be able to handle Alena's funeral without him. I want him—no, need him—at that funeral. My resolve strengthens: I am going to get to Ash.

But then I hear a quick scraping sound. It's my foot, slipping. It slips for no reason. I wasn't trying to climb higher. I wasn't reaching for the window. It's as if some invisible force suddenly grabbed my ankle and tugged. My chin hits the drainpipe with a horrible thud that rattles my teeth.

And as I fall, as the skirt of my sundress billows out around me like a parachute, as my arms and legs dance of their own accord and my hair whips across my face and the scream spools out of my throat, I think, *Eventually, Ash, you will have to let me in.*

JONATHAN IS IN my bed with me, reading aloud passages from Ted Patrick's memoir. He's most interested in Ted Patrick's enemies, who misunderstood him, who were too brainwashed to see the truth: that Ted Patrick was great, that he was single-handedly battling the cult problem. Cult leaders all over the nation called Ted Patrick "Black Lightning" because he was a black man who would strike out of nowhere. They warned their disciples: Black Lightning would snatch you when you least expected it, beat you, rape you, torture you, try to convince you that everything you knew to be true was false.

My head rests on Jonathan's collarbone, and I feel his breath on my hair. His voice dances with the flickering candlelight (I finally invested in scented candles . . . butter cream, three for the price of one). Maybe it would be more romantic if he were reading me love sonnets, but how can I complain? Our feet are touching under the covers and the night is at its darkest point, and if you'd told me a week ago that I'd be naked in bed with a man, and that this man would bring me joy that would flap in my chest like bird wings, I would have told you that you were psychotic.

"Are you with me, Ellie?" Jonathan sets the book down and waves a hand in front of my eyes. "Don't you want to know what happened to him?"

What I want to know is where my kids are, right this second.

I want to know that Bits is getting Ash out of that war zone, away from those lunatics. I want to know that the money I've been giving Jonathan ("Just a little more," he keeps saying, "just another tiny donation to the rescue mission") is going to buy my family back, and that my kids will come stay with me next Thanksgiving during the school break, and that Ash won't say something ridiculous like, "Jews don't celebrate Thanksgiving," and Viv and her family will come over, and I'll introduce everyone to Jonathan. I can just see him carving the turkey, the electric knife whirring to life in his giant hand.

"Don't you want to know the end of the story?" Jonathan asks.

"As long as it's a happy ending."

"Ha!" Jonathan says, because he knows about endings.

Recently, he told me what happened to his wife: Ten years ago, she was terminally ill when she fell in with a community of Orthodox Jews. They brainwashed her into leaving Jonathan. The last time Jonathan saw her, her eyes looked right through him. (Do I know that look? I've seen it on my own son.) When she died a year later, she was in the care of people who were total strangers to him.

How excruciating it must have been, losing complete control, being forced to accept the unacceptable. Do I know what that's like? Better than anyone.

"So what happened?" I ask, my eyes closing. "Where's Ted Patrick now?"

Jonathan sighs. "He had to stop the kidnappings. The lawsuits were rising up around him like floodwaters. Can you believe that? Lawsuits! A revolutionary. A philanthropist. A penniless man who wanted to fix the world and he's dealing with lawsuits! The world is a mess of a place, Ellie. People don't get it. They don't get anything."

I nestle my head deeper into Jonathan's neck and inhale the heat of his skin. Such a contrast, how I feel right now and how I usually feel. Outside of this moment, this bed, this night, I agree with Jonathan: The world is a mess of a place. So unforgiving, so unrelenting, rife with hideous things that can happen to people.

I ADMIT IT: FALLING from a drainpipe is unduly theatrical. But I don't wake up to find a circle of cops pointing guns at my head or to a paramedic asking me who the president is. In fact, there is no waking up involved, because I never even blacked out. I wound up landing sort of on all fours, sort of on my side, in the grass. I have grass stains on my sundress. My knees and the heels of my hands are bleeding, dirty, covered in grass blades. I get to my knees, then to my feet, pick up my purse from where I left it on the ground, straighten my shoulders, and smooth my hair down with my hand. My head throbs. In fact, everything hurts, but not badly. I look at the yeshiva, half-expecting to see the drainpipe spraying water into the air like a fire hydrant, but the drainpipe, the building, everything, looks just the same as always. Everything is still. There's no one around. I made no impact at all.

I hurry back toward the open gate, slip out to the street, and find myself face to face with the hairy guy who believes in both evolution and creation. He's smirking at me as he approaches, as if no time has passed, as if we're still discussing whether or not it's God's will that Ash and I should see each other at dinnertime. His white button-down shirt is untucked and he's replaced his black yarmulke with one of those red, yellow, and green knit tams that Bob Marley used to gather his dreadlocks into. He reminds me of a self-conscious person at a Halloween party, the guy who's too embarrassed to wear a full costume, so he throws on a clown wig or a set of fangs.

He stops in front of me on the sidewalk, blocking my passage. "Did you find him?"

"Don't talk to me," I say. "You make me sick. Every single one of you."

His smile broadens. "Look, was the gate open or not?"

"Ash has a girlfriend," I say abruptly.

"That right?" He's still smirking, but something in his face falters. A light seems to go out. I wonder what it is that bothers him. Does he worry for Ash's soul? Is he jealous that Ash has a girlfriend and he doesn't? "Who?" he asks tentatively.

"Blond girl," I say.

"Monica?" For one split second, his smile disappears completely. He scratches his head through his tam. Then he looks at me again and regains his composure. He clears his throat, resumes his smirk. "You're talking about Monica?"

"I don't know her name," I say.

"Interesting," he says. "Ash likes girls?"

"I just thought someone should know," I say. "She sleeps here. Obviously, that's against your rules."

The hairy guy shoves his hands into his pockets and starts walking backward, away from me. "Who *are* you?" he asks, still smirking.

"None of your business," I say.

He turns away from me like I'm a child having a temper tantrum, and keeps walking in the opposite direction. Over his shoulder, he calls, "I don't think you need to concern yourself with our rules."

I watch him walk away until he shrinks and disappears in the distance. Then I continue through a residential neighborhood called French Hill toward my hostel, past redwood trees and a grocery store, past a cluster of teenage girls wearing too much makeup, past a woman in an apron chasing a dog, past black-hatted men who pointedly turn their faces from me, as if to say, "You are God's garbage, and by shunning you, I am honoring Him." I want to grab those men by their white collars, to spit in their pasty faces. I want to steal their hats from their heads and run, or throw my arms around them and not let go. I want to touch their faces with irreverent fingers to prove that God wouldn't strike us down.

Most of all, I want to hug my brother, to extract him from his yeshiva the way I once, years ago, extracted him from an escalator when his shoe got stuck in the crack.

For some reason, I'm not surprised when I get to my hostel and see the skinny blond girl who was spying on Ash. Her back is to me, but I know it's her. She's stretching, one sneaker pressed to the brick wall in front of her, her upper body curved over, her forehead to her knee. Her foot, or at least her sneaker, looks too big for her leg. She must hear me approaching because she twists to look at me over her shoulder. "Oh, hi," she says. "I knew you were staying here."

"How?"

"It's the closest hostel to the yeshiva." She drops her leg to the ground and turns to face me. "And remember? I'm psychic."

I wonder how much she knows about me, this strange blond girl. I wonder if Ash has told her things, if she understands where he's coming from.

"Do you know anything about my father?" I ask.

She leans back against the wall. "No. Tell me about your father."

"His name's Benjamin," I say. "I don't know. What do you want me to tell you?"

"What do I want you to tell me?" She laughs. "You sneak up on me and you're all, 'Do you know anything about my father?'

Then you're all, 'Why are you asking me about my father?'" She twirls a finger beside her ear.

"He's narcissistic?" I say. It comes out like a question. I don't want to talk about my father. I don't know why I brought him up. What is there to say? Nothing positive. "So since he's a narcissist named Benjamin, he named us after Benjamin's children. You know, the biblical Benjamin."

"Bela, Ashbel, and Aharah," she says.

"I'm impressed." I say it like I'm not impressed, even though I am.

"Why?" She shrugs, scratching her forehead. "That's totally simple."

"But we're Beatrice, Ash, and Alena. Same first letters. My real name's Beatrice, but I never use it. Ash couldn't say it, and 'Bits' stuck. So I consider that my name. It's on my driver's license. But anyway." I cross my arms over my chest, then I uncross them, because I've read that if you cross your arms over your chest, people will think you're hiding things. "Other than that," I say, "our dad wasn't much of a Jew. I guess you probably thought we were super Jews, what with Ash being how he is."

"I definitely didn't think Asher came from super Jews," she says.

"Our father is a weak man," I say, because I always say that to sum up my father, but if I were a fair person, I would say that, like everyone, he's also had moments of strength. I would tell the story my mother likes, about when she brought him home to Brooklyn for the first time, in 1972. My grandmother had just finished making a lawn furniture cover out of plastic grocery bags, and was lying out in their backyard, wearing a faded purple bathing suit with a ruffle skirt. The bags crackled and squished beneath her sweaty skin. It was summer and hot out and my mother was upset that my grandmother, who had survived first Buchenwald, then cancer, was exposing herself to such a fierce sun.

"It is sun," my grandmother said. "This is nothing, a little sun. I should hide in my closet all my life? And anyway, I don't *feel* like moving."

"I'll move you," my father said.

"He will move me!" my grandmother snorted. She was not a small woman, my grandmother.

"I'll move you," my father said again. He squatted, stretched his arms under the chair, then stood, the whole chair and my grandmother in his arms.

"What is he, Superman?" my grandmother said.

My father carried her to the covered deck, set the chair down, and wiped his hands together briskly. "There," he said to my mother. "Now she's out of the sun."

I clear my throat and point at the blond girl. "Is your name Monica?"

"How did you know that?" she asks.

"Someone told me."

"Who?" She pulls one arm over her head by the wrist. "God. I swear. I'm, like, famous."

"Why are you always stretching?"

"It's part of my new image. For seventeen years, I didn't even exercise. Now I'm the exercise *queen*." Monica stops stretching and leans back against the wall again. She tilts her head, as if to study me from a new angle. "I have a psychic feeling about you," she says. She crooks her fingers to inspect her nails. Then she looks up at me and says, "I'll bet all your friends are dumb. You only hang out with dumb people." She takes a step toward me. "It's because you're afraid of your own inadequacies."

"Who *are* you?" I ask.

"Am I right? Okay, one more thing. . . . You're rash and self-destructive."

"You're just saying that because I have grass stains on my knees."

"You know," Monica says, moving even closer to me, close enough to touch my shoulder, "you and I want the same thing. We're working toward the same goal."

"I don't have a goal."

"No?" Monica shrugs. "You have to have a goal. Otherwise you're aimless, and you'll wind up a junky or an Orthodox Jew. Like my dad. He was both. I mean, not at the same time." She rolls her eyes. "He woke up in a gutter one day and realized it was time to find God. That was back in the early seventies. You know what I'm saying. Probably happened to billions of people in the early seventies." Monica flicks her hair over her shoulder. "I know about you," she says. "I know you want Asher to go back to normal. I mean, I know all about these Ba'al Tshuva types. They're nuts-o." She taps at her temple with one finger. "So I totally understand your concern. There was this one guy from near where I grew up? Not religious, right? And he moved to Tsfat. You know, the mystical city. And he got all *frum*—"

"All what?"

"*Frum?* Like Orthodox? And now he walks around Tsfat with a megaphone, screaming about Moshiach all day." She makes an imaginary megaphone with her hand.

"About what?"

"Moshiach?" She drops the imaginary megaphone and grabs my wrist. "The Messiah!" she says. "Are you, like, a totally uneducated Jew? Anyway, he pushes a shopping cart around and screams through this megaphone. Like, 'We want Moshiach *now!*' All day and night. Total whack job." She lets my wrist go. "You came here to rescue Asher, right?"

"No," I say. "I just want to talk to him. I have to tell him something important."

She doesn't seem to hear me. "Well, I want to rescue him too," she says.

I laugh. "You just want what you can't have."

"I already have him."

"You can't have him."

"Why?" Monica asks. "Do you own him or something?"

"I'm just telling you what I know. You'll never get him to love you."

Monica laughs. "Love? Whatever. Lust always comes first anyway. And that's the more important thing. The motivator. Lust is what makes a guy lose his mind, forget himself. You do know that, don't you? I mean, you're probably five years older than me. But anyway. Maybe you should *think* for a second before you decide to hate me." She taps her forehead. "We're on the same team, you and I. We're *teammates*. You have to be a team player." She smooths her hair into a ponytail and holds it in place with one hand. Her arm is string-thin. "The point isn't who gets to Asher first," she says. "The point is that someone needs to get to Asher. Someone needs to get him out of his yeshiva."

"You can't just . . . *remove* people from their lives," I sputter.

"Then what are you doing here?"

"*Look,*" I say. "Ash is *my brother.*"

"So you have a right to rescue him and I don't?" Monica puts her fists on her skinny hips and glares at me.

"I'm just here to visit him," I say. My heart is thudding in my chest.

"What do you want?" she asks. "To see Asher live a normal life? Or to see yourself be a hero? Be honest."

"This isn't about rescuing. He's my brother. I have a right . . ."

By this time, she's already walking away, her blond hair swishing across her back. I watch her round the corner, and then I turn to look at the hostel. It is ugly. The grass in front is overgrown. The paint is peeling off in curls. I wonder if the building would meet safety regulations. I wonder if the foundation is crumbling. I wonder if it's beyond repair.

In the lobby, two girls are sitting across a wooden coffee table from each other, playing cards. One of them has a ring through her nose. She reminds me of a bull. She even blows cigarette smoke from her nostrils. At least one of the two girls has such pungent body odor, the whole lobby reeks of it. I hesitate in the doorway, watching them. The television behind the front desk is tuned to Al Jazeera. I see scenes from the Church of the Nativity: protesters march beside green IDF tanks, punching the air with their picket signs.

The bull asks me, "Would you like to come to a club?" Her British accent makes the question sound like a statement.

Without taking her eyes off her fan of cards, the other one says, "We've been sitting here doing sweet fuck-all since sunup." She slaps a card on the table. "We've got to do something or I'll go mad." Her dirty blond hair falls over the back of her chair and all the way to her waist in thick tangles.

I look down at my sundress and flip-flops. Not exactly clubbing clothes. But both girls are wearing Birkenstocks and earth tones, beaded hemp necklaces, big pants with filthy hems.

"So?" says the one with the nose ring. "You want to come?"

A strange contradiction, body odor and British accents. But here's another contradiction: Jerusalem and clubbing. I think of the guys at Ash's yeshiva, black and white like untouched coloring books. I picture girls in skin-tight jeans, dancing in cages.

"There are clubs in Jerusalem?" I ask.

"Oh, that's brill," says the one with the nose ring.

"What, like, brilliant?"

She chuckles and seems not to hear me. "That is *brill*," she says again. "So are you coming or not?"

I shrug. It's not even completely dark out yet, but I could certainly use a drink. I'll stay for an hour or so, and by then, maybe Ash will be back at the yeshiva. Why not? "Okay," I say, "let's go."

Because it's still early, the club is near-empty, but the techno music pounds up through the floor. From a box on top of a speaker, a strobe light blinks psychotically. At the bar, I sit between the two girls. We order a round of shots that the bartender lights on fire; we drink them through straws, then drink Tuborg beers from sweating brown bottles. My new buddies, Star (the bull) and Greta (with the long hair), are world travelers and best friends.

"Why are you here?" Greta asks, winding a strand of hair around her finger. I see dirt under her nails, tiny brown crescents.

"I'm trying to see my brother," I say, "but he's been brainwashed by the Orthodox Jews."

"That's brill," says Star.

"I've got to get him out of here. And no one else was stepping up to the plate." But it's not true anymore that no one has stepped up to the plate. Monica has. "Can we get more shots?" I ask no one in particular. A new round appears. They're deep green and sludgy. We drink them, make faces, chug our beers. My head begins to buzz.

"What will you do," Greta asks, "drag him out?"

"Oh, I don't know," I say.

I really don't. Even if I did drag him out, what would I do with him? Keep him in my apartment in Boston? FedEx him to my mother? Sedate him and bring him to Alena's funeral in a cage?

"I've heard the real nuts are the Jews who study Kabbalah," Star says. "You know. Mysticism. Like Madonna does."

"Madonna's not a Jew," I say. "She just does that whole Kabbalah thing for publicity."

"Is your brother studying Kabbalah?" Star asks.

"No clue," I say.

I haven't cleaned out the cuts on my knees. They throb and burn. I rest my elbows on the bar and put my face in my hands.

I wonder if Monica could answer Star's question. Does she know things about Ash that I don't know? Probably. She tries harder than I do. She lives here, for one thing. And she has binoculars. I am an impostor rescuer.

The bar is sticky. I can feel the stickiness on my elbows. I don't want to lift my arms. I stay still until someone taps the top of my head. Then I look up. The bartender's holding a shot glass between his thumb and forefinger. It's filled with something Pepto-Bismol pink. He points down the bar. A man with cropped black hair waves at me and smiles. He's holding a matching shot. He lifts it, toasting me, then drinks his. I drink mine.

"He looks smarmy," says Star, and I want to tell her she's one to talk, she who probably hasn't ever shaved her armpit hair.

"He looks like a robot," Greta says.

That I can't dispute. He's wearing a short-sleeved silver button-down shirt and matching silver pants. But I don't care. I smile coyly at him and hold up my empty glass in thanks.

He comes over and rests a hand on my shoulder, bends down, says something incomprehensible into my ear.

"What?" I say. "Speak English."

"English," he says. He smiles. He has a surplus of teeth, crowded together like a fence with too many pickets. "Yes. Okay," he says. "So we will dance."

I slide off my shiny barstool and let him lead me out to the empty dance floor. Really, it is *empty*; we're the only two people on it. Despite the alcohol, I feel incredibly stupid dancing on an empty dance floor in a grass-stained sundress with a guy in a silver suit who actually has glow sticks. Hot pink ones. He keeps one in his mouth, clamped between his teeth like a dog bone, and holds the other in his right hand, which he wiggles over and around his head, and snakes through the air between us. I don't know what to do with my hands. I find myself snapping my fingers, clapping in time to the music. Without a crowd, I don't know how to dance. My partner holds my waist and kind of twists down toward the floor in front of me, so his face is level with my knees. He twists back up and pulls me close to him, practically pressing his nose to mine. I can smell him: alcohol and sweat and cheap hair gel. As he moves, his clothes flash metallically and squeak synthetically.

"You don't like to dance?" he asks.

"I don't know," I say. I don't want to talk. I'm thinking that while I'm drinking at a club and dancing with a stranger, Ash is sinking deeper and deeper into the quicksand. I'm thinking that I stole money to come out here, and I came out here to bring Ash home, and here I am, not even trying. I'm thinking that I'm drinking at a club and dancing with a stranger and my sister is dead. I'm thinking that today would have been Alena's nineteenth birthday; she should be at a club, dancing and drinking and having a good time. I want to tear off this man's silver clothes and straddle him. Under a strobe light, sex wouldn't count. It would be sex you'd see in a flip book.

"This is not good," he says, "you come to a discotheque, you don't like to dance. I think maybe you don't have a good teacher."

"Maybe," I say.

"You don't dress like a clubber," he says, "but maybe in here"—he presses one hand to my chest—"you are a clubber."

"Okay," I say, wondering if it's socially acceptable in this country to touch strangers' breasts.

"You are a clubber on the inside," he says.

"Right."

"In your heart."

"Are you a Palestinian?" I ask.

"I am a Druze," my dance partner says. "You know us, the Druze?"

"How would I know you?"

"We are Israelis. But we are Druze."

"You're Israeli?"

"Me? I come from Lebanon. But most Druze here come from Israel. You will come to my village," he says, "for dinner. Do you like tea?"

I glance at the bar. "Let's do shots," I say, dragging him off the dance floor by his wrist. We sit on the opposite side of the bar from Star and Greta. They lift their glasses to us.

Sweat has broken out on the Druze's hairline. "Those are your friends?"

"No," I say, "not really. I'm too shallow to be friends with people with body odor. I don't really have any friends. Except one. Maggie. But she's kind of an idiot. I'm only friends with idiots."

"Slow, slow, slow," says the Druze. "I cannot understand you."

"Never mind," I say. "I'm not here to socialize. I'm here to rescue my brother."

"Then where is your brother?"

"Exactly!" I say, wagging a finger at him until my hand falls into my lap. "Exactly." I hiccup.

The bartender brings us gin and tonics. People start filtering into the club. The dance floor begins to fill up, and I realize that Israelis could be Americans, but with shorter pants, strange shoes.

The Druze tries to make conversation. "What is your livelihood?" he asks.

"My livelihood? I teach first grade. My brother's the brainy one. He would have been a great scholar. Or a veterinarian. He used to be so nice to animals. I don't know about now. Do Orthodox Jews like animals? My brother wants nothing to do with me anymore."

"Why is this?"

"He thinks he's better than me."

"In my community," the Druze says, "sometimes we think we are better than the religious Druze. We are the educated ones. They are always believing in superstitions."

"Makes sense," I say. And now I wish not only to be in Lebanon but to be a Druze. I move closer to the Druze. I feel the silver vinyl of his sleeve against my bare arm.

"We all live together in the village," says the Druze. "My family. All the families. Religious, not religious, both. We respect one another."

I don't know what a village is. I picture thatch-roofed huts. But that's what I want: a family in a village in Lebanon.

"You are here to save your brother," says the Druze.

"Yes."

The Druze crosses one leg over the other. "*Why* is this your job?" he asks, stirring his drink.

"My family is broken. There's no one to fix it."

"You will fix it?"

Monica flashes into my head, those skinny white legs. "What," I say, "you don't think I can fix it?"

"Dancing will be better now," says the Druze.

I have to lean against him as we walk toward the dance floor. I can feel my eyes closing, my knees wobbling, as if the bass pumping up through the floor is an earthquake. Someone grabs my wrist. I turn around.

"We're going," Star says. "We want to go to a bar in the Russian Compound, try to catch some live music. Something a bit more mellow." She glances up at the Druze. "You coming?" she asks me.

I shake my head. "He'll get me home," I say.

"It'll be fun there," she says. "It's where tourists hang out. Americans and Europeans. Come on. It's creepy here."

"I'm staying."

Star bites her lip, glances over her shoulder at Greta, then looks at me again. "You sure?"

"I'm sure."

"Well," she says. She looks uncertain. "Whatever you like."

The Druze cups his arm around my shoulder and leads me away, giving me the feeling I get whenever I take a wrong turn in downtown Boston, like I'm not positive I've made a wrong turn, but while I'm trying to convince myself that I haven't, I'm passing one unfamiliar landmark after another, until an hour later, West Roxbury or Jamaica Plain or the New Hampshire border appears in front of me like an unwelcome mirage.

I DO SOMETHING TONIGHT that I've never done before: I stay through Arbahim's whole show, through song after song that Todd sings without opening his eyes, through David's thirteen drum solos (I count). Sweat beads fly from David's beard. The keyboardist and the bass guitarist look annoyed. Only Todd smiles serenely and looks content. I don't understand his contentment. If God protects all who love Him, shouldn't Todd worry about what that means for those who *don't* love Him? Doesn't Todd see how good life has been since he became religious? The improvements in my own life are undeniable. Just compare my year in Israel to my year in Boulder. Compare the light in my current life to the darkness of my childhood. It's all so clear: All the bad things happened to me before I came to Yeshiva Hillel.

And ever since, very little has touched me. Even though Yeshiva Hillel is right in Jerusalem, right in the thick of the conflict, not one guy in my yeshiva has gotten so much as a scratch this year. Sure, we've had some close calls. For instance, back in February, Reuven was waiting at a bus stop when a Palestinian guy pulled a gun out of his pocket and opened fire in the crowd. Nine people got shot, but Reuven, who went into shock and didn't even duck, walked away unscathed. Reuven, who can support any Talmudic argument with twenty-four proofs. Reuven, who never misses an opportunity to pray. You think that's a coincidence?

I just don't understand what's going through Todd's head; does he think that studying at a yeshiva is some kind of vacation, that he can just go back to his old life like nothing happened? Responsibility comes with knowing the truth. Once you know it, you have to live by it. How can people like Todd and Monica know the truth but ignore it? Unless David's lying about her, Monica's really gone astray. Not that I care. I barely think about her, really.

Except that she keeps walking into the bar. Or at least, I keep thinking I see her. I don't know when everyone in Jerusalem started looking like Monica. And I don't know why the real Monica didn't show up tonight. I thought she loved Arbahim.

After the last song, I hurry outside before anyone can talk to me. I'm in no mood for conversation or for the lurching brightness of the bus. Besides, it's a beautiful night. I breathe it in, reminding myself to be grateful for it, to appreciate the long walk I'm about to take beneath the stars. But as I make my way through the dark streets, my shoulders slouch.

I don't want to be sad in Jerusalem. One day God will ask me, "Why didn't you taste all my fruits?" and I don't want to have to explain that I was too busy licking my wounds.

Tasting God's fruits doesn't mean giving in to all of your impulses. It doesn't mean having sex with as many sorority girls as possible or traveling to Thailand and—God forbid—praying in a Buddhist temple or doing any of the other things self-important people tell you to do as they offer smug grins and ridiculous clichés like "You only live once" and "Make the most of your youth."

To taste God's fruits is to take advantage of all that Judaism has to offer, to be freed not by secular temptations but by God's beautiful Torah.

By the time I get to French Hill, a blister has formed on my left heel, and all I want to do is fall into bed. I'm practically asleep already. So when I hear Monica's voice cutting through the dark, it takes me a second to understand that it's real.

THE DRUZE AND I find a place on the dance floor. "You want to try my glow sticks?" he asks.

What a question. Who *wouldn't* want to try the Druze's glow sticks? I take them and start moving them in a box shape, in concentric circles, in fast, urgent vertical lines. I have no idea what I'm doing.

"Raksaha jameel," the Druze says approvingly, which I guess is Druze-speak for *Great light show!* He pumps his fist in the air and whistles at the DJ with his fingers between his teeth.

"Yalla!" the dancers yell at the DJ. *"Yalla! Yalla!"* The body heat thickens. Shoulders brush against my shoulders. Bodies squeeze past us. The DJ is perspiring now, sweat glistening on his bald head.

I feel my confidence swell. The Druze dances across from me, as the hot pink lights make trails around us like lasers. I twist the glow sticks over my head, at my sides, in between us, until I'm panting and heady, and then I close my eyes and a memory flashes suddenly, sharply, into the dark. It's the glow sticks that remind me of what was to be Alena's last Fourth of July. Sparklers in hand, Ash, Alena, and I ran around the yard in a wide circle, arms out, creating a light show in the dark. Alena stopped, bent down to tie her shoe. Ash stopped, too, to wait for her, but I kept running, my arms outstretched, unwilling to stop for anything.

Behind my closed eyelids, I see Alena, her smooth face glowing in the light of the sparkler, her forehead puckered as she tried to make sense of her shoelace. And I can see Ash holding her sparkler for her, then reaching his hand down and helping her to her feet.

I stop dancing and open my eyes. The room spins around me, the Druze's silver suit whirling and flashing. I wonder if everyone in his village has a silver suit, if getting one is a rite of passage, if his father took him shopping for his on his eighteenth birthday.

"Hello?" the Druze is saying, but his voice sounds far off, like a scuba diver's voice, muffled bubbles.

I press the glow sticks to my face. "I don't have a father," I say. I wasn't expecting to say those words, but here they are, hanging in the air like a skin I've just shed.

The Druze stops dancing. He is breathing hard. "You have to speak louder," he says. "I cannot understand you."

I back away a couple of steps. The Druze steps closer to me. "Come," he says, grabbing my hand and pulling me off the dance floor toward the neon EXIT sign.

Outside, the air is nice and cool. The Druze leans against the brick wall, and I stand in front of him. He takes the glow sticks from me, tucks them into the pocket on the front of his shirt, and holds my hands.

"I was just saying," I begin, but then I trail off. It's different now, away from the loud music, away from the dancing bodies. Now it's just plain, quiet nighttime.

"What?"

"I don't know why I said it," I say. "I said that I don't have a father. I guess I didn't think you'd hear me. Sorry . . . I'm kind of drunk."

The Druze frowns, thinking. "But you have a brother," he says after a second.

"Yes," I say, nodding. I think of Monica, squatting behind the tree outside Yeshiva Hillel, squinting through binoculars. *I* should be stationed at that tree. *I* should be on night watch. Panic buzzes in my ears. I look at the Druze's silver pants. Elastic waistband? Drawstring? Or do they button and zip like jeans? I reach for his hips, move my fingers in toward his belly. Velcro. I tear it back loudly. The Druze looks momentarily startled. Then he says, "I will tell you something about family. When I was a child in Lebanon, the Israeli army came, and my uncle—my uncle lives here—he was a soldier for Israel, and he came to visit us in our village. In his Israeli army uniform."

"Really?"

The Druze shrugs. "What other opportunity would he have to visit?"

"A Druze in the Israeli army?"

"All the Druze in Israel fight in the army. . . . You know, when the Israeli tanks rolled through our village, in Lebanon, they threw candy. Everyone in Lebanon thought we were traitors. They don't understand Israel, the way the Druze in Israel understand Israel. 'The Druze are friends with the occupiers.' That's what they said about us. That was all they could see. But the Druze, in their army uniforms, they were our family. What should we do, shoot them with a gun? Family is family," the Druze says. The glow sticks in his front pocket create the illusion that his heart is lit up. I touch it. "You see it can be complicated. Very, very complicated."

"Family is complicated," I agree.

The Druze lifts my dress in the front. He pulls me closer. I reposition us so my back is pressed to the wall. Our noses touch. I move my underwear to the side, and pull his hips until I feel the pressure of him against me.

The Druze pulls his face back and lifts an eyebrow. "Is this okay?"

"Yes," I say.

"But you are very drunk."

"Nah. I'm fine."

And then it's over so fast, I'm almost not sure it happened. But he is collapsing on my shoulder, panting. In my ear, he says, "Do not let complicated circumstances stand in your way. You see, my uncle was occupying us, but he was still my uncle. My father hugged my uncle and his gun together. Nothing comes between family. Nothing ever. Do you understand?" The Druze steps back, refastens his Velcro. "You go to your brother now. Do not dance with me."

I'm picturing Israeli tanks shooting chocolate bars into Lebanon. And I realize I don't understand one thing in the entire world. I touch the Druze's wrist. His silver suit shimmers like something precious and rare.

"I'm going," I say, and I run.

I DO NOT LOVE Monica. How could I possibly love Monica? She doesn't even fear God. But here I am hiding behind the redwood tree just outside the gate of Yeshiva Hillel, across the street from Monica, watching her arm reach up to someone, watching her shirt rise to expose her bare skin, and I feel something very much like love. It's probably something else. Lots of things feel like love. Grief, for example. And pain. I can't tell who it is standing there with her, until he steps into the light and I see that it's David. It's David stepping closer to Monica, and placing a hand on that halo of flesh at her waist. He must have caught a taxi from the Russian Compound after the show. And then what? Did he run into Monica? Or did he call her and have her meet him? Or did they plan this meeting ahead of time? Why is he touching her skin?

"You should trust me," Monica says. Her voice is perfectly clear in the empty, quiet night. "I'm pretty much always right. People don't realize it at first and they resist me and resist me until they realize. Like, when I gave up eating meat? All my friends were like, 'That's so stupid,' but I stayed firm about it, and, like, protested when they ate chicken wings, until they finally realized it was wrong to kill animals. Now they're all vegetarians, back in California . . . practically the whole Bay Area is vegetarian because of me, and when I go back there, I'm all, 'Yeah . . . told you so.'"

"I think I'm being tested," David says, dropping his hand from her waist. I can tell by how he says it that he doesn't think that at all, that he just wants Monica to believe that she's torturing him. Where do people learn to be so manipulative?

Monica drops her hand from his shoulder and takes a small step backward. She shoves her hands into the back pockets of her jeans.

"You're like the *pri assur*," David says. *The forbidden fruit.* I can see that he's holding his tam bunched up in his fist. I can't tell if he's wearing a *kipa*.

"Oh, you think *God* is testing you? You think *I'm* the *pri assur*?" Monica sounds delighted. She arcs her arms over her head like a ballerina and spins in a slow circle. "Well, how do I look?" she asks, facing him again and striking a dramatic pose. "Tempting?"

"You're tempting," David says, nodding. "You're definitely tempting."

Yeshiva boys don't act like this! They don't casually touch a girl's skin or tell her she's tempting or admit to her that she might have the power to take them from God. I wonder if I'm witnessing an Exodus. An Exodus in reverse: out of Israel, back into the shackles of the secular world. First Todd, then David . . . they're dropping like flies. I wonder if I should go inside and wake people up, scream in the halls, "We have an emergency!"

This *is* an emergency. A spiritual emergency. My palms are pressed so hard to the bark of the tree, they hurt. I worry for David, I really do, but I'm simultaneously thinking that he's a liar, that he tried to warn me away from Monica so that he could move in on her. He wants Monica, like my fraternity brother wanted Vanessa. And because I think that David is a liar, because he is trying to take something that he thinks is mine—even though Monica is *not* mine, will never be mine because I don't want her—I will not step out of the shadows. Maybe I would if I were a different kind of person.

"Look at it this way," Monica says, pulling the tam out of David's hand. "I'm not asking you to make a life-changing decision right this second. Just come with me for tonight. If you miss your yeshiva?" She flicks the tam at his arm a couple of times. "So you come back. Honestly, though? This place is kind of a shit hole."

How can he let her say that?! He should grab her shoulders and shake some sense into her, let her head careen back and forth on her skinny neck. He should see now that she's a serpent. But instead, he throws his head back and laughs. How can he laugh? What's funny about ruining his life? For a girl, nonetheless. But he's laughing, and now she's laughing, saying, "Yeah, see? I could make you laugh for the rest of your life." She pulls the tam over her own head and adjusts it in the front. "Bet you don't get to laugh much in your yeshiva."

"What do you think," he says, "we all just follow the rules all the time? Not everyone's as crazy as you are maybe, but we party. We do things. We get out."

What?

My breath catches in my chest. All at once, I understand things. I understand that for a year I've been thinking that I'm on the inside, but I've been wrong. As usual, I've been orbiting the nucleus. David is telling Monica a truth that no one has ever told me: that some of the guys at the yeshiva are no different from my fraternity brothers in Boulder. How have I missed it? Does Todd know about this secret inside world? Does Reuven? All around me, people are straying from God, right here at Yeshiva Hillel! But who?

Who is guilty and who is not?

"But I make you laugh the most," Monica says.

"Maybe," David says, still chuckling.

"I bring you the most joy."

"Now you're pushing it."

"But it's true, David. I'm the most fun."

"Okay," David says. "Maybe that's true."

True? There's plenty to be joyful about in the yeshiva! There's plenty of fun. Is David forgetting Shabbat, when we toast one another with shots of vodka, and cry, *"L'chaim,"* and get spiritually high and grow closer to God? Is he forgetting Purim, when we got so drunk we couldn't tell good from evil? Is he forgetting the great joy of learning a tractate of Talmud, of smelling the spice box before beginning a new week?

"You're right," David says.

She's right? She's *right?*

"I can always come back. What's one night away?" He pulls the tam off Monica's head and puts it back on his own head. "I should take things one night at a time." He runs a finger down Monica's cheek. He looks confident doing it, not the way a yeshiva boy who's ostensibly never touched a girl in his life should look. "Why *not* try something new?" he's saying. "It won't kill me."

"Finally!" Monica says, and I remember when she said that to me—*Finally!*—when I came out of my room two Friday nights ago and found her in the hallway. "So let's go," she says, grabbing David's wrist and pulling him.

And then she looks across the street and sees me. Well, I *think* she sees me. She's still pulling on David, and it's only one split second, and I'm hidden, at least mostly, behind this tree, but I swear, her eyes, those evil blue eyes, momentarily meet mine. I feel them like bolts of electricity, feel them so strongly that when she turns back to David, I feel that, too—like an electrical wire was clipped between us; sparks fly from it and die. She drags David out of the light, into the dark, and I hear their voices fade and fade and finally grow silent. But still I keep watching that spot of light on the sidewalk, as if at any second they will reappear in it, as if this is the end of the play, and they have to come back to take their bows. I watch and watch, my cheek pressed to the trunk of the redwood tree, but there is only that light, whitish-yellow, and nothing at all inside it.

I AM NOT THE only mother Jonathan is helping. There is Marion, who shows up at Jonathan's house unannounced and in tears at least once a week, who can't sleep at night because her Scientologist daughter is blowing through some inheritance that was supposed to last her entire adult life.

"She's only twenty-four!" Marion sobs to Jonathan. "Her adult life is just beginning!"

There is Louise, a former runway model, whose son was a model, too, before he joined some cult I've never heard of and moved somewhere in the Virgin Islands to live in a hut. I met her once. She wouldn't look me in the eye.

There's Roberta, whose son is a Hare Krishna who doesn't shower anymore, who lives in New York City and spends his days outside a train station, selling shiny hardcover books about something called Krishna consciousness.

"What are you," I finally asked Jonathan, "some kind of womanizer?" I laughed uneasily, and then he laughed.

"Ellie," he said. "Don't you know me better than that?"

Well, do I? I don't know. I'll give him this: he never acts like he's hiding me. The first time Marion and I met, for example, Jonathan introduced me to her by putting his arm around me and saying, "Marion, I'd like you to meet someone very special." Of course, Marion looked at me like I was the least special person she'd ever met, but that was Marion's attitude, not Jonathan's. Jonathan has never done anything to make me think I'm not special to him. He tells me I'm beautiful. He confides in me. We haven't gone a day without seeing each other since we met. Sometimes, when we're chopping vegetables together in my kitchen, and his shirtsleeves are rolled up to his elbows and I can see the soft hair on his arms, and the veins underneath, or when I'm riding in his car and he's adjusting the heat to make it just right for me, I let myself imagine having a second husband, something I never let myself imagine before.

But other times, I worry. I get quiet and I curl up inside myself and Jonathan wants to know what's wrong.

"Just bring Ash home," I tell him, but that's not exactly what I mean. What I mean is, don't pull the shit Ben pulled on me. What I mean is, my heart is constricting like a question mark.

April 29, 2002

I BOARD A BUS that stops a few blocks from the club. When I look at the Jerusalem buses, I don't see vessels of transportation; I see the images of destruction from the news: the broken glass, the blood, the crushed metal, frayed wires, dead bodies on stretchers. Earlier today, I saw a bus stop where the Plexiglas was gone from one side of the waiting shelter, the metal frame disfigured.

I had planned to avoid the buses in Israel.

Until tonight. Tonight, I feel brave. Plus, cabs are getting expensive. But once the door closes me inside, I feel less brave. Beneath the flickering fluorescent lights, I find myself searching everyone's faces, searching for clues, searching for the beady, tense eyes of a terrorist. I look for suspicious backpacks, for shirts with inexplicable bulges. But for the most part, I can't tell the difference between Israelis and Palestinians. Everyone looks sort of the same to me: a little foreign, a little suspicious. The bright lights remind me how drunk I am. My head pounds. My stomach rolls.

Some teenagers talk loudly in a language that might be Hebrew or might be Arabic. Two IDF soldiers in green berets sit sleeping side by side, Uzis in their laps; they've made pillows with their arms on the seat backs in front of them. An Orthodox couple sits in the seats across from me. The man wears a tall black hat. The woman wears a purple scarf over her hair. The scarf is threaded with gold. She is hugely pregnant. She holds her belly in her hands.

On closer inspection, I see that she's younger than I am. She has the smooth-skinned, wide-eyed face of a teenager. What a different world hers is from mine. She can't be more than twenty, and in just a few weeks, she'll be responsible for a whole other human being. How did she get so mature in so few years? Where are *my* maternal instincts? I want people to say about me, *Bits Kellerman will make a great mother one day.* But I'm pretty sure no one says that. I haven't even bonded with my students. Not really anyway. They like me enough, I guess, but sometimes, I still get them mixed up. None of them really stands out to me as an individual; they're just a hodgepodge of six-year-olds.

The Orthodox girl says something incomprehensible to me. I smile at her. She repeats herself, smiling back gently. Then she bends sideways, over her pregnant belly, and lifts something off the floor of the bus. It's a silver bracelet with a little charm shaped like a hand; the palm is studded with a tiny blue stone. I bought the bracelet in the Old City for ten shekels, from a street vendor who told me it was the hand of protection. The girl holds the bracelet draped over her fingers. The hand trembles like it's uncertain.

"Thank you," I say, taking it, but then, on a whim, I tap her arm and hold the bracelet out to her. "For you," I say. "Or for your baby in a few years."

She looks at me blankly, not understanding. I take her hand, put the bracelet in it, and close her fist around it. Her husband is looking away from us, out his window. The woman shakes her head. *"Lo, lo, lo,"* she says.

"For your baby," I say again.

She hands the bracelet back to me, and says, in heavily accented English, "For *your* baby." Then she smiles shyly, crosses her arms over her chest, and turns toward her husband's window, ending the interaction.

I hold the bracelet toward her again. I know she can see me in the window, but she doesn't turn around, and I can't think of anything to say. I fasten the bracelet around my own wrist.

When I get off the bus in French Hill, even though I have to throw up and would therefore much prefer to go to my hostel, I stumble toward Yeshiva Hillel.

When I arrive, I see no trace of Monica. I sit against the tree she once lurked behind and watch the yeshiva through the wrought-iron bars. This feels right, sitting here, cold and uncomfortable and drunk and sick to my stomach; this finally feels like real effort, real sacrifice. "I'm waiting for you, Ash," I whisper. The night is silent. I listen for Monica's footsteps, so certain I'll hear them, so certain that she wants to beat me to this, that we're like the Americans and the Soviets, racing for the cold, distant face of the moon.

17 Iyar 5762
(April 29, 2002)

I GET UP WITH the sun to pray again at the Kotel, the Western Wall, to start my day as close to God as possible. For hours, I've been tossing and turning, listening to Todd snore and drifting in and out of violent nightmares. I dreamed that Yosi and I were spies and I ratted him out, then had to watch as a man in a ski mask shaved off Yosi's beard and beat him to death with a club.

Joseph, son of Jacob, used to interpret dreams. But Rabbi Berkstein says that prophetic dreams are rare. "Don't look too much into things, except Torah," he says. "In dreams, a person is shown only what is on his mind." What is on my mind is this: the summer I left for Israel, Yosi killed himself. I don't think about that constantly or anything. It's just one of those things that sneaks up on me now and then when other things are going wrong. Last August, one of the Zeff guys wrote to tell me about it, and provided excruciatingly graphic details, about the eight-inch chef's knife Yosi used to stab himself in the chest, about Yosi's wife finding him dead in the kitchen, how she slipped on his blood and injured her hip.

I think Yosi might have been trying to emulate King Saul, who committed suicide by falling on his sword. Saul's is one of the few suicides in the Torah, and the sages have excused him. He was brave, they say. If he hadn't killed himself, he would have been captured by the Philistines, tortured, and made to worship idols. Normally, I agree with the sages. And, of course, it's noble to choose death over worshipping idols. But even though I might never say so aloud, I can't help thinking that Saul was scared, not brave. He was weak and scared, and so was Yosi.

Months before Yosi died, when I told him what I thought of the Zeff Movement and walked away from the Zeff House, he should have been strong enough to think, *Who cares? God and I know the truth.* Instead, he questioned everything.

Well, I'm speculating. I don't know for a fact that I made him question his life. It's more likely that, to him, I was just some stupid college kid in a long line of stupid college kids. After all, how many Boulder kids like me probably drifted into the Zeff House for a little while, and then drifted out? It's arrogant to even *consider* that I might have played a role in his suicide.

I don't want to spend all day thinking about this. That's why I'm going to the Kotel—to make sure that this day, that every day, is as meaningful as possible. It's true when people say that every day counts. You never know what can happen. For example, one day, God created light.

Outside, the girl standing on the other side of the wrought-iron gate looks like my sister. She has the same curly brown hair pulled back from her face, and that frizzy sort of crown thing at her hairline that Bits gets when she hasn't showered. She's even standing like Bits, all her weight on her right foot, her left foot tucked behind her right heel, and she has her head cocked like Bits, only Bits does it because of her astigmatism, and this girl's probably just cocking her head because of the rising sun or for some other reason because I know that this girl could not possibly be Bits.

I walk down a couple of steps and squint, and that's when I see the scar on the girl's shin, the jagged purple line from ankle to knee, the scar Bits got from falling into a sliding glass door when we were little. It's Bits. Bits is standing outside my yeshiva in a sundress.

April 29, 2002

WHEN I WAKE up, I'm still drunk. Birds are chirping like an insult. My tongue has grown fur. I need to be hosed down. Early morning has spread its pink and gold sheet all around me, casting Yeshiva Hillel in a majestic light. I glance around. Still no sign of Monica. I remember the Druze, and squint at the memory of his silver shirt. I smell what will probably be Ash's breakfast, sweet breakfast smells, French toast and powdered sugar.

When I scratch my head, grass blades fall from my hair. I look down at my dress. Grass stains and grass. I'm in camo. I wonder briefly if the gate's open at the side of the yeshiva, and even more briefly if someone would let me in to pee. I look down at my sundress. No way. Besides, why would a men's yeshiva have a women's bathroom? I'll have to pee into the storm drain.

As I squat, I watch the building and send Ash telepathic messages: *Come out. Come out. Come out.* How much of my trip to Israel have I spent staring at these wrought-iron bars, these red and brown bricks?

When I finish peeing, I return to my spot under the tree and lean back against the trunk, remembering a documentary I once saw on telekinesis. Supposedly, we can move things just by thinking about moving them. We can bend spoons and extinguish flames. I stare at the door of the yeshiva. I remember that accord-

ing to the telekinesis expert (I think that was really his title: telekinesis expert), you're supposed to look at the object you're trying
to move and imagine it as your own limb. If you can move your leg,
the expert reasoned, why shouldn't you be able to move a mountain?

I pretend that the door is my leg. I kick it.

It works. The front door opens, and out comes Ash, holding
a velvet pouch under one arm. He is blinking in the early sunlight, wearing what seems to be the yeshiva's uniform: black pants,
white button-down shirt, black shoes. He has those tassel things
hanging down his legs. It must just be someone who looks like
Ash, wearing the outfit that I knew Ash would be wearing. I blink
hard, get to my feet. No, it's definitely Ash. He looks worn-out. His
face is pale, his eyes troubled. And he has earlocks. They aren't
very long, but they're curled into corkscrews. What the hell did
he grow those things for? The other Yeshiva Hillel guys I've seen
don't have them. Or are theirs just less noticeable because of their
beards? Apparently, Ash hasn't been able to grow a beard. Still,
though, he looks a little older than he did a year ago, a little more
grown-up, but also small and vulnerable in his black-and-white
costume, framed by the giant brick building, the bright begin-
nings of sunlight catching him by surprise. I stand, go to the gate,
and hold a bar in each hand. I wait for my brother to notice me.

MY MOUTH GOES instantly dry. I hug my tefillin bag to my chest. And when Bits waves, I don't wave back.

"What are you—" I start to say, but then I stop myself. I walk down the rest of the steps, to the gate. It is Bits; there's no denying it. But I don't want to ask her what she's doing here. I'm in no mood to hear her say, "I was in the neighborhood," or "I've decided to become a yeshiva boy," or "I'm selling Girl Scout cookies." So I ask, "When did you get here?"

"I've been in Israel since Friday. You're not an easy guy to find." Bits rests her forehead against the bars. On the ground, my shadow stretches between us like a tenuous bridge. I notice that her knees are dirty. "Nice hair thingies," she says, motioning to my *payos*.

I reach for my *payos* before I can tell myself not to, and then look past her head to the sidewalk across the street, where Monica and David stood last night like actors in a play. It's amazing how you can't trust a single person. You can't even trust your own sister. Godless people have tricks up their sleeves. Nothing good will come of talking to Bits. She only wants to weaken me, to weaken my relationship with God. And after all that happened yesterday—the terrorist in the Old City, Monica and David—why should I let her kick me while I'm down?

"You need to leave me alone," I say, and the light in Bits's eyes goes dark, but I don't care.

"You're my brother," she says. "I have an obligation to not leave you alone."

"I'm an adult," I remind her.

"Yeah, I guess," she says, "technically, but just barely. And that's really not the point. It's not very adultlike to disappear and not tell your family where you are. Especially in our family. You know better."

I unlock the door of the gate and go out to the sidewalk. What does Bits know about right and wrong? She doesn't even live a Jewish life. She ignores God. She ignores His Torah. And she's here telling me that *I've* been irresponsible? I brush past Bits, clutching my tefillin bag close to my chest. What does she know about anything?

I SHOULD HAVE JUST said it: *Alena is dead. You need to come home.* But how do you speak those words aloud, straight to your brother's face? So now he's walking away from me. Is he going to meet Monica? I slept on the ground outside his yeshiva all night! Drunk! What does he think that was, fun? But I'm not going to get angry. I've come too far to ruin this by getting angry.

"Ash," I call, running after him. The scabs on my knees expand and contract with each step. "I'm sorry I was disrespectful about your hair curls. They look nice. I wasn't thinking. They just . . . surprised me. But I like them, now that I'm getting used to them. Just . . . wait up." But he doesn't wait, doesn't stop, so I slow down and follow calmly behind him. We pass a boarded-up falafel stand, a fancy hotel, an old religious man who walks with his head down, his hands clasped behind his back. And then we're walking on sidewalks along busy streets. Cars and buses whiz past. Still, Ash only speeds up. Once, without even looking both ways, he steps into the street and crosses it halfway, pauses at an island, then crosses to the opposite sidewalk. I speed up, too, follow his every step. Ash begins twisting an earlock around his finger, like a caricature of an old European Jew. What would our grandmother think of this? *Asheleh,* she would say, *what is this, a costume party? Are you dressed as my father?*

I miss our grandmother. When our parents married, she moved to Philadelphia from Brooklyn, so from the time I was born until the day she died, I saw her almost every weekend. We all loved her, even my father; he loved her ingenuity. She saved everything, never let anything go to waste. She would break empty wine bottles and the mirrors inside old compacts, and tuck the shards into a shoe box. When the shoe box started to fill up, she would scour second-hand stores for wooden birdhouses, buy five or ten, spread the wood with a thin layer of plaster, press the shards into the plaster for decoration, then sell the birdhouses at the Jewish Community Center.

Six months after Alena was kidnapped, my grandmother died of her second bout with cancer. My mother pressed ice cubes to her lips in the hospital, as my grandmother whispered in Yiddish to her first husband, who had been dead for forty-five years. My father never visited her in the hospital. He had had enough sorrow. One tragedy a year was plenty for him, he said. On the last night of my grandmother's life, my father stayed home with Ash and me. He told my mother he had to work on one of his projects.

My father always had projects: a crib for me that he never built bars for, a hockey stick he said would be light as air, a rocking chair that had no back. He never finished any of them. He never threw any of them away either. They all just sat in the basement for years to come, half-baked, cobwebbed, hoping to be remembered.

But he didn't go down to the basement that night. While Ash and I sat on the carpet behind him, drawing pictures on construction paper, he stared out the living room window. Maybe he watched the reflection of us on the glass. Maybe he didn't. I remember that night so vividly—Alena absent; my grandmother dying; my father haunted, detached, and perhaps already planning to leave us.

So many people are gone.

I watch Ash's back, his bouncing earlocks. Behind the earlocks and the tassels, behind the bones in his face that have grown more defined in the past year (as if he's finally shed his last layer of childhood), my baby brother is still in there. I know he is. I stop yelling to him. I drop back so I'm following him at a greater distance, but I keep my eyes on the back of his head. I won't give up until he talks to me. He'll have to stop somewhere. He can't walk away from me forever.

After a couple of miles, I recognize the Old City. I hope this is our destination because flip-flops are terrible walking shoes. Also, I'm thirsty, but when a man in the Armenian Quarter invites me into his shop for tea, I refuse. I am on a mission and nothing can deter me. Not tea, not Armenian men. I am going to reach my brother. We snake through throngs of tourists sipping their morning coffee, past covered women chasing tiny, long-haired children, past a group of Hasidic teenagers in black hats with pimples and awkward bodies; they look like strange grandfathers. We snake through the windy little streets paved with Jerusalem stone until we reach the Western Wall.

I watch Ash hurry down the stairs and make his way through security, and I realize that he didn't walk away from me because he had a date with Monica. He walked away from me because he had a date with God. I should have known. As I watch him head through the plaza toward the men's section, I remember the tree in the front yard of the house we grew up in, and how we called it home base when we played tag, and how we could touch it with our fingertips and catch our breaths and no one could tag us it. Now the men's section of the Western Wall is Ash's home base. I look down at the swarm of black hats, and I wonder if all of those men have pasts as painful as Ash's, if they're all running from broken hearts, from the ghosts of girlfriends, sisters, and mothers, from the sharp red fingernails and spiked high heels of women.

I head down the stairs, move through the metal detector and into the plaza. When I approach the divider between the men's and women's sections, I think I've lost Ash. He's blended in with everyone else, gone from me, again, but then I spot his shoulders, the inward curve of them that looks like our father's. He has his arm outstretched, his sleeve rolled up like a junky. He's wrapping a black strap from wrist to elbow to biceps, creating a spiral against his flesh.

I glance briefly at the women's side, at the scattering of women in long skirts bowing up and down over prayer books. I remember reading once about a group of women who wanted to wear prayer shawls and yarmulkes and have minyan at the Wall, just like the men. So they marched here like soldiers, started praying like their fathers and husbands, and got pelted with dirty diapers and heavy chairs. Then I remember how Ash used to hover around the tree during tag, so that if anyone was running for him, he would have quick access to home base. We aren't children anymore; I don't have to respect imaginary barriers and arbitrary rules.

"You're It," I whisper through clenched teeth, heading toward my brother.

I pass a group of men who are bent over a wooden table, reading from the Torah. They look up. They're wearing little black cubes on their foreheads. Someone shouts something in Hebrew. Three men quickly form a row in front of me, their black-sleeved arms stretched out at their sides—a row of gingerbread men. They're shaking their cube heads, pointing to the women's section, screaming things I can't understand. Beyond them, I see Ash, praying obliviously, his back to us. I want to explain to the gingerbread men that I'm not like the women with prayer shawls and yarmulkes. I'm not political. I have no interest in any of this.

"That's my brother," I try to explain, pointing, and the scene strikes me all at once as simultaneously absurd and enthralling, like a scene from *Fiddler on the Roof* gone terribly awry, with me as the star, irreverent and tone deaf. Then I feel something hard hit my left shoulder, and it registers that someone is throwing things at me, and then something else hits my spine.

I DON'T KNOW WHEN I lost Bits, but at some point she stopped screaming "I slept on the sidewalk like a bag lady for you!" and faded into silence. She must have dropped back long before the security checkpoint, but if not, at least the partition between the men's and women's sections must have stopped her. She can't get to me now. Hopefully, she's on her way back to America, where she will read about Palestinian terror attacks and tell herself that Israel is just one big target, that no sane person would choose to live here, that she is therefore superior to me, that Judaism is merely cultural, that religion is dead, obsolete, irrelevant, that Orthodox Judaism is a sexist, backward cult for people who can't find their way.

I face the Wall and I can almost see Shekhina, the Divine spirit, oozing out of the cracks.

I could have joined one of the two or three minyans, or prayer groups, but instead I pray alone, imagining that my tefillin, like Yosi used to say, are antennae, connecting me to God. Tefillin come in two parts: a long black leather strap that you wind around your arm, and a piece that goes around your forehead like a head lamp, with a cube on the front. Laying tefillin is such a humbling way to begin the day, the fulfillment of God's commandment to bind His words on our hands and before our eyes. But I'm distracted by thoughts of Bits. What is she doing here? How did she find me?

I see now that Todd was right: Miriam spoke *lashan hara* about Moses because she was jealous. She was jealous that God had chosen to communicate directly with Moses, instead of with her. I remember Moses' simple prayer after Miriam got *tzaraat*: *God, please, please heal Miriam.* I know I should be as compassionate as Moses, but I don't ask God to have mercy on Bits. She may be my sister, but she's irreverent.

There is a commotion behind me. I don't turn around. I'm sick of distractions. I just want to pray. But then a female voice, *Bits's* voice, cuts through my prayers so loudly, there is nothing else to hear: "That's my brother! I need to get to my brother!"

I whip around, the little black cube still affixed to my forehead, my arm bound by the black leather strap, and my eyes focus in on the turmoil, on the mob of black hats, on Bits's bare arm stretched toward me. Why is she pointing at me? The men will see that she knows me; they will run at me like vigilantes and whip off my *kipa*, yelling, "Look at this impostor, pretending to be religious!" They will roar with laughter.

If I turn back to the Wall and pretend not to notice her, eventually she will have to go away. Won't she? But before I turn back around, I see the rock, like the one David used to kill Goliath, hurtling through the air toward Bits's head.

I hear the rock connect with her skull, hear the little sigh that escapes her lungs, and Bits crumples to the ground like a deflated balloon. And suddenly, my breath goes out of me and I am seven years old with a hockey stick, and a car door is slamming, cracking the air, taking my sister away.

The crowd around Bits is dispersing, some men returning to the Torah as if Bits were just a minor distraction, a mosquito or a couple of raindrops. Others stand over her, staring, looking afraid. I know who threw that rock. I see him in his black hat and black suit. He has long, shiny *payos*. He is smiling slightly, a nervous smile, holding his tefillin bag pinned under one arm. He is watching Bits. He is backing away from her. His rock lies on the ground beside her head. An irrelevant question pops into my head: *Where did he get that rock?* Simultaneously, I ponder the perfection of it—it's round and smooth and gray, like a rock from a gift shop—and I don't even realize at first that I am heading toward the rock-throwing Hasid, instead of toward Bits. I'm not even conscious that I am unwinding the leather strap from my arm, that my anger has turned to sheer rage, and that my rage is directed not at Bits but at the Hasid who tried to hurt her.

Something like a growl escapes my throat, and I charge at the man with all my strength and head-butt him with the little black cube on my forehead. I am holding the man's shoulders. I rear my head back and connect with his forehead again. He makes a panicked sound like a braying donkey, and I am vaguely aware of a searing pain in my own forehead, and of his tefillin bag falling to the ground beside us. All around us, people are screaming. Somehow, I know that they are, even though all I can hear is wind in my head, and now I've got him on the ground, I'm sitting on top of him, straddling his chest. I have the strap of my tefillin pulled taut between my two hands and I lower it to his throat and press it to his Adam's apple.

People are grabbing at me, pulling my sleeve, shaking my shoulder, but I am stronger than anyone, deflecting them with my elbows. The Hasid's glasses have fallen off. They lie beside us on the ground, one frame cracked. His hat, too, lies beside us like an empty vessel. His blue eyes widen. He is screaming, then gargling, *"Lo! Lo!"* I can see the bruise already forming on his forehead from the little black cube, my *shel rosh*. His skin turns bright pink, sweat beads up at his hairline, his eyes are bulging now, full of tears—so weak! a grown man with tears in his eyes!—and behind me, I can feel his legs flailing wildly. With his hands, he is pushing against my chest, his whole body is bucking, but he is no match for me. I realize that this is my first fight ever and I am winning. I don't think immediately about what it might mean if I win.

Not until someone grabs me under the arms and yanks me to my feet, causing me to drop the leather strap, causing my *shel rosh* to slip off my head, do I realize what I was screaming over and over and over, my tefillin pressed to the man's throat, my lips mere inches from his face: "God will never forgive you! God will never forgive you!"

A s I START to come to, my head pounding in a dull, distant way, I see that everything around me is white—sterile, hospital white. Gone are the black coats, the black hats, the black leather tefillin straps, and black tefillin cubes. Everything is the color of surrender. I catch a glimpse of Ash meeting my eyes for a split second, then ducking out of my hospital room, closing the door behind him. I scream to him, then realize that I haven't screamed. It's only in my head that I'm telling him to come back. It's just like praying. Or telekinesis. I have still accomplished nothing; I see that I will not accomplish anything, not in Israel, not before tomorrow when I'm scheduled to fly back to Boston.

Right now, Ash is walking down the long hospital corridor, pushing through the door, stepping out into the sunshine, heading back to the Western Wall or to his yeshiva, or maybe to meet Monica somewhere. Once again, he is gone. And where am I? Still halfway inside a dream, seeing my brother and sister as they once were, years and years and a lifetime ago: sitting on blue carpet in our neighbors' playroom, each holding a joystick, staring straight ahead at a television screen, cartoon light reflecting in their eyes. I remember how still they were, unblinking, breaths held, like two people on a journey. Blasting off. Ash's foot wiggling like it always does when he concentrates. Alena's nose running from her constant allergies. I can practically feel the heat in their palms. The pulse in their wrists. The space in between them where I might have been.

WHEN I SEE Bits's eyes flutter open, I duck out of her hospital room and close the door behind me. I know she's going to tell me something I don't want to hear. Maybe our mother is sick or else so angry with me she sent Bits to try to drag me home.

A doctor walks purposefully down the hall, reading a clipboard. A nurse pushes a woman in a complex looking wheelchair. I reach up to feel the bump that has formed on my forehead. It's sore to the touch. In Hebrew, the woman in the wheelchair tells the nurse, "It hurts! Everything hurts!"

I look longingly at the EXIT sign. But as a Jew, it's my responsibility to visit the sick. So I turn back toward the closed door of Bits's room. I touch the doorknob, take a deep breath, and go inside.

Bits's eyes are half open. I sit in the wooden chair beside her bed. "You okay?" I ask.

"Never better," she slurs. "Nice friends you have."

I let out a sigh and massage my forehead with the heels of my hands.

"Does my voice sound weird?" she asks.

"You're slurring a little."

"How about now?"

"It's kind of getting better. I don't know. Forget that. Let's get this over with. Tell me what you're here to tell me."

Bits clears her throat, her eyes far away. "What, I can't just visit my brother?"

"Visit? This isn't a visit."

"My head hurts," she says, which reminds me of so many days in Boulder, Bits, hungover, sitting in front of the TV in her apartment in her sweatpants, complaining to her roommates about her headache, while I sat beside her, remembering the night before, remembering the guys in baseball caps surrounding her, too close, looking at one another over the top of her head, communicating through glances, touching her upper thigh, her hip, body parts they wouldn't touch on other girls—girls they respected—in front of people.

Not that I can totally blame Bits for being the way she is. Years ago, everyone knew that Bits, at ten years old, was having sex (whatever sex is for a ten-year-old . . . nothing I care to think about). Boys in our neighborhood told me about it. Even then, even though I was only eight, I knew it was bad, and I knew it was my fault. I knew she wouldn't have been doing it if Alena hadn't been kidnapped.

"Ash," Bits says.

I don't look up at her or respond. I open and close my hands in my lap.

"They found Alena's body," she says flatly, and all at once I am floating above myself, hovering, weightless, and now I am crashing back into my chair with a thud that almost hurts my jaw. Here it is: the moment I've imagined for thirteen years, the moment when someone finally says to me, *That's it, it's over, it's irreversible.* There's no more imagining that Alena might be okay, that maybe the kidnapper and his wife couldn't have children, so they'd had to steal one, that maybe they'd loved Alena and cared for her better than my parents could have.

"She was buried at that park where we used to play Capture the Flag."

"Buried?"

"Yeah. Well. I guess that's not exactly the right word."

Not even a mile from home. All these years, Alena's been less than a mile from home. "What do you mean, 'buried'?"

"Hair and bones," Bits says, turning to face the opposite wall. "That's all they found. Or decayed bones. I don't know. A d—" She cuts herself off.

"What?"

"Nothing."

"Just say it."

"A dog dug her up," Bits says. "I mean, dug up her remains."

Remains. I stand.

"Do you hear me, Ash? You're hardly reacting. Do you get what I'm telling you?"

"I'm not an idiot," I say.

Of course I hear her. Loud and clear. She's saying, *You let someone kidnap and kill our sister, and now a dog has dug her up.* She came all the way out here to tell me that I was complicit in Alena's death. She's gloating. She's thinking, *Who are you to judge me, after what you've done?*

"You couldn't have called to tell me this?"

Bits turns away from the wall and narrows her eyes at me. "Are you serious?"

"Yeah, I'm serious," I say, but I know she's been trying to call.

"Don't even start," she says. "Jesus Christ."

There she goes again. Jesus Christ. Does she even know what she's saying? That some guy named Jesus was the Messiah? Our Messiah hasn't come yet! If Moshiach had come, we would all be in paradise.

"Mom wants to have a funeral," Bits says.

A funeral! In New Jersey? To what end? So we can all stand around and cry together and think about how I ruined everyone's lives? I'm not going to a funeral. Especially one at Temple Beth Shalom, my mother's Reform synagogue, where they wouldn't even do things properly. "I live here now," I tell Bits.

"I know that," she says. "You don't have to *move* to New Jersey. You just have to come for a little while."

I'm not going back there, into my past. My past is the long gray strip that sits on the horizon during a storm.

"I'm happy now," I say. I start backing toward the door. "I'm happy here. I'm not going."

"Don't leave!" Bits says. "How can you just leave?"

I open the door.

"The funeral's May seventh," she says. "At ten a.m. At Beth Shalom."

Beth Shalom. Where the men aren't even separated from the women.

"Feel better," I say.

"Ash!" Bits calls. "Don't walk out on me! You're being melo-dramatic! You're being like Mom."

I walk through the door and run down the hall. Through an-other door and out into the sunlight. I take a deep breath and release it from my lungs. This is my life. Israel is my life. God is my life. Not Bits. Not my mother. Alena is gone. We can't bring her back. Not with blame. Not with a funeral. Not with a family reunion.

I head back to Yeshiva Hillel.

David is not at lunch. His is the sort of absence that's noticeable, like a wall that's been knocked down. Normally, I would feel re-lieved, but not today. He's not in classes either. Or at dinner. I can't eat. Of course I can't. Bits is in Jerusalem. Bits is in the hospi-tal. Alena is dead. Alena is dead. Alena is hair and bones.

At dinnertime, I sit in the dining hall, pushing vegetables

around my plate, and the smell of food churns inside my stomach. I am here, but I'm not here. I am Asher, but today I feel like Ash. Nothing is as it should be. I remember Yosi, all those months ago, saying, "The spirit of Shabbat sustains you!" and how I trembled at his Shabbat table. What happened to the person I was then? I knew so much less, I believed things too readily, but I was so full of Shekhina, the Divine spirit, God was coming out of my ears.

Beside me, Todd sits happily, eating cucumber and tomato salad, dipping pita in baba ghanoush. I wasn't imagining it last night: he is more confident and content than I've ever seen him. It wouldn't shock me if he was gone by the end of the month. I'll have to get a new *chavrusa*. It might be someone who knows more than I do. Todd will write me letters once or twice a year because he's so nice, but not because he needs my friendship. I'm not the kind of person people need.

"Asher." Rabbi Berkstein is standing behind me.

I twist around to look up at him.

"Not hungry this evening?"

"Not really," I say.

He lays a hand on my shoulder. "Could I borrow you for a second?"

We go outside to the front steps and sit side by side. The sun is setting. Rabbi Berkstein chuckles and tips his head to the left. "You hear that?" He points up to the redwood tree. The bird, wearing a tight red cap of feathers, has a nondescript call. "I'm not sure I've ever seen a woodchat shrike in Jerusalem. That's a real treat, Asher. A sign maybe. Do you remember what we were talking about in class last week, about birds?"

Birds. Who can think about birds? I force myself to think about birds for a minute. "They used to use two birds for the purification process. For someone afflicted with *tzaraat*," I say. "Which may or may not have been leprosy."

Rabbi Berkstein nods. "And why would people get *tzaraat?*"

"For committing *lashan hara,*" I say. Suddenly, somehow, I know that he knows something. I clear my throat. When I speak again, my voice is smaller. "Or for forgetting God."

"Yes," Rabbi Berkstein says. "We are never to forget Who gave us life. That's why we must honor not only Hashem but also our parents. In fact, we must honor everyone. All Jews. We must be humble. There is no place for arrogance, for judgment . . . for anything negative, because it only means you haven't made room for Hashem."

I turn to look at his profile, the shadow of his black hat against his cheek like a curtain. He is separating himself from me. "Are you kicking me out or something?" I ask, and Rabbi Berkstein sighs and says nothing. "Why?" I'm afraid I'm going to cry. "You think my ego's gotten too big or something? Is that what you're saying? That I need to remember God? I remember God every second! I think about halacha so much, it paralyzes me sometimes."

Rabbi Berkstein pulls at the tip of his beard. "Asher, no one is above breaking God's laws. Unfortunately, everyone forgets Him sometimes. Now, listen. You are like me. Don't think I don't see that. I have a world of love for Ba'alei Tshuva, because I am one. I know how hard it is at first. For a while, many years ago, I was full of hate. Trying to embrace the Holy One, but full of hate. I hated everyone around me who wasn't *frum.* I would go into a rage in my own parents' kitchen because it wasn't kosher. I would throw away their *treyf* dishes. It wasn't right. They had been good parents."

"But they weren't religious," I say.

"They weren't religious because they didn't know the truth. They weren't free, like our people who stood at Sinai. They didn't get to see the miracles firsthand, like our forefathers did, so it was harder for them to come to believe. You and I are blessed, Asher, with a willingness to believe. Of course, I tried to convince them to read Torah, and learn. But who am I to tell my poor parents what the rules are? I'm just a little particle of dust compared with our great Father in Heaven. Look. Asher. I love my parents. I go to their house to visit. I bring my children. I don't eat in their kitchen, but I don't tell them they're wrong for eating in their kitchen. It's their kitchen! My father barbecues cheeseburgers!" He chuckles. "So he likes his cheeseburgers. *B'seder.* May he eat them in good health."

"*What?*" I hold my head in my hands.

"You can't lose sight of the forest for the trees," Rabbi Berkstein says. "We have to overlook cheeseburgers sometimes in order to concentrate on the bigger things. . . . Do you call your mother?"

"Do—? Yeah. Sure. Sometimes."

"Because parents worry, you know. Parents call me because their sons have returned to God and cast them aside. They call because they think we're stealing their children. That's not right that they should think that. Sons should call their parents. I tell these parents, 'Your son is safe and doing beautifully here,' and then I think to myself, 'I should be the one telling them this?'"

I close my eyes and see my mother, photocopying the picture of Alena with the missing front tooth. "Did my mother call you?" I ask.

"No. Should she have?"

"No," I say. "I just thought you were trying to tell me something."

"Look. I can talk to you like this, Asher, candidly, because I know that inside, you are committed. I have no fear that you will leave *frumkeit.* This you would never do."

"Of course I wouldn't."

"But you must understand that there are so many different ways to live."

"But only one right way."

"Okay. Asher, of course, I believe that our way is the right way. But we should feel a little sad for people who don't believe, instead of resenting them. *B'seder?* We need to be the best we can be, fulfill all six hundred thirteen mitzvahs if we can, but should we judge others? Should we become *zealous*? No. All zealousness indicates is that we're hiding things, squashing things down that we don't want others to see. That we ourselves don't want to see. It's meaningless, Asher, to show the world the face of a person who loves God, but then to secretly do things you know God would disapprove of. It should make you ask who you're performing for. For the world? Or for Hashem?"

"Everything I do is for Hashem," I say. "But what have I—"

"I've watched you take a bad turn, Asher. You are blessed with a great gift, you know. A strong mind. You have the capacity to retain more Torah than most people. When you first came here, you were excited and bright-eyed, and you drank everything in like a sponge. Then a dark cloud settled over you. You lost your sense of humor. You used to laugh all the time. You and Todd . . . you would learn together, and you would laugh. Both are important: learning and laughing. Together, you and Todd were ascending to great heights. But when was the last time you laughed?"

I wonder if this is about Todd. Does he know that Todd's leaving? Does he blame me? "I laugh," I mumble.

"You don't laugh."

I look at Rabbi Berkstein. Okay, maybe I don't laugh every second of the day, but really . . . what is there to laugh about? Some things are funny, I guess, but so many more things are incredibly serious. Learning in yeshiva is no joke. It's very intense, and I *like* it that way.

"You have become humorless," Rabbi Berkstein says. "How do you expect to serve Hashem with no joy in your heart? Like you said, you are paralyzed by halacha. Obsessed with the little things. You in the kitchen! A great *chacham* you are in the kitchen. 'Don't cut this on this cutting board. It is sharp and spicy, and for this meal, it will be fleishig.' I've heard you! You know it all! You're just like Asher from Torah. Do you know how Asher's father blessed him?"

I shake my head.

"On his death bed, Jacob said, 'From Asher shall come the richest foods; he shall provide the king's delights.'"

"Really?"

"Really. But what about laughing? You have a responsibility to laugh too. No one wants to see an unhappy Jew. What about honoring thy mother and thy father? Is that mitzvah less important to you than using the right cutting board?"

"My mother and father don't honor God," I say. "My mother . . . well . . . she . . . and my father . . . I barely even know my father. So it's hard for me. . . . I'm just doing my best," I say. "You don't see that?" I wind one of my *payos* around my finger, then release it. Then wind it again and release it. I wind it again so hard, it cuts off the circulation to my fingertip.

"This isn't easy for me, Asher." Rabbi Berkstein sighs and pats my knee, and I feel as though a rope is tightening around my stomach. Then Rabbi Berkstein suddenly shifts gears: "Do you know what used to happen to people when they were suspected of having *tzaraat*?"

"They were quarantined," I say, imagining myself in a cold stone cell, my leprous fingers wrapped around metal bars.

"Right," Rabbi Berkstein says. "They spent some time alone, tried to do some spiritual healing. There's nothing wrong with being alone for a while. Nothing wrong with thinking about things, questioning things, getting your priorities in order, as long as you're planning to return." He holds a hand out flat beside his ankle, then raises it to eye level. "Descend in order to ascend," he says.

"Miriam and everyone else who got *tzaraat* . . . they weren't lepers. Not the way we think of lepers. They were people in spiritual trouble. People who needed to slander everyone around them to make themselves feel better, because on their own, without comparing, they feel pretty bad. A very low point to reach, *tzaraat*."

"You think I'm a leper."

"Of course not, Asher. It's just an analogy." He sighs and steeples his fingers. "Not a very good one, maybe." He is quiet for a minute, then he points to the redwood tree. "I will tell you something about shrikes," he says, brightening.

Get to the point! I want to scream. *Spit it out!* But this is Rabbi Berkstein's way. He teaches like this in the classroom too.

"Shrikes are known as butcher birds," he says. "They impale their prey on a thorn or a twig or a barbed-wire spike. First, they stun their prey with their sharp beaks, then go in for the kill. And then *impale*." He punches his fist into his palm and I flinch. "But they are beautiful, aren't they?" Rabbi Berkstein says.

"I guess."

"Do you understand what I'm telling you? Things are never what they seem to be. That's why we have Torah. God tells us what is real and what is false. What is *truly* beautiful, and what only gives the appearance of beauty." He looks at me.

"I don't want false things," I say quickly. "I never did. Truth is so important," but I remember my secretiveness as a child, how I watched my mother cry for days, watched my father pace back and forth through the kitchen, and didn't tell them about the brown car.

"Asher, we are concerned about the magazines we found under your bed."

Magazines? The memory returns to me in a series of flashes: Monica dropping the stack onto my lap; the huge nipples on the glossy cover; "Bombs aren't usually anything fancy. Just nails and some explosive stuff"; my foot pushing the stack under my bed.

"Not just secular, Asher. Secular I could forgive. *Newsweek* I could forgive. But smut! In your yeshiva!" He sighs. "No," he corrects himself. "Even smut I could forgive. But the ones about bombs." His fingers work vigorously through his beard. "Asher, that is very, very serious."

I could blame Todd. It would be my word against his. He wants to leave anyway. Why should Todd get to stay another day if he's not committed? Why should I be forced to leave when I am here to serve God?

The wrought-iron gate opens. It's David, wearing the same clothes he was wearing last night, his white shirt wrinkled and half-untucked, his beard looking bushier than ever. Tomorrow is Lag B'Omer, I think irrelevantly. A break in the mourning period. David will be able to trim his beard. He has his tam tucked into his back pocket. Rabbi Berkstein doesn't seem to notice anything unusual as David makes his way toward us. He nods at Rabbi Berkstein, smirks a little at me, and goes inside. As usual, he doesn't look the least bit guilty, the least bit nervous. Of course, that's the trick to things: you can get away with murder if you never succumb to guilt.

"Did David tell you to search my room?" I ask, once the door has closed.

"Did David . . . ? Asher, do you know what these two fingers are for?" Rabbi Berkstein holds up his index fingers. "They're for sticking in your ears if you hear someone speak *lashon hara.*" He demonstrates, then drops his hands into his lap. "David speaking negatively about you I wouldn't listen to," he says, but he's not looking at me. "You know we do random searches," he says after a minute. "This isn't news."

All I'd have to do is say it: they're Todd's magazines. Rabbi Berkstein might stick his fingers in his ears, but he would hear me; that's all that matters. He would hear me and I could stay at Yeshiva Hillel. In an hour or so, we're going to count the thirty-third day, which is four weeks and five days of the Omer, the day to take pleasure in fulfilling obligations, and how am I supposed to fulfill my obligations if I'm expelled from my yeshiva?

"They're Todd's magazines."

For a second, I don't realize I've spoken the words aloud. I swear I never felt my lips move.

"I would never, ever have told you that, under different circumstances," I say. "But I don't want to get suspended for something I didn't do."

Rabbi Berkstein sighs. "This isn't a suspension, Asher. Try not to see it that way. At least, it's not a *formal* suspension. Asher, you've been slipping into a deep hole. I see you grappling. You—"

"They're not mine!" I stand up. But when Rabbi Berkstein stays seated, I sit back down, on a lower step. I don't want to be disrespectful; Rabbi Berkstein is a great scholar. "They're not mine," I say again. "I understand everything else you're telling me. I've lost sight of the forest for the trees. Yes. I agree with you. And I want to fix that. But please don't blame me for something I didn't do." I'm starting to feel very sorry for myself. I forget for a second that I really am the perpetrator, that I am being the worst kind of person. My eyes blur up. I swallow hard. I am, of course, giving myself yet another cause for guilt.

IT'S HARD TO imagine my Alena at nineteen. She was the tiniest of all three of my newborns, barely five pounds, covered in black hair like a baby monkey. At age six, she was still tiny, in the twenty-fifth percentile for both height and weight. I still think I see her sometimes. A flash of shiny black hair, a young girl with a sparkly wand, a teenager on roller skates. It will be one second, maybe two, and my heart will leap up like a cobra because God knows I would give anything . . . anything in all the world just to touch her one more time. My skin still aches for her, late at night, as if the shell of me might crack.

I wonder sometimes if Alena was my favorite, or if I just remember her that way because she's gone. Viv says it's not right to rank your children like beauty pageant contestants, but I think it's natural. Alena was the best at showing me her love. Even as a baby, she would snuggle into my neck, sleep peacefully in my arms, whereas all Bits ever did was squirm like a trapped animal, and all Ash ever did was scream, toothless and miserable. Even now, I can't think of the last time Bits or Ash hugged me without stiffness, without patting me between the shoulder blades and saying, "Okay, Mom." Especially Bits. I wonder if she's that cold with men.

If Alena were still here, she would race through my front door, borrow my jewelry, tell me her secrets. She would let me braid her hair. She would be a Broadway actress or a contestant on one of those talent search programs. She would have a loud laugh like my mother's. She would be all grand gestures and splayed fingers, her head thrown back in constant song.

I love all my children. Of course I do. So is it so wrong to fantasize, to imagine? Don't I deserve one little fantasy after all I've been through? Enough with the guilt. I'm drowning in it. But when it keeps me awake at night, I remember Alena, that five-pound bundle in my arms. And then I remember that I'm doing the right thing, that I need to get Ash home at any cost, that I'm doing what I'm doing because I know what can happen: a mother can lose a child if she doesn't keep him close.

A s soon as we walk back inside, Rabbi Berkstein asks Todd, "Can I borrow you for a second?" and leads him out to the front steps.

So what do *I* do? Slip right out the back through the courtyard. I can't face what I know will come if I stay. Of course, once Rabbi Berkstein sees that I've left, he'll know I lied. But his knowing, after I'm already gone, is more palatable than the thought of Todd and him approaching me in the dining hall, Todd pushing on his hearing aid, his freckled eyes wide and confused; more palatable than hearing Rabbi Berkstein say, "Okay, Asher. I think we have a problem here." I could stay here and lie about those magazines forever, deny everything until my dying day, and maybe, *maybe* even get away with it, but the thought of that . . . all that lying, just makes me want to go to sleep.

I bring nothing with me because there isn't time. I don't look back. I don't even care about the framed pictures in my room, about my clothes, about saying good-bye . . . who would I say good-bye to? Todd? Rabbi Berkstein?

For no particular reason, I walk all the way downtown to Ben Yehuda Street, one of the most touristy spots in Jerusalem, a pedestrian mall crowded with shops and cafés. The sun sinks lower and lower, making way for night. I pass a store that sells Ahava Dead Sea products, and I think of my mother, standing at the kitchen sink, massaging Ahava lotion into her hands. Maybe I'll buy her some later, if I can figure out a way to get some money. I can send it to her, get it there in time for the funeral. Then she'll think that I wanted to be there, that I would be there if I could. She'll understand that Israel is just too far from New Jersey, that I can't just hop on a plane and fly there at the drop of a hat. I sit down at an outdoor table beneath a green-and-white-striped umbrella. No. My mother *won't* understand. She won't accept lotion in place of my presence.

Do people look at me and know? Can they see what kind of person I am? I think of the people afflicted with *tzaraat*, who used to have to walk around shouting, "Unclean! Unclean!" so no one would make the mistake of going near them. I wipe my sweaty palms on my pants.

Night has fallen and I still haven't eaten. It's like Yom Kippur, the Day of Atonement, the day we chant, *Who by water, and who by fire; who by sword, and who by beast . . .* the day we don't eat so we can be like the angels.

"It's a mitzvah!" I hear someone yell. "A beautiful mitzvah!"

I turn toward the sound of the voice. A small group of Hasids stands around a big wooden block beneath a green umbrella in the middle of the pedestrian mall, mere yards from where I'm sitting. A boom box sits on the block, playing Yiddish music: "Ay-ya-ya-ya-yai, ay-ya-ya-ya-yai, ai-b'dai-dai-dai-dai-ya-ya-yai." A sign nailed to the front of the block reads, in big red letters, IT'S NOT TOO LATE. The Hasids are helping men—tourists mostly, it seems—to lay tefillin.

In fact, it *is* too late. You're supposed to pray *shacharit*, morning prayers, within the first third of the day. If you miss the first third, you're supposed to aim for the first half. If you miss the first half, then forget it. Move on! Pray *mincha* twice. Pray *ma'ariv*, evening prayers. But these people are laying tefillin like the sun has just risen. The men gathered around the Hasids are beardless; they wear shorts and T-shirts and cameras around their necks, and they smile embarrassed but happy smiles, as they allow themselves to be wrapped in prayer shawls, as they hold out one arm stiffly and, at a Hasid's instructions, lay tefillin.

"A beautiful mitzvah!" one Hasid exclaims again. He grabs a tourist by the shoulders and plants a giant kiss on his cheek.

Maybe *this,* not the woodchat shrike, is a sign. Maybe God is offering me a private means of purification. *It's all right*, He's telling me, *you can start the day over. Forget what happened at the Kotel.* It's such an amazing thing, really, that I'm having this opportunity on the one day I neglected to complete my morning prayers. Of course this is a sign. God is reminding me that this day, one of the worst days of my life, could still turn around if I do my morning prayers properly. I can make up for using my tefillin to attack a fellow Jew.

Gratitude makes my chest ache. I stand on legs weak from hunger and feel so dizzy, I almost collapse. I press my fingertips to the tabletop, wait for my vision to clear, then walk to the wooden block. God forgives. Isn't this proof? I want to fling my arms open and make my presence known. *Hineini!* I want to cry. *Here I am!* Abraham's response when God commanded him to spare Isaac. Moses' response when God addressed him from the burning bush. Instead, I open my mouth and what comes out is a voice I hardly recognize—a timid, exhausted, dehydrated-sounding voice. "May I lay tefillin?" I ask.

The man who puts his arm around my shoulders has a long gray beard like a storm cloud, a tall black hat, a dark coat tied at the waist. He hands me a coin and points toward a wooden *tzedaka* box. I drop the coin into the slot. The man wraps me in a prayer shawl and I let him walk me through the steps, even though I've been laying tefillin every morning since I met Yosi a year and a half ago; even though there are millions of people around and I must appear to them, humiliatingly, despite my *payos* and tzitzit, like an amateur Jew; even though the last place on earth I should be is on Ben Yehuda Street. I should be gone by now, to Haifa, to Tzevat, somewhere far, far away from Yeshiva Hillel.

But I want my new beginning. The Hasid helps me lay the *shel yad* two fist-widths from the shoulder blade of my opposite arm, lining the little cube up so it faces my heart. He helps me carefully wind the strap around in a perfect black spiral, first three times around my middle finger, then seven times around my forearm. Together, we recite the two blessings before affixing the *shel rosh* to my forehead and reciting the next blessing.

I concentrate as hard as I can on the feeling of the leather against my arm, on every bend of the knee, but the strap begins to transform before my eyes. It is the serpent from Eden, winding around its branch. The words I whisper start to hiss in my head; there is a lightness to things that makes my feet float, makes my knees tremble, makes my hands clammy. Sand closes in from the outer corners of my eyes, and I feel the sensation of dropping, like a bird that doesn't know its wings are clipped, and the sky makes a tight hood around my head, the air turns hot, and the ground rushes up and smacks my face.

I AM DIAGNOSED WITH a bump on the head. "It must be a concussion," I say, "at least."

The doctor says, "*No* concussion, Miss Kellerman."

I ask if there's any chance I have head trauma, amnesia, encephalitis.

"Encephalitis? From a bump on the head?"

"I was out cold all day," I remind him.

"Because of sedatives!" says the doctor. "We have let you rest all day. Now it is night. We have other patients. Go! We'll send you the bill."

"Oh, good," I say. "A bill."

So that's the end of my Hadassah Hospital stay. They turn me loose in Jerusalem. It's not that I wanted to stay at the hospital; I just wanted validation. I wanted someone to acknowledge the severity of my attack, to press charges against my assailants. I wanted someone to stick up for me.

I hail a cab to my hostel. I can tell the cab driver's an Arab; his music conjures images of belly dancers. I wonder if it's advisable to ride in Arab cabs. I know what my mother would say: *They're an enemy of our people, the Arabs. What do you want with their cabs?*

In the rearview mirror, the man's eyes are black as Turkish coffee. I lean forward. "Where's Bethlehem?" I ask. I'm thinking of the hostages in the Church of the Nativity. I'm wondering which is worse: being closed in or being closed out.

The cab driver points vaguely and says something I can't understand. He has a long fingernail on his pinky, an eighties-rock-star coke-snorting nail. He makes a *tsk-tsk* sound with his tongue and wags a finger at me. "You cannot go," he says, eyeing me in the rearview mirror.

I never even considered going, but I'm sick of being told I can't go places. "Sure I can," I say. "I'm a journalist."

For a minute, he doesn't answer, and I think he didn't understand me, but then he says, "My sister, she is in Bethlehem."

I lean forward in my seat.

"They have curfew," he says. "No one leaves their houses. The Israeli army does not let them leave. Three times the army comes to my sister's house." He holds up three fingers. "Three times, late in the night, my sister says, 'Welcome,' and they come in and they tear her papers and ruin her home."

"Maybe they think she's a terrorist?"

The cab driver clucks his tongue again. "My sister, she has three babies. She is not a problem to the army."

Maybe that's true and maybe it isn't. Maybe his sister would willingly blow herself up inside Ash's yeshiva. Who knows? My cab driver might be my enemy. But I wish I could tell him that I know what it's like when a sibling becomes inaccessible.

When he pulls over to let me out at my hostel, he scribbles something on a piece of scratch paper. "You are a journalist," he says. He hands me the slip of paper. "This is my sister's name, this is her address. Go to her house," he says. "I want the USA and all the world to see what has happened to my sister."

I tuck the piece of paper inside my purse.

Once he pulls away, I don't know where to go. The very idea of the hostel—the unlikely curry odor, Star and Greta smoking European cigarettes and playing endless card games in the lobby, the TV behind the front desk that blares Al Jazeera day and night—is unappealing. And I can't go back to Yeshiva Hillel. Now that Ash knows I'm in town, he'll be actively avoiding me. Besides, I told him what I needed to tell him. What more can I do at this point?

So I start wandering. Maybe I'll stumble across some sights: tombs of prophets, the Garden of Eden. Instead, I find myself going in and out of neighborhoods, some with graffiti on the walls and laundry swaying on clotheslines, others with well-groomed front lawns and tall fences. And children everywhere. Even though it's after dark, the streets of Jerusalem are teeming with children. I wonder if Ash will raise children here. I wonder if I'll know them.

I'm walking on a street called Hebron Road. In the distance, I see a roadblock, like the kind from the news—a row of stone barriers. I like seeing television come to life, like the time I saw Paul from *The Wonder Years* in an airport. I walk alongside a long line of cars; the drivers lean on their horns, creating a steady blare. I ask a man who has his window open what stands beyond the checkpoint.

"This?" he says, pointing into the distance. "This is Bethlehem."

Bethlehem. I knew that Bethlehem was close to Jerusalem, but I didn't know that the two cities touched each other, joined like estranged Siamese twins. On the other side of the roadblock, hostages huddle inside a church, waiting for things to change. I keep walking alongside the cars, past broken barbed-wire fences and the piles of garbage that lie beyond those fences, past olive trees and a couple of lone donkeys. I'm sure I'm being stupid. It can't be smart for an unarmed American girl who speaks no Hebrew and has a bump on her head to walk toward the barrier between Jerusalem and Bethlehem. But I keep walking, wondering if I'd be allowed to cross over without my passport. All I have in my purse are some shekels, a map of Jerusalem I bought from a child in the Arab market yesterday that I quickly deemed inaccurate, my lip gloss, and the name and address of my cab driver's sister.

As I get closer to the roadblock, I see a commotion. Israeli soldiers in helmets are holding two flailing men. A soldier puts one of the men in flex cuffs, and pushes him to the ground. Another soldier aims a rifle at the back of the man's Coca-Cola T-shirt, right at the words, "Give your thirst a kick." Two other soldiers yell and gesture at the trunk of a beat-up car, then gesture to all the drivers to back up. Limbs and guns swing. Horns continue to blare. And I realize that no one is looking at me.

So why not cross over into Bethlehem? Why not find my cab driver's sister and her family and smuggle them out of the chaos? I'll say I'm a journalist. I'll bring them to Jerusalem. They wouldn't hurt Ash; they would feel indebted to me. Why shouldn't I be able to make one successful rescue, to reunite a family?

I walk right through the barrier and keep walking. No one stops me. I walk past a hill flecked with sheep. A few of them watch me as the shouting and the horns fade behind me, as I venture into a new place, ready to make myself useful.

But suddenly a hand grabs my wrist and a gruff voice is yelling in my ear.

"Okay," I say. "Okay, I give up."

I can practically see that mother, those three babies, reaching out to me, their last hope. But of course, they never hoped for me. I was the one hoping. I close my eyes and go limp. Christmas carols—"O Little Town of Bethlehem," "A Fire Is Started in Bethlehem"—that I hear in the mall every winter swim through my head. The soldier keeps yelling at me, words I don't understand, and turns me around. Turns me back toward Jerusalem, where he thinks I belong.

Because I don't know what to say, I blurt, "I just wanted to see where Jesus was born."

I don't tell him that Jesus' family and mine are the same: an elusive father, a broken mother, and a murdered child, who left in the family a horrible space that no other child could fill.

"EAT, EAT," SAYS the man with the storm-cloud beard. He is crouched above me, his beard tickling my chin and lips. I'm lying flat on my back on the ground, my head resting on a pillow of some sort. A shirt, maybe? The man is stuffing pita bread into my mouth. "Now drink," he says. The glitter of concern in his eyes and the worried V bisecting his eyebrows alarm me.

My mouth is full of bread. I chew and swallow and take the plastic cup of water from his hands. He helps me sit up, and as I drink, pain shoots through my head in a quick streak, appears before my eyes in neon colors, moves from the top of my skull down my neck. I've drawn an audience. I'm surrounded by sneakers and sandals, hairy ankles, shiny black shoes.

"Do you need an ambulance?" someone asks.

"No!" I say without looking up. I imagine an ambulance rushing me to Hadassah Hospital. I imagine riding on a stretcher past Bits's hospital room. "I just hadn't eaten," I say. "But now I'm eating."

"You hit pretty hard."

"I feel fine." My voice sounds clogged and gravelly.

"Keep eating," says the Hasid. "Keep drinking."

I set the plastic cup on the ground, feeling the bread and water expand in my gut as I rest my forehead on my knees. I am no longer like the angels.

But then I hear an angel's voice. It says my name: "Asher."

The voice is shimmering, rippling—a sunset reflected on a lake. When I look up, I expect to see wings. A white gown. A floating halo.

But instead, I see Monica.

She is standing above me in her gold dress, her arms crossed. Her hair is piled up on top of her head, except for a few loose strands wisping down the sides of her face. She smiles the saddest smile I've ever seen and kneels beside me. She grazes my cheek with the backs of her knuckles, then pulls away before I can remind her not to touch me.

The Hasids lose interest and disperse. I hear one of them tell a tourist, "It's not too late."

"Oh my God, Asher," Monica says. "What *happened* to you?"

For a second, I think she can tell, somehow, that I just heard the news about Alena, that I just had to leave my yeshiva. But, of course, she's referring to the cuts on my face. I reach up and feel the side of my forehead. When I look at my finger, I see a speck of blood.

"I fell," I say. My voice sounds thick. I try again: "I had a fall." I squint at Monica. "How did you find me here?"

"David told me you took off. You caused a shit storm at your yeshiva, you know."

"I didn't just . . . take off. . . ."

Why was she speaking with David?

"I've been wandering around looking for you. I thought you'd probably come downtown. . . . Hey," Monica says. "I have a car. Um, Asher? Look at me. You're kind of freaking me out. Are you okay? You look . . . crazed or something. Like you're in a trance. Like you've snapped."

I look at her. She looks older than she did last night, more grown-up somehow. Maybe it's that she looks worried; I probably look a whole lot worse than I feel. Physically, I feel okay. Warm and tingly and numb. I want to ask Monica: Did you spend the night with David? And why? *Why?* I want to ask: Are *you* crazy? Are you a liar? Did you really run away from the religious life? I want to remind her that I want nothing to do with her, that I have better things.

"A car?" I hear myself say.

Monica smiles. "Yes. I rented a car! As soon as David told me what had happened, I was like, 'Asher's going to need to get out of town.' Was I right? Let's go somewhere cool. Let's drive to Eilat and cross over into Egypt. We can go to the Sinai. We can go scuba diving."

"Scuba diving?" I glance at the Hasids and the tourists. No one's looking at us.

"Or snorkeling, if you don't want to go that deep. So you'll come? Asher, you'll never have a better time in your entire life. One time, I went scuba diving in California, and I practically got eaten by a shark. It was the biggest thing I'd ever seen, but inside, I was bigger than it."

I stand up and rub the back of my neck.

"We can go to the base of Mount Sinai. We can build a golden calf if you want! Out of . . . I don't know . . . newspaper. It won't be gold, of course, but so what? It'll be a modern-day version. We can do a reenactment of the giving of the Ten Commandments. I'm a really good actress. I'll be God."

I smell her coconut smell. Her eyes are sparkling. I follow her.

"Maybe we can live there," Monica says.

"Where?"

"Wherever we wind up. That's why I rented a car. I want to travel around and then live somewhere."

"I want to live somewhere too," I say. I feel dizzy. I double over and rest my hands on my thighs.

"Really? So you like the idea of Sinai, or at least Eilat?"

I don't answer her, but I do like the sound of it. I like the sound of having somewhere to go. I like the sound of not going home to Alena's funeral, of not standing in a Reform synagogue with my mother and Bits while they sob over a pile of hair and bones that has nothing to do with who Alena was.

"We could go to the beach every day of our lives," Monica says. "Except for Saturdays, if you're still"—she waves a hand in the air—"into all that. We can stay in on Saturdays and you can study. And pray."

"All right," I say, straightening up again. "We'll see."

"We will? Asher, I can't believe I found you. I mean, I can't believe we found each other. It's like, *finally*. You know what I mean? It's like coming home."

But it's not really like coming home at all, is it, to go back to Egypt. The Israelites went first to Mount Sinai, and then to Israel. Is it okay to go from Israel back to Mount Sinai?

But for the first time, I look—really look—into Monica's eyes, and I see something there that I've never seen before: she needs me. I don't know why she needs me, but her need is clear, almost tangible. So I keep following her. Unlike my father, I'll go where I'm needed. Of course, I'll return to Jerusalem eventually. Just like Rabbi Berkstein said, it's okay to descend in order to ascend.

Monica is skipping and twirling like a child. The Yiddish music fades out behind us. My head aches, but it's manageable; I have a sense now that things are falling into place, like rain into a river. I have direction like my forefathers had direction, three thousand three hundred fourteen years ago.

April 30, 2002

At Ben-Gurion Airport, I buy an international calling card and call Wade. It's five in the morning in Boston.

"Who is this?" Wade's voice is hoarse and sleepy-sounding.

"It's Bits," I say, insulted.

"Bits?" He sounds like the Godfather. "What the hell?"

"Um." I look around. Orthodox men are pushing babies in strollers or wheeling suitcases behind them. An American woman is screaming at her husband. "Look," I say, turning to face the box of the pay phone. I run my fingers up and down the bendy metal cord. "I have to tell you something."

I hear him peeing. "Maybe I don't want to hear what you have to say."

"I'll be quick," I say. "Okay. Here it is. . . . I did steal your money."

Wade says nothing.

"I'm sorry," I tell him. "That was a fucked-up thing to do." I close my eyes and lean my forehead right above the metal buttons.

I hear Wade's toilet flush. "I don't forgive you," he says.

"Okay," I say, sighing. "But can you stop talking shit about me to everyone at work?"

"You're crazy."

"Well," I say. "I can understand your feelings."

The line goes dead. I wait to make sure. Yup. Dead.

Next I call my mother.

"Where are you?" she asks, yawning.

I look around again. I'm in a foreign country. I'm halfway around the world. I'm right back where I started. "Ben-Gurion Airport," I say. "In Israel. . . . I saw Ash."

"You what?!"

"I thought I could get him to come home and—"

"He *is* coming home! He's coming for the funeral. You promised."

"No," I say. I push my fingers through my hair, getting stuck in the tangles. "He's not. I thought I could get him to, but I couldn't. He's not coming. He doesn't want to come."

"Doesn't *want* to?" she shrieks. "What is *wrong* with him? And you! You sneak off to Israel without telling anyone. You fly all the way out there and you can't even get your brother to come home for his own sister's funeral?"

"I have to hang up now," I say. "I have to get on the plane."

"You wake me up for *this*?" She's weeping.

"I'll call you when I get back, okay?"

I clench my teeth. I don't want to hate my mother. I try to remember times when she hasn't been self-pitying, self-absorbed. She is also a good person. She never would have left us like our father did. She worked and took care of us and fed us and clothed us. Sometimes, on Saturdays, she did projects with us: rock candy, leaf-rubbings, yard sales in the living room with Skittles for currency. At my request, she painted my fingernails black for my senior prom. When I played every note wrong during my third-grade recorder recital, she gushed afterward about how perfect I'd been—gushed so effusively, I believed her.

"You don't know what it's like to lose a child," she weeps. "It's the worst thing that could happen to a mother."

I sigh. I wonder if she knows how odd it sounds, her saying that to me, as if I'm a stranger. "Go back to sleep," I say. "I have to catch my plane. Can you go back to sleep?"

"Okay," she says. "Maybe I can."

I hang up, hoist my bag over my shoulder, and head for my gate, wondering about families, about the roles people play. Who assigns them, and when? Who made Alena the strand, holding the beads of us together? Who made Ash the enigma, my mother the victim? Who gave my father permission to discard us? Of course, there is no choreographer, no single defining moment, no cast list stuck to the fridge with an alphabet magnet. It's every single thing that happens to a family, the composite of experiences, that dictates how everyone treats one another.

I WAKE UP BECAUSE someone is shaking me. I open my eyes and everything hurts. Monica's voice: "You sleep like the dead. Come on, Asher. Get up." The world is blurry and throbbing. I am in a car. Monica is standing outside of it, leaning into my open window. "Wake up," she says. She's grinning. "I got us a room."

I try to lift my head, but it's so heavy. I reach up to touch my fore-head and find it rough with scabs and damp with sweat. "A room?"

"We're in Eilat. In the parking lot of a youth hostel."

"We're . . ."

"We'll cross over into Egypt tomorrow morning," she says. "We could do it now, but you're not exactly being helpful." She demonstrates an exaggerated snore. Then she ducks out of the window and spins around in the middle of the empty parking lot with her arms flung open. "Isn't this amazing?" she shrieks. "We're out of Jerusalem. I did it!"

Did it? Did *what*?

"I don't have any money," I say, although what I mean is, *I don't have anything.* I unbuckle my seat belt. Even my fingers are stiff and aching.

Monica finishes spinning and opens my door. "I have enough money for a week or so. We'll get jobs," she says. "Whatever. We'll live off the land!"

How does she plan to live off the land? Will we fish in the sea? Eat plants and bugs? This is all wrong. I should not sleep tonight behind a closed door with a woman. I should not be in Eilat, the secular south of Israel, where I've heard some restaurants even have shrimp on the menu. But I'm too tired to argue with a person who is making decisions for me. I step out of the car. The air is hotter than the air in Jerusalem. I can smell the sea.

"Tomorrow we can go to the beach," Monica says. "Well, first, we'll cross the border. Then we'll sit on the beach all day in Sinai. We can swim or whatever."

Doesn't she know that it's immodest for men and women to swim together? I don't even own swim trunks anymore. She's already walking ahead of me, lugging a giant maroon duffel bag that she extracted from the trunk of the rental car. "Monica," I call after her. "I have to ask you something."

"Ask me later," she says. "Asher. Stop *thinking* so much, will you?"

Stop thinking? That's her advice for me? Thinking keeps people out of trouble. If you don't use your head, you wind up following your heart, which isn't much better than what my college roommate used to accuse me of doing with Vanessa: *You're following your dick, Ash.* What does Monica know about what's good for me? Still, I follow her into a seedy-looking hostel, up a flight of stairs, and into a candle-lit common room, where five travelers lounge on couches. One guy is playing the guitar, Bob Dylan, and the other people are singing. The guitar player is wearing tzitzit, and the kind of *kipa* I used to wear in Boulder when I hung out with the Zeff guys: sort of fez-like, with multicolored embroidery. I want a bed. I want to sleep. I don't feel like hanging out with a bunch of singing strangers in the middle of the night. But Monica drops her duffel bag on the floor and straddles it.

I sit on the worn arm of the couch above her and try not to

look as out of place as I feel. I remember getting stuck at similar get-togethers in Boulder, usually in someone's dorm room, where a joint would make its way around a circle and everyone except me seemed to know the unspoken etiquette of pot-smoking. One awful time, my across-the-hall neighbor clapped me on the shoulder and said, loud enough for everyone to hear, "Dude, you're totally following the joint around the circle with your eyes. You'll get a hit. Just chill." Then he did an impersonation of me, eyes wide, tongue hanging out of his mouth, making everyone burst into hysterical stoned laughter.

"Asher?"

I look down at Monica and see a glimmer of amazement in her eyes.

"Do you *know* this song?" she asks.

The travelers are singing at the tops of their lungs. "You don't?"

"How do they all know it?" she whispers.

"'Like a Rolling Stone,'" I say. "You don't know this song? Really? I didn't know it was possible to not know this song." For a second, I feel a power shift, like I'm in charge, like I'm the one taking care of things, like I'm the person who understands things without having them explained to me and Monica is the type who would embarrass herself at a party. But then the guy playing the guitar shakes his hair out of his eyes and smiles at Monica, and I remember that Monica is beautiful, the kind of beautiful that makes her ignorance of pop culture endearing, not embarrassing.

It's clear that this guy is unfazed by the possibility that she could be my girlfriend. "You want to try playing?" he asks in stilted English. He has sharp black eyes and no chin, like a rat.

Monica giggles. The guy winks at her.

I stand quickly and feel around on top of my head. My *kipa* is gone. I must have lost it when I fell. I feel naked without it, as if it had been covering a gaping bald spot. I squat behind Monica. "Monica," I whisper into her ear. "I need to know something."

She is nodding her head in time to the music.

"Why did you leave *frumkeit*?" I ask.

She glances back at me and grins. "You are so *uptight*," she says.

"I know you've been lying to me," I hiss. "I know you don't go to Hebrew U. I know you left your seminary. What, you thought David wouldn't tell me?"

She yawns. "I assumed he'd probably tell you." She's responding to my whispers in a regular voice. "Honestly, I didn't care one way or the other."

"What do you do, crash on people's couches?"

She giggles.

"David told me your parents aren't even dead," I say.

"What difference does it make?"

"What *difference*?" I am struck momentarily speechless. It makes no difference that her parents are alive? Doesn't she understand how different her life would be if they weren't? What *difference*? "The truth makes all the difference!" I say.

Monica swivels around to look me in the eye, a half-smile on her face. "What do you know about truth?"

"What's that supposed to mean?"

"I told you what you wanted to hear."

"Right. Like I wanted you to lie to me."

"You sure about that? What if you'd known that I *wasn't* an ignorant outsider? I mean, if you'd known that I used to be *frum*—"

"*What*? What are you—"

"Forget it." Monica laughs. "I wanted to help you. But maybe you're a lost cause."

"I'm serious," I say. "Why did you leave *frumkeit*?" I'm barely breathing as I wait for her answer. I need to know why a person who has everything—a religious family, a religious upbringing, the opportunity to study in Israel—would give it all up. "Why did you run away?" I ask, my voice rising.

"Why did you run away from college? Do you know how many people in the world would kill to go to college?"

"That's different!"

The other travelers glance at us, feigning indifference. I can't tell how much they can hear, how much the singing is drowning out. Who cares anyway?

"I don't know, Asher," Monica says. She sounds distracted, annoyed. "Why did I run away? 'Cause I felt like it. 'Cause I didn't believe in it. Why does anyone leave anything?" She leans forward on her duffel bag toward the people on the opposite couch. "The real question is, why are you embracing it? You don't even really understand it. You understand certain pieces, but you haven't been part of it long enough to see the big picture. I know that Asher isn't even your real name. Not that I'm one to talk. I changed my name too. But Asher is the dumbest name in the world. Do you even know who Asher was? The biblical Asher? His mother was a whore. He sold his own brother into slavery. That's the name you chose for yourself."

I can see her spine through the back of her gold dress. I have to remind myself to exhale.

"Look. I left because I'm strong," Monica says. "I wanted a different life so I went out and started living it. You, on the other hand . . . you think you're so religious, but your life now is no different from your old life. Look!" She presses her hands to her chest. "You ran off with the first girl you thought you had a shot with. But you have to feel guilty for being with me. What a drag. You've imposed restrictions on yourself, because depriving yourself—dominating your own desires—makes you feel strong."

"Did you read that in a self-help book or something?"

"Being *frum* doesn't make you strong," she says, ignoring my question. "Living in Israel doesn't make you strong."

I stand up. "Which one's our"—I look down at Monica—"my room?"

She tosses the key up to me. I catch it. "It's room number nine. Hey. Did I ever tell you that my grandpa's one of the greatest *gematria* scholars ever? You know, all that mysticism stuff with numbers? He's, like, the world expert. Madonna thinks *gematria*'s cool. It's not cool. You might have a lot in common with Madonna, Asher. Anyway, the Hebrew word for *banished* has a numeric value of nine. *Banished. Exiled.* Oh, and P.S.? As long as we're talking numbers?" She stands up and says in my ear, "The number of Ba'alei Tshuva in the world equals the number of people who leave *frumkeit*. It's not like Orthodox Judaism is growing. It will always remain static. Which I guess is its appeal. You guys are all afraid of change. You want to live like the Jews in the ghetto lived. Like *that's* rational. Call me crazy, but I *enjoy* moving forward? I *like* progress?"

"You're wrong," I say. "And you're stereotyping. If you were ever religious, you should know better."

"Don't you want to be stereotyped? Don't you want to be like everyone else in your 'community'?"

"We *are* growing," I say. "We're getting stronger and stronger. . . . We're always getting stronger."

"Nope," Monica says. "You and I cancel each other out." She draws a big invisible X over my body, sits back down, and won't look at me. She's watching the European guy with the guitar and the tzitzit. And it's suddenly, horribly clear to me that *I* could be that guy, or he could be me, or he could be David, or David could be me, or whatever; it wouldn't matter. I thought that Monica chose me, that she only latched onto David last night to make me jealous. But I see that that's not it. That's not it at all. Candlelight flickers. Shadows grasp at Monica's hair, at her bare right arm.

"This is a mess," I say, but my voice is silenced by the singing.

I go back down the flight of stairs. Room nine has two sets of bunk beds and smells like cat urine. I climb up to the top of one bunk and lie down, feeling my head throb against the pillow, sensing headlights streaking past the window every few minutes. As I drift in and out of sleep that can barely be called sleep, I listen, for what must be hours, to the singing voices from the common room. They keep going back to "Like a Rolling Stone": "How does it feel . . . to be on your own . . . with no direction home?" The appropriateness of the lyrics is so glaringly obvious, it's humiliating. I cover my head with a pillow, but I can't block out the sound. After a short while, I even hear Monica join in. And I hear her laughter. And I remember the Halloween my father dressed me up like Bob Dylan, complete with a big curly wig. He dressed Bits like Joan Baez, and Alena like Janis Joplin, and the three of us had no idea who we were supposed to be. Our father tried to teach us lyrics: "Freedom's just another word for nothing left to lose" and "I met a young girl, she gave me a rainbow." He kept saying to our mother, "It's just like Woodstock, isn't it?" He even gave Alena an empty bottle of Southern Comfort, but then my mother screamed at him, "What are you, crazy?" and took it away.

Before our mother took us trick-or-treating, the three of us held hands in the warm light of the kitchen, Alena in the middle, so our father could take pictures. Our mother flitted around us, hiding our costumes under winter hats and scarves and heavy coats. Of course, Halloween is a pagan holiday. But I can't help feeling homesick for a place I can't return to.

April 30, 2002

AFTER THE HELLISHLY long flight, the three-hour lay-over, the endless customs line at Logan Airport, and the cab ride home, I walk into my apartment and am immediately knocked over by a wave of nausea. I suppose I'm sick at the thought of returning to the Auburn School, where everyone hates me or about having once again lost my brother, having lost him this time despite my efforts, or about having no family that wants anything to do with me, unless you count my mother or my third cousin Henry, who hits on me at bar mitzvahs.

I barely make it to the toilet before I start vomiting uncontrollably. My skin prickles, my eyes tear and blur, my face feels cold with sweat. I wonder about the *shawarma* I bought at Ben-Gurion Airport. But after a few minutes, I know it's not the *shawarma*. How could I have been so stupid? I missed my last period and blamed it on stress. This was before I found out about Alena. Before Israel. What kind of stress did I think I was under?

I'm puking my guts out, in no mood for anyone in the world, but I crawl to the kitchen for the cordless phone. The worst part about having no real friends is that when I need a friend, I'm forced to resort to Maggie.

"You have to come over," I say, even though it's late, "and bring a pregnancy test."

I hang up, run back to the bathroom, and wait there, hot and cold and sweating and drooling, until Maggie shows up in her pajamas, her blond hair piled on top of her head in a knot. Yawning, she hands me a white plastic drugstore bag. "I don't think you're pregnant," she says. "I think you're still hysterical about Wade. Your stomach is very close to your heart. That's why heartbreak is nauseating."

Maggie leaves the bathroom while I pee on the little stick. I set it on the edge of the sink and collapse to the floor again, draping my arms over the toilet seat.

Maggie cracks the door. "Bits? This is love. Believe me, I know it when I see it. Just call him and say, 'Wade, I'm *sick* thinking about you.' "

"Count with me," I say. "Backward from a hundred twenty."

Maggie comes into the bathroom and sits beside me on the floor. "Who would have gotten you pregnant?"

I rest my check on the toilet seat and look at Maggie. "That's just it," I say. I remember men from parties, men from the coffee shop near the Auburn School, all the men I eyed until they approached me, who took me to their apartments, or into an alley, or into their cars. I can score men like drugs. I know where to look and how to look. I never even have to say much. Men are really very simple, and all more or less the same: an army of soldiers in uniform, marching into and out of me. "It could have been anyone," I say. I'm counting backward in my head. Ninety, eight-nine, eighty-eight . . .

"You don't mean Wade," Maggie says, "do you?"

"It could be Wade," I say. I turn my head and begin gagging again. I have nothing left to throw up, so I dry heave and Maggie holds my hair. Forty-two, forty-one, forty, thirty-nine . . .

"You weren't . . . using condoms?"

"Well, sometimes. As often as possible. But there have been others besides Wade. A long string of men." I sigh heavily.

"A string?" Maggie frowns. "You know, I think Wade would make a great husband and father. He'd be the kind of dad who plays catch with the kids. You know . . . after dinner? And he'd teach you to play racquetball and stuff. Those are the best kinds of guys because they're both manly and playful."

"I don't love Wade," I say. "I don't even like Wade. Okay? And he doesn't like me either. I don't know what the hell I'm going to do. What would I do with a child? I can barely take care of myself. I'm in debt. What am I supposed to do, go on welfare?"

"My uncle's on welfare."

"*What?*"

"Well, he gets food stamps. Maybe that's not the same thing. I mean, he's not my *real* uncle. He was my dad's roommate in college—"

"I don't want to have to get an abortion. I've made it this far without needing one and now I'm twenty-three and it just seems—"

"If you do get an abortion," Maggie says, "I'm sure Wade would pay for it. And then you could work things out. It would be hard, but you could get through it. Together."

"Maggie! What are you *talking* about?"

Maggie pats my knee.

I sit up and close my eyes, lean back against the wall. Nineteen, eighteen, seventeen, sixteen . . . "Fifteen more seconds," I say. I hear the lights buzz in the ceiling. "Five," I say, opening my eyes, "four . . . three . . . two . . . one." I climb unsteadily to my feet and go to the sink. I grab the stick and hold it up to the fluorescent light above the mirror. But it's not necessary, picking it up, holding it in the light. It's as pink as a bad rash: a tiny plus sign in the square white window.

18 Iyar 5762
(April 30, 2002)

WHEN I HEAR Monica creep into the room, the sun is up and I'm awake. I suck my breath into my chest, remembering the night she spent in my room at the yeshiva. Is she going to climb into bed with me? What will I do if she does? I listen to her humming Bob Dylan, settling into the bottom bunk. I keep very still. When I hear her start to snore, I can't decide whether or not I'm relieved.

I climb down the ladder and slip out of the room. I can't believe I didn't think to grab my tefillin bag before leaving the yeshiva. Now I'm in a strange place with nothing but my wrinkled clothes and my tzitzit. I can't even do my morning prayers.

Outside, I have to blink back the bright sunlight. There are only three other cars in the small lot. Monica's rental is parked on a sloppy diagonal. I hear waves crashing. I didn't realize last night how close we were to the Red Sea. I head toward it. The sound of children screeching and playing reminds me of the Jersey Shore, which reminds me that I am no longer a child, and that I have perhaps become what society would deem a loser: a jobless, aimless, homeless, twenty-year-old college dropout.

I stop on a wooden boardwalk and look down on a beach. My headache has subsided a bit. Brown hills surround the sparkling water. It might have been somewhere in those mountains that God gave the Israelites the Ten Commandments and dictated the Torah to Moses; that my ancestors gave up on God and built a golden calf, setting a precedent for guilt. I lean on the railing and watch the horizon. The sun hanging in the sky is a big, blinding ball of gold. It hurts my eyes.

"Aren't you on the wrong side of the country?" someone asks.

I turn around. When I see the man standing behind me, I almost fall over the railing.

"What, do I have two heads?" The man chuckles and pushes his black *kipa* back on his scalp.

I rub my eyes, but there's no denying it: he looks like Yosi. It's not just the beard and the dark clothes. It's the green eyes, the long nose with the broken capillaries at the end of it. It's the way his eyebrows go up when he smiles. It is Yosi. Yosi with a different voice.

"Sorry. . . . You look so much like someone I used to know," I say. "Identical, practically." I wonder about his strange question: *Aren't you on the wrong side of the country?* How does he know I'm from Jerusalem? I take a step backward. "What do you mean, I'm on the wrong side of the country?"

"The fun today is on Mount Meron," says the man. "No?"

I almost laugh out loud at my own paranoia. Of course. Mount Meron. The site of Israel's biggest Lag B'Omer celebration. I can't believe I forgot that today is Lag B'Omer, the only joyous day during the Omer period, the day that commemorates the end of the plague that killed Rebbe Akiba's students. It's the day men can shave their beards, and three-year-old boys can get their first haircuts. How fitting: The celebration is at the northernmost tip of Israel, and here I am, as far south as you can get.

The man leans his elbows on the railing next to me, and we both look out over the sparkling water to the bumpy brown rim of hills. "You know, each day of the Omer," he says, "except the last . . ."

"Represents one path to learning Torah," I say.

"Represents one of our forty-nine soul powers," he corrects me.

I glance at the man again. He must be a Hasid. Hasids are mystical. At Yeshiva Hillel, we didn't talk much about things like soul powers. I don't even know what soul powers are.

"Are you a Lubavitcher Hasid?" I ask. I'm pretty sure he is one, because Lubavitchers approach Jews wherever they can find them and try to help them fulfill God's commandments. The Hasids who helped me lay tefillin on Ben Yehuda Street were probably Lubavitchers. They have centers all over the world called Chabad Houses, dedicated to Jewish outreach.

"I am," he says. "There's a Chabad House in Eilat, you know. Have you been?"

"Me? No. I'm not from around here. . . . Why aren't you on Mount Meron?" I wipe some sand from the railing with my hand, and suddenly I want to know about soul powers. I am overcome by the uncomfortable sensation I got when I learned that Rabbi Zett was a sex offender. Is Yeshiva Hillel *treyf?* Is Hasidism the real Judaism?

"I was planning to go," the man says, "but . . . I had a sense I was needed here."

I feel his eyes on my face, but I keep looking straight ahead.

"I'm Chaim," the man says.

We shake hands. "Asher."

"Asher. Do you have a place to go for Shabbat?"

I don't have a place to go, period, I think to myself, but aloud I just say, "I'm not sure." I hesitate for a second. "Are you related to Yosi Aaronson?" I ask.

"Aaronson," Chaim says, squinting. "I know an Aaronson in Texas. Good family."

"But no relation?"

"None that I know of."

Below us, a tiny girl in a white bonnet squats on the beach, scooping sand into a blue plastic pail with her fists. She looks so focused, the way Reuven looks when he studies a tractate of Talmud, the way I must have looked at one time. Today, the thirty-third day, which is four weeks and five days of the Omer, is the day to take pleasure in fulfilling our obligations. My obligations are to God: to study and pray, to follow the six hundred thirteen commandments. But now here I am in Eilat, suspended from my yeshiva, my *kipa* missing, my tefillin abandoned, Monica sleeping in the hostel room we shared.

"I asked you about the name Aaronson," I say, staring at Chaim, "because I just can't believe how much you look like a rabbi I knew in Boulder."

"Boulder? What's that, Colorado? There are Jews in Boulder, Colorado?"

"Sure," I say, laughing.

"Denver, of course, but Boulder?"

"Well, the religious community is small. But they're there. Anyway, he's dead now. The rabbi. But—" I catch myself quickly and say, "May his name be a blessing. . . . It's like you're twins," I say. "It's just amazing."

I should tell Chaim that he shouldn't be extending himself to me, that I will ruin it, whatever it is, that I always ruin things, that eventually he will wish he never met me. But instead, I turn to him and ask if he has tefillin I can borrow. "I don't have mine with me," I explain, "and I don't have my *kipa*. I'm . . . far from home."

"Of course, Asher," Chaim says. "And you're not so far from home, you know."

Below, the little girl stands, picks up her pail, and starts racing toward the sea. Above her, the fancy V of a seagull dips and glides through the air. Chaim invites me to the Chabad House, and I am grateful. It's not the desperate gulping gratitude I felt toward Yosi; it's more like slipping into an old pair of shoes that I know will fit, or rather, that I know Chaim will stretch to fit me. I look down at the tiny footprints the girl left in the sand, like the footprints my ancestors left. The world is full of Jewish footprints. I look out across the water again to the mountains. I can practically see the Israelites marching through them, and I know now how Moses must have felt, talking with God, and other times, simply sensing God's presence, knowing the route without having to be told, perhaps even experiencing a sort of déjà vu: *I could swear I've gone this way before.*

AFTER THE NAUSEA passes and Maggie leaves, I can't sleep. My thoughts are jumping one to the next like a frantic slideshow. My fixation on getting Ash to Alena's funeral seems so trivial compared to my new dilemma. I can't believe what I just spent the last week doing—falling from a drainpipe, standing my ground at the Western Wall while a bunch of freaks tried to stone me to death. And all the while, a tiny fetus was curled up inside me—a comma awaiting the end of its sentence.

I'm haunted by an old memory of my Aunt May, who, along with my cousins Ari and Reva, lived with us for a few weeks when I was five or six years old, after she left her husband. One day, I overheard my mother say to her, "You have to go back to Gary. Give him another chance. The kids need their father. You want your kids to be damaged goods?"

"Damaged goods." Those are the words that keep returning to me, as I lie sleepless in the dark, one hand on my abdomen, staring up at the crack in the ceiling. *Damaged. Damaged.* Aunt May never did return to her husband, and Ari and Reva did in fact turn out damaged: Ari's been in and out of drug rehab since high school, and last anyone heard, Reva was a street performer in Prague or something. Is it true that fatherless children are automatically damaged? I try to come up with exceptions to the rule—I'm sure they exist but for some reason, I can't. I think of all the people I know with two parents, and all of them are damaged too. Dozens of eggs, cracked in their cartons.

The world is probably inherently damaging. So why introduce a baby to it? Besides, what do I know about having a family, about keeping my loved ones safe, about being a mother? I've never even kept a car for a year without wrecking it, or had a security deposit returned, or held on to a coupon long enough to use it. And I certainly haven't succeeded at being a friend, a daughter, or a sister.

I HANG UP. I shake Jonathan awake.

"Ash is still in Israel," I tell him.

Jonathan won't open his eyes. "But he's left Jerusalem," he mumbles into his pillow. "That's the first step."

His face looks so perfect there on the pale yellow linen, the morning just starting to open, smudges of pink out the window. My tears subside. I sniffle meaningfully. "What are you saying?" I shake him again. "How do you know?"

"Why are you shaking me?"

"That was Bits on the phone," I tell him. "My daughter. Our plan . . . your plan didn't work."

Jonathan opens one eye. He touches my chin. "Ash is out of Jerusalem," he says. "Your daughter is on her way home. Everything's still working. Lie down. Get some sleep."

"Sleep!" I say. "Who can sleep?"

"Just trust me," Jonathan says.

"Trust you! You're a broken record."

Jonathan yawns and closes his eyes again. "There's this girl," he mutters. "She knows what she's doing. It was her job to get him out of his yeshiva, in case your daughter couldn't. I told her to get him out of Jerusalem as quickly as possible. Away from the cult environment."

"Okay. And?"

"And she did it."

"This girl?"

"Yes. She got him out of his yeshiva. Out of Jerusalem. Now he has nowhere to go but home. Just wait. You'll see. Look. It's not important for you to know everything. Just know there's this smart girl, this girl who's determined. She works for me. She has just as much reason to fight the Orthodox Jews as you and I do. She used to be one of them. She knows things."

"What are you *talking* about?"

"Just a girl," he says, yawning again. "This little blond girl named Monica."

BACK AT THE hostel, Monica is missing. Standing in our room in my new *kipa* (courtesy of Chaim), I can hear that European guy strumming his guitar in the common room above me, but I don't hear voices. Monica's duffel bag is open, and clothes are strewn all over the floor—a yellow-and-blue flower-print bikini, the gold dress (inside out), two pairs of sandals, a tank top that looks like it would fit a baby. I grab a beach towel that Monica left on her unmade bed, carry it down the hall to the bathroom, and take a shower. Afterward, I have no choice but to put my dirty clothes back on.

When I return to the room, Monica is there, wearing cutoff jean shorts and a white bikini top that's probably see-through when it gets wet. She's squatting over her duffel bag, digging through it. When I walk in, she glances up, then goes back to her digging.

"Are you going to stay inside all day or what?" she asks. Her hair falls down her back in a single messy braid. She stands up, puts her hands on her hips. "It's summer! Practically."

I look away from her bikini top, up at the ceiling. "Monica," I say, sighing. "What are you going to do here?"

Her eyebrows knit together. "Here?"

"Are you going to stay in Eilat?" I go to the bunk bed and hang the damp towel on the bedpost.

"I thought we were—"

I hold up one hand, cutting her off. "I'm not going to Sinai," I say. I go back to the door and lean against it again.

"But yesterday—"

"Yesterday was different. I was going through . . . some stuff yesterday. And I had just hit my head. And I had hardly eaten. I wasn't thinking."

Monica squats beside her duffel bag again and pulls out a tube of sunscreen. "Okay, fine," she says. She sits on her bed and begins slathering sunscreen on one arm. "We can go to Jordan," she says. "Hey. Wait a minute." She points a finger at me. "Do you even have your passport?"

"No!" I say, throwing my hands up. "Don't you get it? I have nothing!"

"Okay, okay. So we'll stay here. I know you're freaked out about money."

"It's not that I'm freaked out about money," I say. "It's that I don't *have* any money. Do you understand that? And you and I have nothing in common." The words tumble out of me like marbles from a sack.

Monica rubs sunscreen into her hands and says nothing.

"What do you want from me?" I don't ask it in an accusatory way. I'm not angry. I just want to hear her say something honest for once.

"Nothing!" she says. "I want to help you."

"You don't want to help me. You want to change me. You want everyone in the world to quit believing in God, so you can feel better about your choices."

"You don't even know me, Asher."

"How am I supposed to know you if you lie all the time?"

"You're just scared of being free!" Monica says, her voice rising. Anger turns her cheeks pink.

"Free? I'm perfectly free."

"You want to leave me here, Asher? Fine! I'm not the one who needs to be taken care of. What are you going to do, seek out the Orthodox Jews of Eilat?"

My face feels hot. I won't tell her about the Chabad House, where Chaim fed me sweet rolls and coffee and prayed with me and invited me to his house for dinner. That's none of her business.

"You're not going to go back to Jerusalem, are you?" Monica stands and bangs her head against the frame of the top bunk. She cries out and her eyes squeeze shut into wrinkled little slits.

I step toward her. "Are you all ri—"

"Don't touch me!" she screams, and when her eyes fly open, I see a single tear beaded on her lower lashes. "You think you're the only one who gets to decide when and if we touch each other?" She bends down to grab a T-shirt from her duffel bag and pulls it over her head, making her blond hair stand on end like sun rays in a child's drawing.

I want to put my fingers in her hair, to smooth it back behind her ears. I curl my hands into fists.

Monica is packing a beach bag: towel, sunscreen, one of her American magazines. Without looking up, she says, "You know, I used to have this dog? Stanley? This giant white dog," she says, pausing in her packing to open her arms out to demonstrate, "with long hair all in his eyes like a stuffed animal? Anyway, this one night, my dad got mad at me for some reason. This was when I was little. Like ten. He got mad at me because I didn't clean my room or something, and we had a fight, and then the next day, I got home from school and Stanley was missing. I was all, 'Um, where's Stanley?' Right? And my dad's all, 'Yeah, I put him to sleep. Stanley was very sick.'" She finally looks up at me. Her face is hard, expressionless. "He wasn't sick," she says flatly. "He was only four years old. My dad killed him to get revenge. On me. I was *ten*. Do you see what kind of person my father is?" She's holding something—a sock?—twisting it angrily in her hands. "And that's not even the half of it!" she says. "That's just one little example."

Everything is crystallizing now. "So your father's *not* dead."

"My father is a heartless man!" Monica screams. And then she says what I guess I saw coming: "And you're just like him! You don't care about me."

"I don't care about *you?*"

"A heartless person wearing a religious mask," she says, and I'm not sure whether she's talking about her father or about me. "You're all the same. David too. There's a piece of work. He's been in love with me, like, forever. When we're together, he acts all tortured, like he knows he shouldn't touch me, but like he just can't help it. I know it's an act. David's had sex with tons of girls."

"He *has?*"

"But around his parents, around his friends, it's like he's Mr. Frum. You're all the same. Full of bullshit."

"David's had . . . ?"

"Whatever, Asher. Grow up."

I clear my throat. "Listen. I'm not as heartless and weak as you say I am. I serve God the way He's meant to be served." My voice sounds odd, unlike my own, a muscle that's atrophied.

Monica looks like she might explode from frustration. Finally, she just screams, "You're no better than me!"

Of course she's right. But she's wrong to think that religious men are interchangeable. For the first time, I understand something that should always have been obvious: some people will disappoint you and some people won't. And life will always work that way. I touch my fingertips to my chest, where my heart may or may not be. I almost want to tell Monica the things I know. But instead, I say, "Good-bye."

Monica's head snaps up. "I almost blew up your yeshiva," she says. The light in her eyes is gone.

I close my hand around the doorknob behind me.

"I still could too," she says. "I know how to build bombs. I could blow your yeshiva to pieces. It wouldn't be hard. And then what? Would your friends get a good spot in the world to come? Would it be worth it then that all they ever did was study and pray? Or would people feel sorry for them because they'd missed out on life?" Monica climbs to her feet.

"Good-bye," I say again, turning the doorknob. I am already gone from Monica. I am down the street in the Chabad House, returning to a life of Torah. "I hope you find the things you need," I say, and I open the door and leave her.

May 1, 2002

OKAY, IT'S NOT true that I have no family. When I
have a problem, a problem that has to be a secret from
my mother, there's one person I've always been able to
call. It's my Aunt Viv, and yes, she's my mother's sister and best
friend and practically her neighbor, too, but she can keep her
mouth shut, and she doesn't judge. It's six in the morning, but I
know I won't wake her. She's up every morning at five, knitting or
doing yoga or gardening if it's summertime. The very thought of
her puttering around her house, her hair a mess, her face not yet
freshened with makeup, comforts me a little, like I'm still a baby
instead of someone who's pregnant with one.

The sound of her voice makes me want to cry.

"Bits? Is that you? God, honey, I haven't heard from you in
forever."

"Well, I just got back."

"Back?"

"I was in Israel."

"What?! Your mother didn't tell me that." I hear her move her
mouth away from the phone for a second. "Phil, did you know Bits
was in Israel? . . . How's Ash, honey? Does he look like himself?
Was he wearing the black hat and the whole getup?"

"Aunt Viv," I say, sitting up in bed. "I really need to talk to you.
Do you have a second?"

"Sure," she says. "Your Uncle Phil and I are just lounging around, drinking coffee. Would you believe he just turned fifty?"

I wince. "Shit," I say. "I spaced that, didn't I?"

"Oh, honey, who cares. Believe me, by the time you get to fifty, no one's celebrating a damn thing."

"Aunt Viv," I try again. "I know I'll see you at the funeral, but I need to talk to you now. I—"

"The what?"

I hear a sudden alertness in Aunt Viv's voice, the high note of terror. "Bits?"

"Yeah?"

"Did you just say . . ."

"Aren't you coming?"

"Did you say . . . funeral?"

"Yeah."

Aunt Viv is silent. Then in a small voice, she says, "No one called me. My God. Who died?"

"No," I say. "I mean at . . . whatever it's going to be. The memorial service or whatever."

"The what?"

My head feels empty. Something is terribly wrong. "Aunt Viv?" I say, and my voice sounds detached from me. It's like I'm listening to this conversation, instead of participating in it, and I know all at once, know like I've never known anything else, that there are no bones. There is no black hair. There was no dog digging anything up. There is no Alena. There will be no funeral. I know all at once I've been lied to.

PART III

21 Iyar 5762
(May 3, 2002)

EVERYTHING I THOUGHT I understood is murky. What
I thought was the ultimate Jewish life is simply *one* Jewish life. Yeshiva Hillel's way is not the only way. There is
also the Chabad way. There is also the Zeff way. There is also the
Satmar way, the Belz way, the Viznitz way, and on and on. There
is not just Jerusalem. There is also Eilat. There is also New York.
There is also Montreal, and London, and Chicago.

After I left Monica, I returned to Chaim, who gave me a bedroom in his home, even though he has seven children. At all hours
of the day, there are babies squawking. There is the smell of food
cooking. I'm grateful, but these are not my sounds and smells.
They belong to another family.

Yesterday, my third day at Chaim's, I wrote Todd a letter and
mailed it to Yeshiva Hillel. I asked him to forgive me. I asked him
again to forgive me. And I asked for his forgiveness a third time,
in accordance with Jewish law. Afterward, I still felt far from absolved. I can't imagine ever feeling absolved.

This morning, Chaim and I have been at the Chabad House
since we woke up. He was teaching the *parshah* class he always
teaches on Fridays, and I had to struggle to stay awake during it
because I haven't been sleeping well. I've been having nightmares

about Yosi again. Now we're walking back to Chaim's house, and maybe because I look so exhausted, or maybe just because he's been wondering since he met me, Chaim asks, "Are you planning to settle here, or do you have unfinished business elsewhere?" He looks at me hard, and I see Yosi in his eyes.

"Unfinished business?" I laugh. "I have a lot of unfinished business." And then I take a deep breath and tell him all about Yosi.

When we get back to his house, I'm still talking, so we sit outside on the stoop and watch three of his children pick dandelions from the front lawn. I keep talking. Chaim listens attentively.

When I finish, he's quiet for a long time. Then he says, "We have free will."

"I know."

"It's tragic, but people can choose suicide if they want. They stop believing that Hashem has a plan for them, that Hashem gives them only as much as they can handle. They stop believing. But that is their choice. A very sad choice, but a choice nonetheless."

I think about what he's saying. Adam and Eve chose to eat from the Tree of Knowledge. The Israelites chose to build the golden calf. And I've made my own choices.

"Everything is a choice," I say, but I'm not even sure I've said it aloud, until Chaim responds, "Even guilt is a choice."

One of Chaim's children, a tiny boy who hasn't had his first haircut yet, brings me a fistful of dandelions. I take them from him. "Thank you," I say, straightening them into a bouquet. But then, inexplicably, inappropriately, I'm overcome by the sense that I don't want to be holding this child's weeds. The bright yellow-gold of them turns my stomach. The word "purge" forms in my mind like a command. I'm just sick to death of holding things.

"Do you understand what I'm telling you?" Chaim asks.

"Yes," I say.

"Guilt is a choice," he says again.

"All right," I say. "Okay."

I open my hand and shake the dandelions out. I wipe my palm on my pants. For the first time in thirteen years, I feel like I can breathe.

ACCORDING TO JONATHAN, Ted Patrick used to collaborate with parents to learn their children's schedules; then he would physically snatch the kids from cult headquarters or from their college dorms, stuff them into his car, and speed off, the brainwashed teenagers in the backseat screaming like raccoons in a dumpster. Ted Patrick had volunteers all over the country who let him use their homes, lock all the doors and windows, and do the deprogrammings, no matter how long they took. Sometimes, they took only an hour or two. The longest one took eleven days. Deprogramming was a lot like the brainwashing the cults did in the first place: sleep deprivation, thought reform, withholding food. Some kids would get violent, but Ted Patrick fought back, throwing them onto beds, screaming in their faces to stay put, pinning them against walls.

He wanted to undermine everything they'd been taught by the cult leaders. He would point out the hypocrisies, the injustices. He would blow holes through the cult's doctrines, make fun of the leaders, and basically force the kids to use their brains, which cult leaders teach their followers not to do. The snapping back to reality was always sudden and dramatic. One minute a kid would be telling Ted Patrick that she hated him, that he should die, that she hated her parents and had no loyalty to anyone but Krishna, or Moon, or whomever, and the next minute

she would burst into tears and hug her mother, apologizing pro-
fusely.

I want that. Hugs and tears. So I've seen one too many made-
for-TV movies, read one too many Hallmark greeting cards. Well,
sue me. I don't think I'm asking for much. According to Jonathan,
Ash is on his way home, on his way to what he believes is his
sister's funeral. Okay, so I lied to my kids. As if they never lied
to me! What about the time I found a pack of cigarettes behind
the sofa cushions and they both played dumb? What about two
months after Ash's bar mitzvah, when he swore he'd written his
thank you notes?

The important thing is that Ash is coming home. I want to
hear my son say, "What was I thinking? Mom, I'm so sorry. I'll
never leave you again." I want to hear him say, "You lost Alena.
You lost your husband. But you will never lose anyone else."

25 Iyar 5762
(May 7, 2002)

AFTER TALKING TO Chaim, I made a decision: I needed to stop doing things that made me feel guilty. So simple! Why hadn't I thought of it before? I knew that nothing would make me feel guiltier than missing Alena's funeral. So I made up my mind to go. The trip didn't have to be a long one, and as soon as it was over, I could come back to Israel, figure out my next step, find a new yeshiva.

Chaim called Yeshiva Hillel for me and had my passport sent. He even bought me a plane ticket and gave me extra money for a taxi. Of course, I promised him I would reimburse him in full within two weeks. I'll have to borrow money from my mother or Aunt Viv. Maybe that won't go over so well, but what else can I do at this point?

And now the plane is landing. Now it's speeding down the runway. My window is framing America. I will make my mother happy. I will spend time with Bits. If I have to, I will shake hands with my father. I will carry Alena's casket to the cemetery and shovel dirt onto it. I will leave a pebble on my grandmother's grave. I already feel lighter—I do—like that split second on the roller coaster at Six Flags Great Adventure, when you're going over the first big hill, when gravity gets all mixed up, when it hasn't had time yet to ground you.

America is bright. Were the traffic lights always so green? Were the lines on the roads always so yellow? I'm squinting in the backseat of the taxi, en route from the airport to the synagogue. I whisper prayers to myself and squeeze my tzitzit in my fingers. I won't have to be here forever.

These are the things I know about Buckley Quinn: He was forty-two years old when he killed himself. As a child, he could put puzzles together more quickly than any other child in his class. He alternately worked odd jobs and collected government assistance. His sense of humor included a tendency to sneak up on people and scare them by grabbing them abruptly or covering their eyes with his hands from behind. He was just under six feet tall. He wore thick glasses. Through the lenses, his eyes were magnified. I know these things because I read an article about him ten years ago and saw the picture. My mother had unintentionally left the magazine lying out.

Of course, Buckley Quinn is not at the synagogue, but also, he is. He follows me into Temple Beth Shalom, a gust of wind as the door closes. He mingles with the familiar spicy smell in the hallway. He accompanies me past the Judaic art that lines the walls—a brightly colored abstract painting of a shofar, a brass replica of the Ten Commandments, a marble statue of Aaron and Chur holding Moses' arms in the air—past the temple gift shop, past the bridal lounge and the function hall and the main sanctuary, and into the small chapel where Bits and I used to come for junior choir practice. Buckley Quinn settles into every pew.

Aside from him, I am alone. I must have gotten the time wrong. It occurs to me that it's been a lot of hours since I last showered. I'm lifting up my arm to sniff my armpit when I sense a presence in the room with me. I turn to the back of the chapel to see a giant, huge like Goliath, wearing a suit that doesn't fit him. A man too big for human clothes. His head is shaved clean.

"Ash," he says. He holds up a finger, signaling me to wait. "Or Asher. Which do you prefer?"

For a second, I think he's Buckley Quinn. It doesn't make any sense, of course, but my chest is constricting.

"I'm Jonathan," the giant says, moving down the aisle toward me, holding his hand out. "I'm a friend of your mother's."

I stand. For some reason, I don't want to touch him, but I give his giant hand a limp shake. "Does she know I'm here?" I ask. "Where is everyone?"

"I wanted to talk to you, Ash." He steps closer to me, closing in on my space the way Israelis do. Americans don't get this close.

My ears pulse. My palms start to sweat. "I have to go," I say. "I have to find my family." I move past him, walk down the aisle. For a second, I think he's going to try to stop me, but he's not moving, not saying a word.

I push the chapel door with all my weight. Nothing happens. It's locked.

M Y MOTHER CALLS to tell me she got the time of the funeral wrong. "You can take a later train," she says.

"Maybe I'll come early," I say, testing her.

"Don't," she says. "I mean, why rush?"

I don't let on that Aunt Viv and I know what she's up to. I don't tell her that Aunt Viv noticed how much she's been talking about some guy named Ted Patrick. Aunt Viv looked him up and read about the man who used to try to deprogram cult members. (And once, a lesbian. Or a girl whose parents thought she was a lesbian. Or something.) I don't tell my mother that we suspect that she tricked me into going to Israel, or that we suspect that she's planning a deprogramming for Ash. Why say anything? Why try to stop her? I know I wouldn't be able to; I know how myopic a rescuer's vision is.

I used to think I knew what happened when you tried to rescue someone. If he was drowning, he'd panic and drag you down with him. If he was suffocating, he'd grab your throat. If he was freezing, he'd leach all your body heat. If he was crying over the kitchen sink and you slipped an arm around his waist, he'd lean on you until you toppled to the linoleum.

I used to worry that I was selfish. I thought I should be more helpful. But no one is more selfish than the pushy helper, who launches rescue missions so she can win the medal, the pat on the back, the gratitude.

Here's what happens when you try to rescue someone: you find out you're the one who needs rescuing.

Jonathan has asked me to give him an hour alone with Ash. Actually, he asked me for two hours, but I bargained him down to one. Not that I don't trust Jonathan—I've trusted him with everything else; why not with the first hour of the deprogramming?—but I want to see my son. I can hardly wait. I want to put my arms around him. I want to breathe him in, to smell the scent that only a mother can smell, the faint undertone of the way he smelled as a baby. I want to touch his hair and push it out of his eyes.

I'm pulling on my stockings, planning to leave for the synagogue in fifteen minutes, when the phone rings. What if it's Jonathan? What if something has gone wrong?

But it's a woman's voice.

"Um. Mrs. Kellerman?"

"Who is this?"

There is a second of silence. "You don't know me," she finally says.

The voice is soft, distant. I sit on the edge of my bed and press the phone hard to my ear. Of course, I'm expecting bad news. Something has happened to Ash or to Bits. A car accident. A plane crash.

"I have some information that might be important to you," the woman says. "My daughter knows your son. My daughter . . . is troubled. She's . . . do you . . ."

"What?" I say. I can hardly breathe. "Is Ash okay?"

"Do you know a man named Jonathan?"

"Oh. Yes," I say. But I wonder if I should be admitting to knowing him. What if she's one of his enemies? Jonathan is always talking about Ted Patrick's enemies, how they sabotaged Ted Patrick and landed him in prison. Jonathan says that he has enemies, too, people who don't understand him.

"There are some things I think you should know," the woman says. And then she begins. She tells me everything. She tells me what I suppose I've suspected all along. Deep down. Deep, deep down. That I've put my trust in the wrong person.

Ten minutes later, when I hang up the phone, my brain returns to me.

Snap. Just like that.

I put on my shoes. I grab my purse. I call Viv. I call Bits. I come clean.

"Okay," Viv says. "It's going to be okay."

"I already knew," Bits tells me. "Did you think I wouldn't figure it out?"

Here's what happens when you try to rescue someone: You can forget your priorities; you can even forget your children. You forget all about the person you're rescuing.

I'M SANDWICHED BETWEEN the door and the man who calls himself Jonathan. I feel his breath on my neck. He speaks, and I hear the lilt of questions in his voice, but I can't understand him. Fear is pushing through my head at top volume, a gust of wind. When I force myself to make sense of his words, what I hear is this: "Just explain it to me. Explain how the Holocaust could have happened if the Jews are the Chosen People. Explain to me what kind of God would allow someone to kidnap your six-year-old sister, expect His followers to wear tall black hats, and command women to wear wigs? Why wigs, if they already have divine God-given hair?"

Divine God-given hair?

"I'm trying to get you to think," he says. "I'm trying to show you that the things you've been told aren't true. Ash," he says, and now his enormous hand is on my shoulder, "I'm trying to help you. I'm trying to give you your life back."

"I'm happy with my life," I tell him, trying to keep my voice steady. He doesn't need to know what my life has consisted of this past week. He doesn't need to know about Monica, about the magazines. Before that, things were good. After the funeral, things will be good again. I love my life. I love Israel. I love learning in yeshiva. Who *is* this man anyway? "I need to find my mother," I say. I finally turn around to face Jonathan. Saliva glistens on his big white teeth. He is an animal, a predator, backing me into a wall, his eyes boring into me.

"It's normal, you know," he says, "the way you feel about Monica. I know how it is. I'm a guy. It's natural. It's how we're wired."

"How do you . . ."

"Just because your rabbis tell you she's off-limits doesn't mean you can stop your feelings. Your urges. What has ever been wrong with love?" He gives me a big smile. So many perfect, shiny teeth. I wonder irrelevantly if they're dentures. "And between you and me, there's nothing wrong with lust either."

I wonder how long I could hold my own if he attacked me. That's what this is leading to, isn't it? I remember my fight at the Kotel. If I am angry enough, I can hurt someone. The problem is, I'm not angry. I'm jet-lagged and disoriented. I feel like I'm having one of those dreams where I'm being chased, but I can't run.

Where is my mother? Where are Bits and Aunt Viv and Uncle Phil and all the neighbors? Where are my mother's friends from the JCC? Where is the rabbi? At the very least, where is the janitor who cleans the chapel, or the security guard who watches every room in the synagogue on a split screen in his office?

"Can I sit?" I ask. "Do we have to stand like this?" I need to get my bearings, catch my breath, collect my thoughts.

Jonathan looks like he's debating for a second; then he steps aside and I go to a pew and sit. He sits in the same row, a couple of feet away from me. "You realize," he says, "don't you, that you're in a cult?"

I look at Jonathan. He has a twitch in his left eye. It's slight but unnerving, like the jerking leg of a sleeping dog. "Now I know you're not lying about being friends with my mother," I say.

Is he my mother's boyfriend? Has my mother begun dating? I wonder what other weird things have happened since I've been away. And how does my mother's boyfriend know Monica?

"My mother thinks I'm in a cult," I say. I bite my tongue to keep from defending Orthodox Judaism, to keep from losing my temper, to keep from telling this guy to mind his own business. I know that anger will only make me seem weaker. I have to make him think I'm calm and confident. I know this from my years of being a vegan. People love to preach meat-eating to vegans. They would get angry with me, telling me I was ruining my body, disrupting the food chain, condescending to the common man, putting farmers out of work, and my best defense was to respond with cool amusement. "I live and let live," I used to say. "*I'm* not preaching to *you*."

Jonathan says, "Do you know *why* your mother thinks you're in a cult?"

"No. Do you?"

"Yes," Jonathan says. "Because you are."

Really? I think. *No one's ever asked me for money. No one's ever tried to keep me at the yeshiva. On the contrary, they were trying to expel me when I left.*

"What do your rabbis say about the secular world?" he asks, sliding closer to me. "They say it's poison, that you should avoid it like poison. Right?"

I try to give a light chuckle, but it sounds weird in the high-ceilinged chapel. It reverberates mockingly in the rafters.

Then Jonathan says something that sends a chill up my spine: "Laugh all you like," he says, "but I'm going to deprogram you. You're going to resume a normal life."

That word: "normal." What does it even mean? Is America normal? Was my life before Israel, life after Alena, normal? Besides, is normalcy something to strive for? Jonathan is staring at the side of my face. I can feel it, but I keep my eyes straight ahead, locked on the holy ark. I am remembering Monica, her voice, her words, her aunt's boyfriend, the one who called her Fish, the one

who David said she ran away to. And suddenly, things start to fit together.

"Are you Monica's Uncle Jon?" I ask.

"Uncle." He laughs again.

"Did she send you to talk to me?" I ask. But I realize almost instantly that she couldn't have. She doesn't know where I am. The only logical conclusion I can draw is that Jonathan sent *her* to *me*. But why?

"I'm here for my sister's funeral," I say. "And that's it. When it's over, I'm going back to Israel." For some reason, I feel like I'm lying, like I'm weaving a story to trick him. "My sister's dead," I hear myself say, and as soon as the words are out of my mouth, it occurs to me that maybe she's not, that maybe I've been tricked. But I'm not yet sure who tricked me.

"I know why you're here," Jonathan says. "I want you to know things too."

"What do you want me to know?"

"I want you to know that your yeshiva has brainwashed you."

"Whatever you say." Cool amusement. Calm and confident.

"I'll prove it to you."

"Fair enough," I say, "on one condition."

Jonathan wrinkles his brow.

"I want you to explain to me how you know my mother and how you know Monica. I want you to tell me the whole story from the time you met my mother until right now. And then I'll listen to or say anything you want. Okay?"

"We're not bargaining," Jonathan says, "but I have nothing to hide. What do you want to know? Monica's aunt hired me."

"When? For what?"

"Couple years ago. She wanted me to help Monica. Monica's parents are brainwashed."

"They're religious."

"They're Orthodox Jews. Ba'alei Tshuva. So I helped Monica and now Monica helps me. It's a labor of love. For me. For Monica. It was for Ted Patrick, too, and for everyone who helps me, and everyone who helped him."

"Who?"

"Black Lightning," Jonathan says.

And then the door at the back of the chapel bursts open. "Bursts" is the only way to describe it because it's like a super-hero comic strip, the way Bits comes crashing into the chapel. (She should be wearing tights and a cape. . . . Is Black Lightning a su-perhero? Maybe she's Black Lightning.) My mother and Aunt Viv are behind her, and Bits, sweaty and out of breath, heads directly for our pew, pushes past Jonathan, plops herself in between us, and screams in Jonathan's face, "Leave my brother alone!"

I look at Jonathan, who is wearing an expression like we all just barged in on him sitting on the toilet, and I look at my mother, who is sobbing makeup down her cheeks, and at Aunt Viv, who is holding my mother's hand, and I can't help it—I laugh.

This is what happens when you try to rescue someone: there is embarrassing, ineffectual melodrama, like a fire truck blaring sirens, speeding toward a cat in a tree.

MY MOTHER'S BOYFRIEND just looked at my breasts.
I saw him do it. He looked at my breasts, then looked
past me at Ash, then looked at my breasts, then turned
around to look at my mother and Aunt Viv, who are still standing in the aisle. I'm leaning on Ash, blocking him from this man
who is supposed to be my mother's boyfriend, supposed to be a
"deprogrammer," but who looks nothing like a guy who could
rescue someone and a lot like a guy who should sell encyclopedias.
He's wearing a beige suit. His arms are too long for it. Incongru-
ously, his head is hairless.

Jonathan scoots out of the pew and into the aisle. He puts his
hands up like we're going to shoot him. He says, "I'll step outside
and let everyone get reacquainted."

Everyone ignores him. We're all staring at Ash. Ash is staring
back at us.

Jonathan says, "I'll come back once the smoke has cleared."
He's backing away. He says, "Ellie, come get me if you need me.
I'll be right out here."

My mother doesn't seem to hear him. She is squeezing Aunt
Viv's hand, her eyes still on Ash. She's hysterical. The fingers of
her free hand are pressed to her trembling mouth. I know she's
thinking, among other things, *Why does my son have* payos?

"Okay, Ellie?" Jonathan says. "I'll be right out here."

My mother glances at him for the briefest moment. He probably doesn't know her well enough to recognize that look. It's the look I got when she caught me using her car before I had my license. If she weren't so fixated on Ash, she would breathe fire on Jonathan like a dragon. It occurs to me that she was sleeping with this man. My mother. Having sex. I quickly flick that thought away.

I say, "We need to get something straight here." There are things I want to say. Things I want to scream at my mother and, of course, at Ash. "We need to get something straight," I say again, but I can feel tears in my throat, and my brother's breath on the back of my head, and I'm thinking that maybe there's nothing to get straight. Not right this minute anyway. I'm thinking that life just isn't so straight. For the most part, it's a mess. And I don't have to make it messier, but I don't have to fight it either. I'm thinking that my baby will be damaged. Sure. But who isn't? It will fit right in with the rest of the world.

WHY DOES MY son have *payos*? I wasn't prepared for *payos*. His fingernails are dirty. He has scabs on his forehead. I want to hug him, to breathe him in, to feel the weight of him, the fact of him, in my arms.

Bits is saying, "We need to get something straight."

"I misjudged," I say. I squeeze Viv's hand tighter. "I shouldn't have trusted Jonathan. I thought he could help. He said he could." I don't say, *I was lonely. Haven't you ever been lonely before?* I don't say, *I didn't know I needed a man, and then there Jonathan was and it turned out I did.* I don't say, *You can't imagine how your father wounded me.*

Ash says, "How do you know Monica?" His eyes are hard and cold. Is his voice a little deeper? Is he a little easier in his own skin? My son is growing up. My son is basically a man.

Bits's eyebrows go up. "Mom, you know *Monica*? That blond girl?"

Ash looks at Bits. "How do *you* know Monica?"

"Your girlfriend!" Bits says.

"She's not my girlfriend."

"I don't know her," I say. "I swear. Jonathan was pulling all kinds of strings in Israel. I didn't know anything. He wouldn't tell me anything." I stop and take a deep breath. I tell them what Monica's mother told me—that Jonathan worked with (read: slept with) her sister, Monica's aunt; lured Monica, a troubled girl, away from her parents; and then, they suspect, slept with Monica. Before she was even eighteen!

"Not that I agree with Monica's parents raising her to be an Orthodox Jew," I say quickly, "but I agree less with a man who is a pervert, not to mention delusional."

"So being religious is a little better than being a pervert?" Ash's voice is prickly.

I lower my voice. "He thinks he's Ted Patrick," I say, jerking a thumb toward the door of the chapel.

"So, wait. They didn't find . . . ?" Ash's eyes widen. He looks past me to Viv. "So Alena's not . . . Aunt Viv? They didn't?"

Viv shakes her head. I can tell Bits is trying not to cry. Ash glances at her profile, then slings an arm awkwardly over her shoulder. How did this happen? Have I stopped existing? I made a mistake! One little mistake! How could I have known that Jonathan uses this Ted Patrick act on women all over the country, that his story about his wife isn't even true, that he gets women into bed, pushes his own agenda, and collects people's money? How could I possibly have known?

"Ash," I say. I hold my arms out. "Come give your mother a hug."

For a few awful moments, Ash just stares at me. Then he sighs, rises like a robot, and slides past Bits. I take him in my arms, but he stays limp. He smells like he hasn't showered since he left Boulder a year ago. But he also smells like my son.

"I tried to give you a good life," I weep into his shoulder. "Both of you. I wanted what was best. After what happened . . . I don't ever want to let another child out of my sight. Can't you understand that?"

"But we're not six," Bits says. "That's the thing."

I hug Ash more tightly. He pats my back. He says, "Mom, this is crazy. Maybe you need to see a doctor."

Me? A doctor? Jonathan's the one who needs a doctor! I'm about to say that aloud, but then I remember something Monica's mother said to me on the phone, and something occurs to Viv and me at exactly the same second. *He collects people's money and vanishes without a trace.*

Viv and I lock eyes over Ash's shoulder.

"I'll go make sure he's . . ." Viv says, and she's running toward the door of the chapel, flinging it open, and now I can hear her high heels in the hallway, and I know instantly that we were all very stupid, especially me. Of course. Especially me. Jonathan is gone. Why *wouldn't* he be gone? He has vanished without a trace.

PART IV

May 30, 2002

ACCORDING TO MY doctor, I'm about three months along, but until this morning, you never would have guessed that. First of all, I've gotten sick to my stomach only twice in the past month. Second of all, as soon as I finished the last two weeks of the school year at the Auburn School (where hardly anyone, except Maggie, spoke a word to me), I started waitressing at this restaurant, Bailey's Grill and Tap, on Brighton Avenue, so it's not like I've been sitting around acting all *indulgent* about being pregnant. Third of all, I was barely gaining weight. Until this morning, when I woke up and looked . . . well, pregnant.

I couldn't get into the navy blue pants that I have to wear for waitressing, but I don't have another pair—who has more than one pair of navy blue pants?—so I had to squeeze, and now I'm walking to work and my legs are numb because they're more or less each in a tourniquet. I can't feel them. Blood is not circulating through them. And by the way, pregnant women should not wear skin-tight pants.

When I graduated from college, I thought I could kiss my waitressing days good-bye. Guess not. Ash keeps telling me to quit. He says what did he bother coming home for, what did he bother getting a more-than-full-time job for if I'm just going to keep working straight through my pregnancy? (That's right. He's gainfully employed. In America, of all places.) I want to answer, *You came home because I gave you a good excuse to come home. You came home because Mom got involved with that weird guy and lied about Alena. You came home because Monica seduced you out of your yeshiva.* But I'm not stupid. I keep my mouth shut.

Ash says there's no need for me to be working a potentially dangerous job, that it's not just my life anymore, that I owe it to my unborn child to take it easy. That's sweet of him, but let's look at the facts: He's a twenty-year-old virgin. Well, maybe he's not a virgin. But he's definitely not a pregnancy expert. Or a money expert, apparently. I admit he's working hard and saving up, but he's not on his way to his first million or anything. (He's lucky to have work at all, considering he's a college dropout with no practical skills.) So what am I supposed to do, lie in bed with my feet up for the next six months? I want to be out of debt by the time the baby comes. That means I need to pay off my credit cards, pay back my mother the rent money she lent me, and, last but not least, save up five hundred sixty dollars for Wade.

Wade. I still haven't told Wade that he might be a daddy. But there's a chance the baby's not his. And even if it is his, what's he going to do, propose to me? Right. He'll see for himself once school starts back up in September. In the meantime, I have other things to worry about. For example: It's eighty degrees out and I think my pants are about to rupture like sausage casing. Another example: I'll be going back to the Auburn School at the end of the summer, twenty-three years old, single, detested by all my colleagues, and fat. (I know, I know, pregnant's kind of different from fat. But still.) A third example: In six months, I'm going to have a child, and I might look into that child's face and see reflections of Wade, or of a stranger, or of someone I remember only in a hazy drunken-memory sort of way.

But I might also see reflections of myself—a fresh, pure, unscathed version of me.

25 Sivan 5762
(June 5, 2002)

I F YOU JUDGED by movies or greeting cards, you'd think nostalgia was something cozy, like a cup of tea and an arm around your shoulder. But that depiction is inane. I'm teaching Yehuda, one of the full-time students at the Yeshiva of Brookline, how to make *cholent*, the traditional Sabbath dish that we ate every Saturday at Yeshiva Hillel, and I'm so nostalgic for Shabbat in Jerusalem, it's like an ice pick stabbing my throat.

I wonder if finding nostalgia painful is a prerequisite for becoming religious. After all, don't we, the observant Jews, know enough to pine for the way things used to be, for the days when Moses spoke with God, then delivered divine messages to the children of Israel? Don't we cringe when we compare the world as it must have been to the world as it is now? Don't we strive to preserve the past? It's just as easy to be nostalgic for the life you lived last month as it is to be nostalgic for a thing you've never known. I should know because I'm as nostalgic for the Jerusalem of 5762 as I am for the Jerusalem of three thousand three hundred fourteen years ago. And there's nothing cozy about any of it.

"It's better to put the chicken in a plastic bag with the matzo meal," I say, demonstrating. "Then you can just shake the bag, and then the chicken's coated. See?" I pass Yehuda a plastic bag.

It's not that I don't like the Yeshiva of Brookline. I do. I have three roommates instead of one, but that's okay, because room and board are part of my compensation. I also get a somewhat meager salary, in exchange for being a full-time odd-jobs man. That means not only do I work in the kitchen, but I do anything and everything that needs to be done: I change lightbulbs, I stuff envelopes, I do wake-up sometimes. Which means I have less time for learning, but at least I'm making a little money.

The main difference between the Yeshiva of Brookline and Yeshiva Hillel is that the Yeshiva of Brookline is kind of a commuter yeshiva. Lots of the guys don't live here, so there's not the same sense of community, but being back in yeshiva is still a tremendous relief. After that guy Jonathan locked me in the chapel, and my family broke in and "rescued" me, Bits told me her secret: she'd just found out she was pregnant, and no one except Aunt Viv and her friend Maggie knew about it. I saw then that the Holy One had brought me to her, had brought me where I was needed. Bits was alone. She needed me. Of course, it's not like pregnancy just *happened* to her out of nowhere, but we all make mistakes; mistakes aren't really the point. So I agreed to stay with her for a while. I drove back to Boston with her. I wanted to get away from my mother anyway. I will forgive my mother, of course. Rosh Hashanah and Yom Kippur are coming, and I know how important forgiveness is.

"She's the person who gave you life," Aunt Viv reminds me, but there are some things you don't lie about, Alena being at the top of that list, and yes, she's my mother, and okay, maybe she did what she did out of misguided concern for me, but still. Pretending a dog dug up Alena's hair? Taking up with that pervert? Sending Monica to seduce me, like I'm some kind of animal that can be swayed by the promise of treats? I can't think about it yet without feeling sick.

Anyway, within days of arriving in Boston, I had found the Yeshiva of Brookline and befriended one of the rabbis there, Rabbi

Shimon. I told him my whole story right off the bat—about Alena, about what my mother did, about Bits's pregnancy. I was tired of keeping secrets. And I told him that my stay at the Yeshiva of Brookline would most likely be temporary. "I want to be in Jerusalem," I explained. "As soon as Bits is back on her feet, I'll go back. I'll find a new yeshiva. I'll start fresh."

Rabbi Shimon smiled. "You're doing the right thing, you know. Your sister needs you here. You did what Moses would have done. You will have a very special relationship with that baby."

"Maybe," I said. "I don't know. I don't know what kind of relationship I'll have with it. I mean, my sister's not religious. . . ."

"Family is family."

"It's not *my* baby."

"Asher," Rabbi Shimon said again. "Who is Chur?"

"Chur?" I had to think for a second. "I can only remember one thing about him right now," I say. "This is terrible. I'm already starting to forget things."

"What do you remember?"

"When we fought the tribe of Amalek in the desert during the Exodus, Moses had to keep his hands raised in the air. When his arms were raised, the Israelites would prevail. Whenever he lowered his arms, Amalek prevailed. Chur held up one of Moses' hands for him."

"Right. So Chur was very special to Moses."

"Yes."

"Who was he?"

"What do you mean?"

Rabbi Shimon glanced at the ceiling. "'What do I mean?' he asks me," he told an invisible third party, opening his arms to the heavens. Then he reached across the desk to clap me on the shoulder. "I mean that Chur was Miriam's son, Asher. *Miriam's son* held Moses' arm for him. Do you understand? Chur was Moses' nephew."

HERE'S WHAT I'VE learned in my five-plus decades of life: Some people disappear so easily. One minute you can smell the clean scent of their hair, watch their eyes change color in the sunlight, notice how they scratch their ears when they're nervous and how they double over when they laugh too hard; and the next minute you're like a dehydrated person in the desert, drinking from an imaginary stream.

Other people can't disappear. Even when they want to. Take me. I'm always right where you think I am. I'm washing dishes wearing yellow rubber gloves. I'm glancing at the phone, wanting it to ring. I'm blowing warm air on my knuckles, shivering inside my car in the cold early morning. I'm not saying that I miss Jonathan. Me? Miss *him*? Ha! I feel like I slept with the town whore. Good riddance. I'm just saying, enough with the disappearing acts. I've had plenty for several lifetimes.

I'm using this Jewish dating Web site now. Guess whose idea that was. Viv's. Of course. On my profile, I had to answer the question, *Who is your ideal mate?* I thought about it for all of three seconds before writing, *Someone who won't disappear.*

This afternoon, I'm sitting in Starbucks. (Chain coffee shops never disappear; they just keep cropping up like chicken pox.) I'm waiting for a man whose screen name is professor40. The message he sent me last week said, *People disappear on me too.*

Professor40 and I talked on the phone for two straight hours. He has four grown kids in foreign countries, a wife who left him for the man who was renovating their basement, and a dog who ran off with another dog from the neighborhood. Do I think he's the answer to my prayers?

Please. I stopped praying years ago. But maybe Viv is right that it's time for me to meet a nice Jewish man. Maybe she's right that it's time for us all to get on with our lives.

July 9, 2002

I HATE SUNDAY NIGHTS because there's always a band at the restaurant and it gets way too loud and gives me a headache, but the band tonight isn't bad, and the guitarist seems to be checking me out, despite my fat ankles and my ugly new pants with the baby-shaped pouch. Or maybe I'm imagining it. What are the chances that a musician is turned on by a pregnant waitress? The only people who love pregnant women are other women, particularly other women who have had babies. More women have talked to me in the last month than in my whole life. Everyone has a pregnancy story. Some are sweet. Some, like the story one woman told me about her friend dying during childbirth from a ruptured something or other, are not sweet. But talking to women is nice. Generally. I had begun to miss it a little, I think.

So women are all over me, but the men have disappeared. Or rather, I have disappeared from their vision. I suppose there's nothing sexy about a woman who is carrying another man's child. Whatever. I like the break. But I also wouldn't mind talking to that guitarist, even though I guess it's sort of cheesy to drool over some guy in a band like I'm one of those teenage girls who gets her breasts autographed.

Anyway, one woman who is not all over me is my mother. After the shit she pulled, I figured she'd be eager to make amends with me, but when I gave her the news that she was mere months

away from being a grandmother, she said, "What?! Are you trying to give me an attack?!" Then, after hyperventilating for a few
seconds, I guess she realized there was no attack in store, so she
declared herself "traumatized" and hung up on me. Traumatized.
Like a Vietnam vet. She won't even talk to me.

I'm not angry. I mean, it's not like I could have expected her to
congratulate me. But I forgave her for lying about Alena, and that's
unforgivable, in some people's opinions. At least Ash is excited for
me. He doesn't say so, but I can tell because he gives me lots of
spiritual advice, like that if it's a boy, there will have to be a bris.
("Disgusting," I said. "No way in hell I'll let some rabbi chop my
son's penis." But I was just saying that in a sisterly way.) I don't
mind Ash's spiritual advice. I'm not bothered so much anymore by
Ash's being religious. I mean, if I had the choice, I would prefer
him to be a nice, laid-back agnostic, but whatever. He can be what
he wants, as long as he's still my brother.

In his spare time, he's been building a crib. I don't remind
him that our father did the same thing, built a crib before I was
born even though he knew nothing about building things. I don't
remind Ash that our father never finished it. Never finished any of
the projects he started in our basement. Ash will finish. I know he
will. Ash is not the half-assed type.

I'm wrapping up my shift when the band takes a break, and
as I'm clocking out at the bar, I see out of the corner of my eye
the guitarist approaching me. I pretend not to notice. He walks
right up to me, and what he says surprises me: "You're not Asher
Kellerman's sister, are you?"

I turn around to face him. His red hair hangs over his forehead
in a thick fiery flop. I stare at him as I untie the apron from my
waist. If he's calling Ash "Asher," he must be somehow affiliated
with the Yeshiva of Brookline, but he doesn't look religious. He's
clean-shaven. No *kipa*. None of those tassel things that Ash wears.

He's wearing jeans and a T-shirt with an American Express card on it, one of those preemptive consolation prizes you get when you sign up for the credit card that will ruin your life. "I am Ash's sister," I say.

The redhead has beautiful hands. I notice them when he reaches up to absentmindedly touch his ear, the way people with nose jobs do to their noses. "I knew it!" He cocks his head, and I see that he's wearing a hearing aid. "You look a lot like him. Way prettier, though. I'm Todd," he says, holding out his hand to shake. "I used to live with Asher. In Israel. We were roommates at the yeshiva." He laughs. "So how is he?"

"Ash? Fine. He lives here. In Brookline."

Todd's eyes widen. "You are *kidding* me."

"Nope."

"I live in Somerville," he says. "I'm going to the Conservatory in the fall. This is unbelievable! What's he doing here?"

"Oh. Well. I'm"—I glance down at my belly—"pregnant. So he's here. Helping. He's working at the Yeshiva of Brookline. See, I'm not married. . . ." I want to run my hands through his red hair. I want to say, "so I'm available." I must be starved for male attention. I haven't had sex in months, haven't even wanted to, but suddenly— No. No, no, no. What do I want with some yeshiva boy?

Todd is staring at me, shaking his head. "You know," he says. "It's amazing. I looked at a picture of you for a full year."

"Ash had a picture of me?"

"Well, you were probably eight years old in it. But somehow, I recognized you anyway."

"I guess I haven't changed much," I say. "At least, I haven't matured much. . . . Well, I mean, I'm pregnant. But other than that." I'm rambling. Saying ridiculous things. I bite my lip.

"I knew you lived in Boston," Todd says, "so maybe I always sort of expected to meet you. I don't know. . . . Ash is *here*? Re-

ally?! Man." He laughs. He has freckles in his eyes. He points to
the apron I have balled up in my fist. "Stay," he says. "We're on for
another hour. Then I'll buy you a drink."

"I'm pregnant."

"Oh. Right."

"I'll have water," I say quickly.

He smiles. He has a beautiful smile, like the first notes of a
song that I've never heard but I can tell I'm going to like.

7 Av 5762
(July 16, 2002)

I STILL HAVE TO wonder about forgiveness. In a couple of months, it will be Rosh Hashanah, the Jewish New Year, when God will inscribe the names of the chosen in the Book of Life. And ten days later will be Yom Kippur, the Day of Atonement, when God's decisions will be sealed. That means I don't have much time left to clean my slate. I don't want to stand in shul chanting, "Who by water, and who by fire," and wonder if it is I who will die by water, or by fire, or by sword or beast, if it is I whose sins have finally accumulated enough to exclude me from the Book of Life. Not that God's decisions are always so clear. People who seem perfectly good and righteous die too. But after the Israelites sinned with the golden calf, God did say to Moses, "Whoever sinned against me I will blot from the book." So I'm worried. By sinning against my fellow man, I have sinned against God. The truth is, it's easier to apologize to God, because you don't have to look Him in the face. But you have to apologize to people too.

I apologized to Todd, but my apology was cheap. Handwritten. I never had to look him in the eye, never had to wait for his response. He didn't write back to me and I don't blame him. I guess he doesn't know my address, but even if he did, I wouldn't expect a letter. Why should he forgive me?

I also owe an apology to Monica. It doesn't matter if I think she wronged me. I wronged her too. At least, she thinks I did. And she might be sort of crazy, also, considering her bomb obsession, considering her sketchy relationship with Jonathan, who is more than twice her age and used to date her aunt, considering the fact that she's devoted her life to pulling religious men away from the Holy One (I know she doesn't just do what she does for Jonathan's sake, or for money . . . after all, David's parents didn't hire Jonathan. She preys on all religious men, whether their parents want her to or not), so I should have a little sympathy. I should try to make things right on my end. I don't know how to find her. But I suppose I should start looking.

The other people whose forgiveness I want are gone. I want to apologize to Alena for letting her get into that car. I want to apologize to Yosi for the mean things I said to him, for judging him, for pushing him away after he'd done so much to help me.

After I got my plane ticket back to the States, I had another long talk with Chaim. I asked him what I could do to atone for transgressions I committed against people who are no longer living or available to me.

"If you are really, truly sorry," Chaim said, "Yosi's soul knows it. He forgives you."

Well, maybe that's true and maybe it's not, but I just wish so badly that I had easy access to the people I need to apologize to. It takes great strength to look someone in the eye and apologize, and I want the opportunity to do that. I want to see how strong I can be. A few weeks from now will be the anniversary of Yosi's death. I will light a *yartzheit* candle for him. That's one thing I can do.

I don't know if Alena's soul has forgiven me. When I imagine our souls hashing it out, I think of her last Fourth of July, when we burned sparklers in the backyard. I remember her reaching up to touch the flame of her sparkler to mine. I remember how the two flames became one, and how Alena pulled hers away and said it was brighter than mine. At the time, I said, "No, it isn't!" But now I agree with her—it was always the brightest—and wherever she is, I hope that she knows that.

I suppose I could ask Rabbi Berkstein where Todd is. I've been exchanging e-mails with Rabbi Berkstein. I had to contact him as soon as I got here because I needed him to send me my stuff. He feels guilty that I wound up back in the States. He thinks he made a mistake, that he should have reached out to help me rather than push me away. He said this even after I came clean about the magazines, which wasn't such a dramatic confession, since he wasn't the least bit surprised; even though Todd had readily taken the blame, Rabbi Berkstein never believed that the magazines were Todd's. Anyway, he didn't mean for me to leave the Land and he wishes I hadn't. So there's one person who wants forgiveness from *me*. And I've given it to him now, more than once. At this point, I'll forgive anyone who asks my forgiveness.

July 30, 2002

S O I HAVE a boyfriend. He's my first. I'm the only person
I know who got pregnant before having her first boyfriend.
Ash still doesn't know that Todd's even in Boston, let alone
sleeping in my bed every night. We're going to tell him, of course,
but we've been together only a few weeks and we haven't had time
to do *anything*, really, except go to our respective jobs and then
meet back up at my apartment and stare at each other a lot. We're
not having sex. It seems weird to have sex while I'm pregnant. I'm
not exactly feeling sexy. We just kiss a lot, like thirteen-year-olds.
Well, not like me at thirteen, but like other thirteen-year-olds.

I don't even know who I am anymore. A celibate girl with a
boyfriend? How did *that* happen? Actually, I understand it a little. It's strange: I'm not as anxious as I used to be. Maybe that's
because Ash has come home, or, ironically, because I'm going to
be a mother. I don't really know, but I feel pinned to the ground
now, rather than like I'm floating above it. That's how I imagine
my old self: hovering a little, grasping at handfuls of loose earth.
And now I don't crave men the way I used to. I don't need them
anymore to stare at me like they want to suck the very blood out
of my veins or to swear they will die if they can't have me. It's different with Todd.

I'm better than I used to be because I'm not wasting so much
energy keeping secrets, but here's one secret: I kind of miss my old

self. Even good changes feel like loss. Plus, I don't trust sudden change. Maybe the way I used to be is the real me, and this is just a phase.

But I can't complain. Todd should complain. His girlfriend is pregnant. But he says he has nothing to complain about. Not one thing in the whole world. See, an amazing thing is happening to him: his hearing in his right ear has begun to come back. He realized it one night when he took out his hearing aid before bed and noticed that he could hear the water running from the bathroom sink more clearly than usual. Since then, his hearing has been gradually improving. It's not perfect. It might not ever be perfect. But it was almost completely gone, and now some of it is restored.

He's amazed by the whole thing, obviously—I mean, he should be; it's amazing—but I finally had to ask him if this meant he was going to feel indebted to God and start going to the yeshiva and wearing those tassel things again. I was afraid it would mean that, but he said no, he doesn't have to be in a yeshiva to thank God, does he?

Well, I don't know. I'm not the God expert. It creeps me out when people talk about God too much. It reminds me of those weirdos in Boston Common who wear sandwich-board blueprints of Hell and preach through megaphones about being saved. I guess it also reminds me of Ash.

But Todd doesn't talk about God much. He thinks his hearing came back because he gave up some of his worries. He had lots of worries, he says, mostly unfounded ones. Everything used to worry him. He says some people—like him and like me—just hold their anxiety closer to them than other people do. He says he was kind of paralyzed by all the worrying, constantly pressuring himself to do impossible things, like find meaning in the world, and that was how he wound up getting all religious in the first place. But later, he decided to take a risk and pursue his music, and he thinks God or the universe or whoever rewarded him for making his peace.

He thinks his hearing is part of his reward, and I'm the other part.

I like that theory. I don't think you could prove it with the scientific method or anything, but who gives a shit about the scientific method? It's a nice idea: if you listen to yourself, you get your hearing back. Maybe something similar has happened to me. I wonder what I did to spark my own good luck. Try to help Ash? Start saving money to reimburse Wade? Whatever it was, I got three surprising but ultimately good things in quick succession. Boom, boom, boom: baby, brother, boyfriend. Not that I can very well declare myself a great person. I can't. I'm not a great person at all. I'm kind of an appalling person, if you think about it. But what's the sense in thinking about it? You can't waste your life harping on your flaws.

1 Elul 5762
(August 9, 2002)

I'VE GOTTEN BITS to agree to meet with the *rebbetzin*, Rabbi Shimon's wife. Do I think my sister will become an Orthodox Jew? No. But it's a step. I wish she would consider her baby; she needs to nurture her baby from a young age if she wants it to have a connection to God. She says she doesn't care whether or not her baby has a connection to God. She says she just wants her baby to have ten fingers and ten toes. I said, "Where do you think those fingers and toes come from, Bits?" and she said, "You are so retarded, Ash."

Anyway, she's coming to the Yeshiva of Brookline tonight because the *rebbetzin* is giving a women's seminar for Rosh Chodesh, the first day of the Jewish month of Elul. I'm waiting for Bits outside because after her experiences in Israel, she doesn't believe me that you can just stroll right in to the yeshiva. Yeshiva of Brookline isn't gated like Yeshiva Hillel is. Yeshiva Hillel is in Jerusalem; Yeshiva of Brookline is in Brookline Village. You can see why one would be gated and the other wouldn't. But Bits said I had to meet her outside anyway because she has something exciting to tell me. She wouldn't give me a clue. She said it was a surprise.

I made her promise me something: "Wear a long skirt and long sleeves," I said.

"It's August."

"But still."

"Ash," she said. "I don't think I'm going to fool anyone into thinking I'm modest. I'm pregnant and not wearing a wedding ring."

"Just . . . please?" I said, and eventually she agreed.

She doesn't fight me on every little thing, now that I've moved to Boston. She knows my stay is temporary, but she's still appreciative. When I first got here, she was so accommodating, it almost made me uncomfortable, but that's starting to fade. The other day, for example, she made an unsolicited comment about Orthodox Jews having body odor. "Enough," I said. "Seriously." And she did let it go, which is good, but a week ago, she never would have made that comment in the first place. Well, what did I expect, moving to the same city as my sister who's my polar opposite? Now I see her coming from way down the road, and she's holding someone's hand. So I guess the surprise is that she has a boyfriend. That's good. Well, it's immodest and tacky, all things considered, but I guess it could be a good thing. As long as he's Jewish. Maybe he'll have the decency to marry her, and then her baby can come into the world with two parents. Even from this distance, I can see that Bits's boyfriend has red hair. In the sun, it glares gold for a second, then dims, and guides my sister toward me like a light.

ACKNOWLEDGMENTS

THANK YOU, JEFFREY DeShell, my first mentor; Melissa Glass, my first *chavrusa*; my teachers at the University of Montana; my amazing friends, Aryn Kyle, Jen Kocher, and Cristina Henríquez, who read early drafts and provided priceless critiques. Thank you, SR. Thank you, Josh Shamsi, for giving me a home in Jerusalem; Jon Malki, for always offering assistance; the scholars at askmoses.com and the many yeshiva students and rabbis who answered my strange questions. I am particularly grateful to Rabbi Noah Weinberg for his *48 Ways to Wisdom*. Thanks to the folks at *Moment* and at *The Greensboro Review*, and to Yona Zeldis McDonough at *Lilith*. Thanks to the organizations and institutions that gave me funding and writing time: the Anderson Center, the Martha Heasley Cox Steinbeck Fellowship, and Portsmouth Abbey School. Thank you, thank you, thank you, Kate Lee, agent of my dreams, and Jeanette Perez, editor extraordinaire. Thanks and love to my grandmother, Claire Spechler, who has taught me so much about Judaism; to my brother and sister, who graciously tolerate having a writer in the family; and to my parents, who make many things easier for me.

About the author

About the book

Read on

Insights,
Interviews
& More . . .

A Conversation with Diana Spechler

Joanna Foster

Let's start simple—where are you from?

I was born and raised in Newton, Massachusetts, but I've moved around a lot since graduating from high school. So far, I've lived in Colorado, Israel, Montana, Texas, Wyoming, California, Rhode Island, and now New York. I've lived for brief periods in other places too.

When did you start writing?

I can't remember a time when I didn't write. It always amazes me when I hear a great author say something like, *I wrote my first story at forty*. It seems impossible to me that I could have become a writer had I not been working at it my whole life. When I was in the second grade, I wrote a story called "Shana and The Magic Quilt" about a girl whose quilt comes to life. Shana had really long hair, down to her hips; when I was seven, hair of that length, in my mind, was synonymous with mind-blowing beauty. The story was twenty-four pages long, handwritten. My mother still has it.

Do you remember the first book you fell in love with and why it affected you so strongly?

It was *The Catcher in the Rye*. I remember reading it when I was thirteen years old and thinking, *You're allowed to write like that?* It sounded more like one end of a fascinating conversation than like a work of literature. As soon as I finished reading it, I started it again. The last line breaks my heart like nothing else. "Don't ever tell anybody anything. If you do, you start missing everybody."

Who are some of your writing influences?

J. D. Salinger was the first, but in graduate school I learned so much by reading Raymond Carver, Joy Williams, and Lorrie Moore, although I'm not sure anyone would guess that by reading my writing. While writing *Who by Fire*, I learned a lot about specific techniques from different books. For example, *The Secret History* by Donna Tartt taught me a few things about plot, and *That Night* by Alice McDermott really made me think about the necessary mixing of simplicity and complexity.

When you're writing, do you have an audience in mind? Are you writing for someone in particular?

I try really hard not to think about audience when I'm writing. I could never have written the sex scenes in this novel if I'd allowed myself to imagine my father reading them. ▶

A Conversation with Diana Spechler
(continued)

Are there any lessons you learned, having attended the University of Montana Creative Writing Program, that you would pass along to other up-and-coming authors?

I learned most of what I know about writing at the University of Montana. I would tell anyone who wants to be a writer to go to an MFA program (although, admittedly, there are plenty of writers who will say just the opposite). Beyond that, I would recommend paying attention to constructive criticism that comes from trustworthy, knowledgeable sources; developing a thick skin; and writing every day. Also, try to have as many experiences as possible, be an excellent listener, and surround yourself with interesting people. But I guess that last bit is my advice to everyone, not just to writers.

How much does your background—whether it be the city you grew up in, your family, your experiences—make its way into your writing?

It's in there. All of it. It wears many full masks and thin veils.

Are you working on anything now?

Yes! I'm writing a novel based on the summer I worked at a weight-loss camp. Fat-camp life is a far cry from yeshiva life, but I guess I'm drawn to microcosms. ❧

66 I learned most of what I know about writing at the University of Montana. 99

4

A Life in Books

Best short story I've ever read: I feel like I fall in love with a new short story every week—recently, Rebecca Curtis's "Big Bear, California" and Julie Orringer's "The Isabel Fish," but a couple of my all-time favorites are "What We Talk About When We Talk About Love" by Raymond Carver (actually, almost anything by Raymond Carver) and "Brokeback Mountain" by Annie Proulx.

Best "film of a book" I've seen: *No Country for Old Men*, but I have to confess I didn't read the book.

Favorite bookshop: I love them all.

Favorite heroines in literature: Chloé in Charles Baxter's *The Feast of Love* and Carmen in Ann Patchett's *Bel Canto*

Favorite hero in literature: Holden Caulfield

Author I'd most like to meet: Moses, or whoever really wrote the Torah. I'd like some answers.

Favorite "guilty pleasure" reading: I'm a sucker for shockingly candid memoirs. One of my favorites is *Borderlines* by Caroline Kraus.

Best writing advice I ever received: Padgett Powell used to warn us against "poetic potatoes." It's great advice— don't overdo the prose; it just doesn't sound good. ❧

Blame

I HAD BEEN WORKING on *Who by Fire* for about a year and was spending the summer teaching fiction at Interlochen Arts Camp in western Michigan, when I got a strange phone call from my mother. Since I spend most of my life in anticipation of catastrophe, and despite the fact that my mother calls me several times a week, a family member on my caller ID always sets off emergency vehicle sirens in my head, so I felt momentarily dizzy when the first thing out of my mother's mouth was "Okay, don't blame yourself, but—"

"What?" I said. "Oh my God. But what?"

I was standing outside the cafeteria wearing the Interlochen uniform: a light blue polo shirt tucked into navy blue shorts, socks, and sneakers; I wasn't dressed to receive bad news. In movies, women look beautiful when they get bad news. They might be beautifully disheveled—messy ponytails, nothing but their boyfriend's oversized button-down—but they're never dressed like a dad on a sailboat. Their shirts are never tucked into their shorts. Oh, and they're never at summer camp.

"Relax," my mother said. "It's nothing tragic." And then she told me what was up: My brother, who was spending the summer in Israel before starting law school, had decided to become an Orthodox Jew.

"*What?*"

I would have laughed out loud if I hadn't been so baffled. *Bits* was the one whose brother was an Orthodox Jew in Israel. I was the one whose brother lived in a college town in a house decorated with collections of empty liquor bottles and a gold-framed Natty Light mirror.

"It's not your fault," my mother said. "It's just a very strange coincidence."

> ❝ I wasn't dressed to receive bad news. In movies, women look beautiful when they get bad news. They might be beautifully disheveled—messy ponytails, nothing but their boyfriend's oversized button-down—but they're never dressed like a dad on a sailboat. ❞

I thought about that after I hung up.
Usually, when I tell someone "It's not your
fault," what I really mean is the opposite.
I don't consider myself insincere, but I am
decidedly averse to a few things in the world,
and one of those things is confrontation.
(Others include milk, mice, the sound of
my neighbor's television through the wall,
and people who use the word "ironical.")
I say "It's not your fault" in response to
"Sorry I forgot we had plans," "Sorry I cut
in front of you in line," and "Sorry I bumped
into you so hard my elbow knocked out six of
your teeth."

So I wasn't convinced of my innocence.

But let me back up for a second: It's
important to clarify that my brother is
nothing like Ash. He's the most even-keeled,
outgoing, considerate person you'd ever hope
to meet. He's one of my favorite people in the
world. He's one of a lot of people's favorite
people in the world. His decision to become
more serious about Judaism was neither an
affront to me nor a threat to his character. So
words like "innocence" and "fault" shouldn't
even have crossed my mind. But I was really
freaked out (and apparently so was my
mother) that I had caused an event by
writing about it.

"Don't you think it's weird?" I asked
my friend Janée, the Interlochen poetry
teacher.

We were sitting on the steps of her cabin
in our matching blue outfits, my sneakers
beside the black boots she wore that laced
straight up to her knees (she's one of those
admirable people who refuses to see ugly
shorts as a fashion obstacle).

"There's that quote," she said, adjusting
her black plastic-framed glasses.

"What?"

"I can't remember. Something about how
the poet speaks the truth. You have to be ▶

> **"** I was really
> freaked out (and
> apparently so was
> my mother) that
> I had caused an
> event by writing
> about it. **"**

Blame *(continued)*

careful what you write. Writing can be prophetic."

"But I'm not a poet," I said. "I suck at writing poems."

"Look," Janée said. "Sometimes these things just happen."

They do?

I kind of liked the idea that maybe I was a prophet, but I had a sense that my prophetic powers, if they did in fact exist, were tinged with darkness. After all, if I were the good kind of prophet, like a fortune cookie, I would have written a much more uplifting novel—a story about the end of world hunger or about a girl with a functional family.

Maybe I was bad luck, the opposite of a rabbit's foot, something like the tiki that Bobby Brady found on the beach during the *Brady Bunch* Hawaii trilogy, the trinket that cursed his family's idyllic tropical vacation.

A few months later, in early November 2004, I was packing to go to Israel. My brother was back in Austin, Texas, where he had moved into his own apartment, made his kitchen kosher, and was somehow finding time to both attend law school and study Talmud with a rabbi.

In current events, Yasser Arafat, who had been a Palestinian leader in one form or another for four and a half decades, had slipped into a coma. Rumors were flying: He was in a coma because he had AIDS! He had AIDS because he was gay! No! Actually, because he was bisexual! No! This wasn't AIDS; it was the result of a high-tech laser attack by clandestine Israeli soldiers! Some said he'd been poisoned. Some said he had a hereditary form of cancer. Some said he'd eaten bad meat.

Whatever it was, my friends kept calling to

> ❝ My friends kept calling to ask me, 'Do you think this is the best time to go to Israel?' ❞

ask me, "Do you think this is the best time to go to Israel?"

Repeating the mantra of many Jews worldwide, I responded, "There's never a *good* time to go to Israel."

But okay, I was nervous. Who knew what would happen if Arafat died? What if Israel took the brunt of the blame? Who was to say there wouldn't be riots, attacks, chaos throughout the Middle East? And there I would be in Jerusalem, alone, knocking on the doors of yeshivas, trying to do research while violence erupted all around me. The image (which for some reason included land mines, peasant clothes, and a walking stick) made me feel very sorry for myself.

In Jerusalem, as soon as I got to my friend Josh's house, where I would be staying, he said, "Guess what? Arafat died."

Of course he did, I thought. *Probably the second my plane landed.* Now I was convinced: My very presence caused high drama. I was the Hawaii tiki. The one that nearly killed Greg Brady in a terrifying surfing disaster.

For the next couple of days, it seemed that every school, business, and sightseeing stop in Jerusalem was closed, some because of the mourning period, others because of heightened security. Everywhere I went, guards or "sagoor" ("closed") signs turned me away. Frustrated, I asked Josh and his friend Nabiha, a Christian Arab, to take me to Bethlehem.

In earlier drafts of *Who by Fire*, Bits actually makes it into Bethlehem, makes it all the way to the Church of the Nativity (I had been inspired by an incredible news story from the time of the siege, about two eerily oblivious Japanese tourists who wandered, somehow unnoticed, into the war zone, forcing journalists in flak jackets to ▶

Blame *(continued)*

come to their rescue), so I needed to see it for myself, to make sure I got the details straight. But Bethlehem was even more shut down than Jerusalem. The few things that weren't already permanently closed because of the ailing economy were closed temporarily as a nod to the late Palestinian leader. The cars flew black flags from their antennae. Posters of Arafat and stenciled drawings of suicide bombers adorned the city's walls. The security fence was covered in angry graffiti. At the bullet-pocked Church of the Nativity, a tour guide said to Josh and me, "Israel created Hamas. And America created Osama bin Laden."

I stepped back from him, alarmed, glimpsing blame for what it often is: a vacuous oversimplification.

Back in Jerusalem, on the last night of my trip, I was on Ben Yehuda Street eating my final falafel before heading to the airport when a guy wearing a black *kipa*, jeans, and a T-shirt walked by the door of the café I was in, saw me, and came inside. "Diana," he said with no hint of an Israeli accent. "Right?"

I had seen him earlier that day near the Western Wall, at a yeshiva where I had been attending classes. He had been sitting in the back of the classroom, taking notes, his dark, shaggy hair hanging in his eyes. The rabbi teaching the class had addressed him by name: Noah.

Noah asked me what I was doing eating falafel surrounded by suitcases. I explained to him that I was a writer, that I had come to Israel to do research, and now I was on my way home.

"You're writing a book about Israel?"

"Kind of," I said. "Some of my novel takes place in a yeshiva. Most of the students are

66 At the bullet-pocked Church of the Nativity, a tour guide said to Josh and me, 'Israel created Hamas. And America created Osama bin Laden.' 99

American. One of the main characters is a Ba'al Tshuva."

"Like me," he said. "Do you want to ask me questions?"

This was truly amazing. Most yeshiva boys I had met had been hesitant to let me interview them. I wasn't sure if it was because I was female, or because I wasn't religious, or because I was a writer who swore I had no opinion one way or the other about Orthodox Judaism. But now, suddenly, a yeshiva boy who wanted to help me had fallen out of the heavens and into my lap. I wondered: If by writing about Bits's brother's religious awakening, I had caused my own brother's religious awakening, and if by writing about the Arab-Israeli conflict, I had caused Arafat's death, then maybe by writing about nice yeshiva boys (Todd? Reuven?), I had summoned a nice yeshiva boy. Perhaps it was a stretch—okay, it was all a stretch, I was stretching like Gumby—but I went with it. After all, I didn't want to be the Hawaii tiki; I wanted to be a rabbit's foot. Noah wrote his e-mail address on a napkin.

By the following March, when my friends Jen and Aryn came to visit me in California, I had been corresponding with Noah for four months. "I have my very own yeshiva boy!" I gushed. The three of us were driving from San Jose, where I lived, to the Napa Valley, this great place in northern California where tourists can be not boozehounds but urbane wine enthusiasts. "I ask him the most obscure questions," I said, "and he knows the answers. He has all kinds of useful information. Like, the kitchen guys at his yeshiva are Arabs. I never would have guessed that. And also, when Miriam had leprosy, Moses drew a circle around himself and said, 'Please, ▶

> **"** But now, suddenly, a yeshiva boy who wanted to help me had fallen out of the heavens and into my lap. **"**

please heal Miriam.' And then another time, a rabbi did the same thing—drew a circle around himself and asked God to end a bad drought, and then the drought ended."

"Who's Miriam?" Jen asked. But she was gazing out her window.

This was back when I was spending a lot of time talking to people (read: anyone who would listen or anyone who was in my car and therefore couldn't escape) about Orthodox Judaism, Talmud, and yeshiva life. I was so immersed in my novel, it was hard to remember that most people weren't interested in discussing, for hours on end, the ramifications of the golden calf. At that time, when I saw Orthodox Jews in the streets, I would stare, openmouthed and awestruck, a reaction most people reserve for the Swiss Alps or the Rolling Stones.

The next morning, after a day-turned-evening of wine-tastings that were less tasting, more guzzling, we woke up in a motel room, our heads pounding, all three of us sounding like Marge Simpson as we discussed the most efficient way to find coffee to inject directly into our veins. Still in bed, I checked my e-mail on my cell phone.

"Oh no," I said. "Oh my God."

The e-mail I read came from Noah's account. It had been written by his friend and sent to everyone in Noah's address book.

"What?" my friends wanted to know.

"I can't believe this," I said. "My yeshiva boy died."

Aryn flopped down on the bed next to me. "What are you talking about?"

I read the e-mail aloud. Noah's body had been found on the floor of his apartment. He was only thirty-four years old. Since autopsies aren't in keeping with the tenets of Orthodox

> 66 Noah's body had been found on the floor of his apartment. He was only thirty-four years old. 99

Judaism, his cause of death would remain unknown, but he had probably had a brain aneurysm. His parents were flying to Jerusalem for the funeral.

"I feel like such an ass," I said. "He sent me an e-mail the other day and I never responded. I was planning to respond, but I hadn't gotten around to it yet, and now . . ."

"And now he's dead and it's all your fault," said Aryn, who invariably refuses to indulge me.

"Right," I said.

"Right," she said.

By the third of the *Brady Bunch* Hawaii episodes, Bobby Brady wanted to do whatever it took to wash his hands of the tiki. Because of its evil powers, Greg had almost drowned, a heavy wall hanging had almost fallen on Peter's head, and a deadly spider had almost killed Marcia. I guess Bobby thought that if he got rid of the tiki, things would stop being his fault.

Right after Noah died, I thought a lot about blame. I realized that because it was a theme in the novel I was writing, I had turned it into a theme in my life. All the weird things that had happened while I'd been doing my research—had I unconsciously caused them or at least encouraged them? Could I have prevented them had I wanted to?

I finally made myself admit that those questions were unanswerable, not to mention narcissistic and teetering on delusional. Around that time, I wrote the scene in *Who by Fire* about Bits wondering whose fault it was that Ash had dropped out of college and run off to Israel. She notes that "you can make yourself crazy" wondering who's to blame for things.

Yes, I thought as I wrote that. *Enough.* ∽

Author's Picks: Top Ten Favorite Novels about Families

Revolutionary Road by Richard Yates

This is a timeless page-turner about the struggle between embracing discomfort and submitting to complacency. I love the darkness of it, the complexity of the characters, and Yates's subtle use of dialogue to propel the themes (for example, the characters are always commenting on how good it feels to sit down). The center of the novel is the Wheeler family, a young couple and their two children living in the suburbs.

Middlesex by Jeffrey Eugenides

Middlesex, an epic novel about a Greek family that settles in Michigan, is narrated by a child from the third generation who is born as a hermaphrodite. The story is so authentic, so well researched and detailed and convincing, it reads like nonfiction.

Housekeeping by Marilynne Robinson

In my opinion, Marilynne Robinson's writing is as beautiful as it gets. This coming-of-age novel about two sisters, Ruth and Lucille, living with their eccentric Aunt Sylvie, contains one of my all-time favorite quotes: "I have observed that, in the way people are strange, they grow stranger."

The Poisonwood Bible by Barbara Kingsolver

Reading this novel around the time I started working on *Who by Fire* taught me a lot about how to write a story from multiple points of view. It's narrated chapter by chapter by four American sisters who move to Africa with their mother and their missionary father. Each sister's voice is

> **❝ In my opinion, Marilynne Robinson's writing is as beautiful as it gets. ❞**

unique and endearing, the setting is captivating, and the undercurrent of impending doom makes the book impossible to set down. I sacrificed a night of sleep for this novel and read it in one gulp.

The History of Love by Nicole Krauss
     Many of the family ties in *The History of Love* are broken by death and secrets, but the story is as intricately woven as an ancient tapestry. I don't think there's any other book in the world that could have made me fall in love with the name Alma.

The Namesake by Jhumpa Lahiri
     This novel about a second-generation Indian in America, Gogol Ganguli, captures and magnifies a part of youth that everyone can relate to: feeling embarrassed by your family.

The Invisible Circus by Jennifer Egan
     Jennifer Egan's debut novel is about Phoebe O'Connor, an eighteen-year-old girl whose childhood was shaken by the losses of both her father and her sister. Haunted by the mystery surrounding her sister's death, Phoebe travels to Europe in search of answers. This isn't exactly what you'd call a feel-good book, but the writing is sharp and the story is riveting.

Dinner at the Homesick Restaurant by Anne Tyler
     I love almost everything by Anne Tyler. Her novels read, structurally, like long short stories, and her characters are pleasingly, quietly flawed. Also, I can't think of a writer who comes up with better titles. *Dinner at the Homesick Restaurant* is my favorite Anne Tyler novel, the story of Pearl Tull and the three children she raised after her husband abandoned them.

Read on

Author's Picks: Top Ten Favorite Novels about Families (*continued*)

Family History by Dani Shapiro

Dani Shapiro is a master at turning quiet suburban family life into a thriller. *Family History* poses a difficult question: If you think your husband is trustworthy and your child is not, can you choose between them?

Portnoy's Complaint by Philip Roth

It's not as beautiful as *Goodbye, Columbus*, and it's a little dated now, forty years after the publication date, but it's a humorous take on growing up with overbearing Jewish parents.

Don't miss the next book by your favorite author. Sign up now for AuthorTracker by visiting www.AuthorTracker.com.